THE DESTINED ONES
BOOK 1

SEASON
OF
ANGELS

DESTINED
PRESS

JAIME KIMBLER

Acknowledgements

There were a small number of people who took time out of their busy lives to read my first manuscript. It began with a chapter sent to my mom for some brutal honesty—whether to give writing a try or stick to what I'm good at, painting. It was her excitement for every following chapter that got me started. And starting is the hardest part.

Thanks to Command Sergeant Major (Ret) Robert Pruitt and Francesca Simons for your time and constructive criticism and for genuinely liking the story. It kept me going. And very special thanks to my husband, Command Sergeant Major Matthew Kimbler—my support, my soundboard, my safe harbor—for helping me every step of the way.

I would like to thank the people in my life who have been my friends, companions, coworkers, and neighbors. Every player in this, my life's film, the good and the bad, it all made a difference. It all brought me to this wonderful time in my life where I could put my stories to paper and pour from the soul.

Table of Contents

This book was inspired by all the creative minds who are bold enough to share their art with the world, but it's dedicated to those wonderful beings who say magical, life-changing words such as

I believe in you.

Chapter One

O urs is a love eternal, golden cords stretching beyond life and death, finally meeting and weaving our stories together, lifetime after lifetime. This world is cold, and love is scarce, the reason for people like us to bring love back into it, to leave a spark of light before we go, even if in some lives, we are forced to go alone.

We were the souls betrothed in each lifetime, the destined ones, tethered, the red thread; and in this life, we were destined to share a home grown over with love and roses, but you can't change the course of the wild winds. The night of my high school graduation, and only days since our last embrace, I drank too much whiskey with a friend and got behind the wheel of my grandpa's old truck. I swerved to miss a cat in the road and crashed into a giant old oak tree. I died on impact. I died thinking of her.

The full moon glowing, the cool wind sweeping through my fingers, the perfect song on the radio. The evening was mystical. When a good song plays on the radio at the right moment, you turn it up. That's what I did, and that's why I saw the black cat in the road at the very last moment. Every driver wonders what they would do if that happened to them. They tell you not to panic, not to swerve, that you might lose control. Maybe I was just startled, but it was probably the whiskey, and the rest was fate.

We live our whole lives afraid of these, the final moments of our lives. We wonder what they'll be like and hope they're not horrible. Fear of the unknown, and I can't think of a bigger unknown than how or why we die. I can tell you that I never expected my life to end so early, so few of life's precious moments experienced. I don't feel like I had enough time to contemplate my ending, when I was so busy beginning.

Most people envision crossing over to be fearful and chaotic, though it can be as simple and soft as a breath. Screeching tires, grinding gravel, and the sound of Bob Seger singing "Shame on the Moon" from my radio filled the air until all fell silent. It was only moments in clouds of dust that I felt my truck strike the tree and my body smash into the steering wheel. I was blurring through the motions of driving poorly, overcorrecting, and losing control in my last few seconds of life, but my mind was focused on memories of Audrey. Those were the last times I would ever see her on the same side of the veil.

But beyond the veil I stood now. I was water, I was air, I was fire and earth. The tide of the universe swept upon me with its wisdom. I could feel and see the energy of all things; I now know we are all connected far more than I ever imagined. The earth and its inhabitants sing songs just by being, a symphony of life, and I could hear it all. Even that giant old oak hovering over me.

Looking at the wreckage, hearing the creeks and moans of a terminal vehicle, smoke and steam rising, drips of gasoline and water, I saw my bloodied arm hanging out of the window. It seemed as if at any moment it would begin to move and open that tricky door handle. But I knew my arm wouldn't be moving. I knew I had just felt my last breath leave my body, but I stood there, frozen. The younger we are, the more immortal we feel. How closely we dance on the edges of life, unaware of the veil's longing eternal embrace. Helpless I was, until I saw two familiar faces approaching through the settling dust. I couldn't recall where I'd seen them before, but I knew I had run into them a time or two. Of all times, what were they doing here now?

A calmness and peace like I'd never known swept through me, and without words being spoken, I knew these people, these beings, were my guardian angels. They had been by my side even before I crossed into this world, though I was meeting them officially for the first time after my life on earth had ended. They walked together, joined in the union of a shared purpose, both with concern and compassion in their eyes. The closer they came to me, I was able to notice small things about them. Their features, their clothes, their gait, all things I had always wondered about were here before me. Paroh was my height, he had light brown hair and eyes the colors of storm clouds. He was dressed nicely as was she, in what looked like clothes you'd wear to church, but from a different time. Nessa was shorter than me with tan skin and dark auburn hair. Her eyes were piercing green emeralds, holding back tears. Most people are greeted at the end of their days with happy angels celebrating the joyous occasion of returning home. But my life was cut short. I hadn't listened to them. They had tried to warn me. They'd tried to hide my keys. I could blame the cat in the road, I could blame my truck, shame on the moon, but this was my doing, and with one decision, I had cut short this beautiful life that was destined for us.

They reached out to comfort me with their hands on my shoulders. As I stood in the here and now, I looked down and saw that I was restored to perfect health. People had begun to approach the truck and had alerted the authorities. Clovis Police and Fire were always fast to respond to any kind of emergency; the reason why it was such a sweet and safe little country town to grow up in. I could hear the sirens now, and lights came into view. Moments later, the area was filled with emergency vehicles and uniformed people rushing all around me. I stood silently and felt the rush of wind brush against me, though to them, I wasn't there.

The fire crew opened the old truck door and was able to lay my body down, as CPR was attempted. They tried longer than I expected to revive me, but my bones had been crushed, and I'd suffered a severe blow to my skull. I was a healthy young man, I was an athlete, but there's not much you can do when your number is called, and those wild winds blow.

A barrel-chested police officer stood over my body with his hand over his heart and recognized me. "Oh no, no, no. That's Harrison's kid. He just graduated from Clovis West." He ran his hand from his brow and into his short hair in disbelief. "Nights like this make me want to retire. I better head over to the ranch and let 'em know."

Soon, the commotion was over. They moved my body from under the towering oak to the hospital in an ambulance, but there was no need for lights and sirens. One by one, the vehicles left the scene much quieter and slower than before, and then the area was cleared. All except for my old truck left there, crushed into the giant oak. The black cat lay low in the brush, watching it all. Watching me.

Guardian angels are with you from the beginning of your life. They are assigned to you, to protect and guide you and help you from making bad decisions, whether you heed their warnings or not. Here mine stood, trying to usher me toward a billowing bright light above me. That's usually where you meet Peter at the pearly gates, checking the big book to see if your name is on the guest list. My name was on the list, which wasn't the issue. I know I've bent God's ear plenty, I've prayed, I've asked Him questions relentlessly, and feel that He has answered me, but in the end, I believe He knows my heart. But just as free will reigns here on earth in life, you have one more choice in the hereafter.

"I can't leave her. We were supposed to..."

"We know." Paroh interrupted me, placing his hand on my arm, consoling me. A simple gesture, to reassure a wayward soul, but I noticed waves of calming energy fill me from his hand. It was a familiar feeling. I realized how many times in my life, when troubled, he had been there, comforting me.

Nessa, with a slow, wise smile, insisted, "Let's take this elsewhere."

In a single deep breath, I opened my eyes, and we were all sitting in the warm sand at Pismo Beach. I smiled as soon as I saw the waves crash along the unmistakable stretch of heaven on earth I'd loved my whole life. The only person who loved this beach more was Audrey, and my heart and mind focused again on her. She always talked about his place. That it was magical. It always caused her worries and cares to fade like the morning cloud cover. That first tide to rush around her ankles, the chill of the water, and sinking sand beneath her feet made her feel connected. She belonged to this earth, to that moment, and no other present moment ever felt as visceral. This beach inspired her. She rose at first light each morning to hunt for sand dollars, working up an appetite for traditions. After the sand was washed from her feet, she'd walk into town for those one-of-a-kind cinnamon rolls. Nothing else would suffice. Each trip to Pismo, she loved looking through the seaside shops for fun things, but her favorite was to buy a new zip-up hoodie that had the words Pismo Beach somewhere on it.

There was a weekend when our families had both ended up at Pismo at the same time for vacation. She took me on her adventures. We played in the water, collected seashells, climbed rocks, and gazed into tide pools. We'd spent our entire days on that beach, and sand dollars were our treasure. At first light, we began all over again. It was the best weekend I think I'd ever had. Yes, there was something magical about this place, and that's why my angels brought me here, for such a decision. It wasn't going to be an easy one, so let it be in a place that brought me peace.

Beyond protecting us throughout our lives, an angel's job is also to usher us into the light once we've reached our life's end. That's what most of us do. Immediately after crossing, our souls are drawn to this exquisite purity, a home that we had long forgotten. What most of us call judgment day, thinking of it as some biblical punishment—and it will be for some—is actually your life being played before you and all of heaven like a film, and you get to experience the joys and pain that you caused others. If you're a kindhearted, giving, serving, and forgiving person, you have a wonderful experience to look forward to when your film plays on. Granted, there's only one man who walked the earth that has the perfect story to tell, but for us simple souls, we'll have our ups and downs, our disappointing scenes and proud moments, and hopefully some triumphs and redemption. It takes all of that to make a film a good one. God help those who led a life of selfishness and greed. If you hurt people, you will feel every bit of sorrow that you caused them and, subsequently, the ones they went on to effect by your actions. You'll feel shame, pain, and embarrassment before all of heaven. I guess you could call that pain hell. But hell is a real place, and luckily for me, that's not where I was going.

I did have a choice in this matter, though. If I didn't go into the light with them, I could see her again. That's what my angels and I sat there in the sand discussing. My choice. I could stay here and make sure that she's safe. I could watch over her, but this is where I'd have to say goodbye to my angels for now. When the time comes that I decide to take the luminous journey toward Peter and the pearly gates, I will see them again. I could see a sadness in their eyes. I was a job left unfinished, and no master likes that. But they had also been beside me for 18 years of my life, and goodbyes always weigh heaviest on the heart. They were excited for me to finally see friends and family, my grandpa who I'd missed so much, all eagerly awaiting a grand reunion, and so many surprises. That would just have to wait. They had one last task left, and it was to deliver me to my next destination.

We traveled at the speed of breaths, and in one, we were standing before another angel. This was Audrey's guardian angel, working in a garage on his motorcycle. He was entranced in his work, a grease-covered brute of a man. It just went against every idea in my mind of what a guardian angel should look like, especially the one who was responsible for protecting her. Audrey's angel should be more in a suit than looking like he belonged to a biker's club.

"There must be some mistake. This can't be Audrey's guardian." I shook my head in disbelief.

Audrey's angel peered around the bike with an irritated glare, tilting his nose down to look above the line of his sunglasses. A hand-rolled smoke rested gently between his lips. His brow furrowed, his head was bald and shiny, arms bigger than any gym rat I'd ever seen, and with a deep, resounding voice, he asked, "What did you drag into my garage?"

"This is Josh, Josh Harrison. He has recently crossed." Polite introductions were made by my angels. "You two are about to get to know each other quite well. He's made the decision to stay and keep watch over Audrey with you."

Audrey's angel grimaced, stood up angrily, slamming a grease-ridden rag to the floor with frustration. He was absolutely terrifying. He walked directly over to me, stood over examining me with contempt, and to my utter surprise, put out his hand and said, "Glad to have the help, brother!" He and my angels broke out into laughter. Though it was at my expense, any tension was disbursed, and the energy in the room lifted. Shaking my hand, he laughed, "Hey man, I was just messing with ya. My name is Gavri."

So his name, Gavri, meaning warrior of God, was fitting. When he was laughing, he didn't appear as terrifying as he once had, but still, I'd hate to be the poor soul that crossed him. It took me some time to adjust to all of this. I wasn't expecting the day to be so…much. Truth be told, I was exhausted and overwhelmed and somehow at peace all at the same time. I felt the hands of my angels on my shoulders to comfort me once again.

"We have unfinished business and a lot to talk about, but your journey continues," Paroh said, looking at me and then the ground with a sigh. "We'll be watching. Never too far, but you're in good hands now."

And with a heartfelt embrace, my angels wished me well and were on their way. I had only just met them face to face, but I could feel a tug at my heart as I watched them go, having felt their presence, their closeness my whole life, and now I had to go on without them. No longer a man but a spirit, no longer watched over by my angels, but being led by new ones, into unfamiliar territory, with an impossible mission.

Gavri started cleaning up. He put a few of his tools away and washed his hands, then invited me through the back door of his garage that led down a stone path to the backyard of his place. It had a scenic, heavenly peace about it. The yard was flat, with the occasional towering trees blowing and bending in the wind. The yard overlooked a deep canyon, so the view was, well, angelic. It looked like you could leap off the edge at any moment, and who knows, he probably did. I was still trying to wrap my head around the idea that angels had their own homes. All this time, I'd thought they just hovered around and flew off wherever they were needed, but they could be anywhere, anything, anyone, any time.

Gavri tapped my shoulder with a cold beer. "You want one?" Half smiling, he continued, "Or is it too soon?" He smirked. "It's okay, kid. I know all about ya."

He took a long sip followed by a longer sigh. "I've known about you your whole life. I know Audrey loves you. I watched the two of you grow up together. We always knew that this might be the outcome, but things could've changed in an instant. We were hoping for a miracle, Em and me. But God has bigger plans for her. She has a special calling this time, and maybe that's why you're here with me, to help her through it all. She's gonna be devastated when she hears the news."

We both paused in silence, our hearts pained at the thought of what this would do to her.

"She doesn't know yet?" I questioned him. I questioned time. "I thought she would've found out by now."

"Time moves differently on this side. It's still the night you died, brother. She won't learn about you for another two mornings. That's when we'll really need to go to work. I had a feeling you'd be showing up here. You two are destined, and that's usually what happens if one life is cut short, and the other is left to go on alone," Gavri explained.

He went on to warn me, "It won't be easy. In fact, it's gonna feel like hell sometimes. You'll watch the woman you love walk her whole life through, feeling alone for most of it. She'll live her life looking for the love she shares with you, wondering why it never really works with anyone else. Can you stand by and watch her live a lifetime of heartbreak?"

"There must be something I can do for her. I know it. I made a promise to her and I'm keeping it. I will make a way," I vowed. I could have been with my heavenly family right now, celebrating my return, but my heart was here, for as long as she needed me.

"You're not the only one who has tried throughout a lifetime to reach the other. Ultimately, that's what you're trying to do, right? To capture a moment, an understanding, that elusive connection?"

I listened to every word and nodded ardently.

"Honestly, some people live their whole lives missing the signs we send them, or they ignore them altogether. The pain of life clouds their connection with their Creator. Connection is everything. It's the only way she'll survive out there with her heart and her soul, still her own, in the end." Gavri paused for a sip. "It's gonna be all right, brother. There are things we can do. I'll show you. God has given us unmatched abilities and strength, but our hearts still break for her. God is within her too, though. She won't fail. And we won't fail her."

Chapter Two

I n another life, the first life we shared together, Audrey and I were two round-faced little Lakota children playing in the plains below the jagged rocky terrain of the Black Hills. They called me Ohanzee, which means shadow. Her name was Wichahpi, meaning stars. We came from a long line of vibrant, wise, and generous people, but as compassionate and peaceful as we were, we always had to be prepared for war. We were about to be tested.

Our holy men passed down our spirited history and legends at night, a dramatic display in the firelight. We were always happy to hear them. It was a simple time then. We were young and still being taught about our land and the values of our ways. We were taught about Mother Earth or Unci Maka as we knew her, believing that whatever happened to her would surely happen to us. The greatest of all the earthly spirits was Unci Maka, but everything covering Unci Maka's robe had a spirit. When you believe that everything has a spirit and is all connected, you hold things in higher regard.

As children, our duty was to learn skills, collect chokeberries and herbs for the healers. Wichahpi was more excited to discover feathers in her path than anything else. Our people believed that a feather was a gift from the sky that brought you, your Creator, and the bird it came from closer together. As I followed her around, I came to believe that feathers lined her path, wherever she went. They always seemed to fall at her feet, and I came to look forward to that sparkle in her eyes when she would find them.

We watched the women prepare bison hides and grind dried meat into dust for pemmican cakes. Wichahpi was drawn to the decorated tipis of the healers, watching the wise women prepare herbs for outside wounds and tonics for those wounds within. When we were much smaller, we would play hunter and buffalo. Sometimes the buffalo would win, injuring the hunter, and Wichahpi would change form from raging beast to wise healer, covering me with leaves and brush as those wise women did.

The medicine women were keen to cultivate her interest. I was different. I longed to be brave and hunt, to be celebrated for the kills I brought home for feasting. The holy men would wait for a vision that would bless the right time for the hunt. I watched the men as they covered their horses in war paint, believing it would offer luck and protection. I ran beside them as they thundered through the village, wishing I could go too.

By firelight, the holy men told us stories passed down from our ancestors. I loved the stories about wolves and buffalo. Wichahpi loved the story of the prairie rose. They say that Unci Maka grew sad that her robe was only covered in dreary colors. She longed for flowers and colors to make her happy. A prairie rose heard Unci Maka's wishes and grew from deep below, hoping to grant them. The prairie rose fought her way to the surface and bloomed in the sunlight. This greatly pleased Unci Maka, but the Wind Demon was angered. He didn't allow such a flower to bloom in his land, so he blew and blew until the little prairie rose was no more. Unci Maka was even more saddened, but soon all the prairie roses down below grew to the surface, together. They grew in force. The Wind Demon was angered by their presence and swept through the land, screaming. He blew and he blew until he ran out of air. As he took a moment to catch his breath, his lungs expanding, he smelled the sweet scent of the prairie roses, and their redolence overcame him. He was no longer angry. He was no longer a demon.

We both loved the stories of the wolves and the moon. The holy men told stories of the moon possessing great powers and the Wolf Moon being the most powerful. The Wolf Moon got its name from hungry winter wolves howling outside our camps. Holy men spoke of such beasts that were the body of a wolf and the spirit of a vengeful man. During the Wolf Moon, these wolf spirits roamed the earth in packs, making the Wolf Moon the most dangerous moon of all.

Holy men said that the Great One saw the night was too dark for Unci Maka, so he called on his wolves. As the story goes, the wolves howled the moon into existence one night. Wichahpi would watch the holy men as they waved their arms to the sky and howled, while I sat there, watching her. They called me Ohanzee, shadow. I was her night sky. The holy men would tease Wichahpi, that maybe before she was in human form, the Great One had called upon her to run through the night sky, and what we see, shining at night, are her footprints.

Seasons changed, and our people did too. In time, our people lost connection to the Great One, and our land began to suffer. A great famine plagued our people. Did we do this to ourselves? Were we being punished?

We soon ran out of food. Our people were starving. Our oldest and our weakest were called home to the Great One, along with our ill and injured. Our healthy and young grew weaker. Our leader called for the two strongest scouts to ride into the Black Hills and search for buffalo. It was our very last hope.

As the sun was sinking the day before they left, we set the bonfire and sounded the drums. We danced around the fire and prayed for mercy and blessings. Our prayers surrounded the scouts, and the smoke swirled to the heavens. We stirred the spirits of our ancestors who twirled in their buckskin shawls and fringe, sweeping great clouds across the sky in many colors with the wild, wild winds.

The men had been gone for days. Our people, who had once reveled in the abundance and blessings of the Great One, were now feeling forgotten. Hope was fading. Wichahpi and I hadn't lost the playful spirit of our childhood, so we swam in the spring water and ran through the tall sweetgrass. We climbed the rocks to the peak, where we sat and watched for eagles. But one day, it wasn't an eagle we saw; it was a lone scout, returning from his journey. We ran back down the hill, bringing news to our elders. All of the tribe appeared from their tents, grateful for the news of his return. We all gathered and listened to every word of his story. He was trembling as he told it.

As he and the other scout grew tired and hungry, about to give up hope, they both saw a distant vision of a woman walking toward them. The closer they came to her, the more blindingly her beauty shone. One scout boasted that he'd make her his own, that he would overpower and have his way with her. It was the ramblings of an exhausted and ravenous man. It was finally time to approach the woman standing before them. The boasting scout walked to her, and with each step, a great angry wind grew, twisting around him. It turned into a raging storm, which enveloped the scout completely, and as the storm and angry winds quieted down, lying at her feet was a pile of the bones of the boasting scout. The lone scout was left wavering. She knew the reason for their journey and gave him words to take with him back home to his people. He brought us news of this holy woman's arrival. He instructed us to make a great tent for her, so with what little strength we had, the grand tent was built, and we waited.

It was Wichahpi and me, two children running through the field of dancing sweet grass, who saw her first appear. We both stopped the moment we saw her—this radiant being, unlike anything we'd ever seen before. We called out that she was coming, and the message was passed on through the village like wildfire while we stood watching this beaming holy woman walk before us. She was surrounded by halos of fire rainbows. The breeze caught strands of her long black hair and the eagle feathers that were braided in and lifted them into the air behind her as she walked. With each step, we could hear the fringe and beads on her white buckskin dress all sound together, like rumbles of distant thunder. I took Wichahpi's hand as this mysterious holy woman looked over at us with her glowing golden eyes. She smiled and bowed her head to greet us as she passed. As Wichahpi and I held hands tightly, greeted by the holy woman, something came over us. Our hands were now bound by a golden prairie rose cord that could never be severed.

The holy woman gave our people a sacred pipe carved from the blessed earth. With it, our holy men could speak to the heavens. She gave us instructions on how to live, how to grow, how to love, and, most importantly, how to pray. She was an angel and a legend to all our people. We thrived after the blessings that followed, and we starved no longer.

When she left that day, Wichahpi and I followed her to a field where she knelt, covering herself in her white buckskin shawl that the blessed pipe was once wrapped in. When she stood, she was no longer in the form of a woman, but that of a white buffalo that ran until it disappeared far in the distance.

Though our lives were full of big changes, I noticed subtle changes in Wichahpi. She would disappear to quiet places and look up to the sky. She was connecting with the Great Spirit. I found her to be the most beautiful in those moments, and I found myself praying more as well, wanting to experience whatever it was that made her glow.

We were never the same after our hands were bound by the holy woman's blessing. As we grew older, we spent time together just as we did when we were kids. I once led her down a path away from the others, just so she could discover the eagle feather I knew to be there. She smiled the same childlike smile that always warmed me. In the stillness of that moment, I swept the hair away from her eyes, my hand gliding past her cheek and to the back of her neck, as I drew her lips to mine. It was a respite in time when the only thing that mattered was the closeness we felt, of our bodies, of our hearts, and our spirits. We clung to that moment while the wild winds began to stir.

The father of Wichahpi was saved when Mato, the great bear, was angered one night. Our bravest hunter spared the life of the bear as well, in heroic efforts. His name was Otaktay, meaning to kill many. Her father wanted to reward the brave hunter with a precious prize for saving his life. The prize was Wichapi. I became the darkness of my name from the pain I was feeling. My whole world fell dark. Every day I prayed for another way. She was always mine, she would always be mine, no matter who decided her fate.

The day before the wedding ceremony arrived, and our people were busy, preparing for a celebration. Wichahpi was surrounded by the women of our tribe, blessing her and braiding her long black hair, as an owl flew into her tipi. It fluttered low and frightened the women, causing a great commotion, until it landed high in the top. There it stilled and stared down at Wichahpi with its glowing golden eyes. The women became silent, looking at this foreboding figure. Owls are omens. Omens of death. A few moments passed, and the mysterious creature flew out quietly, leaving the women uneasy. Not one word was spoken about the spirit visitor. One by one, the women touched Wichahpi's shoulders lovingly on their way out, until she sat alone.

I stepped into her tipi, startling her. She put her hand over her heart but was relieved when she saw it was me. She stood to greet me, and I stepped closer to her. Again, I brushed her hair from her eyes and held her face in my hands as I kissed her. A forbearing kiss, weighted by the sorrow in our hearts. I held her hands and looked into her eyes that were filling with tears. I said nothing. My eyes conveyed my sentiment, until I kissed her hands and walked away.

To celebrate their union, our people had planned a great feast. And for a feast, we must hunt. Most of the young men joined in on the hunt, riding faster than the other. It was customary to allow the celebrated man to make the day's kill, so we all taunted the lucky man until it was time for him to draw his bow and release his arrow.

The brave hunter came too close to one of those dangerous beasts. The buffalo halted and swiped at his horse with his sharp horns, narrowly missing the horse's nose. The horse stopped at once and reared back in fear, again and again, finally throwing the brave hunter to the ground. As he tried to rise and run to his horse, his horse ran further from him while the buffalo was close behind. Other riders tried to distract the beast from his target. They yelled and called out to it, running past it and shooting arrows. Arrows sank into its flesh while his horn tore deep into the side of the brave hunter. Blood was shed by both man and beast that day. Both were laid to rest.

After a time of mourning and seasons painted the trees around us, our people had a reason to celebrate once again. I feel it was the blessing we received from our angel that day, the golden cord of the prairie rose, that allowed Wichahpi and I to become man and wife, raise a family, and a long line of our name. We were called home the day our time of peace was broken and our village was burned. We died together in our tipi, holding each other close, holding hands as tightly as the day we saw our angel in the tall blades of sweet grass. Our tipi was afire, burning and filling with smoke, but an angry wind swirled at our feet and surrounded our bodies. Within the smoke, I could see our angel twirling with her white buckskin shawl, the fringe and beads floating in the air as if time had slowed to a still. The wild wind carried our spirits to the other side. We never felt pain or shed a tear. She wouldn't let us. Our family was able to escape and find help. Our angel is still watching over them, as angels do.

This was the first life that we shared. Our connection began at the dawn of this life, our friendship grew, and our love, blessed. We grew up knowing each other from birth, running through the village with a pack of our dogs playing behind us. We were the curious, watchful eyes of our tribe while learning to become the strong backbone of it. We had survived famine and tragedy together. We had loved and lost. But most importantly, we had been blessed by an angel with a cord that bound us together, which could bend but will never ever break. Not even in death.

Chapter Three

My family bought a large property in a small town I'd never heard of. The town of Clovis had great schools, a charming main street with historical old buildings and many antique shops. There was an innocence to the town, a kindness, the perfect place to raise a family. I was just a little blond-haired boy, more concerned with changing schools and making new friends than anything else, but that quickly changed when I saw the place. This was a real ranch, acres of it, pastures for boarding horses, barns and arenas. It was wide fields surrounded neatly by white fences. The property would be one giant square except for the five-acre lot on the northeast corner where our neighbors lived.

Our little old country house was blue with white trim, two stories, close to the road aptly named Peach Avenue, as we were surrounded by miles of peach orchards. My room was upstairs, facing the property on the corner, which made me curious what kind of people we shared fences with. A twin bed was situated in the corner opposite the window; I also had a bookshelf, a plain wooden desk, and a chair that had been stacked high with moving boxes. My brother's room overlooked the hay barn and smelled of horses, but he was older and got the room ever so slightly larger than mine. He had no idea I was the lucky one with the view.

My mom kept me busy moving boxes, all the ones with my scribbled name, Josh, up to my room for unpacking. All I wanted to do, though, was grab my mountain bike and take a ride around the neighborhood. When you're a kid, that's the greatest taste of freedom you can get, and I was lucky, I could stay gone all day. This town looked like a good place for escape. My family life wasn't turbulent by any means. I had loving parents, and my older brother was fun from time to time, but I was a quiet, contemplative kid. Okay, maybe some people might even call me a little strange. I got along with most people, but for the most part, I just kept to myself and was curious. I had so many questions about life and God and why we were here, but most people couldn't answer those questions for me. Maybe they didn't know either. So I tried my best to act like a normal kid. I liked bike rides and the wind on my face. I liked the grinding of gears shifting and, someday soon learning how to ride without using my hands.

Before we moved to Clovis, when I would ride my bike to a friend's house and miss dinner, my mom would punish me by allowing me to ride my bike only to the library. At first, I thought that was the worst thing that had ever happened to me. I didn't want to sit and read all day when there was a full summer to explore outside. But one day, sequestered in the library, I just happened to walk past a table that had a funny-looking book sitting by itself and no one around to claim it. I sat at the table and flipped through the pages, and it was one of those rare occurrences in life that you'll remember forever. That funny-looking book contained strange words and sayings from all over the world and their meanings. These were words I had never heard before, in foreign languages, but they explained feelings, experiences, and profound things that the English language, or as much as I had learned of it, had no words for. I call myself strange because I became obsessed with a little book that showed me a new world. I used these words in conversation with my friends, and they just looked at me peculiarly. My mom wondered where I was learning these foreign words. She thought perhaps I had met a stranger who might not be a good influence on me. But funny enough, she decided to walk into the library one day, thinking I'd be evading my punishment, but to her utter surprise, I was sitting at the same table where I first found the book. She sat down with me and took the book from my hands. She flipped through the pages and giggled at some of the words.

"Do you know what a gheegle is?" She asked me, smiling.

I shook my head.

"Apparently, it's the urge we feel to pinch something incredibly cute." She put the book down and pinched and tickled me while shushing my laughter. That marvelous, funny-looking book just stayed my sentence early, but I'll remember it always.

Our unpacking got to a manageable point where my mom could find her cooking utensils, and soon, I smelled some familiar scents swirling in the air and up to my bedroom.

"These aren't for you. They're for the neighbors on the corner," she warned, checking the oven. "Okay, maybe you can have one." She winked with a straight face that turned into a grin.

My mom packaged her specialty cookies neatly into a basket covered with a cloth, sighed, and nervously asked, "Ready to meet the neighbors?"

My mom wasn't your typical mom with manicured nails and pretty dresses. My mom loved horses and was more of the outdoorsy, hardworking, not afraid to get her hands dirty type. She was usually in a pair of dusty jeans and boots and some sort of flowery button-down shirt. She was a very kind and generous woman, but you would have to get to know her first. Many people saw my mom's rough, dusty exterior as too high of boundaries, but the ones that saw past that were the lucky ones. As if to look beyond one's crooked garden gate, to admire their blooming roses.

We walked from our house down a long lane that separated our property from our neighbor's. We could see into their horse arena and pens filled with quiet, sleepy horses swishing their tails back and forth. I saw bunny cages that faced the tallest, thickest vegetable garden full of ripe red tomatoes. I was so curious about this place that I just wanted to stand there, peering over their fence to admire all the interesting things that caught my eye, but the crunching of gravel beneath my mom's swift steps kept me from my musings. I had to run a few steps just to catch her. Finally, we saw their house from the front. It was so beautiful. Everywhere I looked, it was enchanting. Overgrown blooming wisteria hung from a giant arbor that had a winding, inviting pathway beneath it. A sprawling lemon tree stretched toward the sky above the east side of the house, begging for its fruit to be picked and made into sweet summer lemonade. I could almost taste it, which made me grow ever so thirsty. There was also a plum tree, so rich with violet orbs, the fruit so ripe. I watched a plum fall from its branch, and I wanted to run over and devour it. The plants looked happier there than I ever remembered plants looking. It seemed like an oasis. It was only fitting that it had tall palm trees lining a long circle driveway. In the center of the driveway was an eight-foot black fountain, ornate in detail and spilling and sloshing with water. I couldn't take my eyes from it. Maybe that was the point—being so captivated by this beautiful fountain that you don't see the dual Rottweiler welcoming committee. My mom squeezed my hand as they started barking, and I jerked to attention.

Just then I could hear a woman with a thick southern accent say hello. "Y'all come on in!" she waved. "They just look mean, but they won't hurt ya." She was tall and tan, with shoulder-length auburn hair, close to my mom's age, wearing jeans and a shirt that looked like she might have been gardening. So she was the garden enchantress.

We walked up a couple of steps to the front porch and through two old carved wooden doors. Everywhere I turned, I saw remnants of an old world. An old world I had never known. My mom's decorating style was just simple country stuff and a few antiques that had been passed down through the family. But this house was just as dark and mysterious as it was enchanted and warm. Every pathway enticed you, every painting romanced you, even the air filled with orange blossom and clove begged, breathe me in, and I did.

"Hi. My name is Jane, and this is Josh. We just moved in behind you and wanted to say hello. We made you some cookies. Hope you like them!" my mom said, smiling and then looking at me.

"I'm so glad y'all came by. I'm Adele, and somewhere around here is Audrey. She's just about your age, Josh." She smiled, turning her head to look for Audrey. Then she graciously accepted the basket of cookies and made some oohs and ahhs at them.

She pulled two cookies out of the basket and handed them to me. "Josh, if you go out the back door, I bet Audrey is out on her trampoline. You should go say hello."

In a matter of moments, Adele's welcoming personality had our nerves dissipating. I could hear our moms asking all kinds of questions about each other and the neighborhood as the back door closed behind me, and just then, the enchanted garden continued. I could see a topaz shimmering gem of a pool calling me on this hot summer's day. Morning glory vines weaved around wrought iron gates and wooden fences.

I walked under a patio cover, which had a whiskey barrel fountain flowing down into a river rock bed, and through the other side of the patio was a sunny patch of lawn surrounded by tall, purple cherry trees. The wild winds I had been feeling suspended, my heartbeat calmed, my breath deepened. It was the first time I felt this current pulling me toward something special. And there she was.

The trees provided a partial canopy that allowed the light to beam through and cover her and the trampoline with both shade and droplets of light. Time slowed. As she jumped on this massive trampoline in the corner of the yard, she stayed in flight for a few moments. Her long, light blond hair floated all the way above her head, danced around her face on its way back down, to bounce in curls below her shoulders. She was in a white T-shirt that had a faded heart on it and pink shorts. Her feet were bare as they normally would be on a trampoline. She jumped up and down on her feet a few times and then would bounce on her backside and back to her feet again. It looked so fun, but I was having more fun just watching her.

"Oh, hi!" she laughed, embarrassed knowing someone was watching her. She stopped jumping and walked to the edge to meet me.

"Hi, I'm Josh. I just moved in over there." I pointed and then handed her a cookie, "Here, my mom made these for you guys. Our moms are talking inside."

"Nice to meet you. I'm Audrey." She chewed as she said her name, giggling and covering her mouth. There was something about that gesture, that moment, that made me feel more comfortable around her. Audrey was so genuine and sweet that I felt like she might be someone I could finally be my strange self around. "Come on up. It's fun." With that invitation, our summer began.

Our mothers found us jumping and laughing and talking as if we had been friends for years. They watched us for a few minutes and laughed at our goofy landings until my mom was ready to head back to the house. "All right, Josh, we still have some unpacking to do. Let's get going, okay?"

I shrugged my shoulders, and we both started climbing down off the trampoline. She stood in front of me on solid ground, and I could see that I was taller than her. She just tilted her head to one side with a frown and waved goodbye. I found myself doing the same thing back to her. I felt sad that this had ended too soon, and I didn't have enough time to ask her any questions. All we did was bounce and laugh, and I had to leave now, wondering.

"You should come over tomorrow and go swimming, Josh," Audrey's mom encouraged, "…as long as it's okay with your mom."

My mom nodded, grinning at me. I looked over at Audrey, and we both smiled wide and quietly celebrated as kids do. I remember walking home that afternoon, realizing that was the first time in my life I was excited for what tomorrow might bring. I was excited that I'd met a new friend, and I couldn't stop smiling about it.

"In the fall, you and Audrey are going to the same school together. She's not in your grade, but at least you'll have a friend there. What did you think of her?" my mom asked, several strides ahead of me.

"She seems nice," I answered her in my simple, vague boy terms.

I went straight up to my room, taking another cookie when my mom wasn't looking. I sat near the window and could see the fence to Audrey's backyard. Just behind that fence, I saw her blond hair flying up into the air and back down again from the bounce. I ate each bite of my cookie slowly, chewing, watching the rise and fall of that beautiful girl. I had just met someone my soul recognized, and my young mind was still trying to understand it all.

A slap on my shoulder broke my concentration. "What's up, dude?" my brother sighed. He stood behind me, looking out the window. If he didn't know what to look for, he wouldn't be able to see her. "Hey, I heard you met the neighbors. What are they like?"

"They seem nice. Their house is so cool. They have a pool and a trampoline. I got to jump on the trampoline with the girl. Her name is Audrey." I sat on the bed, and John sat at the edge of it. "I get to go swimming over there tomorrow."

"Cool. I wish we had a pool." John frowned in disappointment.

John was the quintessential cool older brother. He was athletic, attractive, charming, and everything I wanted to be. I was just a skinny little brother, more of a quiet, daydreaming bookworm. But in the time I'd have to grow into a man, I'd be taking notes from him.

I turned back to the window and looked for the long, blonde bouncing curls, but she must have gone inside. I wondered what she was up to now. I wondered what she liked to do during the day, during the night. Was her favorite color pink? What were her dog's names? I knew tomorrow I'd have these questions at the ready. I knew I'd have trouble going to sleep. I knew tomorrow would really be something.

The sounds of horses stirring, lark sparrows chirping, mourning doves cooing, bees buzzing in the tree just outside my window, and my mom downstairs, cooking breakfast, roused me from dreamland, awake enough to contemplate my senses. The sun peaked over the tops of the trees in peach and pink tones, vibrant oranges and rays of sweet morning. It was all so beautiful, I wished a painter had their easel and paints set up to capture it. I would come to learn that what I thought was a rare glimpse of heaven as I woke was just your average sunrise in the country, and summers were ripe with them.

My dad and brother were just grasping handfuls of food and rushing out the door as I came down the stairs. I watched their commotion and sat at the kitchen table, still sleepy and quiet. My mom rushed around me, serving me heaping piles of scrambled eggs, seasoned country potatoes, sausage links, and toast. I thanked her and dug into the warm country feast as if I'd gone hungry for days. My mom was just happy that I had a healthy appetite and seemed to be adjusting to the new surroundings well, so while holding a wooden spoon and kitchen towel in one hand, resting on her hip, she wrapped her other arm around my shoulders and kissed my head. Then roughed up my blond hair with her hand to bring the trifecta to a close as she always did. It always made me giggle, even with my cheeks full.

As boxes emptied and began to disappear one by one throughout the old house, our ranch was a busy, bustling dust cloud of big trucks and horse trailers. Rigs, as they call them. I could see my dad directing traffic and my brother leading horses around by the halter to their new temporary home. We were going to offer boarding services to local horse people, so our job was to feed and water them, see to any minor veterinary needs, and exercise them if the horse was of a special working type. I didn't pay much attention to all of the details. I was just excited when my dad saddled up a horse and let me ride one once in a while. We had a few horses of our own.

They were sweet old tired souls that each one of us in the family had developed a connection with. They loved us and were glad to do anything we asked.

When you want a dependable, stable horse, there's nothing better than that, but there are sometimes when you just want a horse that's full of life and vigor, and unpredictability. These were the kinds of horses we were boarding. They were beasts that struck at the ground with their hooves and ran wild through our pastures, kicking and bucking, only to stop at a thicket of grass to nibble on. It dawned on me when I saw these wild beasts playing that they weren't beasts at all, but more like big puppies. They'd kick a giant ball around this field if they had one. Just big puppies, and we were a puppy daycare.

I jumped on my bike and started riding along the lanes that separated the pastures, lined with white painted fences and the occasional thirsty rosebush. I rode west all the way to the railroad tracks that lay just behind a very tall line of eucalyptus trees. On the other side of the row of trees was a long lane that wrapped all the way around to the front of our property. I took time to explore it all. I noticed all the squirrel residents, who stopped what they were doing to stare at me, the new kid. I pedaled quietly and slowly through the barn breezeways not wanting to startle the friendly long faces that peeked out of the stalls to greet me. I said hello to each one, and some of them gave me a big chin raise, greeting me in their horsey way.

It seemed I was making one giant circle down the lanes I traveled, until I got to the lane that took me to Audrey's house. There were more rose bushes along this path than the others, which figures, since I was entering the land of the enchanted. And suddenly I saw her. There she was, riding an aqua blue bicycle toward me. She liked bikes! I immediately took a hand off the handles to wave a big, silly wave, and she did the same. We met halfway down the lane and came to a dramatic halt, digging into the gravel. I was happy to see her, as if I'd discovered something magical, and I couldn't wait to learn more about it. She was a blond-haired, sun-kissed, and freckle-cheeked new friend. Her eyes were a topaz blue-green, and had dimples when she smiled. All things I silently made note of as she was talking to me.

Serendipity. A common word most of us know. It means finding something wonderful without even looking for it. Apotelesma is a lesser-known word, ages old, that references the effect the stars have on destiny. You could say both of these words apply to the day that changes a life forever, but there's a Japanese phrase that captures the feeling I had when I first met her. Koi No Yokum is what two people feel upon meeting, a knowing that one day they are destined to fall in love.

"Let's pick some peaches for your mom," she said and waved on as she led the way. She rode her bike like a boy, to my surprise. I was a little shocked at the tomboy before me, but I liked it. She looked back at me with voice raised, "Follow meee."

She pedaled down the lane and across the street from her house. She leaned her bike against the soft tilled ground. Our feet sank into it. Out of her pocket, she pulled a bag and began to fill it. "Do you like peaches? They're perfect right now."

I picked a couple of round, fuzzy peaches, blushing in pinks and soft oranges, along with her, and answered, "I do…I think. I can't remember."

She giggled, "We'll have some later by the pool." By that time, the bag was full. "In the springtime, all of these trees are covered in little pink flowers. It's so pretty! It's like a dream."

Her face lit up as she described the scene to me. I would've stood there trying to imagine the pink peach blossoms, but I was too caught up in her smile. The dimples on her cheeks and the sparkle in her eyes. She stood her bike up and walked it to the road.

"Let's go to your house and drop these off," she said, with a squinted smile and wrinkled nose from the sunlight in her eyes.

"Yeah, let's go." I nodded and climbed on my bike behind hers.

We rode just down the street to my blue house and pedaled into the driveway, leaned our bikes on the lawn by the front door, and ventured inside. My family was all outside, handling horse business, so luckily, I could show her my house without some awkward family encounter. She was very observant but quiet. She smiled when she saw something that she liked. There were those dimples again.

My mom always had a big bowl of fruit on the kitchen counter, but it had been empty since we moved in, with so little time for grocery shopping. This was the perfect place for all these big ripe peaches. It made a beautiful display. But I didn't care; I was a boy with big afternoon plans. One of them being...should I let this girl see my room? The words escaped my mouth before I really had time to think. "Hey, you wanna see my room? It's kinda messy, but..."

"Yeah!" She was way more excited to see a messy boy's room than I ever anticipated. Panic thoughts ran through my head, like did I leave any underwear on the floor?

Luckily, my mom had swept through my room with all the tell-tale signs. My bed was made, and my things were tidy, with no underwear lurking. Thank you, Mom. She'd had no idea that I'd have a friend over to see my room; she had just done her normal mom things that she did every day. It had gone unnoticed and unappreciated...until now.

"I like your room." She glanced over my things, toys, and books, and I didn't mind. Then she went to the window. "You can see my backyard from here. Do you like it here?"

I glanced out the window at where she'd be on her trampoline with her hair floating. "Yeah, I'm starting to." The smile on my face was growing. I had to remind myself to be cool, cause that's what my brother would be telling me. He told me many times, whether he's right or wrong, that you can't let girls know that you like them. "You gotta play it cool, man." He'd pat me on the shoulder and then rough up my blond hair like Mom did.

"Are you ready to go swimming?" she asked, not knowing it had been on my mind since the offer was made.

I eagerly nodded, and in a flash, we were spinning tires and kicking gravel, going down the lane and rounding the corner to her house. Now that this was my second time to the enchanted garden I called her house, I noticed that her pasture had unpainted wooden fences, and her backyard fence was made of wooden posts in a row, framed by adobe brick towers. At the top of the brick towers were large black lanterns. They must've looked spectacular at night, all lit up, and I tried to make a mental note to look out my window after dark to see them. Perched on one of the fences was a big black and white cat, with long, fluffy hair, who seemed to be resting until her favorite person, Audrey, returned from her ride. Sure enough, the closer we got to the cat, it stood up and stretched slowly, then came meowing up to her. Leaving her bike and rushing to her cat, she made introductions, "This is Bednight." She held the big fur fluff in her arms and giggled.

"Bednight?" I tilted my head, questioning.

"When we got her, I was too young to say midnight. My family thought it was funny, so it kinda stuck."

"That is funny. Hello, Bednight." I scratched the fluff's forehead and around the ears. The kitty looked up at me with her big golden eyes, sizing me up and searching my soul. I passed the test, I suppose, when the cat wrapped her paws around my hand. It made Audrey giggle. She was young, but she already knew the value of an animal's judgment of character.

And there, finally before me, a glittering, glistening, beckoning jewel in this California desert. I took my t-shirt off, kicked off my shoes, and ran five steps, gaining speed for a most impressive cannonball right in the middle of the pool. She stood at the edge of the pool in a one-piece suit that was pink and gray. She was laughing at my spectacle but was hesitant. There are two types of people in this world when faced with a pool or big decision. There are those who dive right in and deal with the rush of cold water with a scream and laughter. Then there are those who dip their toes in the cold and need a little coaxing. They need someone to tell them it's ok…jump in…everything's fine. And that's what I told her. That's what I was here for.

In minutes, we were laughing and playing, splashing water all over her backyard and floating on giant pool floats of different shapes. There were a couple of beach balls, a water slide, and speakers playing my favorite radio station. Her mom soon appeared with plates full of snacks. Sure enough, there was a sliced peach on a plate with strawberries and sliced watermelon, cheese, and crackers. Audrey's mom asked if we were having fun, and I wanted to tell her right then that I wanted to move in. I wanted to tell her that her house was magical, and I never wanted to leave it, and that I really liked her daughter. But I played it cool, man. I said yes and thanked her for the food as I made my way through the water to the decadent poolside display. Her mom also brought out two giant folded beach towels for us to wrap up in when we were done. We quieted down while we were chewing. I told her, "Your mom is really nice."

"Sometimes." She giggled back.

Suddenly, Audrey's older sister opened the backyard gate and stomped through. She was tall like her mom, blond and tan, but definitely seemed different than Audrey. Have you ever been irritated with someone just by how they carry themselves? It was a snooty walk with big steps and a bounce, her nose so high in the air that she didn't see Bednight dart across her path but not fast enough.

"Damn cat!" she screeched, trying to collect herself. That's when she looked down at the pool and saw the two of us. "What are you looking at?" she snapped, bent down to steal a slice of watermelon, and continued her snooty walk into the back door of the house.

I bit into a slice of peach, the colorful fruit, shades of gold and oranges and magenta that work a spell on your tongue. I remembered tasting a peach before but not like this one. Soft and sweet like a mixture of honey and summer and countless dreamy pink petals, the best way I could describe the taste of it, with a warm feeling in my chest as I looked over at my new friend. Her tiny frame, bronzed from hours of summer sunlight, her blond hair slightly darker when wet and slicked back against her head, her eyes red from chlorine, while her green irises seemed brighter than I remembered them being before.

I noticed Audrey had become disheartened. She looked down at the water and ate another bite. She was embarrassed by her sister acting so rudely to her new friend, as if there was anything she could've done about it.

"You wanna see my hiding place?" she asked me with the slightest curve returning to the edges of her lips. "I like to go there and get away from my sister."

Everything about her house so far seemed fun and mysterious, so I nodded eagerly. With our beach towels wrapped around our soaked bodies and flip flops on our feet, we walked to a massive double gate made of large wooden spikes and iron latches. Standing on her tiptoes, she reached for the top latch that would open the gates, just enough for us to squeeze through, and then latched it back again from the inside. A closed gate usually meant that no one was out with the horses, and she was less likely to be found.

On my left, I could see a single-story, plain building she called the tack room. It had a sliding door that was already open just enough to see the same riding equipment we had at home. There were numerous saddles and bridles, halters, ropes, hackamores, brushes, horse blankets, and various other things horse people need. There was even a feed bag or two and a string of bells that you'd drape around a horse's neck for a parade event. And on the right were the two big bunny cages, high off the ground. The rabbit's cages faced a most ripe, robust, and colorful garden. I remembered thinking it must've been torturous for the little guys being so close to something they wanted so much but couldn't have.

We continued walking past the garden, the arena, and beside a long hitching post to a high, rusty open hay barn. It was stacked to the roof full of hay bales. Audrey walked with her arms out, keeping her balance in front of me, into the stack of bales. We climbed a stack of them to a certain level where she had laid out a blanket and a book, James and The Giant Peach, from an earlier visit. I could see now that with seclusion and the view, this was an ideal spot to disappear to. Once we got seated and comfortable, she reached beside her and pulled a small plastic bag that contained my mom's cookies. She handed me one with a big grin. "These are really good."

You truly learn a lot about a person when you spend time in their environment. The enchanted house and her friendly mom had seemed so perfect until I saw what her sister was like. I recognized the differences between Audrey and her sister immediately. It was night and day, storm clouds and sunlight. I could tell there was a lot more to the story, but I wasn't sure how to ask, so I went with a good one. "Do you have a favorite color, Audrey?"

She looked up to the sky and pursed her lips in thought. "My mom buys me pink stuff cause I'm a girl, but I think my favorite color is blue, like the sky or water." She looked over at me and asked the same question.

"That's my favorite color too. I really like dark blue."

Her eyes sparkled, "Yeah, like when the stars come out. That blue." She paused to smile, and her dimples appeared. "My favorite time of night is when the sun goes down and the sky is getting darker, and one by one the stars peek out. I always point out the first couple of stars I see."

Just when I thought I had her figured out, I found new hidden layers. I knew deep down that she was quite different from anyone I'd ever known. She was a gentle free spirit. She had a deep connection to nature, to the land, the animals, plants, music, and art in mysterious ways I'd never known possible. I loved how she found so much beauty from the earth. She was drawn to anything with soul, and the deeper the better. I felt so at peace in her presence. She always marveled at the beauty around her. She seemed to always be searching for the miraculous creations of the earth and never hesitated to point out their beauty. I knew even back then that she was a wise, old soul disguised as a sweet little girl.

She introduced me to all her horses and the two Rottweilers, Pete and Pepper. She told me about her very first dog, a wolf hybrid named Sam, who had been her closest companion and protector. He would follow her everywhere, on daily trips to the garden, while riding her bike, and would sleep next to her at night. On Valentine's Day, years back, Audrey heard a knock at the door in the pouring rain. As her mother opened the door, a tall man in a long black coat, holding a shotgun, informed them in the coldest of terms, "Your dog was chasing my sheep, so I shot him." Audrey was quiet for some time.

"That's horrible." I shook my head and stared at the ground.

"It hurts when I forget. Sometimes I look for him or call his name, and then I remember that he's gone. But I think he's watching over us. He sent someone in his place," she said, pointing to Pepper. Several days after her family heard the sad news about Sam, when Audrey was out playing, she kept seeing a dog hanging around their property, coming closer but still cautious, and pointed it out to her father. That dog was welcomed into the family and given the name Pepper, and weeks later, she delivered a litter of puppies that looked an awful lot like Sam. Pete was one of Sam's pups. She showed me a drawing of Sam, and I learned then that she was artistic, and drawing was her favorite pastime.

I learned that her favorite food was her mom's lasagna, and her least favorite foods were pickles and mushrooms. I learned that she was really afraid of spiders after an incident in the hay barn. I'm afraid of spiders too, but I had to play it cool, man. My brother would be so proud. As we sat in the haybarn, a strong gust of wind blew through the old sheets of metal, rattling them, like they would fly off at any moment. The wind carried a dove feather, spiraling slowly down in front of us. Audrey rushed to pick it up, smiling widely, gently running her fingertip down its soft edge, "When feathers appear, angels are near. Did you know that?"

That was the first time I heard that saying. As she waved her feather around, excitement changing her expression, I realized how much it meant to her. I soon noticed feathers everywhere she went.

From that day, we became great pals—the "let's do this again tomorrow" kind of pals. I left the enchanted garden and headed down the gravel lane toward my house with my heart so full. She was the kind of pal you couldn't wait to spend time with, and my smile lasted well into my sleep.

Our summer comprised riding bikes all around the lanes and quiet country roads, riding horses at her house and at mine, and cooling off in her pool, with her mom bringing us poolside snacks every time. We became inseparable, a heart connection of the purist form that two young friends could have. We were just two good pals, good kids, who were usually out of sight and out of trouble. What more could our parents ask for? Before we knew it, we had splashed our summer away and stood in a new season.

Our moms dropped Audrey and me off at the entrance of this new school one bright, sunny early morning. They took pictures of us standing next to each other holding our lunchboxes and squint-smiling into the sun. Moments later, our different classrooms were located, and we drifted into the mix. I was happy knowing she was there. I sat wondering how she was doing most of the time. Was she wondering about me? Would we see each other after class?

I formed friendships fast there, to my surprise, and usually found myself busy playing with my new friends at recess and lunch. Our break times were not typically at the same time, so we didn't get to see each other then. Somehow, I'd miss her after class as well. But we made up for lost time on weekends and crammed in our storytelling and laughing the best we could.

One day I looked out my classroom window and was able to see her playing with her friends at recess. They were playing on these bright yellow bars that we used for pull-ups, but they were also great for climbing on. Close by I could see two older boys tossing around a baseball and hitting it with a bat. For some reason, I was watching at the particular moment when the baseball bat hit a line drive straight at Audrey. It hit her right on her forehead and knocked her unconscious. I could see lots of kids on the school grounds running in her direction, so I jumped out of my seat and ran outside, all the way to her. I pushed kids out of the way until I saw her on the ground in front of me. She wasn't moving. I grabbed her hand and yelled her name. I yelled it over and over again until I saw her eyes open a bit. She looked at the crowd of people around her and drifted back out.

I put one arm under her neck and the other under her knees, gently picking her up off the ground. The crowd of kids slowly moved out of my way with nothing but a slight whisper among them. They were scared. Even though Audrey was a quiet little girl, she had become well known with the kids, and there was a real dread that came over everyone watching me carry her away. It felt like the longest walk of all time to get her to the nurse's office on the other side of the campus. Would she be okay? Had I gotten there in time? What could I do? The nurse greeted me and pointed to the bed in the other room. I rested her head gently on the white pillow and fixed her blond hair around her shoulders. I fixed her hands and her dress and sat down beside her. The nurse was busy talking to teachers and staff, a plan was made to call Audrey's mom right away, and then the nurse came in to see her. I held her hand and wouldn't let it go. The nurse didn't have much room to get around me, so eventually I had to let go and step back. She instructed me to get back to class right away, but I hesitated. How could I go back to my classroom after this? How could I leave her? Even then, I couldn't leave her.

The principal stepped into the room and asked to speak to me outside, so I followed. He praised me for bringing Audrey right into the nurse's room and helping her as I did. He told me that Audrey's mom was almost here to take her to the hospital, and that she would be just fine. With a heavy pat on the back, he told me I should go back to class and not worry about a thing. He also rewarded me with a brand-new Lincoln Lion number two pencil for my bravery.

But I didn't want a damn pencil. I wanted to stay with Audrey all day. Or at least until I knew that she'd be okay. I was not ready to let her go. I doubt I'd ever be. I went to the boys' bathroom, sat in a stall with my head buried in my hands, and cried more tears than I ever remembered. The tears just flowed. And my heart panged.

My teacher that year happened to be one of the best teachers I'd ever had. Mr. Spurgeon was his name. After a while of crying, apparently, I had been missed, so Mr. Spurgeon came into the boy's bathroom looking for me. That day, he was probably the only person in the world who could've coaxed me out of that stall before I was ready. He had short rusty brown hair and a mustache. He was an athletic guy, always wearing hiking shoes and cargo shorts instead of your usual teacher stuff. Once a week, when there were meetings he had to attend, the class would see him dressed up in jeans, a short-sleeved button-down shirt, and a knit tie. The man had some unusual taste in attire, but he was fun and made things interesting, and that was real currency as a teacher.

Mr. Spurgeon tapped on the stall door and asked, "Hey buddy, are you all right in there? My friends are firemen and can get the jaws of life to open that door if you need 'em."

I stood up and slowly unlatched the door. I didn't have much to say; I just looked up at him with my tear-soaked face. His mustache moved to one side of his face as he reached into his back pocket for a neatly folded bandana. It almost looked pressed with an iron. He stood aside and shook it out like a magician, trying to afford me some comic relief, and then ran the cloth under the faucet for a few seconds. Once it was evenly wet, he wrung it out on the concrete floor and gently placed the cool cloth against my face. It was a relief. It was a kind gesture that instantly made me feel better.

"Ok, Josh, I know today was a rough day for you, so I called your mom, and she's headed here to pick you up." He added, "You know, you did a really brave thing today. You just bolted right out and helped that little girl when no one else even knew what happened. I'm proud of you. You're like a guardian angel."

My teacher led me all the way out to the parking lot and waited with me for my mom. It seemed Audrey had already left, and when my mom was pulling out of the parking lot, I could still see teachers gathered together, Mr. Spurgeon joining them now, discussing the day's events. Probably wishing they had answers just like me.

The next day, I woke up and couldn't focus. My clothes were barely on, my shoes untied, my hair unbrushed, and all I wanted to know was if Audrey was okay. I still didn't know. My mom cleaned me up. At the breakfast table, she brushed my hair as I ate my cereal. She packed all my school things up, and soon I was walking into the commotion of my classroom. Before it began, Mr. Spurgeon took me aside and gave me the good news. Audrey's mom had called the school and updated them on her condition. She had a concussion but was resting and doing fine. I suddenly had a smile on my face that beamed all morning.

When my mom picked me up at the end of the day, we both buckled in, and she paused, looking at me. "Hey, you wanna go see Audrey?"

My mouth gaped open, and she added, "This isn't a play date. It's only to say hello, and that's it.

"Yes, please. Let's go!"

"I picked up some goodies for you to give her. That's what you do when someone's feeling yucky." She pointed to the grocery bag in the back seat.

Clovis was a small town, and in minutes, we were driving down Audrey's road toward Peach Avenue and came up to her long circle driveway. But just before driving in, I yelled, "Wait!" and my mom hit the brake pedal sharply. I jumped out of the car and looked both ways before running across the road to the orchard of blooming peach trees. I carefully broke off branches with the most blooms, remembering how much she loved this time of year. I saw my mom smiling at me in a way I hadn't seen before. She was proud of me, but I think she knew then that this wasn't something a boy did for just any friend. Audrey's Rottweilers came running toward the car, bouncing around, curious what I was carrying.

"Oh, Pete, come on," Audrey's mom yelled from the door. "Y'all come on in."

Audrey's mom and my mom began chatting, but I remained quiet and concerned. I just wanted to see her. I craned my neck to see into the next room, but she wasn't in view. I wandered into the living room that was just off their kitchen, which was where I found her. She was resting on a foam folding chair that had been laid out like a big bed. She was surrounded by doodles and drawings of all her favorite things. She was watching a movie and had snacks and drinks on the coffee table next to her. I tiptoed into the room, not wanting to startle her, but I think I did anyway.

"Oh wow, you're here!" she whispered excitedly. However, her thousand-kilowatt smile was not able to hide the giant goose egg on her little forehead where the baseball had hit her. She had black eyes and looked pale. Man, I hated seeing her like this, but she was alive and happy to see me, and that was everything. A new kind of smile graced her face when she saw the peach blossoms, as if to say, "You remembered."

My mom brought a package into the room that contained cupcakes from the grocery store. She pulled one out for each of us and rubbed the top of my head, which left my hair a mess, then went back over to chat with Audrey's mom, and let us visit.

"Mom says you're my hero," Audrey said, with white frosting on her lips.

"Me? Oh, I just saw what happened and had to help you. I ran out of class and didn't even get in trouble." I shrugged off the praise and replaced it with a bite of cupcake.

"Thank you. You're always looking out for me." Her little grin at me spoke volumes more than her little words did.

"I always will."

"Promise?" she asked, whispery.

"I promise," I whispered back, and I meant it.

Our eyes met, and there was something about it. We held our gaze, a hidden language discovered therein. We could cross our eyes and smile, we could shrug our shoulders, breathe out a huge breath deflating our cheeks, or just simply read each other. While most people shyly avert their attention, we can just be. We were open, like strange little books, full of wonders like that book that changed the way I looked at life.

We sat holding hands in a way our moms couldn't see, and when it was time to go, I hugged her and kissed her cheek. I could see she was surprised by that gesture, and I'll never forget the smile she had from it. What the heck just came over me? Then I stood up and pinched her toes teasingly, to play it cool. As we left her house and continued home, I began to notice how peach blossoms would bloom in my mind at the thought of her.

Peach blossoms are loved all over the world, signifying true love. There's ancient folklore about the peach blossom, that travelers in an ancient time followed a trail of peach blossoms that led to an otherworldly place. In this place of utopia, time stood still, and the inhabitants of this strange place were protected from the perils of the outside world. Over time, the story would develop into a parable about unrealistic expectations, but I knew better. Our bond was a peach blossoming trail that led to otherworldly places, and time would tell if we can find our way back again.

Chapter Four

Yugen is a Japanese word describing the concepts of beauty and mystery and the heartbreak of our world and how sometimes that could bring us to tears. It's also attributed to art and love and life, sweet and bitter, happiness and pain, love and loss, and how you can't have one without the other. When you cross over, or depending on how much life you've already lived, you'll find that yugen describes life perfectly.

Gavri's Mediterranean-style home was open, with curved doorways and lots of indoor plants. The pathos plants had been there for many years, as they had grown long stems from their pots that hung and draped with care. There were huge ceramic pots that held leafy palm trees near his windows. And the windows had sheer white, long curtains that caught gusts of wind that blew in. The wind filled them with air like a sail on a ship, and then they would fall gently back down again, repeating over and over. There was something soothing to it, watching the breathing rhythm of his home, though an unpleasant reminder of this veil that separates me from the ones I love.

His house was filled with fascinating things he'd collected from all over the world, throughout time. This collection was absolutely priceless. I was standing next to artifacts that the world would clamor to see. I just stood there and studied each piece, trying to remember its place in history, and wondering what Gavri's role was in all of it. Visions began to play out in my mind so vividly that I had to wonder if I was getting a glimpse of his history playing out before me or if my imagination was just still overstimulated. I was starting to understand that the man who had quite literally taken me under his wing had been around for centuries.

He had jewel-encrusted crowns resting on plump velvet pillows. He had a progression of swords that looked like they had developed through the ages. The collection was masterful. He had skulls of creatures I'd never seen before. I stood in awe. Had these creatures roamed the earth? They were both enormous and terrifying, as if they were from the dinosaur era, and then there were some that were tiny. These were too small to be human at all. They had oddly shaped skulls and long, thin bodies, almost as if they were miniature human skeletons. But what were they? Humanlike skulls with elongated brain cavities. Where did those come from? My questions were multiplying until I paused. Questions on this side of the veil were answered differently than we were ever taught growing up. Usually, it took asking the question to the right person, and you might get your answer back then. All I had to do now was seek the answer within.

This was a startling revelation, that all the answers were lying within us, the whole time. All we had to do was quiet our minds enough to find them. In a chaotic world, by design, some would say, the answers within us stay buried and grown over, like treasures waiting to be tripped over. All it would take is a journey inward, self-discovery, and meditation. Strange how most of the people who have caught onto the revelation are thought of as strange by society. And yet that society is the most confused and disconnected of all.

Just then, distracting me from my fascination, I heard the roar of a motorcycle pull into the driveway out front. I could see through the blowing curtain a faint figure of Gavri in a white T-shirt, jeans, and boots throw one leg over the side of the bike and walk in. No need for helmets here because there was no traffic or wrecks or injuries—only the purest open road view and biking experience one could dream of having on earth. "Hey Gavri, you're an angel. So, why the bike?"

Amusement came over him as he answered me, "Just something

I've always wanted to do." He walked over to me. "You found my collection, I see. What do you think?"

"It's incredible. I still can't believe I'm standing here seeing all of this."

"I have a bunch more to show you, but we'll get to that." The amused expression on his face turned somber. "This is the day, brother. It's time."

He pursed his lips in consolation and bowed his head as his hand firmly grasped my forearm. In a breath, we were in Audrey's circle driveway, where a lot had changed in the years that had passed since we were kids.

The black fountain in the middle of the driveway didn't seem so giant now that I was no longer a boy. The palm trees had grown taller, and the garden was even more grown over, though it had lost a bit of its enchantment since my last visit. Something had happened here. In my heart, I knew the passage of time hadn't been kind to this family. Time rarely is. We were met by a smiling woman with long black hair and glowing golden eyes. She had such a lovely spirit, some kind of gentle aura surrounding her, and I knew this was Audrey's other guardian. Her smile was for me, the kind of smile you have when holding a heavy heart.

"Hi Josh. How are you feeling?" she asked politely, though already knowing I was worried out of my mind, my stomach wrenching.

I shrugged. How does one answer that question? But she knew.

"This is Emuna. It means Faith." Gavri wrapped his muscle-bound arm around her, making her look tiny.

"You can call me Em," she told me as she patted Gavri's forearm that rested on her shoulder. These two went way back. You just assume that guardian angels develop a friendship while watching over you, but still, it was a pleasure to see right before me. It was as if Audrey had two sets of parents caring for her, adoring her, and she didn't even know it.

"It's time to go in." Em pointed to the front door.

Audrey's mother was cooking breakfast and calling her to the table, losing patience with every call. Audrey was a teenager in high school now, and mothers and daughters go through a normal irritation with each other during this time. I could see there was more under the surface. Audrey's mother wasn't the friendly, charming woman I first met all those years ago. You could see deep-rooted disappointment and sadness in her eyes. Unresolved problems in her marriage had soured into resentment. You cannot carry these heavy feelings without it taking its toll on you. It was sad to see how life had changed her.

As I was studying the change in her mother, Audrey rushed into the room and sat at the table. Pouring a glass of milk, she thanked her mom for making breakfast and scooped scrambled eggs onto her plate. Her mom stood quietly while she finished cooking the sausage and then walked toward Audrey to add a few links to her plate. Her mother lingered behind her and apathetically delivered the news we were dreading for her to hear.

"Hey, did you hear about that kid you used to play with, Josh, I think? He died the night of his graduation. He had been drinking and wrecked his truck."

Audrey sat frozen in her chair. The shock of the news overcame her. Her body was completely still, her breathing nearly nonexistent. Her mother couldn't see the heartbreak in Audrey's eyes, the welling up of tears that spilled out effortlessly over her cheeks. She wanted to scream but couldn't. Em whispered into Audrey's ear, telling her to go to her room and rest, and she listened. Ever so quietly, without saying a word or eating a bite, she left the table and closed herself off in her room. She buried her face into a pillow and broke into pieces. We were all there with her, though she had no one to hold her together. I would've done anything in my power at that moment to change things. Reverse time. Refuse the drinks. Lose that friend. I lay on the bed beside her and wrapped my arms around her tightly.

I'm right here, Audrey. I love you. If only I could fix things.

But I could feel her pain radiating through me. I felt her confusion and despair. It was unbearable. She felt our connection severed by my passing. But it was much deeper than that. The course of her life, as it was meant to play out, had just been drastically altered, forever. The red thread that connected us, the prairie rose cord that bound our hands and hearts, was still very much intact, though to her, was no longer.

I looked at her angels, and they were standing silently together, eyes closed, with their hands reaching toward her. They were healing her. They were surrounding her in love and peace as beams of different colored light streamed from their hands and gathered into a pool around us. I felt that too. It was one of the purest things I'd ever experienced. If only this broken world had more of it.

My eyes wandered around her room. Beyond the typical mess a teenager makes, there was her kind of beauty covering the walls. If it wasn't photos of her and friends, it was her sketches and art inspiration. There were so many of the beach, mermaids, and flowers. It would seem that she identified with mermaids, the lonely creatures that they were. There was one sketch she had named Sand Dollar Beach, which she had just turned into the painting now resting on her easel. It was our happy place, Pismo Beach. One of those paintings you could step right into—if only we could. A sinking, sparkling tide revealing shells and sand dollars, treasures in her path. Dark clouds moving in, and rain showers in the distance. So much healing poured into the imagery, the rich colors and softness. In the coming days, Audrey would learn from this very painting that there was healing radiating from her work. This painting would mark the beginning of the discovery of her purpose.

Audrey fell asleep clutching one of the only photos she had of us together. It was our first day of school after our first wonderful summer together. We were just two little blond kids, arms around each other and smiling, as we were about to embark on a journey.

That journey, though starting out together at the same school, quickly changed, and different schools became different lives. We had new friends, began to spend our free time playing sports and hanging out with the same sex, trying to understand the opposite. We were growing up quickly. Audrey had gotten involved in volleyball and softball. There were times I could see her practicing with her friends out in her arena. I could see that she was getting better and better and growing taller. There were times I'd ride past her house and could hear her plinking away at her piano. She had always wanted to play, and each time I passed her window, I could hear the music improving and flowing. There were even times I could faintly hear Beethoven and Mozart from my bedroom window, and it always made me feel proud. Though we didn't hang out as much as we had when we were little kids, I still paid attention even if it was here and there, from afar. I still saw her blond hair floating in the air as she jumped on the trampoline. I could see much more of her now that she had grown up a bit. I wanted to see her again to catch up, and I knew that someday soon, we would get our chance.

One afternoon, I came to the stop sign at the corner of Peach and Nees. The corner of land before me was her pasture dotted with grazing horses, and there she was. She was riding one of her horses without a saddle as if she had just spontaneously jumped on, surrounded by her playful panting dogs. They just ambled through the grass, her bare feet dangling, her blond hair swaying with the movement, and her whimsical dogs making her laugh. I was captivated again, in a moment when time had slowed. She was even more beautiful than I remembered.

I had grown to love baseball and had a letterman jacket to prove it. All the girls loved the jacket, and being a tall blond with blue eyes didn't hurt things. But I didn't have a girlfriend. Some of my friends did, and I heard all about it, but I was just too busy with sports and studying for all that. I worked hard on my grades. I wasn't the smartest guy in the class, but I managed to get impressive marks and, with my sports achievements, was awarded a full ride to Fresno State, the local university that wasn't even five minutes away. My friend, Brandon, was on the team too, but the girls and the partying kept him from getting a scholarship. I could tell deep down he was a little jealous, and it bothered him, but he tried really hard to hide it from me.

One particularly beautiful night, I was Brandon's designated driver. He liked to visit his dad's liquor cabinet and hit the whiskey. He had a decent job at the hardware store, and he was clever enough to replace what he drank so his dad never noticed. But on this beautiful night, I was tasked with driving Brandon and his little brother around. We teased his little brother a bit before dropping him off at the junior high dance. Just a few years ago, I was going to the same school for these dances, and as a rite of passage, I gave him the same treatment I had gotten.

We tooled around town and had just enough money for a cheeseburger at our favorite spot. It was a great place to eat while watching the people stroll by. I loved people watching. I was an introvert and an observer, so this was a time to enjoy good food and be entertained by people and their silly ways, silly clothes, and funny walks. We had several drink refills when I realized the time. "We better get to the dance. He's probably waiting for us."

"Eh, it's still early. Let him squirm." Brandon chuckled sinisterly with his straw between his teeth.

I started cleaning up, and he followed my lead. We headed back but were not in too big of a hurry, and when we got to the school grounds, we just waited out on the big lawn in the middle of campus. The school lights were on, but the moon was brighter that night. We stood out in the calm, warm evening air and listened to the music escaping the school gym. Kids were scattered here and there, most of them were sitting down, waiting for their parents to pick them up from a dance they were more than eager to leave. Apparently, our boy had himself a fun time in there, and we were happy for him. We were laughing at the idea of him dancing with girls when a beautiful girl caught my eye.

She was walking with a friend across the edge of the grass. I could only see her from a distance, but she held my attention. She had long tan legs in a light peach-colored sundress. Brandon never noticed me watching this girl walk all the way into the gym. He was too busy making fun of his brother and telling me funny stories. We were laughing at one when, after maybe ten minutes had passed, the girl in the peach sundress appeared again. I was consumed. Who was this girl? Her hair was blond, and her skin was kissed by the sun from a poolside summer. Our laughter at one of Brandon's stories made her turn her head in my direction, and it was then that I recognized her. It was Audrey.

The blood in my body raced, my face flushed, and my mouth hung open in shock. This beautiful girl—woman!—was Audrey. My Audrey. She was almost as tall as I was, long and lanky as young kids are, but she was all grown up and absolutely stunning. "Audrey?"

"Josh?" she echoed. She walked toward me in slow motion as if my mind were recording her movements, frame by frame, so that I'd never forget. When she was only a few feet from me, as if she were that little girl I grew up with, she ran up to me and hugged me. I wrapped my arms around her and had just enough time to breathe in the scent of jasmine and strawberries. I wanted our embrace to last forever, but it couldn't.

"You look amazing. How have you been?" I asked without thinking. Still captivated.

"Thank you. Wow. It's so great to see you! It's been so long." She beamed through her smile.

"Hey, let's meet up soon. We need to catch up. I have so much to tell you." By this time, we were both surrounded by our friends and their tired younger siblings who were all wanting to move along, but somehow, we felt encapsulated in our own world.

"I'll call you soon, okay," I said, releasing my grip. My hands reluctantly fell from her back, but I held her hands in mine. Our gazes lingered. Our smiles widened. Our hearts swelled.

"Promise?" she asked in a whisper, her whole face smiling, reflecting the anticipation of what her heart dreams.

"I promise!" I assured, as my face reflected the same.

How could I even describe that slice of time? The sizzling electricity of our touching skin, the harmony of our words. The energy fields of our hearts mingling, and all of the things our eyes meeting, lingering, connecting conveyed. I don't think I could. I don't think there were words yet developed in any language that could express what that moment meant to us.

She tilted her head with a frown and waved slowly, just as she had the first day I met her. I did the same. After a few steps, we both turned and looked back. The exuberance we both felt for our spirits to reconnect again, the idea of having the opportunity to explore a new level of our friendship, the hope for time, time together as wonderful as we had always known it to be—we both felt it.

I had girls swarming me at school, vying for my attention in ridiculous ways, but all it took was one smile from this gorgeous, sun-kissed creature, and I was in love. Or had I been all along and only man enough to know it now? I had a date with my dream girl, and that was all my mind could focus on. For days, that's all I cared about. All this time, I had known right where she was and was lost without her. But we found each other again, and that was all that mattered. I just needed to graduate, and our story could begin again.

Chapter Five

Mizpah is a wonderful Hebrew word that describes the deep bonds between loved ones, especially those separated by great distances or the veil. Is there someone you love just beyond the veil? The love and connection between you never dies. It's merely expressed differently now. Connection is what we want, the living and the departed. As if sending out a signal into space, asking, "Are you still here with me somehow?" And by some miraculous event, something small and quiet that whispers an answer, "Yes, I'm here."

On our side of the veil, we love and feel, maybe even more so now, with heightened empathic ability to feel the pain of others in real time. Angels especially. I learned that many people on earth have this ability, empaths, as they call them. A complex and misunderstood ability where Audrey would feel a lot of pain in her life, which was not even her own, because she is one of them.

I had to come to terms with the fact that I was watching her life being played out before me, without me. I felt all her emotions, I knew other people's intentions, and I could see lies being told to her that she couldn't. And there wasn't much I could do about it. I could scream and curse and break things, but it still wouldn't change the course of those wild winds. I just had to let certain things play out as God and free will intended and stand by in good faith for the moments that I actually could help her. I'd do anything for her. Paradise could wait.

Audrey's life was steeped in artistry, generations in her family contributing to that. At home, her father's leather shop was one for the senses. Leather has such a subtle, soft scent, but in his shop, it was strong. High shelves were stacked with rolls of hides in different thicknesses and colors. Thick wood countertops on either side of the room were covered in scraps of leather, leather working tools, and papers with scrolly designs and notes for future projects. A cantankerous antique sewing machine, the size of a washing machine, was in the corner of the shop that smelled of oil and was a constant source of contempt for her father, as it often broke down in the middle of a project. A waist-high saddle rack, a wooden stand with a curved top for saddles to rest on while being assembled, was always somewhere in the middle of the room. Her father liked to keep his knives sharp and, after use, throw them at the counter like a throwing knife so they would stick vertically deep into the wood. Though her father kept quiet and to himself mostly, she grew up used to the sound of him hammering the stamps into the soaked hide, in which he'd cut intricate designs and patterns of depth and beauty. After a few weeks, there would be a fully functional piece of art sitting atop that saddle rack, which would soon be meeting the person for whom it was crafted. He never had a disappointed customer, and word spread throughout the horse community that her father's saddles were the best there was.

Audrey often talked about art with her father. She'd point out a sunset that she found extraordinary and express the wish to paint it. Her father would usually tell her that no one would believe her painting of a sunset that beautiful. Was he discouraging her? Was he challenging her? There were a couple of things her father told her that affected her work from then on. "Look at things as if you're about to paint them." It trained her to see things artfully, what colors to mix for that moment, perspective, focal points, and lighting. From then on, she may have seemed to be sitting quietly, but her mind was busy painting. The other thing he told her was to never force a style. Style is an artist's calling card, a most identifiable character in their work, but it shouldn't be imitated or falsified. He told her this so that in the work and time it takes to become an artist, she would find that her true style would slowly emerge, naturally.

There was a dark room in her grandparents' house, windows

draped with heavy fabric, but once the lights turned on, every inch of the room was found to be covered with some type of art. The walls were decorated with magazine clippings, sketches, scriptures, and great-grandma's pen and ink barn drawings. The windows were covered to protect the shelves that lined the walls, which were full of her grandpa's wax sculptures that had yet to be cast into bronze. A closet, removed of its doors, was in the corner with stocked shelves of every art medium ever invented. Drawing pencils, oil pastels, chalks, charcoals, graphite pencils, ink pens, sculpting tools, and a whole bunch of things that Audrey hadn't figured out yet, all in creative disarray. It was a tidy mess, but she and her grandpa knew just where to find things. Organizing everything might stifle an artist's delicate spontaneity. The closet was also home to her grandma's sewing machine and swatches of fabrics in every color, used for the vibrant quilts Audrey loved watching her make. Notebooks could be found throughout the room, many pages filled with Audrey's early childhood sketches of dogs, birds, horses, and rainbows. Sometimes all of them together. Her grandpa was both frustrated and amused that he'd have to flip nearly to the back of the notebook to find a blank page to use.

Audrey's grandpa was a different kind of mentor to her. If she expressed an interest in making something, he'd tell her, "Go for it!" and by the example of his work, she learned not to be afraid of things looking terrible on the first try. In fact, it was expected and embraced, but the growth and the fun were in the improvement of each attempt thereafter. Two exceptionally talented men influenced Audrey artistically. Her dad just seemed to play it safe. She wished he would try something so incredibly different, to risk seeming ridiculous for the small chance of a brilliant new discovery. In contrast, her grandpa was bold. He took artistic risks all the time. He could laugh at himself and not take mistakes too seriously. Mistakes are proof of growth, he would say, of movement and change, and there shouldn't be any shame in that, unless you quit. Two men influenced her artistically, but she was inspired to be bold.

Just once, she wanted to see her father let go and be vulnerable with her, bring down the walls, have fun, laugh, but just like his art, he stayed within the lines, he remained in his comfort zone, and anything new and surprising rarely happened between them.

It was only natural for her to be drawn to art. It was light in the darkness, a healing companion, and the perfect escape. She drew on anything she could get her hands on, and her mind could drift into the worlds of her imagination. If something wasn't right, she'd practice until it was. One Christmas when she was still quite young, Santa surprised her with Bob Ross art supplies, oil paints, books, brushes, a big easel, and blank canvases. Not many artists can say that they weren't inspired by the oil painter, Bob Ross, the drill sergeant turned unintended art therapist. Most of these things can still be found in her art studio to this day.

All through school, she was known as the artist. If a group art project was assigned in her classes, everyone wanted to work with her. If she was assigned an essay about a historical figure, she would sketch a portrait of the person and use that as the title page. Audrey knew that if she turned in an artistic assignment, she'd most likely never get it back from the teacher. If the teacher kept her work, it was one of the highest compliments in those days. Her teachers were amused at the sketches they'd find on the back of tests and quizzes. Teachers and her classmates regarded her as an artist, though deep down, as many artists do, Audrey struggled with the idea that she may not be good enough to be a real artist. It only made her work harder.

When we were little, Audrey made me a birthday card with a painting of the two of us riding horses, side by side, sharing a long path toward the light. It was something I treasured. I didn't proudly display it in my room for others to comment on. But it became a well-worn bookmark for every book I read, from then on.

An authentic style soon emerged. Still the same little girl I grew up with. The blue jeans, the green eyes, the free spirit. While her friends were clamoring for the latest trends, she remained a classic. As art became the most dynamic, colorful thing about her, her outward appearance softened.

I sat beside her while she painted, radio playing, songs spinning memories in her mind, and the corners of her mouth turning up now and then. I followed the process from blooming ideas in her mind, to sketches in her notebook, to streaks of paint on a canvas. I knew the reason she chose each idea.

"Peach blossoms," I whispered into her ear as she was searching for new subject matter to paint. Close beside her, I watched her expression warm, she wrapped her arms around herself, as she remembered telling me about the pretty pink blossoms when we first met. On a blue canvas, she painted brown branches covered in delicate pink petals facing all directions, some wide open, some closed, some buzzing with bees. True love. That's what she heard. That's what she felt. That's what she painted. And I had the privilege of witnessing every minute of it.

Those were the times I longed for. It wasn't the big connection I was craving, but it was something. It was enough for me to be heartened by what could have been and would be. But we were entering a time in her life in which dark storm clouds were approaching. These were the times Gavri warned me about, but sunshine or rain, I am keeping my promise.

I really had no idea how high school affects young ladies. The thought never entered my mind, me being too wrapped up in my own world. The lucky girls have two doting parents who fill their world with encouragement and wisdom all their lives, preparing them for adulthood. The unlucky ones are thrown into the deep end and sink or swim, it's up to them. It didn't take long to learn why it was a grim time for Audrey. Rock and hard place, meet thorn and barb. It seemed she had few places of real sanctuary to go to. All her life, she watched the relationships of her school friends, the mothers and daughters who were so close and did everything together. She'd see them out shopping, getting lunch, dressing similarly, as best friends would do. But Audrey and her mother were never like that. Her sister came from Adele's previous marriage. They had that best friend relationship and never hid it from Audrey. She longed for that connection, the bond between mother and daughter, and no matter how hard she tried, it just never happened. Audrey always felt like she was in some type of Cinderella fairytale. The callous ways the mother and daughters treated Cinderella, the whispering behind her back, the exclusion, the favoritism, the sneers—Audrey had to face all. It broke me to watch the people she loved treat her this way, for no reason at all.

To me, Audrey seemed like the rejected lamb. If a ewe has a troubled birth and experiences a lot of pain, it will associate that pain with the baby lamb, and it will blame the lamb and reject it. Unless someone steps in to care for the little lamb, it will most likely perish.

Audrey's mother was an empath too. When empaths are unaware of their condition, they have a tendency to be codependent on other people, manipulative ones. That's what made the relationship between Audrey's sister and mother work so well. They both fed off of each other's energy. Audrey's sister wanted Adele to gush over her and dress her and control her life, when it was actually Adele being the one manipulated and controlled. When Adele tried to control aspects of Audrey's life, even at a very early age, Audrey said no. She wanted to be independent, and though that's exactly how a strong young lady should be, it made her mother feel unneeded and unappreciated. The wedge began to grow.

Adele's marriage to Audrey's father was failing, and instead of comforting her children, she felt as if Audrey had chosen sides, her father's side. Fighting and blame, bitterness and weaponized words. Her mother allowed a very insecure and jealous daughter to alienate the other.

Unhealed empaths yield bitter fruits. There were times when Audrey was too afraid to even open her bedroom door and walk down the hallway for fear of hateful confrontation. So school became her escape, but high school was no real escape; it was just the least traumatic. But even that changed.

If you walked behind her through the hallways at school as I did, you would see that she waved and greeted or smiled at almost everyone she passed. She wasn't the super-popular girl; in fact, she went out of her way not to be involved in cliques. She was selectively extroverted but mostly a shy kid like I was. A quiet observer. She was a wonderful, warm, and caring friend, but for her, friendship never seemed set in stone but more like rapidly shifting plates beneath her feet. Few knew the depths of her as I did, looking beyond that crooked garden gate, to admire the roses.

In one class, there was assigned seating, and four desks were arranged to face each other. Audrey was seated by two very shy students and one boy who, for years, had had a crush on her. He was the strange type that showed his admiration in torment. He teased Audrey incessantly about everything from her looks to her clothes, the way she walked and talked. Everything she did was under fire from him. It was really getting to her. She dreaded the class and missed it if she could. She was in tears at night about the ugly things he said to her. She tried ignoring him, and that only made things worse. So there finally came a day when she stood up for herself. She fired back at him with a nuclear force and scorched him in front of anyone within earshot. The paper tiger was set ablaze that day, and he never spoke a word to her again. She was so proud of herself for standing strong, and other students who heard his daily torment were happy to hear her defend herself as well. Several days later, after the boy's many absences, the teacher pulled Audrey aside and told her the news. The boy who had been tormenting her had committed suicide, and because the teacher always saw him talking to Audrey, he assumed they were good friends. He wanted to give her the news personally.

Audrey carried a heavy weight, a burden of blame for his death. The news came in just days after she unloaded all the suffering he had caused her, right back onto him. She didn't mean to hurt him, to make him feel worthless enough to send him to his grave. None of this was her fault. I watched as he returned to his turbulent home life on a daily basis, fighting with every toxic member of his household. His father drank and created violent situations almost every night. His mother rendered herself unconscious every night with a dangerous roulette-like mixture of pills and vodka. The father had a tendency to sneak into his little sister's room, entertaining bad thoughts. The boy knew what his father was up to and always tried to get there in time to protect her. This one tragic night, his anger got the better of him. His mother was unconscious, he found his father beginning to act on those bad thoughts, and in the height of his rage, he beat his father to death with his baseball bat on the floor of his sister's room. The boy was terrified of going to prison for what he had done. It all happened so fast. His emotions overcame him, of the worst kind, and in the depths of his grief and shame and confusion, he felt there was only one way out. He apologized and hugged his sister, kissed his mother's forehead, and found a rope and a tall tree. His aggression toward Audrey was a broken boy's cry for help. We always take our problems out on the ones we love, don't we?

Bruce was another boy at school who liked Audrey. He was a big football player and a generally feared guy. He had a bad reputation, and most people steered clear of him. The whole school began to learn that he had a crush on Audrey, so no other boy was brave enough to cross Bruce and ask Audrey out. Audrey never paid any attention to gossip, so the rumors about his reputation never influenced her. Bruce became a great friend to Audrey, and soon the rumors were swirling that they were an item. Audrey's first job was hostessing at the best Italian restaurant in town. Her mother would drop her off for her shift, and sometimes, if they let her off work early, she would walk down to Bruce's house. The town was safe and peaceful. She enjoyed walking along the streets of charming old Victorian homes in that area. Bruce's house was the least charming of all. It had broken down old vehicles and rubbish stacked in the yard, overgrown with weeds and neglect. The house would be beautiful if someone loved it enough. She usually called Bruce from the restaurant, so he'd be expecting her, sitting outside waiting. On most nights, these two teenagers, who were rumored to be having wild interludes and probably going to have a baby out of wedlock, were actually finding solace in each other's company. Nothing more. They did lie on the mattress on the floor of his room, his arm stretched out and Audrey's head resting on it, but in those few stolen moments, this feared brute was merely a misunderstood boy to her. He was a big bear with a thorn in his paw, and she was the only one brave enough to remove it. They spent this time telling each other their darkest secrets and pain.

Audrey, being an empath, found that people would just open up to her. Strangers would tell her their life story or problems and be in tears before they knew it. She had this healing energy about her that other people could sense, but she was unaware of. She let Bruce tell her stories about his abusive mother and father, and I watched as she absorbed all of his pain like a sponge. She listened to his dreams of the future of fixing up classic cars and having his own garage someday. Another thing Audrey was blessed with was the ability to not only absorb the pain of others, leaving them feeling lighter and freer, but also encourage, nurture, and inspire people to chase their dreams. Those few nights that she walked down to Bruce's house and spent an hour or two talking with him healed him. It set his whole life on a different course than it previously was. People can accomplish greatness when they heal and feel like someone believes in them. He would forever remember her for her friendship and their talks. But soon new rumors circulated at the high school that Bruce was having a fling with a girl named Julie, and there was truth to those rumors. Audrey was finally set free. If rumors were to swirl about her, they'd have to make up new ones.

She was entering a new phase of her life where women were showing signs of jealousy, the men were becoming more forward, and the boys were becoming shy. Even her male friends were beginning to treat her differently. She was no longer one of the gang, but this beautiful girl who made them all nervous. It confused her. It isolated her even more, so she turned to the only things she had left, her art and music.

She was smart enough to get straight A's, but for some reason, she didn't apply herself that extra percentage. It wasn't for partying like the rest of them. She avoided parties. She loved getting invitations, but after a while, the invitations ceased. They realized she wasn't the partying type. When the kids were at a house party, Audrey could usually be found hanging out with her closest companion. Someone who had seen her through her worst times, wiped away her tears, and provided a kind distraction from all the pain. Her companion had 88 black and white keys and was one of the most loyal friends she had. Together, they played music spanning decades of genres. She could play anything from Andrew Lloyd Webber to Brubeck to Beethoven and all in between.

On rare occasions, when no one was home, Audrey would break out certain songs that were sentimental to her. She learned to play this particular song because it was her mother's favorite, but after some time, it took on new meaning. There are some songs that are tightly bound to the past, and "Rainbow Connection" was one of them. The lyrics talk about rainbows and what's on the other side. "Someday we'll find it, the rainbow connection."

I sat beside her as Audrey began to play this tune on her upright piano. She faintly sang the words with her eyes closed and tears building. She was singing to me. I could see our memories play out along with the tune. The first day we met, jumping on the trampoline, splashing around in her pool, riding horses together down the lane, hunting for sand dollars, and the few times we got to watch the stars peek out of the night sky. I wanted the song to last forever, her voice so sweet, the song so sentimental, but that's just why it ended. There it was, the connection, and I knew then that she was looking for it, just as I was.

Selah is a word with several meanings, but one means to pause and reflect. The keys absorbed her tears that dropped between them. She pushed her fingers gently back and forth along the length of the keys, her fingertips getting lost within the black keys and back out again. It was a slow movement of her hands, her eyes closed tighter now. Her heart, weary of carrying the burdens of loss. This song reminded her of her best pal in her life at the time when she was learning how to play it. And it reminded her how alone in this world she really was.

Selah, to pause—somewhere in the meaning of that word, it implies that we might begin again. Someday we'll find it, that rainbow connection. If only she knew I was right beside her, my arm around her, my entire world orbiting hers, all the love she could ever ask for, so close.

After dinner and homework, Audrey was about to sneak out alone to watch the stars appear and brighten, but her mom stopped her at the back door and mentioned the dirty dishes in the sink. Audrey was disappointed and slowly brought the sliding glass door back to a close. She walked up the steps into the kitchen and ran the water until it was warm. The dishes were done in a few minutes, but she had grown tired, so she returned to her bedroom and turned her radio on to a whisper. She rested her head on her pillow, filling her consciousness with soft sounds and drifting through levels of sleep.

When we were young, her bedroom had been decorated by her mom in pink and ruffles. I could see that those things had not been of Audrey's choosing. Things like astronomy charts, rock and feather collections, a bookshelf of Hardy Boys mystery books, and her sketches could be found throughout the room. As a high schooler, her room was no longer pink, but her collections and feathers and drawings were still there, in greater numbers. She traded the Hardy Boys for Hemingway and Austen. I enjoyed looking at the photos she had displayed, her smiling face and kind eyes hiding the weight of all she carried behind them. Though she hid it well, I could see it. Her paintings were changing, improving, taking on a light like no other art I'd ever seen. I reveled in watching her become the artist I know she would be someday.

I held my sleeping beauty. She was sleeping on her side, and I gently pulled her as close to me as I could. I smelled the familiar scents of jasmine and strawberries. I closed my eyes and took us to dreamland. I took her to the top of a hill, at the edge of a glade, at dusk. Blankets and pillows arranged, all we had to do was lie back and watch the show. Audrey watched as the stars came out one by one, far brighter way up here. She was pointing them out to me and smiling. All the while, she was the star my eyes were fixed upon. The star that charted my course. She got to see her stars appear that night after all. With me. Rainbow Connection's melody softly resonating. After she pointed to another star, I took her hand and kissed it, promising, "Someday we'll find it."

Chapter Six

I ndizi is an Italian word that describes signs or indications of a supernatural and miraculous nature. Oh, how I would love to sit with Audrey and talk like we used to, even just five minutes in the flesh, her eyes seeing me, reading me, her smile being returned by mine. If only I could listen to all the small details of her day, her wishes and dreams, the things that trouble her, all while comforting her. The veil would forever obscure my presence in her life, but I was learning the ways I could return that signal she was sending out into space.

The Mizpah remains, and your loved one is trying to connect. They can't call you up and ask how your day went, or text you goodnight. But in quiet moments, you'll see something that reminds you of them, and the memories begin to play in your mind. It's the significant song that plays on the radio. It's that special thing you find out of the blue. Signs are everywhere.

My mom's dad and I would play gin rummy a lot. We'd tell old stories and laugh, taking turns beating each other, round after round, as fast as we could. I remember the frustration, waiting on that last card to win, but my grandpa would ask me, "Hey, what tastes good with juice?"

I'd fall for it every time. "I don't know. What?"

"Gin!" He'd blurt out before his victorious laughter.

Whenever I'd see playing cards, or numbers in threes and fours, my mind was directed to our fun days together, bonding between shuffles and cans of his favorite ale, gin-ger ale. Somewhere deep down, I knew it was him giving me a nudge. You're told those sorts of beliefs are silly and to shrug them off, but that couldn't be more wrong. My grandpa's old truck was given to me after I got my license, but every now and then after we lost him, I'd find his card, the ace of hearts on top of the stack of papers in the glove compartment, when it wasn't there before.

When I crossed over, I could see how he sent those messages to me, those memories, out of the blue. I do the same things now. My family is reminded of memories and shown small things that remind them of me frequently. I try whenever I can to show them I'm still here. I send them love in any way I can. I celebrate their victories in life, jumping up and down wildly, like a parent at a

Little League game. I'm there to comfort them in their disappointments too. I hug my mom and hold her hand when the tears fall. I cannot be with her, but I can make her roses bloom bigger and brighter than ever before. I'm there with her when she makes her delicious cookies. I try to make my brother laugh at memories of all the fun and trouble we got into. I watch over my beautiful nieces and guide them as their life is just beginning. I watch over all of them and send messages. Every year, they gather at my grave, with balloons and prayers to celebrate my birthday. They send me balloons, I send them rainbows. If they only knew how close I am. It will all make sense to you when you cross over, but I hope you see the signs and receive your messages far before then.

Every living thing, even the earth is energy taking form. The form may change, but energy remains constant. I may be energy that has crossed over, but in some miraculous way, I'm able to transfer my being to different things to reach Audrey. I was the monarch butterfly that glided and twirled through the air only inches away from her eyes, circling her with my big black and orange wings until she laughed and forgot all those concerns for a moment. I was the ladybug that lit on her hand and startled her into laughter. Yes, that was me. Will you know those signs are from us? That's the miracle we so long for, existing on this side of the veil. When we send you messages, will you receive them?

Audrey's aunt passed away from a cancer that first seemed to go into remission but came back and spread throughout her body with a fury. Her Aunt Diane was her mom's closest confidant and best friend. They would spend hours on the phone catching up and laughing to tears, at any old thing. Audrey grew up knowing exactly who was on the other end of the line. Hearing her mom's laughter was always a breath of fresh air. Adele, an empath just like Audrey, had few friends that she could trust and allow to get close to her, so losing her sister was the most tragic of losses. Though they lived on opposite sides of the country, they called often, and their bond was strong. Diane was one of those innocent souls who could heal anyone, within moments of being near her. A contagious laugh, a nurturing spirit. She was a painter, a crafter, a cook, a mother, raising two boys and loving them dearly.

Diane believed that finding dimes was a sign from heaven that angels were watching over you. Adele remembered visiting her sister, grocery shopping with Diane, and watching her stop abruptly in the parking lot to pick up a dime. It seemed like she found them everywhere she went. The look on her face was pure joy, as if discovering a treasure. Diane received the messages from her guardian angels, just the way they had been intended.

As Diane lay in a hospital bed, fading quickly, she was visited by her sister, friends, and family. In a peaceful breath, as her body slept, her spirit crossed the veil and was greeted by even more friends and family, with tearful and joyous celebrations of a life well lived and purpose in life fulfilled.

Diane's husband, Harold, was holding her hand in the hospital bed when she passed, and when the time came for him to make his way to his car and finally head home, alone, he opened the car door, and before he could step in, there on the pavement was a shiny new dime. He knew it was a message from her. A strong man, a loving husband, their boys' father, and a bit of a skeptic. He'd roll his eyes when she talked about messages from her angels. He stood beside his car, his toes inches away from the dime, tears falling onto the pavement. An undeniable message, in the simplest of terms. The dime hadn't fallen from the heavens to light in his hand. It didn't sparkle dramatically. It was a soft and subtle sign to him, in one of the toughest moments he would ever remember, assuring him, "It's all okay. I'm still here with you." Harold got her message.

A couple of days after the passing of her sister, Adele pried herself from the house, deciding to go to Hinds Hospice Thrift Store to search for treasures. This was always a therapy for her, and on that day, a lovely handbag hanging on the wall caught her eye. The lady behind the counter was happy to retrieve it for her, so Adele could have a closer look. Normally bags in these stores are thoroughly cleaned out, but on this day, she was overcome to find a new dime inside its pocket, as if someone had just dropped it there. Visions flashed through Adele's mind of her sister. They were not of Diane fading, lying sick in a hospital bed, but of her happy and healthy, with that young-at-heart, joyful spirit she always had. Adele stood there in the thrift store, holding the purse, eyes filling and flowing with tears as these visions played on.

Diane's message was received. She stood beside her sister, arms around her, trying to wipe those streaming tears and telling Adele in her thick Mississippi accent, "Oh, don't you cry, honey. I'm right here. You can't get rid of me that easy! I wish you could see how thin I am now, dang it. Buy the handbag. I love you."

And with a kiss on Adele's cheek, Diane stepped away, and her energy disbursed into the ether. Wherever Adele went, from that day forward, she would see glints of silver on the ground and have to pick them up. She knows it was a sign from her sister, so she looks up with a smile and drops the dimes into her pocket. Dimes everywhere. Messages received.

"I have an idea for you," Em told me, with a broadening, wise smile on her face. It was the last string of hot days of summer, and we were enjoying the sun as much as Audrey was.

"Well, let's hear it!" My curiosity was instantly piqued. Em and I had grown close since my crossing. She had taken me under her wing, as a little brother, and I was grateful. On this hot sunny day, complemented by the occasional gusts of cool wind, we were up high on Audrey's patio roof with our typical bird's eye view. Down below was Audrey on her usual lounge chair, listening to her favorite radio station and dividing her attention between her sketch book, dogs, and cat.

Music is immeasurably healing. This was the time when I realized the significant role music played in her life. She always had music playing, fitting the mood, soothing the senses. She loved the way music could lift her spirits, no matter what kind of day she was having. She felt that when the music stopped, feelings of loneliness and haunts of life would begin to creep in. She felt a deep spiritual connection to music, and when she closed her eyes, it almost seemed like she could see it too, the rise and fall, the rhythm and harmony, creating evolving shapes and colors. Certain lyrics spoke to her, reminding her of me sometimes, wondering if we would've slow danced to this if given the chance. She wondered if there had been a song that made me think of her when I was alive.

"Em, what was your idea?" I pressed.

"Play her a song on the radio. Do you know you can do that?" Em grinned, her eyes sparkling, already knowing how important this lesson would be for Audrey and me.

I jumped to my feet with excitement. "No way! Show me how."

She taught me all I needed to know. It's not as if I can pick up the phone and call Audrey. My communication demanded more creativity now, but could these messages possibly reach her?

Audrey lay on her back in her metallic glacier blue bikini. It was the kind that tied into bows on her hips and her back. She had white sunglasses that had the same color glacier blue lenses that matched. She was the perfect California vision. She was my dream girl, and I was about to remind her. The radio sat on the table beside her lounge chair, so when the DJ came on, announcing the next song, she definitely heard the dedication. "All right, all right, I hope everyone out there is enjoying the last heatwave of summer! This next song is from Josh to his dream girl, saying he's keeping his promise. So, here is 'The Promise' by When In Rome."

Audrey sat straight up, her mouth open, hand on her racing heart, though in disbelief that the message she just heard could possibly be for her. But it sure sounded like it was. She remained sitting straight up, listening to the words. A strange tingling ran down her spine, and she felt goosebumps on her skin.

She slowly lowered her head back down on the pillow, holding onto every word being sung. The words were perfect. That was our song, and I will keep reminding her. Soon enough, her mind would play tricks on her, convincing her that it was a silly coincidence. But that's how these signs work. Loved ones on this side play songs all the time for the living. We fill your mind with a rush of memories and love. It's so terribly sad that so few recognize the signs. We all just want the living to find the dime and look up and say, "I know that was you. I miss you too." Or listen to a song we play, hear the words, and get the message. Time will tell if Audrey will know I'm sending her all the love I can, but after that dedication, she realized there could be something there. She was open to the possibility, and if there were signs to be seen, she would be looking for them.

Audrey had always wondered how she fit into this world, and growing into a striking, tall blonde didn't help matters. It only seemed to alienate her even more. At her hostess job, flowers and gifts from anonymous admirers were being delivered now and then. Audrey wasn't used to this attention. In her mind, she was still the nerdy girl who stayed home on Friday nights, hanging out with her old friends, Wolfgang Amadeus Mozart and Ludwig von Beethoven. Attention was nice, but only if it came from the right sources. She felt at times like an unanchored ship adrift in a raging sea or a leaf floating in a wild wind. I saw her for what she was, though: authentic, eclectic, bohemian, and somehow wild and shy at the same time. She was a free spirit if there ever was one.

What did she want in a companion? An anchor, a shelter, a champion, or maybe an angel? She wasn't quite sure yet, so she entertained herself, learning about the weirdness of the world. She studied ghost stories and UFOs, Stonehenge and the Great Pyramids, strange healing temples and rock formations, and found that the oddities of the world helped her feel a little less otherworldly herself. She had felt the presence of the spiritual realm around her all her life. This mysterious connection to the other side was always felt but never quite understood. She longed for that understanding. She felt drained by people, socializing, crowds, and negativity, so she isolated herself often, reading and painting, knowing that only when she was alone or near bodies of water that she was able to fully recharge.

I knew what she wanted. Deep down, she wanted a love both deep and light as a feather, a one-of-a-kind connection, profound understanding, but believed that, for someone like her, that didn't exist. I was all of those things for her, embracing her tightly, adoring the things about her that she thought were unlovable. If only the veil could part for a moment, just a moment, I'd show her all of it. My promise to her was to spend every day of her life trying.

The little artist I grew up admiring, who loved to draw her horses, dogs, and cats, was now driving forty minutes to attend college art classes. Most of her friends scattered into the wind after graduation, attending universities all over the country, but Audrey was content blasting the radio in her red Jeep Cherokee along the scenic drive to class each day. She excelled in that environment. The students were creative, the curriculum engaging, and the professors challenging. The little artist back then was definitely an artist now, finding the escape she needed in life. The great escape, the light in the darkness, the cactus flower in the desert.

One foggy morning, in a hurry to get to her early class on time, she drove her jeep into the thick fog and got to a stop sign where the visibility dropped sharply. That's where Em and Gavri stepped in. On any normal day, angels are there to help you, eagerly. All you have to do is ask them. They will never disrupt your free will unless your life is in danger. Angels are there to protect you throughout your life, and on this particular morning, she needed it. They calmly whispered in her ear, "Turn around and go back home. It's too foggy. Too dangerous." She sat alone at that intersection, being faced with the voices of her intuition. She heard their voices. She felt the sinking in her stomach warning her of danger ahead. It was from that moment on that she felt a real connection with her angels. She didn't know their names, she didn't know what they looked like or how many there were. She just knew that angels intervened on her behalf that morning. They protected her from God knows what, and she was grateful. She turned her jeep around and spent the afternoon listening to music and painting, knowing something special had happened that day. She didn't feel quite so lost and alone, but this marked the beginning of her feeling guided and cared for. The message was received.

If Audrey hadn't listened to them, she would've continued down about fifteen miles to a spot in the road by the river where the fog was terribly thick. The oncoming traffic would not have seen her lights or the road and would have hit her head on. I can see the path not taken, and all I can tell you is when your angels speak to you, please, please take heed. And always look for the signs.

In another life, I found my Audrey near a shimmering body of water. My angels had led me on a trail of a thousand signs, right to her. My father and mother were avid hunters, though everyone at some point or another had to be, to survive back then. Some just learned better than others. My parents taught me how to track animals and had even been known to track criminals and lost children. My skills were what landed me a tentative job with the US Marshals. My parents learned their tracking skills from an old Sioux Indian they had befriended and traded with back home. He even took time teaching me a thing or two. When you know the things to look for and quiet your mind and allow yourself to be led by spirit, the path is revealed. I spent much time with animals, learning their behavior, expressions, and tells. If you can read an animal, reading a human is easy. The three marshals that I rode with teased me relentlessly for seeming like a savage. I learned to be quiet, listen for signs in the wind and upon the earth. I didn't say much. I'd always been a quiet observer. If you are quiet, really listen to people, they reveal so much more than they ever intend to. These men were uncomfortable with my silences, even confrontational like animals, but once my skills were put to use and proved invaluable, they began to respect my place in the ranks.

The marshals needed me to help them track a six-man killing crew that had raped and pillaged their way from the East Coast down through the south and had recently crossed into Mexican territory. We were on a mission to kill or capture these men before too many more graves were filled with the innocent. Most of the time, we went from city to city, arriving upon a scene that depicted the savagery of these animals, but we were gaining on them. Once they crossed into Mexican land, they seemed to stop their terror. The mood changed for some reason, and we were trying to understand why. I tracked them to a growing river town of cautiously friendly people. When they realized that we were not murderous thieves, their hospitality was unmatched. These families had poor ways but loved richly, so much so that God himself would be proud. "Do not forget to entertain strangers for thereby some have entertained angels unawares" (Hebrews 13:2). We were fed, we had shelter, drink, song, and stories. It was enough for four tired souls to be replenished and continue the good fight.

The trail was long and tiresome, feeling like it was grinding us into dust. Before the marshals found me, I had been praying for work. I had been praying for a direction, for love, and for signs. As we moved from town to town, my conviction was fading. This mission tried our souls, our hope wore thin, our bodies ached. But something within me kept me focused. We had a mission: to save lives and deliver justice. Sometimes you find the strength to see a mission through to the end when you remember who you truly work for. The marshals would pay me at the end of this, but the real boss

I answered to was my Creator. Remembering that helped me hold myself and the work I did to a higher standard. My pay would be good, but my reward would always be greater.

One afternoon I broke from the pack and wandered alone by the river. Other people would be advised to stay with the group when hunting dangerous men, but I was different. People didn't sneak up on me. I found them. And at the river, I felt a strangely familiar sensation. The wild winds I had been feeling suspended, my heartbeat calmed, my breath deepened, and there it was. The pull of the cord of the prairie rose that bound us, willing us closer. I followed the river quite a way to a quiet, overgrown, and almost eerie part of the bend. The water seemed to slow. My caution rose. I tied my horse yards away and walked to the bank, connecting with earth and spirit, and that's when I saw her. She was connecting with water, bathing in the center of a pool in the river. In this life, my Audrey had long black hair and brown skin, and I saw all of it. She cooled her body, bathed, and then began to slowly walk to the bank where her clothing lay. I had to remind myself to breathe. She was a mirage to me, a spirit, a siren to a lonely man, and I would have followed her to the depths. I watched her take every step out of the water as it streamed off her glistening brown skin. Her arms lifted, hands wringing her long black hair as she ascended the bank. I walked closer for a better view. I couldn't help myself. I placed my hand on my sidearm, ready to pull when I saw a man approaching her. She was already wearing a cotton slip, seemingly unaware of the man creeping up behind her, but the wind changed. She was distracted by the suspicion of my presence while slowly reaching into her leather bag. I wasn't about to let this beautiful woman be harmed by an animal, but just as he made his move and grabbed hold of her, in the struggle and commotion, she drove a six-inch blade up under his chin and deep into his skull.

I watched the man stagger steps away as his blood flowed out of his body. His hands clutched his neck as if there was anything he could do to stop the bleeding. He finally fell to his knees and then face down into the dirt. I'd just watched the most beautiful woman I'd ever seen just kill a man, and I'd never been more entranced.

There's a moment when you kill a man that feels as if time is going to cease forever. You're in shock, you're in shame, even if you were only trying to defend yourself. She was trapped in that moment, that whirlwind of feelings, and I felt the need to comfort her. I put my hands in the air and stepped into plain view, so she knew full well I was there and had seen the whole thing.

"Aléjate!" She panicked, but I tried to tell her not to worry. That I was no threat. I told her that I saw him sneaking up and that I was ready to kill him myself. After a few minutes of angry rambling in Spanish, she calmed down and told me in English that this man had been following her. He had been caught looking into her window at night and was chased from her father's property many times. She'd turned down his wedding proposal, and he had never gotten over it, being so used to affording everything he had in his life. This was not his first attempt to take what was not his. She had reached her limit, and always looking over her shoulder in fear was no way to live. She said that he had terrorized her for the last time and kicked his dead body. I might have heard ribs breaking.

She looked down at her slip, which was covered in spatters of blood, and returned to the water. She washed the garment while still wearing it, then walked to the riverbank with it clinging to her skin. That sight was almost enough to make me forget about the dead man by my feet.

With hat in hand, and once she was properly dressed, I introduced myself. "Miss, my name is Elias." I offered to take care of it all for her. I offered to take the dead man to the sheriff's office. She was grateful and invited me to her father's estate for dinner that evening.

"And does the river siren have a name?"

"Oh…," she started, slightly smiling, amused at the name I'd given her. "Please, call me Angelina."

I draped the dead man's body over my saddle and rode into town to find the local sheriff. The town looked like a combination of an old west town and little adobes. It was windswept and dust covered, but that didn't take away from its charm. It had two-story buildings that were covered with thirsty old blooming prairie rose vines, which added a splash of bright color to the dull desert landscape. The marshals and nearly every resident saw me stroll through town with this sorry son of a bitch bleeding down the main street. While the sheriff greeted me with scorn and suspicion, the marshals rushed to my side. Apparently, this man was a friend of the sheriff, and it didn't matter what he was guilty of. On this afternoon, the marshals and I had become enemies of the state, and we hadn't even killed him. We dropped off his body, but we learned that in this territory, the law was regarded differently depending on your wealth and connections.

While the marshals were being entertained by our gracious hosts, I had a dinner to attend. It was a rough, transcendent countryside that brought me all the way to her massive iron gates. Two guards greeted me with suspicion, reluctant to open the gate for a gringo. I rode my horse up to the stables. A young boy took the reins, and I tipped him, telling him to keep my horse ready. I might need to leave early.

The grounds were lovely and well maintained. Their home was a Spanish jewel in the desert. I came up to two giant carved doors that opened before I could knock. I was greeted by el mayordomo, or what those up north call butlers. He was a kind, smiling old man who took my hat and sidearm. I knew enough Spanish to ask the gentleman to keep my things close to the door, and he winked. It seemed that I was not the only one making requests for an early retirement. All of these requests were in vain as it were because once I was formally announced, I was treated as if I had been the one who saved the young lady from her aggressor. I was regarded as a hero. The river siren had told her father that I saved her. It was the only way to explain why I was there. Her father was a gracious man, the host of the evening. However, I felt her father had some secrets lurking beneath the surface. He was a wealthy man. He was far wealthier than just a cattle rancher in Mexico. Some side business perhaps?

The finest steak, potatoes, fresh vegetables, and wine were served in excess. We all sat at a hand-carved wooden table that had high-backed chairs reminiscent of medieval times. He had rugs of cowhide and bear strewn about his home, wild game hanging on the walls, and large, colorful oil paintings in every room. Angelina sat quietly through the entire meal and let the men talk about life and politics, land and law. We were polite enough to avoid the events of the day, leaving that for a later, more private discussion. After dinner Angelina asked me if I would like to take a walk with her, and of course, I accepted. Her father had given her the name Angelina, and there couldn't be a name more fitting. I could tell by the way she spoke and carried herself that she had spent most of her time educating herself not only in the arts of language, music, and history, but also in protecting herself and learning the ugly ways of the world. She would have to, to be able to drive a knife into a man's flesh that way.

We walked through the gates and into the open territory, where it was a more natural, rugged landscape. It was a warm, late summer night when the sun seemed most hesitant to set. We came to a point on a hill where one would be enchanted by the view, but I was too busy taking careful steps and catching glimpses of her. I couldn't keep my eyes off of her, and it wasn't because I had seen her form from far away, though that was a dream to me. She had that long black hair, which, when let all the way down, reached her lower back. Her eyes were the color of meadow grass. It's funny how, through our lifetimes, we could look so different, but our souls remained unchanged.

"Stop! Dame tu pistola!" she whispered. Her eyes fixed on a target I hadn't yet seen. "Your gun! Now!" Not a second later, she pulled my gun from my belt and fired. My gun was a lot louder when I was not the one shooting it.

She handed the gun back to me, dangling it on her dainty finger from the trigger guard. When the dust settled, I saw that she had blasted a rattler nearly in half at the base of a prickly pear cactus. It was still moving, the final pangs of death, though far less threatening. My God, I loved this woman. Both maddening and intoxicating, and I could not tell which was having more effect on me. The view was romantic, and I suspect she had a motive for bringing me here. I stepped closer to her, perhaps closer than she had allowed anyone in some time. I was not easily surprised, as I was used to reading creatures, but she was a different one altogether. She took those final few steps that brought us together, and in slow, intentional movements, she wrapped her fingers around the lapel of my vest and pulled me in. First our eyes met, then our lips, then our hearts. It was a kiss to set the sun, to spark wildfires, and even bring down barriers. When it came to a close, I realized I had passed a test. She was reading me. Could she finally lay down her weapons with someone, after so long? Could I be someone she could trust with her life? Of course. But with her heart? A kiss reveals more than we expect.

She began to tell me about her family. She confided in me that her brother and his friends had been up north for most of the year and had just returned. Pausing for a moment, she slightly squinted her eyes, as if to read my intentions, curious to know if that had something to do with my sudden arrival in her town. She talked about her father being a cattle rancher. Then she spoke of how dangerous the family business was. Raising cattle was dangerous, but she knew her father and brother were keeping things from her. The family business, whatever that was, had affected her life deeply. Attacks had been made on the estate. People had tried to burn it down. There had been shootouts and men trying to kidnap her. She had a difficult time trusting people, trusting men. She was having difficulty even trusting God. That is why she had to become so good at protecting herself, though it was as if she was asking me for my help now.

The evening concluded not long after our walk, with many thanks to the host and help and a kiss on the hand of my river siren, my crack shot maiden. I departed with hopes of seeing her again soon. I was grateful for a quiet night. With a full belly and weary head, I retired early, drifting off into visions of her.

I arose to gunfire. It wasn't a shootout but rather just some still drunken Mexican shooting off his pistola in the barrio. I peered out my window in time to see his family rush the drunkard home, scattering a cluster of feeding chickens in their way.

I washed up and dressed, stepping out of the front door of the casa, looking down at my pocket watch. I was stepping into a dust cloud of thundering horse hooves. I looked up to see Angelina and her long, bouncing black curls, stopping her buckskin mare just before me. She was a delicate, exotic bloom among the thorns and prickly pear landscape. Beauty beyond what I'd ever known, yet my ways kept me in a state of cautious refrain. "Bueno dias. I came to invite you to dinner at the house again. Please, won't you come?"

I laughed in surprise. Surely God was smiling on me that day. "Buenos dias a ti y si. Mi encantaria. You haven't found any more snakes, have you?"

"No, not yet." She slyly smiled. "Something tells me that they reveal themselves when you're around."

"You might be right about that, miss."

As swiftly as she appeared, she turned her mare around in a rising cloud of dust, shouting, "Hasta esta noche!" and was gone. She had such a presence about her that as she left, it was as if she took the air and all the angels around us with her, and all I was left with were a few pecking chickens.

I spent the day with the marshals. They were eyeing the gang we had followed into town. The marshals weren't sure where they were staying at night, but from daybreak to sundown, they could be found at the gambling hall and chasing women. It had been tough for the marshals to keep their positions quiet when a young soiled dove turned up dead at the hands of one of the gang. However, we could not just arrest one. It must be all of them. And that time would be quickly upon us.

The smoky gambling hall was full of card tables and scattered grumbling gamblers. They all seemed to be sleepy all day and livelier as the day grew long. We sat in the distance with watchful eyes. All I gathered from our observations was that they had to take up a life of thievery because they all were god-awful at poker. I also observed that the piano picker was extraordinary. I could listen to him all day, and under different circumstances, I'm sure he could play all the classical greats and could break your heart with tender melodies, but to appease all these drunkards, he played their silly favorites on that chimey old upright.

I had to excuse myself from the festivities at the gambling hall and head out to dinner. I told the marshals not to get into any trouble, and they told me not to go falling in love. We all laughed, knowing we'd be guilty by nightfall.

I was ecstatic to see Angelina, my river siren, my crack shot maiden. Mi mujer peligrosa. But there was something more in the air that night. There was an electricity, a foreboding feeling I couldn't shake, no matter how much I thought of her. I approached her home this time with much less apprehension. I was a welcome guest, but I still paid the young boy to keep my horse handy and tipped the old man at the door to keep my hat and sidearm close by. Just as before, the food was decadent. A man could get used to the things on this menu. Her father was cordial and made the politest of conversation with the occasional cloaked jab at the guest that drew his daughter's gaze a little too long.

Suddenly, through the front doors arose a commotion. The stable boy ran in to alert the family of trouble. Her brother had just arrived home, having been shot in the side at the gambling hall. The boy told her father that men were close behind him. Her father stood to his feet, slamming his heavy cloth napkin on the table. He ran to the stables to find his son. Still seated, I looked across at Angelina, sitting very still, considering the news we all just heard. I saw tears run down her cheeks as she whispered in fear, "Snakes, everywhere."

I rushed to her side, to hold her. I wiped her tears away with the silk kerchief from my pocket. "Listen to me. I've been tracking a band of criminals with the US Marshals. We were at the gambling hall all day, and your brother was there. He's in the group we're tracking, and he's in trouble. You need to tell your brother to turn himself in."

"My brother is a bad man. He got involved with the wrong people. He became cruel. He wronged bad people, and they follow him here.

That's why I had to become strong. That's why I..." Her emotions overcame her, and she broke down in my arms. But we only had moments before the marshals would arrive. I had to do something.

We both went out to the stables where her gravely injured brother had lain against the doors. Blood had dripped its way into a pool, but her brother was gone, and so was his horse. Her father was gone too. He must have taken mine.

I went to the front of the estate and flagged down the marshals. They didn't charge in as fast as I thought they would. They were bandaged and hurt. It seemed that the marshals had made their move tonight, and the outlaws fought back.

Angelina rode up to the gate of the estate on her buckskin mare, with another horse for me. The marshals rode out looking in all directions for the escaping men. I took the horse's reins and walked back to the pool of blood. This was where my tracking began. The blood stopped where fresh horse tracks began out the back of the property, with the occasional drip, drip, drip. I rode for a while, but when the tracks failed to lead us in a direction, the blood did once again. It was the same as if I had been out hunting.

If I shot an animal but only wounded it, it would limp off, leaving a trail of blood behind it. I either caught up to the animal to end its misery, or I found that it had already succumbed to its injuries. But one never tracks an animal down because there is hate in the heart. On the contrary, in general, it is usually a beautiful full-grown elk or deer, bear, or boar that is caught—you hunt all out of love for the people you feed or protect. However, my life had been centered around a different hunt. This was about saving lives, by hunting down vicious creatures. There was only one left, bleeding his way into the body of water where I first encountered my river siren.

We cautiously rode into the trees toward the bank of the river. We expected gunfire but heard sobbing instead. There, sitting against the base of a tall tree, was a grieving father holding his dead son in his arms.

"I wanted him to die in peace. I could not let them hang him," his father sobbed. Angelina rushed to her father's side and held them both.

The marshals and I had finally put an end to the evil of the outlaws and saw that they were laid in the ground for good. The marshals took a night to rest and gain strength for the long ride home. I spent the evening with Angelina, comforting her in any way I knew. That night, Angelina and I made a pact to meet at the train station and ride the last car out of town together. In the morning, I bought the tickets. The marshals took my horse back with them. By dusk, I was left waiting as the train captain stood calling. Time was running out, and there was no sign of her, so I climbed the steps and took one last look across the platform. I felt the train move beneath me. I was leaving town alone.

Angelina saw the devastation it caused her father to lose his only son, and she realized that losing his daughter would wreck him beyond repair. She didn't have the heart to leave him. She stayed and took care of her father as the events of losing his son sent his health into a downward spiral. She was there until the end for him, and that's exactly where she was supposed to be.

While I traveled alone, I began to realize the strain asking her to leave with me had put on her. We all make hasty decisions, especially in love. I was about to make another one. As soon as I arrived back at my home, I collected my pay from the marshals, sold my belongings, and traveled back to that Mexican river town. This trail of a thousand signs, the signs that led me right to her, was the trail that led me home. I rode up to the gates on my new horse and friend, whom I'd named Marshal, where the two guards smiled when they saw me. I rode up to the stables, and the stable boy was happy to take my horse. The old man at the door was still winking when he took my hat but a little slower on the move. Angelina, at the top of the stairs, stopped in surprise to see me. I could tell she was overjoyed, and as she ran down the stairs, I rushed up the bottom steps to meet her. She had been waiting for me and believed I would return. From that day forward, we never parted. We raised children and farmed cattle and lived our long and happy lives in that old estate. Natural causes took me to the other side in the twilight of our lives. In exactly the same number of days it took me to get back to my home, sell my belongings, and return to her, that's how long it took Angelina to join me in the afterlife. All of this, because I followed a trail of a thousand signs, on a mission to save lives, but in the end, it was answered prayers and Angelina who saved me.

Chapter Seven

As the Earth breathed, wild winds ushered in new seasons. Audrey had a way of honoring each one. I couldn't tell which was her favorite. The new life springing forth and blossoming after a bitter winter, the sweet smell of summer roses, strawberries, and late cool evenings. Unci Maka's painted robe in ambers and wines as the garden readied for a winter's slumber, or the Season of Angels, as she so lovingly called the spirit of Christmas; when the veil seemed slightly thinner, just enough for a little light from heaven to warm the hearts of even the coldest souls.

The Japanese have a saying about seasons. Ou Bai Tori is a way of honoring each one, knowing that in our own time, we will blossom too. Those wild winds were stirring. If I could slow life to a still and slip through the veil that held us apart, I'd steal her away to that peach blossom realm where time couldn't find us. I would tell her all the little things that I wished she knew. I would hold her until the feelings of loneliness were gone forever. If I could restrain those wild winds, I would, but I knew what was coming. And now these three remain—faith, hope, and love. The greatest of these is love, and this was to be her new season. We all look forward to this season in our lives and are rarely prepared for it. I knew I wasn't.

I admit, I chose my path. A string of lousy decisions led me to this place where, just out of sight, I see Audrey, I can be near her, and I can love her, but most of my efforts go unseen. There's no heart on earth more deserving of love than hers, so all I can do is make sure that the one who holds her heart is worthy of it.

In the time before Audrey and I were born, we had chosen the lives we wanted to live together, where we would battle against time for our paths to cross and our souls to remember, following the golden cords of the prairie rose until we finally meet. But this wasn't just a spinning wheel of reincarnation. We were different, set apart, for purposes and lessons yet to be revealed.

We are destined. Our connection is one of a kind. That's what makes the love we share so compelling, even as it is veiled between life and the beyond. Plato believed that at one point, we all might have been one, and by coming into this world, we craved that oneness, and discovering our soulmate was the closest to that oneness we could find. He also wondered if Zeus cursed us mere mortals to search throughout our lifetimes for the soul we were split from at birth.

There is a Celtic phrase, Anam Cara, meaning "soul friend," the one with whom you share your deepest bond. The belief is that this one person in our life will hear our confessions, those deep, dark secrets we keep locked away, our pain, our shame, and no matter what, they will love us unconditionally. There's a Japanese legend of an old man who lives on the moon, and late at night, he searches the world for kindred spirits, destined to tell a special story together, and when he finds them, he ties a red thread on both of their pinky fingers, linking them together. This assures them that they will find each other eventually. Shakespeare wrote a line that seems to relate to the idea of the red thread, saying, "the journey ends when lovers meet."

But all kinds of love exist in life, like that of the soulmate. There is only one destined for me, but as one goes through life, there can be many soulmates, and they can take on many different forms. The trusted friend, the loyal companion, the pet that rests at your door, eagerly anticipating your return. In Urdu, it is called raabta, the soul connection. The stored honey of life.

Audrey's classmates invited her to a bar one evening to hear a live band. A musician herself, she loved hearing live music and being immersed in the energy it created. It was a fun atmosphere with happy people and clinking glasses.

She drifted through the crowd toward the bar and caught the attention of the bartender. As she waited, a glance around the room revealed her friends gathered at a table, waving her over. She noticed a rowdy table of men had grown quiet as she walked closer to them and the bar. She could tell they were all watching, whispering about her. Audrey had been the subject at many tables, she accepted that with grace. She had time to accept that she was different. Her looks, her personality, and many aspects of her being would always cause her to stand apart from the rest. Being different was a good thing that garners attention, though often not the attention one sought.

Tequila sunrise. That was the drink she ordered, sweet and strong, a great song by the Eagles, and the name of her latest painting. A cause for celebration that evening, having just signed her name on it. A few extra cherries dropped in her glass when the bartender wasn't watching. The band was talented and played some of her favorites over the buzz of the lively crowd. And there was always that one table that tended to be a little louder than everyone else, or certain people who didn't realize how far their voice carried. It was the rowdy group of guys she had noticed before. A few obnoxious outbursts from the table drew her attention. One of the men at that table noticed her side eye.

Audrey weaved her way to the bar to buy a round of drinks for her table, and that man decided to break from his table and join her. His name was Beau. He was 6'4", wearing a pink button-down untucked shirt, the sleeves rolled up, and jeans. He seemed comfortable in his own skin, carefree, happy. He reminded me of Paul in Breakfast at Tiffany's, about to meet the loveliest lost soul. He was tall and tan with a friendly smile, and what's not to like about that? But a handsome face was simply not enough for Audrey. In fact, it was the handsome and charming ones that she was most suspicious of. He introduced himself and apologized for his obnoxious friends. They were out celebrating a friend's recent engagement, and the drinks were flowing. He was sincere and funny, trying to make up for his earlier impression. He bought the round of drinks for Audrey and her friends, and as she was walking away with her hands full, he asked, "Would you like to have dinner with me tomorrow?"

He watched as Audrey's long blond hair swayed as she turned back to answer with, "Maybe." After glances and simpers across the crowded room, maybe turned into yes. She rarely gave out her number. If a boy really wanted her number, she made them memorize it. If they had too much to drink to remember the next morning, well then, problem solved. But Beau remembered.

Audrey was scheduled to work that night but switched shifts with a friend and decided to live a little. A red Corvette pulled into the driveway, and a bouquet of red roses approached the door. She hadn't expected that. Most boys she knew drove old trucks like I did. Red roses were a nice touch, but I knew red was not her favorite. This probably worked well on other girls. He took her to one of the most treasured restaurants in town. It wasn't the hottest, newest place, but it was the type of restaurant where the chefs went for good food. He knew the people who owned it, and they made sure their dinner was superb. He was funny without even trying. I closed my eyes and reveled in her laughing.

He made her feel comfortable. It was as if he tore through the fabric of her reality and created a safe place for her to duck into, to forget about the heartache and haunting of her life. That's what they say about healing, that you're holding a space for someone, a safe, quiet place where one can heal themselves. Holding a space, in my mind, looks as if the walls in the Indiana Jones movies were closing in, but there's someone strong holding the walls apart, saving you, and giving you enough time to plan your escape. I liked to think that when the walls were closing in on Audrey, it would be my part to play in her film. I would be the one in her life, even if it was in the periphery, where she knew me to be, keeping my promise, but someone else had that privilege. It created in me a longing like I'd never known, watching someone holding a space, in her life, at the beach, in her arms, doing things for her…that I desperately wish I could.

Beau thought that with his attention to detail, the flashy car, and the romantic nature of the evening, he was beginning to steal her heart, but that wasn't it at all. Over time, it was the way that he made her laugh, the soul connection they were making, the young-at-heart, genuine spirit he had that drew her to him. She gave her heart willingly, and though my tortured heart ached within me, I was happy for her.

Limerence. It's a lovely-sounding word describing intense infatuation and the desire to have someone all to yourself. Oh, I was quite familiar with the feeling. But the word loses its shine when watching others feel that same way about the one you love.

This was a painful time for me to witness. I couldn't understand it. He was not her type. He was the center of attention with his charisma, but she didn't want someone who made everyone laugh all the time. She wanted someone really only interested in making her laugh. She was a lone wolf, looking for a similar creature. I couldn't figure him out. I could see him interact with his friends, a big group of guys that he'd known for years, and I just didn't know if he could separate himself from his friends long enough to give Audrey the attention she deserved. The time that a soul connection needed to develop. I didn't know what kind of creature he was, but beauties do love beasts.

They became inseparable. He was unpredictable and exciting, warm and affectionate. He was enamored by her artistic ability. He was a creative himself, so he challenged and encouraged her. He made her feel like the world needed the art she was creating. He was right. And that sentiment, that gift of encouragement, stayed with her for all of her days. She felt both free and loved at the same time with Beau. On some weekends, he'd sweep her away to Morro Bay, where his family had a beach house. They'd walk the length of the sandy shoreline, collecting seashells and running from rogue tides. They played in the sand like children until the sun began to set. He stood tall behind, with his big arms wrapped around her, admiring the bright Alizarin crimsons and golds of the sun's farewell. The rest of their night was spent drinking wine on the balcony of his beach house, telling funny stories of their younger days, waves crashing in the distance. To her, it was as perfect as she'd ever known.

She always gauged whether a situation felt right or not by a particular haunting feeling. In that moment, was there that uneasy feeling, that emptiness, did she feel like she belonged somewhere else? Oftentimes, with others, yes, but with Beau, sipping wine and hearing the waves roar, crash, and grow quiet again, his big hand gently holding hers, was one of those rare and wonderful times she felt like she belonged.

One of her fondest memories was the night she locked herself in her room, studying for an exam she'd have to take the next afternoon. Her bed was covered in open books, notes, and papers. She was in her pajama shorts, a white tank top, and a loose-fitting silk robe. With her music down low, she heard a quiet knock on her window. Her blinds were down, and she was startled at first until she heard Beau's voice calling her. He knocked again as she pulled the blinds up. With a little coaxing and a handful of pink roses this time, he carried her out the window and off into the night. She was never going to get an A on that exam anyway.

But her favorite memory of him was a time when she came down with a cold and couldn't go out. She stayed in bed for days, and they missed each other terribly, so one night he went out with friends and decided to do something wild. Beau was not the karaoke singing type, but on this night, he called Audrey and asked her to listen while he sang one of her favorite songs. He sang "It's Now or Never" by Elvis Presley to her and a bar full of people. He was great. I really didn't want to like this guy, but I had to admit—he came up with some great ideas. Singing to her that night was a memory she'd never forget.

Sadly, time changes people and their feelings. That haunting feeling of needing to be elsewhere began to creep in, but not for her. She began to feel like there was somewhere else he needed to be. She loved Beau; there was no question about that, but she was still that same leaf in the wind. She was still that boat adrift in a raging sea, and Beau was no anchor and showed no interest in becoming one. In her heart, she felt that Beau had a bold future ahead of him, but it no longer felt like she was destined to be a part of it. She had this growing feeling that she was one of those really good previews in his life, before the real film begins. If she really wanted to, she could've tried to solidify their relationship, but it would only be postponing the inevitable. Audrey knew he wasn't the man to offer her safe harbor just yet, so hearts were broken, and tears were shed, and their paths reluctantly diverged. So how does one move on after that, besides putting all those fond memories away in a box, to perhaps be found later, when the pain of broken hearts isn't as arduous?

Audrey was at work one evening, standing near the front door of the Italian restaurant, when a group of firemen walked in, dressed in their blue Clovis Fire Department t-shirts and blue slacks. They weren't there to eat. They were there on official city business, performing the restaurant's annual inspection. Jack led the team. He was tall, with dark hair, handsome, and polite. He introduced himself and his crew and why they were there. Jack wasn't flirting or smiling. He was keeping it cool. I could tell by the way he would sneak glances at Audrey from different angles of the restaurant, pretending to inspect certain things while she was seating guests. He was definitely interested. He was familiar to me. Though he wore his blue casual uniform that day, I recognized his face from just a few years back. He had been only a rookie then, when his team pulled me from my truck. It was one of his first fatalities. I remember seeing the look on his face when he saw that I was just a young kid driving around at night in a truck much like his own. By now, he'd assisted many wrecks, saved many lives, but there were always going to be the few he couldn't save that haunted him.

A couple of nights later, as she was adding notes to the seating charts at work, Audrey saw two smiling faces walk in. It was Jack and another fireman from the day of the inspection. It was a really busy Saturday night, but she found them a table quickly.

After they ate the best Italian food in Clovis, Jack pulled Audrey aside. "Hey, we're headed over to the corner bar. I don't know when your shift is over, but you should come join us." Jack's big smile made it impossible for her to refuse.

"Maybe." Smiling, she rushed back to work. Audrey's stressful shift was nearly over, and there was no better way to forget it all than to have a couple of drinks with Clovis's bravest. She had a pen woven through her hair, keeping it in a tight bun, and when she pulled it out, her soft curls fell below her shoulders. She sniffed her shirt, a rich scent of spaghetti sauce, but to some people, that might smell like heaven.

She walked into the corner bar, and the firemen were strategically seated to see her entrance. Audrey had no idea she was walking into a setup. As soon as she was invited to sit down, the other fireman was called away suddenly, leaving the two alone that night. Jack was older than Audrey, and he was clever and witty. I felt I needed to keep an eye on this guy. With Beau, there were times he would have a wandering eye or charm the waitress. Audrey noticed. Beau wasn't that slick. But Beau made up for his impropriety in many other ways. Though I hated to admit it, he did have a good heart.

Jack was a smart man. He seemed wise beyond his years and a little too manipulative for his own good. He steered the conversation in creative ways that kept her interest. He had to, as he wasn't her type. His fireman job, the persona attracted the eyes of many women, but Audrey was different, and if the crowd was interested in something, it typically repelled her. He knew it too. He had to try harder and liked the challenge.

He sent her flowers often. He made grand gestures of his affection that really moved her. Their romance was smoldering. One afternoon, Jack invited her to visit the firehouse for a tour. He showed her their breakroom and bedrooms, the kitchen, and the lounge. The guys were all piled there on a giant sectional couch, watching a movie while their food simmered in the firehouse kitchen. They all waved and greeted her from their comfortable positions, and then Jack walked her out to the rigs. She felt small standing next to these towering red trucks. In their own little world, tucked between the rigs, Jack kissed Audrey like she had never been kissed before. A noise was made in the periphery, and the kiss ended abruptly. When Jack knew they were alone, he put his hands on her shoulders and backed her up against the truck and kissed her again. His hands ran through her hair and traced down the sides of her neck. He kissed her with more passion and intensity than she'd ever known. She thought being kissed like that only happened in movies.

"Hey brother, you wanna go grab a beer or something?"

Gavri elbowed me, about to drag me out of there if he had to, but God works in mysterious, marvelous ways. Just then, lights flashed, sirens screamed, and men from all over the building came rushing from where they were to jump into their boots and jackets and pile into the rigs. They had six seconds to be on the rig and out the door, including Jack.

Blutterbunged is a goofy word describing someone like me, standing there with a surprised, gaping smile. It wasn't my business what Audrey did with her love life; she deserved love and happiness, even if I was not the one to give it to her. I didn't usually peer around walls to watch the intimate moments of her life, but for some reason, Gavri and I were there, and I think he sounded that alarm just for me.

One of her favorite memories with Jack was celebrating the Fourth of July on a boat at Bass Lake. All day was spent drinking and sunbathing as they occasionally did, but this time, they waited for the sun to go down and the fireworks to fly. It was the most spectacular sight she had ever seen. Not only was the fireworks display a massive show, but it was all reflected on the black rippling water. She was so moved that she fought the tears from her eyes. She had so much appreciation for her life, for that moment, and for the amazing country she had the privilege of calling home. She was grateful for Jack, but looking up at those sparkling lights, high in the heavens, she couldn't help but think of me. She wondered what my view was like seeing the fireworks from above. I could see the show from all angles, glorious as it was, though it paled in comparison to my view of her. Colors of the blasts reflected on her tan, oiled skin and glittering eyes—my Audrey, more beautiful than ever.

Then came that haunting feeling Audrey just couldn't ignore. It was the feeling of belonging elsewhere. Never talk about politics or religion in polite conversation, as the saying goes. They eventually learned that his Jehovah's Witness faith and her Christian faith were incompatible. The clever man that he was had hidden his faith as long as he could, knowing that Audrey would have to leave her faith behind if they were to share a future. I could see his intention. His endgame was to convert her, to change her, the ultimate conquest, the grand prize. No man, no matter who he was or what they shared, was worth trading her faith and foundation for. She ended the relationship, but for months, Jack tried to change her mind. He tried everything. He bought expensive gifts and invited her on long vacations. He wrote her letters, pages long, attempting to clear any confusion about his faith, but it always came down to the same conclusion: she'd have to abandon her faith for him. His attempts failed, and he soon faded away into memory.

She grew up going to church just as I did. We were raised in a family that every now and then would say grace at the table, if we remembered to, before digging in. The foundation of her faith was there, though everyone's walk was different. Hers was still in its infancy. Her walk was just beginning, though far enough along to avoid wrong turns.

There was a lively little Irish Pub on the edge of town where Audrey met up with her friends for a pint. Everyone loved Fibber McGee's. It was plastered with Irish memorabilia and neon beer signs with a charming and cozy atmosphere. As she weaved her way through the crowd of standing room-only people to get to her friend's table, she saw a familiar face smiling back at her. It was Anthony, a friend she'd known all her life. He had been in her kindergarten class and several classes after that. He hugged her immediately, elated that their paths were crossing again. Audrey had always had a crush on Anthony. He was a very handsome Italian, with tan skin and light green eyes. He'd always been the cool kid, a star athlete with a ton of friends, and for some silly reason, Audrey thought he was out of her league. Strangely enough, he thought the same thing about Audrey. He grew up adoring her, never telling her. She always saw him driving past her house in his red and white hotrod. He loved driving down her street in hopes of catching a glimpse of her riding her horses. There was even a time when Audrey fixed Anthony up with a beautiful friend of hers for a double date. All the while, Anthony had been wishing Audrey knew how he felt. It was a tough secret to keep, but it wouldn't be the last.

He graduated from Purdue University and moved back into town. This was his moment. That night at the bar, he never let Audrey out of his sight. He was in love all over again. As they walked to their cars after the last call, he invited her to dinner the next night, to catch up. He was tall with dark hair and striking Italian features. He would've been Caravaggio's muse had he only been born in the right century. He was her age, vibrant and interesting, but not quite the dueling and manipulative intellectual that Jack was. And he wasn't the young-at-heart, innocent spirit that Beau was either. But he had a uniqueness, an authenticity about himself that she admired. He was a curious soul, outgoing and funny, charming even. He made her feel extraordinarily special, as if she were this rare, one-of-a-kind jewel. She most definitely was, but he was smart enough to realize it.

He went out of his way to impress her, but in ways that might work for other women. It only revealed that he didn't know her, deep down, not like I did. She wasn't like other girls who found fast cars, the powerful job, and money all that interesting. After all, those are the things men sell their souls for. But could he connect on a soul level with her? Did their spirits feel at ease together, or was it just a passing physical attraction, amplified over time?

They caught up on all the years that they had known each other and laughed at the revelation that they had been mutual admirers all along. They regretted the wasted time of their past and dreamed of a future together. They spent an entire summer escaping the heat in his swimming pool, way out in the country. It had large rocks at one end where a waterfall flowed. The bottom of the pool looked like sand, their own private desert oasis. He was in awe at times, watching her glide through the water, the golden mermaid that she was.

Just like all those years they'd known each other, he still carried a secret, unsure of the time to share it. Their summer was drawing to a close, and time was running out. They had built a bonfire in the field near the pool as the sun was setting. There, he revealed his big plans of moving to Hawaii, where his brother was waiting for him. The arrangements had already been made to ship all his belongings, even his car, to Hawaii through military transport. His brother was a lucky Marine stationed there. Plans had been orchestrated months in advance. When she heard the news, she expected them to come to the mutual decision to break things off, but he surprised her with an invitation to move to Hawaii and live with him. He wanted to spend the rest of his life with her, and he put all his cards finally on the table.

Move to Hawaii with a beautiful man who was crazy about her? She had entertained worse ideas. She allowed herself to daydream and let the island visions steep in her mind for a while. I thought he was a decent guy, he had good intentions with her, and I couldn't blame him for wanting the best of both worlds. Who wouldn't want to live in paradise with a mermaid of their very own? But she recognized a pattern with certain people. Why did their love come with a cost when she loved so freely? Anthony had plans set in motion, a life in paradise awaited him, but she didn't want to make him choose between leaving or staying with her. Deep down, I thought she already knew what his choice would be. She dropped him off at the San Francisco airport and cried all the way home, believing that if love was truly meant for her, it wouldn't cost her anything. She wouldn't have to make such sacrifices, but she would recognize love that was meant for her, because it would be as freely given as her own.

There were many dates in this season, though only a few ended in the same fashion. Just before Audrey's date dropped her off at home, she'd make them take her down a dark country road and turn on the radio. They found a slow song to dance to and swayed in the beams of the headlights. I wish I had a chance to dance with her. I'd play "Angel Eyes" by The Jeff Healey Band, and for the full four minutes and forty-one seconds of it, I'd kiss her and hold her close to me, wishing this moment could be looped in time, forever.

The only thing Audrey felt she understood about love was that it was as dangerous as fire. It could warm a home, or it could burn it down. Love scared her, but her heart longed for its mate. He was out there somewhere. So what did Audrey want? She wanted love and to be understood. She wanted Pismo vacations and an art studio. She wanted to watch the stars and play guitars and spend her life making beautiful things. I could hear her prayers for love to find her, and it broke me. I cried out to her, "I never left you. I'm right here, Audrey." The intensity of my voice scattered birds from their trees and swelled the wind around her, whipping through her blond hair. Chills ran up her spine, feeling there was much more than just the scattering of birds around her.

"I love every little thing about you. I love all the little things that no one else knows. I love how your eyes sparkle at the sight of stars. I love how you show your emotions on your face. You can't hide anything. I love how you bite your lip when you're painting. I love watching you mix your colors and how you're not a perfectionist about anything, except for your art. I love how you stop to say hello to every cat and dog you pass. They love it too. I love how you make raspberries with your mouth when you make a silly mistake. I love how you can't help laughing when someone stubs their toe or trips, even though you're one of the clumsiest people I've ever known. I love how you can't resist a plate of grated cheese, and when you try to pinch a bite with your fingers and bring it to your mouth, you end up spilling cheese everywhere. Just everywhere. I even love how when you cry, your eyes turn an unimaginably beautiful color of topaz. I love how easily and innocently you blush. I love how I can tell when you're thinking about me. I know the signs. I see you stare at the ground for a moment and get quiet and then look up at the sky with this bittersweet little smile, while that big heart of yours sinks. Right then, I wish I could tell you a funny story or trip over something. I wish I could tell you how stunning you are when you're putting on makeup, but even more so when you're taking it off. There's just something about how you look when you're finally home and you put on that silk robe and twist up your hair with a paint brush." Images of me filled her mind at that moment. There's that bittersweet smile.

Those dimples. If she only knew how close I really was.

"I love you for the things you keep hidden too. The deep wounds you just can't seem to heal from. And because you can't heal yourself, you love the feeling of helping others, the shoulder to cry on, the sounding board, the guardian angel. It's almost to a fault because if you're too busy helping other people, you don't have time to take your own inventory and do the hard work inside yourself. The distant father, the mother who can't bring herself to love you; they make you feel weak. They make you feel like you don't deserve those A's in school, deserve that good job, or dare I say…people in your life you can trust. You sacrifice, and you sell yourself short and let the voice of the enemy tell you over and over that you're not worthy. But my job is to remind you that you are. My job is to love you and remind you of who you truly are and the purpose you have, even if it's only in dreams, where you may or may not remember. But one of these days, I pray that you finally remember on your own."

What is love, really? I used to think that being destined meant romantically destined, but that's not always the case. Agape is a word that describes the highest form of love. It's a selfless love, an all-enduring, unending, all-encompassing love. Love is a friend who loves the light inside you, whether dim or blinding, and finds it all beautiful. Love is the friend that sees you through. Love is keeping a promise. I want her to have it all.

Many months had passed, and she finally heard from Anthony in Hawaii. He was delighted to hear her voice and repeatedly told her how much he missed her. But again, he had a secret to tell. He broke the news that he was going to be a father. A little fun with a cute girl at his house party turned into a life-altering event. He lamented the past, asking for Audrey's forgiveness. There was nothing for Audrey to forgive. She was happy for him. She knew he'd make a tremendous father, and this adventure would be good for him. She, too, had a secret to tell. In those months, a life-altering event had happened to her as well. She was engaged to be married. When she told Anthony the news, the line fell silent. He just couldn't speak. He had no breath for his words. A rush of regret and despair washed over him, and there was nothing he could do about it, having traded a time in paradise for the rare jewel he once held.

Chapter Eight

If only there were a language all the world could understand, that could somehow fill the void between us all. And if not between us all, then just between the hearts of two people. Ludwig van Beethoven spoke of music, saying that music is a mediator between the spiritual and the sensual life.

Sound is a precious thing. Our Creator spoke the heavens and earth into being. All living things have a communicative repertoire and create a kind of music just by existing.

Seatherny is a word to describe the peace we feel while listening to songbirds. Deamflum describes the serenity we have from the sounds of a waterfall. Brontide is such a great word, describing the rumbling of distant thunder, and psithurism is the sound of wind sweeping through trees. The oceans roar, storms crash, the wind whistles, wings flutter, bees buzz, cats purr, and it's even more pronounced on my side of the veil. Sound, bells, laughter, and music were some of the first healers. Music is a language we all share, and we don't have to read sheet music or play an instrument for it to change our lives, our mood, our hearts.

I think Audrey's first love may have been music. She loved to wander into her father's music room, a piano, various stringed instruments lining the walls, and on the shelves in the back of the room held fascinating noise makers from all over the world. A thumb piano, a didgeridoo, a concertina, a jaw harp, maracas, and harmonicas. Kids wander off, but her parents needed only listen to know where to find her.

Audrey's mother wanted to give her a well-rounded education but didn't know where to start, so she dropped her in the deep end of every activity her mother ever wanted to try. She involved her in ice skating, though too unforgiving, then in gymnastics, but not really a sport for lanky girls, tap and ballet, practicing her pliets on the soccer field. No matter how hard she tried to connect with those activities her mother introduced her to, something never felt quite right. But there was always that old upright piano that sat quietly to everyone else, though softly calling to Audrey, saying, I'm here for you. Won't you give me a try?

Finding the right piano teacher was an obstacle in itself. She began with a very old teacher with outdated ways of smacking hands when a wrong note was played or a note at the wrong time. Over the next few years, she was instructed by boring teachers who taught page by page out of expensive piano lesson books. When Audrey was on the brink of giving up, her mother introduced her to Dave Calvin, who was about to change everything. He was in his thirties but looked as if he'd stepped out of the seventies. This guy looked and sounded like a hippy, but you'd never guess the musical genius hidden beneath all that shaggy hair. He was laid back but encouraging and discovered that Audrey was motivated by challenges. He told her that he wanted to introduce her to classical greats, but he wasn't sure if she was ready or advanced enough. She instantly wanted to prove him wrong. He expanded her view of music, changing the black and white notes on a page into art, feelings, colors, emotions, love, heartache, anticipation, anger, and joy. She was learning Bach, Beethoven, and Chopin, while also learning his favorites, being Ellington and Brubeck. For some, playing music is an ability they wish for; some have tremendous talent, and for some, it's simply found in the soul.

She would play soft tunes at night until she heard her father snoring. She wore that as a badge of honor. But this learning process was driving her sister mad. Her sister wouldn't just ask politely for Audrey to stop playing. She would sneak into the music room and pull the wooden cover over the keys in hopes of smashing Audrey's fingers. It caused Audrey to memorize the songs so that she could watch for signs of an approaching sister.

When her sister would walk away defeated, Audrey would play certain tunes for her, like that of the Witch's theme from The Wizard of Oz. Strange how Audrey's playing really irritated her sister, not when she was an awkward beginner, but more so when she was playing complicated pieces beautifully.

We all start out as awkward beginners. My mom took me to the same old lady on a different day of the week. Unlike me, there was a time when Audrey sat at the piano and didn't have to be forced to play thirty minutes every day, for practice. One day, the light just came on for her. She and that old piano became the closest of friends, spending hours at a time bonding. But it was always going to be a lonely instrument to her. While her fingers learned muscle memory and could play on autopilot, she would frequently look out her window and daydream of playing guitar on the beach with friends. She thought of what it would be like sitting by a campfire with her husband someday, strumming guitars and singing their favorite tunes. It was something to do together.

While in town, Audrey passed by a big guitar store. She had no intention of making a purchase that day, only to see if anything called to her. She strolled through the rooms of electric guitars, the walls covered in instruments of every shape, size, and color. She pulled down an alluring ivory Fender with a natural blond wood neck and held it. It was heavier than she had imagined. She lightly strummed the strings with her thumb. It felt good in her hands. Electric guitars are capable of so many sounds and sing in the right hands, but she didn't feel ready for electric just yet. Throughout the room, there were boys plugged into amps, demonstrating their varying abilities. It was loud chaos. But there was that special room tucked away, temperature controlled, usually empty. She left the noise of aspiring rock stars and entered the hushed room of hollow bodies and artistic inlay. Audrey always loved the look and sound of acoustic guitars. They weren't the attention getters, loud and bold. Acoustics are softer, the extraordinary sound of a plucked string, capable of so many voices, desiring days spent on the beach.

In the corner of the room, there was a man in a black t-shirt and jeans, with his back to the door. She recognized the tune he was playing, "Patience" by Guns and Roses. She could hear the differences in the tune and tempo that he added to the song as she slowly admired each hanging guitar. They were each works of art, all having exquisite wood finishes, abalone inlay, wood designs. They all spoke to her, pull me down, pluck my strings. Hear how I resonate.

The man with his back to her had stopped playing and turned slightly to see her. "That sounds great." She said. "Don't stop because of me. I'm just window shopping."

He smiled and began a new tune she tried to recognize.

As she gazed at the guitars that brought her closer toward him, he asked, "Which one is your favorite?"

"Oh, they're all so pretty. It's hard to choose." Audrey took a moment, making her way back to a certain guitar. "This one. The abalone inlay is really something."

He returned the guitar he was playing to its place, and she noticed how much taller he was and the broadness of his shoulders. He pulled the guitar she pointed to from the wall and sat down with it. He played arpeggios up and down the neck, demonstrating its deep resonating tones. "Wow, it sounds beautiful too."

He laughed and said, "Well, you have very expensive taste. You just picked out the most expensive guitar in this whole store." They both laughed; the ice had broken.

He went through the room playing different guitars that she liked, demonstrating how each brand varies in sound and why he preferred certain ones over others. It was quite the experience. She watched him as he played. She watched his large hands, his fingers moving effortlessly across the strings. They finally came to a guitar that was calling her, so he put it in her hands. She sat down on the stool behind her, and he moved her fingers along the neck, into a position to form a chord. Audrey didn't seem to mind him touching her hand. She strummed the strings and smiled brightly back at him. He was so knowledgeable, helpful, kind; she was sold. "Hey, will you be here on Thursday? I have to wait for payday, but I think I found the one I want. Will you hold it for me?"

With a puzzled look on his face and after a hesitant moment, he said, "Yes, I'll be here on Thursday. What time?"

"Same as today. What's your name, by the way? You've really been so helpful."

"I'm Ethan," he said, shaking her hand. "It's been fun. Looking forward to Thursday."

The week seemed to move slower than usual for her. Was she more excited to see the tall blonde with blue eyes or to buy her first guitar? Thursday afternoon had finally come around, with swirling butterflies in her stomach. She walked into the store and was approached by an associate in a black t-shirt, asking if she needed help. She declined but asked, "Do you know if Ethan is working today?"

"Ethan?" he repeated, his expression perplexed. "I don't know an Ethan who works here, but I'm pretty new."

"Oh, don't worry about it. I know what I'm looking for, but thanks anyway." She left the associate and stepped inside the acoustic room. That's where she found him. He was sitting in the same spot, playing a different tune. After a moment, she recognized it. It was Waiting On a Friend by the Rolling Stones. As she hummed along, he turned around, amused by the exchange. They greeted each other, small talk, pleasantries, and then went to look for the guitar she wanted to buy. The associate that she spoke to earlier informed her that the guitar was unavailable. He looked at Ethan, confused. Ethan watched the disappointment come over Audrey, while she graciously smiled and thanked the associate.

"Have you eaten already? Want to grab some lunch with me?"

he offered as a consolation.

"I'd love to, but don't you have to stay for your shift?"

Ethan laughed and finally told her, "I actually don't work here."

"But…" Audrey laughed at herself, putting her hand on her cheek, clearly embarrassed. "You were so helpful, and you were wearing a black t-shirt and jeans. I just thought…And you're here today?"

Their lunch began with laughter, and time flew by while talking about guitars and good music. He was self-taught, and she had years of training on the keys, but somehow, they found themselves on the same page. He had a quiet, humble, and witty personality. He was easygoing and attentive. They shared a second language of music, something she had never known with anyone else. It was a real connection. It was refreshing. She discovered that he was exceedingly intelligent, but not manipulative with it like Jack was. He was easily the smartest guy in the room without anyone needing to know. He was the surreptitious, quiet guy in the corner, who could play anything, build anything, do anything, but didn't have the need to broadcast it. She really liked that about him.

She was drawn to his style too. He drove a 1965 slate blue GTO. He was a former navy man, and military men were always just a bit more attractive to her. The idea that they turned their lives over to their country, selflessly for years, was endearing. Although Ethan seemed a simple, jeans-and-t–shirt kind of guy, there was a mystery brewing just beneath the surface. She couldn't put her finger on it, but would that edgy, hotrod image that she was slowly chipping away at give way to reveal a big teddy bear underneath? The problem with that, in my own opinion, was that he was a dangerous combination of trouble and disarming blue eyes, when she should be loading for bear.

They began to spend all their time together, a musical romance in full bloom as if it were spring, though it was that amber and wine time of autumn. One afternoon, she made him take her to a pumpkin patch where they picked out a few pumpkins for carving. They blared good music, and cut into the pumpkins, joking about the gooey insides, even throwing it at each other. They laughed till it hurt. Once they cleaned up, he made her dinner, prawns and steak, cooked just the way she liked them. She could tell that he poured love into his cooking, and she enjoyed watching his process. After he spoiled her with dinner, he took her up to a loft where all his musical instruments were kept. She was dazzled by the number of amps and guitars spread all over the room. There was even a keyboard. She wandered around the room, silently taking inventory. It took her back to the days of playing in her father's music room. But there was something special he wanted her to see. "Hey, come over here. I think you're gonna like this."

He was standing next to a couch that had something lying on it, covered by a throw. He pulled it back to reveal a rectangular guitar case, all black with small gold details. Audrey looked at him and looked back at the case. "Open it." He nudged.

To Audrey's surprise, it was the very first guitar she pulled off the wall. It was that blond and ivory Fender, the electric beauty that she had shied away from. During that week, he returned to buy the guitar. He bought it knowing she'd have the desire and talent to connect with it someday. He watched her take it down from the wall, the first guitar she loved, believing love at first sight existed at that moment, for both of them.

When I was watching her with the other boys, it hurt me, but only superficially, as a flesh wound would. But there I was, watching her find what she was starting to believe was the one, and if I were still alive, the wounds I would suffer by watching this would've surely been fatal.

Is there any better reason for being alive than being in love? You can love lots of different things, but the state of being in love is life, illuminated. It's intoxicating and exhilarating. Audrey had been in love before, but not like this. She had never felt the same love requited. She had a light that rivaled the glittering night sky and full moon glowing, and though seeing another man have this effect on her was agony for me, I couldn't take my eyes off of her.

The two of them could appreciate the music on deeper levels than most. Meliorism is a belief that one can create a positive change in the world through creativity, love, and kindness, and that was something they shared. It was often they'd look up the chords of a song and learn the lyrics. In a matter of minutes, they'd be playing the songs on their guitars. This was uncharted musical territory for her. Ethan was a great teacher. Not just for Audrey. He was the type of guy that if you visited his house, after a while, you'd have an instrument in your hands, and music would be flowing. Even if you were new to music altogether, he made it fun. It was a universal language that he wanted to share with everyone. It was one of his most unique and admirable qualities to her. It set him apart from the rest of the men she had ever known.

They spent their weekends driving to different beaches, collecting sand and shells in small glass jars for a special shelf that hung in Audrey's bedroom. Ethan took her to Pismo, staying in her favorite room that had the perfect view, but as soon as they got there, they both unpacked their guitars and found a good spot down in the sand. They played tunes they had been practicing. Audrey felt she was not at all as good on the guitar as she was on the piano, but it was fun catching up. This was a dream come true for her, whether it sounded good or not. She'd found someone who finally spoke her language. Those deep feelings of loneliness were no longer. No longer feeling like there was somewhere else she needed to be. She felt as though her heart had finally found safe harbor.

Several months into their soundtracked romance, Ethan surprised her with two tickets to cruise the Mexican Riviera. They set sail from a dock in San Francisco for those exotic Mexican destinations, but it was Catalina Island where her life changed forever. The ship docked early in the morning, leaving them with an entire day for exploring. After renting a golf cart, they toured the island along its small, winding mountain roads, Ethan driving in varied ways to spook and startle Audrey into laughter. They kissed at stop signs, crosswalks, and lookouts, and though it was only their beginning, they felt like old familiars. They returned to their ship to cool off in the pool and rest up for dinner. Audrey was excited that the evening was going to be a formal affair. The warm ocean air caused Audrey's hair to show its natural form, cascades of golden waves, befitting the mermaid she was. Her dress was a deep aubergine color, draping on her figure and pooling at the floor. The straps were aubergine jewels that gleamed off her bronzed skin. Ethan wore a dark charcoal suit, a crisp white button-down, and a pale pink tie that had hints of purple to match her dress. The pair was the most stunning couple on the vessel. All of the passengers and crew looked lovely and glamorous; they sipped on champagne and dined on lobster, while the ship's photographers captured it all.

With two champagne flutes in one hand and Audrey's hand in the other, Ethan led the way to the very top moonlit deck. The faint sound of music played from the party decks below, the canopy of stars put on their most sparkling display, and Ethan seized the moment. With a toast to their amazing time together, he pulled her close to him and revealed the ring he was holding in his hand. He didn't do the grand gesture of the dramatic one-kneed proposal; that just wasn't his style.

He simply stood beside her, holding her as close to him as he could, offering his heart, baring his soul, promising a future together. It was genuine and heartfelt. It was perfect. Moonlight reflected in the happy tears in their eyes as she said yes.

Had I not indulged in so much whiskey, foolishly driving my old truck into the night, had I done everything differently that night years ago, I would be the one proposing to Audrey. On our special day, I would've spent the whole day sunbathing and playing on the beach with her. Just before sunset, I would have taken her hand and led her down the shoreline looking for shells and sand dollars. I would have hidden a unique shell, holding her ring, in a tidepool, which I knew she loved exploring. I was going to tell her how I'd fallen in love with her at first sight all those years ago and always have and always would. I was going to tell her how my soul rejoiced when it finally found its true mate. Audrey and I had enjoyed elaborate engagements throughout our lifetimes spent together, but that one, the simplest of gestures, the raabta, the history of our love, the one that never had its chance, would have been the best one of all. If only.

The rest of their night was spent on that moonlit deck, dancing and twirling about to the faint music from the decks below, finishing the bottle of champagne in their unforgettable Catalina Island party for two. Gavri and I, in our suits, and Em, in a velvet sapphire gown, watched over our Audrey with tears in our eyes. A bittersweet, heavy-hearted moment seeing Audrey the happiest she'd ever been, though knowing how things were supposed to be with me. Gavri and I loosened our ties and let them hang freely. Em took off her high heels, and we all sat on high, clinking our glasses, somber as it was. We should be celebrating them, the two songbirds. This was where I should've given her one last kiss, let her go, and allowed my spirit to drift up into the beckoning light above me, but I couldn't shake the feeling that there was still a purpose for me here. Perhaps she was about to need me more than ever. The angels knew all the answers, and instead of popping champagne on the calm waters of Catalina Island, they were bracing for an imminent storm. I couldn't leave her now.

Chapter Nine

M etanoia has Greek origins, describing the journey one takes to change and grow the self, the heart, mind, and soul. Some call it the long journey inward. Nepenthe is another Greek word that means the elixir for sorrow. There is medicine for pain, but what is the medicine for physical pain in the spiritual sense? Nepenthe is something that relieves our suffering and soothes the mind enough to forget, be it a place, an action, a person, or even an animal. This was to be a dark season, Audrey's long journey inward, the nepenthe, the discovery of her purpose in life, and I was there to witness it all.

Few know what dark night of the soul is until they survive it. From birth, we have been conditioned by the people around us, our loved ones, our friends, teachers, television, and radio. We don't think we are, but these messages are seeping into our subconscious, telling us who society thinks we should be in order to fit into it. Most people who survive the dark night of the soul have lied to themselves and others, built a façade, worn an ornate mask to blend into the masses, to avoid bringing unnecessary attention to themselves. The dark night of the soul is about a time in one's life when the façade, the false skin, is shed. The old self dies, while a new one emerges, and the process is a painful one. The pretenses that were once clung to are found absurd and useless; the activities that once brought pleasure are of no interest. You feel as if no one can relate to what you are going through and that they all think you are crazy. Isolation, depression, and darkness set into your reality until you have no choice but to retreat to the only light you can find, and that is hidden deep within you.

After a lifetime dedicated to studying art and sharpening her skills, Audrey's hard work finally paid off. Once she began selling her large oil paintings, happy patrons led her into a business of painting murals in their homes. Before she knew it, she had a waiting list months long. She was painting in restaurants, salons, and mansions. Her work differed from one job to the next. One week she was painting a beach mural, the next she was painting giant marble columns, a kid's pirate-themed bedroom, and grapevines in a Tuscan-themed kitchen. People shared her business number like wildfire, and she found herself to be a professional artist, a female artist in a field usually dominated by competitive males. She painted her whole town and the surrounding towns too. Soon she found herself being flown all over the West Coast for her work. Audrey was exceptional, and her clients knew it. She was making more money than she ever dreamed an artist could make.

She tasted the sweet success of her calling, and after several years, it was all gone. The business was crashing, but it wasn't only hers. It was Main Street, Wall Street, and the world's economy was all feeling the brunt of bad policy and politics. Audrey learned that the first of any business to dry up in a shaky economy was the arts. Her waiting list soon disappeared, and she found herself crashing from the high of her own independence into joblessness.

Audrey's father had been a saddle maker and leather crafter since he was in high school. He was taught by legends in the field, and it wasn't until he was fired from his corporate job at fifty years old, that he poured his heart and soul into his work, full time, and became a legend in the field himself. As an artist, you would think he'd be delighted for his daughter to charge into her calling with such passion and find success doing so, but he wasn't. Sadly, he was the type of man who seemed to find more worth in a person by how their résumé measured up. If they looked good on paper, if they had their ducks in a row, or if they graduated with a prestigious degree. He wanted a daughter who made him look good. It wasn't only for his sake that he wanted her to be successful. All parents want their children to be secure in their careers so that they don't have to worry about them so much. He was an artist. He knew that art was a fickle business.

Her father had learned how to shape leather, carve patterns into soaked hides, and use tools and stamps to adorn them with details. It was a beautiful craft, and his artistry was marvelous, but leather work was the only lane he seemed to stay in.

Leo, her grandpa, was always making new things for Audrey's grandma. If she saw something in a magazine, he could make it in an afternoon, typically looking better than the original. He had a kind soul, just the same as Audrey, and that resonated in the work they both did. Everyone could see their similarities. They made each other laugh all day by goofing off—water fights in the summer, card games in winter, playing dominoes, and watching old western movies. They were the best of pals. He called her Puddy Tat. Inspired, she followed him around, learning new techniques, getting an education in life and art and faith that would never be gained from any classroom. "Somewhere Over the Rainbow" was his favorite song, and it became hers too. As a little girl, she fashioned a mud kitchen, and he was her best customer. He would ooh and ahh and beg for seconds. He would pull her around in a rusty little red wagon until she was big enough to pull his dog Fritzie around in it. Fritzie was her grandpa's schnauzer and a terrific sport. She was pulled all over that yard most days, through mud and over bumps, sometimes even tipping over, but the dog was so happy to be loved and included that she'd hop right back in and hang on.

Her grandparents came up with the idea of making Audrey her own big playhouse in their backyard, where her mud kitchen once stood. Audrey's mother and sister wanted to go on shopping sprees but never wanted little Audrey to tag along, so they would drop her off at her grandma and grandpa's house, promising to take her to the zoo as soon as they returned. She waited eagerly for them, and by nightfall, she was devastated. The first time it happened was considered an accident. The second time was too, but it didn't matter how many times it happened or what excuses were made; she felt terribly abandoned. Her grandparents resolved to make their garden a place better than the zoo or anything her mother and sister might promise. They worked together to make the cutest playhouse on the planet for her. It was a Tudor-style cottage with Dutch doors and latching windows. It had a cutout in the counter for a bowl, which was the sink, a desk full of art supplies, a play oven, and all the plastic food and kitchenware to accompany it. In the corner of the house, her grandpa built a small bunk bed. It was the perfect size for her teddy bears on the top bunk and Fritzie on the bottom. She had everything she needed, but her grandma added the final touch. She installed an intercom and told Audrey she could radio out anytime she wanted a snack delivery. Outside her playhouse, there was a wine barrel cut in half where her grandpa planted his favorite flower, the prairie rose. He always picked a rose or two for her when he'd come knocking on her playhouse door.

When Audrey was visiting, she watched him use saws and drills, hoping someday to be able to make things as he did. He was a busy man and hard worker until one day, a heart attack sent him rushing to the hospital. Three heart attacks later, the doctor made it clear that working was out of the question, so he was now free to follow his passion in sculpting. He would fill their little house full of the sweet smell of melting beeswax on the kitchen stove. He would slowly shape the wax into a figure that came to life before Audrey's eyes, then he'd take it to be transformed into bronze. He created cowboy scenes like a blacksmith hammering iron, as Audrey's great-great-granddad did. A cowboy riding a bucking horse, right out of the chute, a cow defending her calf from wolves, and then there was Audrey's favorite. Every time she went to her grandparents' house, she saw all of his bronze pieces, but the cowboy sitting on a whiskey barrel, singing and playing the guitar next to his howling dog always made her smile. That feeling she got from seeing his works of art was the same feeling she wanted people to have when they looked at her own work someday.

Leo was ecstatic about the mural work Audrey was doing. He wanted to hear about the details of every job and see the photos when she was finished. If Leo was proud of her work, that was what truly mattered to her. During the last year that her business was still going, she learned that her grandpa was sick. She visited him more often, brought food, and helped with the housework. He was getting worse and fast. Audrey sat at their kitchen table where she had enjoyed their company, morning toast with strawberry jam, Chinese takeout, crates of fresh-picked strawberries, and hearing good old funny stories her whole life, and was told that he was dying. She stood up with conviction, saying, "No, let's get you to a better doctor, and we'll fix this. There's got to be a way."

"There isn't a way to fix this, Puddy." Audrey's grandma bowed her head.

Audrey refused to listen and vowed to get him help, but it finally took a beautiful sunny afternoon in the same yard where her playhouse still stood, where he told her, "I'm ready to go, Puddy Tat. I've lived a long life, I've fought for my country, I've loved, I've raised a family, and even eaten mud pies. But my body is tired...and I'm ready to go. And I know where I'm going." With tears pooling in his eyes, he pointed his shaky finger up to the sky. He hugged Audrey with all his might. He prayed this would help her understand, and he put on a brave smile for her. She returned a defeated smile as best she could, with quiet tears streaking down her cheeks.

Audrey couldn't understand how he could just give up. The hardest thing Audrey ever encountered was having to stand by helplessly and watch someone she loved suffer while there was nothing she could do about it. This crushed her because she wasn't only losing her grandpa. She felt like she was losing one of the only people who truly loved her unconditionally and, most importantly, who understood her. Audrey would soon lose the last deep soul connection she had on this earth.

Her relationship with Ethan was becoming rapidly strained. It seemed they were in love and in bliss until they moved into a small apartment together. She discovered that he had an affinity for alcohol. She wasn't used to being around someone who drank heavily, so she didn't understand the change that occurred when alcohol hit the bloodstream. He seemed on certain occasions to have a case of Dr. Jekyll and Mr. Hyde, but she assured herself this was just a phase.

The loss of her business and flow of income caused a rift between them. She learned he held a similar belief as her father, that she had played around with paint long enough, and it was finally time she finished her degree and got a real job. That was a devastating blow, having worked so hard to achieve this level of artistry…for nothing. It felt like the things most dear to her had little to no value to him. It felt like Ethan was losing respect for her, but she hoped his perspective would change.

With money problems multiplying, Ethan knew there was only one thing left for him to do: become a soldier. He fought this decision. It was the last thing he ever wanted to do. He waited weeks, hoping their financial situation would recover, but it never did. It was something he dreaded doing, though it was not displeasure about the act of serving his country because he had already served willingly. Having to sign that contract, making those sacrifices again, going through boot camp as a soldier this time, and losing a rank to join a different branch was all asking too much, and deep in his heart, he resented Audrey for it. Military life meant a lot of goodbyes, and they were faced with their first one when he flew off to boot camp, and she stayed to finish the last few mural jobs she had left.

Audrey was alone again. If I could've ripped through the veil, I would have. She came home every night to an empty apartment, and the weight of it all crashed down around her. I was beside her, holding her every time I saw her cry. I wished she knew that. I am her destined one, there's no one who understands her more. I see it all, I know why it all happens, but I can't comfort her with that. But there are things I can do.

Em showed me how to leave signs for Audrey, while Gavri was the one who showed me how to protect her. The two were such a perfect balance for Audrey and such wonderful forces for good in her life, if only she knew. Angels are messengers. They are sent in God's place to care for the living, and if only the living knew how much their angels loved and adored their people, earth would be such a different place. If the living only knew they had so many more angels than friends, if they only knew that angels are standing by, cheering them on as they go through life, they would never want to give up.

So, Em gave me another idea for Audrey. She set up a meeting for a kid's room mural with a new client and was dressed and prepared for the meeting, leaving her apartment when a beautiful young cat came walking directly up to her. Em showed me how to communicate with the kitty. That beautiful creature with smoky gray and charcoal colors wanted to be loved and to find a home, so I told her to find Audrey. Animals are multidimensional creatures, making communicating with them easy. This was the first time I'd ever spoken to an animal before and felt understood. That morning, as Audrey was rushing to her car with her hands full of notebooks, her drawings and portfolio, she was greeted by a very persistent and vocal kitty. She walked right up to her feet and weaved between them in an affectionate way. Audrey put her books down and picked up the kitty. It was love. But after a few moments, Audrey had to put her new friend back down and hurry to her meeting. Before that, she told the kitty, "I want to take you home with me, but I have to go now. Please be safe and come back tonight. Come back and find me. Promise?" After she heard a few meows back at her, Audrey reluctantly drove away.

The meeting was a flop. The people wanted too much for very little, and Audrey wasn't about to be taken advantage of. She changed into her lounge clothes and silk robe, sitting by her open front door for hours, sipping red wine and listening to soft music play. She waited for the smoky kitty to return, but sadly, there was no sign of her.

Later that night, after finally closing the door, she grew weary and drifted into a dream, where I met her. She found herself in the same place where she was waiting for the kitty to return and, instead, watched the flowers bloom around her as if it were a moon garden, then noticed the air smelled sweeter. She saw me appear from the shadows. I played her a song that spoke to my heart, about waiting, called "Aspettami" by Pink Martini. This waiting and patience and longing sure tries a man's soul. I knew what it was like to wait and hope, and at least in these few moments we shared in dreams, whether she remembered my visits or not, it kept me going. It was the electric, thrilling stolen moments. And yes, stolen is the perfect word. We weren't meant to share this time ever again, but somehow, here I was, walking into her dream and seeing her smile with those dimples; these stolen moments where I was able to do all the things I never got to do.

I sat beside her, holding her hand in mine. "It's okay, she'll be back soon," I assured her. She smiled warmly back at me. The news she so desperately wanted to hear. She wrapped her other hand around my arm and rested her head on my shoulder. I got to ease her worried heart. I got to make her smile and look into her eyes. I felt the warmth of her embrace, these stolen moments that might fade when she woke, but I would never forget. If only I could spend eternity in moments of my choosing, this might be one of them.

Days later marked Ethan's return from boot camp. Both of them were nervous about what his return would mean for their relationship. Audrey believed that giving Ethan a lot of space to adjust to being home might be best, so she worked in her studio, and he had time to tinker in the garage and work on his car.

One windy afternoon, Ethan was lying on his back working underneath his GTO when he encountered a furry visitor. He had never been around cats before and had this notion that they were all skittish and feral. But that same smoky kitty rubbed her head against his shoulder and meowed in his ear. He felt paws press down across his stomach while part of his body was still beneath his car. This kitty was the first thing that made him laugh since he returned, and it was love. This time, he walked into the house with her in his arms and gave Audrey an incredible surprise. Ethan was the hero that day, even if he had a little help.

They named the smoky kitty Roxy, and she was the rock star of the household. She provided comic relief when things became too serious. All I had to do was ask. There was a heated argument between Audrey and Ethan that turned into a screaming match. Something had to be done. I told Roxy to do something funny, lighten the mood, now! I expected her to leap through the air or run around the room really fast. I was stunned to see her jump up on the table between them and puke off the side of it. Cats take a few gags to vomit, and that actually made them stop arguing. They both stood there and watched her gag and puke off the table and splatter on the floor below. They went from screaming to belly laughs in seconds as I stood there, entirely dismayed. But it worked!

The call came in that Audrey had been dreading for so long. Leo's time was running out. Sometime in the night, he'd had a massive stroke, and it left him unable to speak. Audrey entered his bedroom and sat beside him. It was a giant California king-size bed. The same bed where she used to fall asleep between them as a little girl. The décor hadn't changed much in all those years. She held his hand, resiliently fighting tears, having so much to say with so little time. His eyes were always so playful and expressive to her, and even now, in his final hours, though unable to speak, his eyes said so much. All she could do was tell him over and over, "I love you, Grandpa. I love you. I love you. I love you."

Her father ushered her out of the room, and that was the last time she ever saw the man who ate mud pies and pulled her around in a red wagon. The last time she ever saw the man who'd inspired her to become a real artist, who knew her flaws and loved her anyway, the man who understood her. Understanding someone, or even trying to, wanting to, is one of the richest and rarest gifts you can give another living soul. Audrey would have fleeting moments of understanding in her life but never again feel understood in the way he made her feel.

I watched Audrey sink further and further into a deep depression. She closed herself off and self-medicated with hard alcohol. She was never a big drinker. Even in her condition, she hated the feeling of being out of control that alcohol inevitably left her in. So, she decided to try cannabis instead. At first, she didn't know how to use it. She was unsure of it and its effects. We have been living in a world built to support the profit margins of Big Pharma. If you have an ailment, chances are they make a pill for that, but the good book speaks of herbs of the land to heal, doesn't it? For Audrey, the herb opened her mind so that she could clean out those neglected dark corners. It leveled the spiritual playing field. It helped her relax and cope with the pressures of life and treated her pain while she mourned. But like any medicine, it was to be taken in small doses and only intended for a limited period of time.

She tuned the music to fit her mood, piled the paint on her palette, and was able to apply brush to canvas, freer than ever before. Her usual creative mind was stimulated and inspired. In the past, she'd hesitate to make bold moves; she'd overthink, but with the herb, she tried new daring things on a whim, and they turned out beautifully. Even though this was one of the darkest paintings she'd painted, the colors were more vibrant as she brought meadow flowers to the warm morning light from the darkness of Prussian blue. Her paintings were alive and illuminated. She was simultaneously nursing a broken heart and discovering abilities and a whole new world within herself, all at the same time.

There's a Japanese word that comes to mind. Seijaku is a word that implies that solitude isn't only loneliness but perhaps a wonderful place of self-discovery and renewal. I suppose it depends on the circumstances, and when we're mending a broken heart, it would be difficult to see solitude like this, but it was in painting, her therapeutic escape, that allowed time for seijaku.

While the music played and the paint spread across the canvas, the mind wandered. In this time, she was being confronted by all her demons. Demons are real, and they all have specific tasks, but all have the same goal. They are sent by their master to destroy you with your worst fears, greatest failures, deepest regrets, and most painful memories. They whisper into your ear all those negative and repetitive thoughts and lies. That's how you know they aren't angels. Angels are only positive energy. They only lift you up and make you feel better, whereas demons will only drag you down. Audrey had done a good job her whole life outrunning her demons until now.

This was Audrey's "Dark Night of the Soul," where she could run no longer. She faced each painful memory in her life, one by one, forgiving herself and others in the process. It left her demons powerless, and they failed their mission. This was a grueling process, but in time, she realized that she had worked through every wicked thing from her past that kept her up at night. She would tell herself, yes, this happened, and you know what? It's okay. That happened too, and that's okay. She let things go. She had spent her whole life fighting things, fighting for things, fighting battles within. That was usually a sign. It was a sign to surrender. She took the fight and surrendered it all to her Creator, who had wanted for so long to fight those battles for her.

She was finally free from it all, and her journey began to take on a different light. Her mind and her body were no longer a haunted mansion but now taking the shape of a temple. A battle-worn, overgrown, and unkempt temple, growing a garden inside, but Audrey wasn't afraid of the work she saw before her. She knew it would be worth it. So how do you clear away years of brush? It takes time being by yourself, being vulnerable and exposed, pruning away that which doesn't bloom, and waiting for your garden to grow in new ways.

It was a means to a beginning, a learning that she credited to the cannabis, that this newfound expansion of abilities was found inside all along. The herb just made her fearless enough to find it. It was a portal to a land not yet explored, which helped her address the negative spiritual world around her, leveling the playing field. But when the game is over, win or lose, we all have to leave the field at some point. Staying would grow tiresome for the soul. Upon learning she didn't need the herb to find her way and that it had served its purpose, it was left behind her. After all, true medicine is not meant to be taken forever.

She noticed that this was a time in her life when God seemed to clear distractions. He removed family and friends, drama, and confusion. It was as if He said to her, "Now that I have your full attention, create, write, paint. Get to work." She became very familiar with the process of her alchemy. Her nepenthe, her purpose. She had this incomprehensible way of turning her pain into works of art. With each painting, she was healing herself, but in time, she would learn that the healing didn't end with her. The healing could be felt in the admirers of her work. The people who couldn't help but gaze into her painted scenes, feeling changed by them.

There was a night I planned to visit her in a dream, but instead I watched while someone else made a visit. There in her sleep, I watched her grandpa, Leo, fully restored to his former glory, take her on a walk to show her various scenes from their past and in her future. These were things she didn't quite understand yet but soon would. There came a time when they walked upon an old wooden dock. This dock had been there through the ages and creaked beneath their feet, though what seemed to be water that a waiting boat was floating in was perfectly still and bathed in a myriad of soft pastel colors, just as the sky. Leo believed she deserved a better goodbye than what she got the last time they saw each other. He even smelled of sweet beeswax. It was the goodbye and embrace she needed from him to be able to let him go. In his bold and passionate way, he told her once more, with a proud smile on his face, "Go for it." Then he boarded the waiting vessel, and as he blew her a kiss and waved from the deck, it slowly and quietly crossed the sky, into the cloud cover and through the veil.

Audrey's last mural job was in a big public building downtown. She preferred working late hours so that people wouldn't distract her on the job. Ethan went to pick up a few late-night burgers and fries, the perfect fuel to put the finishing touches on this mural and call it a night. As he was pulling in the driveway, in the dark of night, somehow he saw a tiny black furry kitten. Gavri, Em, and I ushered this kitten from the middle of nowhere, right into Ethan's line of sight. We shone a heavenly light on the little guy so Ethan would see him, but before that, I told the little fella, "Promise me that you will love Audrey and Ethan with all your heart." Ethan walked into the building and set the bags of food on the table while Audrey was still focused on the last few brush strokes. He giggled and said, "You're not gonna believe what I found outside."

Audrey turned and saw the little black kitten peek out of Ethan's half-zipped jacket. "Oh wow, you found a little baby!" She dropped everything, carefully pulling him from the jacket, holding him. He was so loving and cuddly, she melted right then and there, along with every pressure, every worry, every sorrow. She gave him a proper lover's name, Romeo, and smiled her way through the rest of the work that night. They brought their new furry baby home, Ethan thinking it was the craziest coincidence how both cats seemed to find him. Audrey, in a silent prayer, thanked God for sending an angel into her life after such a loss. To her, he was a gift from heaven and from her angels. Just that she believed that was good enough for me. She was recognizing when we were at work in her life. We were getting closer.

Audrey always prayed for wisdom, and when asked for it, God gives it generously, but you should be warned that with great wisdom comes experiences of all kinds. He'll show you that your value is worth more than any elaborate mask. He'll give you the courage to step beyond the comforts of facades. Peaks and valleys, storms and sun, all to get to the light of the battle-worn temple within you. But the long journey inward is always, always worth it.

Chapter Ten

In a year, 365 days, a rotation around the sun, four colorful seasons, a lot can change in that time. We can only expect that we are about to change as well, a chance to grow stronger, develop deeper roots, withstand the wild winds, but then there's the possibility that one little thing can change everything.

There's a word for the sadness we develop when our world isn't the way that it should be. It's a German word, weltschmerz, translating to "life weary." Things could be so much better, but our world is tempestuous; those wild winds blow against us, and there's nothing we can do about it.

Audrey and Ethan fought like titans. The heavens could hear their commotion, and their neighbors unfortunately did too. There were times when their neighbors called the Clovis police when they heard crashing and yelling inside their apartment. Trouble was building there, just as the surface of the earth reveals signs of an impending volcanic eruption.

What happens when you bury your worries instead of communicating them? Unintended consequences. Audrey felt Ethan was hiding things from her and distancing himself. He was. Having trust issues, her mind wandered and jumped to conclusions until all she could do was confront him. Ethan had always had a rough time being vulnerable, opening up, and trusting as well. In his past, he'd never had the opportunity to learn healthy communication, to know what that feels like, and that there could be a peaceful outcome. Audrey hid her worries away too, but out of any relationship she'd have, she wanted this one with Ethan to be the safe place to talk, her safe harbor. The longer things went unsaid, the more tension built, until the inevitable confrontation. This process happened over and over, more volatile each time.

When too much is suppressed for too long, it's fire in the earth's belly, and rising to the surface, it's dangerous. Audrey was all fire. Sadly, it seemed like the only time Audrey heard the real truth from Ethan was when he was shouting it. She was never one to back away from an argument. She just wanted the truth, and she would confront and push and prod until Ethan's limits were reached. She would keep at it, Ethan would want to leave the room, but instead, holes were punched in the walls, and doors were torn off hinges.

Audrey knew he had anger and resentment issues, but she never believed those weapons would be pointed at her someday. These are the things many military spouses face. The military teaches its own to fight battles to win, but when these people come home from battle, their battle continues internally. They learn to bury their feelings deep down, only to surface in combustible ways. Ethan was a man who dealt with years of childhood trauma, of the likes he never spoke of, then pile on the years of military service in two branches. He wasn't just a bear with a thorn in his paw that Audrey could bandage up. He was deeply wounded, and from her own past trauma, she couldn't help but "poke the bear" when she was angered. It only made things worse. I saw two people who loved each other tremendously, though communicated their feelings poorly or not at all and resolved conflicts the only way they knew how. Loudly and violently.

It was in the middle of a screaming match that I reached my limit. I was screaming too. I had seen Ethan go too far; I heard the meanest things two people could say to each other. I was yelling at the angels to intervene; I was cursing and throwing things until Gavri put his hand on my arm. "Shhh." He had a look in his eyes that I'd never seen before, and I froze immediately. In that moment, as Ethan was screaming and gnashing his teeth like a cornered animal, Audrey could only see him, but there was no sound at all. It was like someone hit the mute button on him. Everything seemed to slow down around her. It all felt so strange until I heard the voice speak to her. "Is it not enough that I love you?" Eight words that changed her whole life from then on. Eight words spoken to her by her Savior. The angels and I looked at each other in amazement. It was earth shattering, hearing the Most High speak.

Audrey was quiet. When Ethan ran out of words, he left the house. Behind closed doors, she fled to the light she found in that battle-worn temple within her. His words repeated over and over in her head. "Is it not enough that I love you?" A simple question but what the Savior was asking of her was complex. She had grown up in the church. She wore a cross. She memorized scripture at summer camp, but He needed more from her. He'd grown frustrated that a young lady, so loved by her Creator, hadn't realized it yet. She was fearfully and wonderfully made. Her Creator delights in watching her live her life and shows her all the time that He loves her, but the messages had not been received.

She was about to learn one of the most valuable lessons in life. She felt like her family didn't love her, and she relied heavily on Ethan for love to make up for what was missing in her life. But that wasn't his role in her life. Not just yet. She needed to learn that her Creator loves her, and it took removing almost everything in her life before she stopped looking to people to fill the void in her heart that only her Creator could fill. He'd left her no choice but to look up.

Following the eight most important words she would ever hear in this lifetime, instructions followed. She was given a task. "Just love him. Just love Ethan, faults and all. Allow Me to fight your battles from now on. I will take care of him." In the Good Book, there are 594 chapters that come before Psalm 118 and 594 chapters that follow, leaving that verse to be the center of it all. "It is better to take refuge in the Lord than to trust in man" (Psalm 118:8). It's easy to develop trust issues in this cold world, where love is scarce, but the Creator is reassuring you that you can trust Him.

Audrey's parents were in a loveless marriage. Even Audrey sensed at an early age that something wasn't right. Her father was always busy every Saturday morning. He was a big-time, cigar-smoking executive and had to entertain important businesspeople. It didn't leave much time for playing catch with his daughter or mowing the lawn. He blamed his absence on work a lot, but when he was let go at fifty years old, he no longer had golfing as an escape. Audrey's mom had a good job and kept the family afloat as an office manager, but the tensions at home were at an all-time high. Audrey knew divorce was imminent. The fighting was constant. She and her sister had a routine when they were very young, to shelter in her older sister's room, drowning out their voices with loud music. I remember Audrey told me that I provided her with an escape, but I never really took her seriously. Even though I was just a silly boy, I could see now that she'd forgotten it all when she was with me. I'd made her laugh, and she'd felt normal, happy, and safe.

The foundation of her home had been crumbling beneath her feet. She'd gotten used to living in survival mode very early on. Her parents remained married for a grueling twenty years. Wondering why her mother stayed, Audrey walked away from that experience, vowing to herself that she would never stay in a loveless marriage. I hoped that she would keep that promise.

When Ethan's mother turned eighteen, she spent a fateful evening at a house party with friends. Her birthday wish was to escape from home, from her life, and from California. But the wild winds had other plans. She met Ethan's father at that party, a very handsome James Dean look-alike. They had a fun night together but lost touch for some time, until he was informed that he had just become a father. There were no photos of Ethan's father holding his son. At the age of twenty-five, Ethan's father was in a car wreck that took his life, quite similar to mine. He was hot-rodding. He liked fast cars and good music. He had just gotten off work and was headed to meet some friends but happened to be late. He never made the gathering. His greatest regret was not being a part of this little boy's life, but he made up for it in the hereafter, in every way he could.

Ethan's mother and her parents raised him, giving him the stable, loving, and nurturing home he needed. At five years old, his mother fell in love with a retired navy veteran who lived in the Midwest, so she followed him there, finally finding an escape out of California, never revealing that she had a son. This man had red hair, a thick beard, and broad build. He looked like he should be living on a fisherman's boat with a thick cable knit sweater and a pipe in his mouth. Ethan's mom and the veteran were married and soon had a little girl. Now that she had made him a father, she broke the news to him about her son and finally brought Ethan out to the Midwest to join them.

Lifequake sounds as ominous as its meaning. It's that one little thing that changes everything.

All Ethan remembered was being ripped from the loving home of his grandparents, only to be dropped into a loveless home in a strange place. His stepfather could be cold and cruel. He was an alcoholic with a temper. Ethan grew up under the constant threat of a belt. His stepfather was raised the same way, but by an even heavier drinker and more violent man. It's a terrible shame when people don't learn from their experiences, allowing a vein of brutality to flow. Soon, Ethan was old enough to find escape as I had done, on a bicycle around town, usually staying out of trouble, fearful of what his old man would do to him.

There came a time when Ethan's mother and stepfather reached their end. Once again, his mother abandoned him and left town. She left him in the care of a man who didn't love him, and if he did, he didn't show it. This broke Ethan's heart into pieces, wounds he was yet to recover from. This was when he learned the skills of compartmentalizing, but he was emotionally stunted from the trauma he had suffered up to this point. Still, he went to school and got good grades, like a good boy. His mom took a bartending job at a country club where she met her new love interest, a wealthy, old money lawyer from Oklahoma.

Ethan's stepfather had a big building he used for car repairs and fine-tuning classic cars for good money. He fixed them up with new upholstery, paint jobs, body work, and more. This was where Ethan learned an invaluable education. He learned everything he needed to know about cars. He became a valuable asset to his stepfather's company, though he never received much compensation. Never a thank you or I'm proud of you. Only a backhand or two when Ethan overstepped his boundaries as young men often do.

Ethan was in high school now, and drinking was prevalent among the bored youth in his tiny town. He was taking after his stepfather. He might have been taking after his real father as well. That DUI he got might have been the thing that saved his life. Soon thereafter, Ethan's mother, with her newfound wealth, tried in apathetic ways to seek her son's forgiveness. Each attempt seemed disingenuous. Years of hearing about his stepfather's navy days influenced his future decisions. Just as his mother wanted an escape from California and the turmoil in her life that followed, Ethan found an escape as well. He joined the navy and left the Midwest life and his callous mother behind him.

Ethan lost himself in reading and his duties on the ship until he was free to eat good food and to drink himself silly in each new port. The dark vastness paired well with his emptiness. His favorite thing about being on the ship was the good rest he experienced, being rocked to sleep each night by the sway of the vessel. After six years of serving his country on the high seas, he was finally free to live life as he pleased. He moved to California. His family's roots were there, so he gravitated back to where he had come from. He searched for answers about his real father, who he was, and what had happened to him. But for some reason, the answers were never given freely. It seemed they were guarded secrets, and Ethan was given little or false information. It was a painful dead end that continued to haunt him. He would never know how his father, after all these years, watched closely after him. He advised him on important matters. He visited him in his dreams, laughed and bonded with his little boy, only to be forgotten upon waking. But I got to see it. I saw how much his father loved him and cheered for him, hoped for him, was proud of him, and longed for a time when he could tell Ethan everything, just as I yearn to tell Audrey.

Rock and hard place, meet thorn and barb, but that's why he and Audrey bonded so quickly. They had survived traumas in their past, and maybe by being together, they could survive the future.

She knew the beginning of his life lacked love, and all she wanted to do was love him so much that he might forget all about that. But can a man learn from the cruelties of the past and become the man he needed as a child? Or is he doomed to repeat the past and ruin his future?

She tried to reach him. She tried to fix things. She tried to make a connection, but nothing worked. All she had left to do was leave it in God's hands and wait. Time was passing, and this turmoil began to take its toll on her body. She was showing signs of sickness, a terrible feeling in her stomach, though she didn't know what was wrong. Military life kept Ethan away from time to time, and medical bills were piling up, so Ethan decided that when he returned from his next trip, they would go to the courthouse and get married. This would put Audrey on his insurance plan. This would help with the bills. It felt like mostly business.

The once-happy couple had dreams of escaping to an island beach to say their vows. They researched various places all over the world, different seasons and weather. There, they planned on simple attire, Audrey in a light, flowing white dress with flowers in her hair and Ethan in tan linen pants and a white linen shirt, barefoot in the sand. An island getaway to exchange vows but a big reception back at home for their families to attend. I loved that idea for Audrey. I wanted to see what she would look like as a bride, even if she wouldn't be walking down the aisle to meet me.

Audrey had been a bridesmaid to many brides in many elaborate, elegant weddings. Each one seemed to outdo the next but always had the big poofy dress and expensive flowers. But when it came to her own, she and Ethan wore their everyday clothes, with their everyday smiles. They went through the ceremony downtown beside an arch covered in dusty silk flowers in the corner of an empty room of the courthouse. Vows were exchanged that day, though I was sad to see that it was nothing like the island plans they'd once dreamed of. A holy union such as this deserved so much more. A wedding marks the joining of two people to become one entity. In a very spiritual and even physical way, possibly down to your DNA, you're linked with that person forever. It deserves a celebration, with adoring family and gifts. But some things in life don't work out the way you plan them. Sometimes your dreams don't come true the way you think they should. Weltschmerz. It wasn't the wedding they had intended, but they still held onto their hope for a future together.

From the courthouse downtown, Ethan drove Audrey to St Agnes Hospital's ICU where her grandma was being treated. The family thought she was dying, so the two newlyweds spent their time in a hospital room, telling her grandma the good news.

The newlyweds were so hospital weary that they never had a wedding night. They never even had a honeymoon. Audrey never got to have all the wonderful traditional things that a wedding brings. She never got to design her wedding cake or share smeared icing bites as husband and wife. She never got to choose the song for their first dance. She never had the father–daughter dance. In fact, word got back to her father that there had been a wedding without him, and he never quite forgave her.

With weeks of love, care, and prayer, her grandma made a miraculous recovery and was back in her home. As Audrey was growing up, her grandma would talk about the day she'd finally get married and the traditional gift her grandma wanted to give her. Most gifts are chosen off of a lengthy registry, a Cuisinart, kitchen gadgets, cheese knives, and glassware. Her grandma had saved a roll-top trunk for this incredibly special occasion. Inside, she had placed hand-sewn satin pillowcases and enclosed gifts of fine housewares for the couple. A treasured collection of crystal and silver, linen and lace, and pieces of their lineage, passed down to her when that special day comes. Audrey loved the idea of her grandma's hope chest. From that early age, it caused her to daydream of what that special day might be like and the lucky man meeting her at the end of the rose petal path. Audrey was finally given her hope chest, that priceless gift from her grandma, that could never be found on a registry, just as it was described all those years ago.

There was another gift that sat on her grandma's kitchen table. This was a gift from her grandpa. It was a simple white box with a raffia bow tied around it. Audrey sat at the kitchen table with her recovering grandma and opened the box. A rush of emotions overcame her when she saw her favorite sculpture by her grandpa. It was the man with his dog and guitar, singing atop an old whiskey barrel. They could both feel grandpa's presence in the room with them in that moment, with the faintest scent of beeswax in the air. Her grandpa and I stood together in her grandma's kitchen. He pulled a pressed white hanky from his back pocket and wept into it. We both felt the same longing, to join in at that moment, to hug them both, to celebrate the news, to reassure them that we were still here, watching over them.

Ethan left the same week of the wedding for a year-long training course at Redstone Arsenal, Alabama. He too sent her music. He found that "Time in a Bottle" by Jim Croce fit their situation, reminding him of when their lives were much simpler. From Redstone, they spoke often at first, and then sometimes, and then seldom. She played the song when she felt lonesome, the lyrics speaking to her in so many ways.

If I could save time in a bottle. I had to hand it to the guy; the song was perfect. It made her think of people she loved in her life, some living, some beyond the veil, and how precious time is as we go through it.

A lot can change in a year. This was the first time Audrey felt that she didn't have to survive anything, so she began living. She began to take better care of herself—she read more books and worked on her art. She took her grandma grocery shopping and to lunch a couple of times a week. She played her guitar as she sat watching the television every night, and her skills steadily improved.

Audrey had defeated her demons and had forgiven the past, but now she was faced with a tremendous decision. The year Ethan and Audrey spent apart was coming to a close, and he was to return any day. Was this a relationship worth continuing? Would things ever get better between them?

Upon his return and successful year, he was offered a job about two hours north of Clovis. Ethan and Audrey were standing at a fork in the road. He came back from Redstone a slightly different, more collected man than before. Audrey was in a different mindset herself. Her own trauma caused her to react to Ethan in confrontation. She wouldn't hesitate to "poke the bear," but she was different now. Even more understanding. It seemed they both had changed for the better, but were they still good for each other?

It was finally time to make a decision about where life would take them. With faith and forgiveness, they moved forward, together. After many weeks of searching for the right place, they finally rented a lovely, sage green house with ivory trim and a big front porch, in an even smaller town near his work, where their new chapter could begin.

I was worried for Audrey, sure. But I never knew how strong she was until I saw how bravely she faced her demons and Ethan's demons as well. She didn't even know how strong she was.

Confronting one's demons is something people all over the world are too scared to do, and one by one, she sent them packing. She didn't need someone to rescue her; she freed herself. She didn't cower in the face of rage. She didn't give an inch. Just more and more things I'm learning about her that I love, and I thought I knew everything. I wasn't surprised she didn't back down from this challenge. Walking away would've been the easy thing to do.

She wanted to be loved and understood as well as forgiven. But I was learning more about why she chose Ethan. Perhaps in the grand scheme of it all, we are here on this earth to learn new things, and for an old soul as she was, that was hard to do. Maybe Audrey fell for a man who could teach her lessons of forgiveness, patience, and healing, like no other.

Perhaps that's why the Good Book tells you to forgive people, time and time again. Maybe it's because people need forgiveness and love and time to heal. Maybe Audrey was the only person in the world brave enough to help Ethan this way. And maybe someday, having healed, he too could face his own demons. A lot can change in a year.

Chapter Eleven

There's a word that describes a place that makes us feel like we belong there. There's a familiarity, a reassuring and nurturing feeling, a welcome that it offers, like no other. That word is cynefin. Another term is querencia, meaning a safe place, offering the peace of mind that it takes to let your guard down and become who you truly are. If you were lucky enough to be born into a place like this, chances are that at a certain age, you are eager to escape it, looking for adventure in your life. But the ones who weren't as fortunate, who were dealt a far more traumatic hand, search for this place their entire life.

Home. It looked like a quiet cottage tucked away in the woods. The house had a long wooden porch that ran the length of the house, with ivory beams and a railing. The bushes and shrubs were mature and sprawling, happy in their environment, under the shade of three towering redwood trees. The front door was a deep-stained wood with an oval-cut glass window in the center. Audrey's very first visit to the house was to look for a sign that this was the place God had set apart for them. Deep cuts within the oval glass window revealed shapes of the Ichthus, the fish, the ancient sign of Jesus. During that first visit, it was a time in the afternoon when the sun cast large reflections of the fish across the walls of the entry in a prism of colors. That was the sign she needed. That's when she knew.

Artists don't like bare walls. Audrey turned up some good decorating music, found a hammer and nails, and hung her favorite paintings in perfect places along those walls. Most of them were finished and framed. Some incomplete pieces were also hung on the wall, still needing time and work. When she sat and sipped her morning tea, they spoke to her, revealing just what changes they needed. By the time she got to the bottom of her cup, she was pulling that piece down and marching into her studio. Another work in progress would later take its place. Also on the walls, hung like works of art, were their guitars in distinct colors, each chosen as a painting's complement. That was all Ethan's doing. A heavenly display of stringed instruments and canvas art that would make any bohemian feel at home. Mismatched, interesting furniture pieces began to come together to make an inviting, comfortable place. Upon entering their home, you were greeted by scents of sage and roses. Worries and the world, left at the door, good music, food, and drink—one might feel so at home they may never want to leave.

As old-fashioned garage sales moved online, she searched through the items, not knowing what she wanted until she saw it, saved it, and thought about it for a while. One by one, piece by piece, she filled their home with furniture that they could actually live on. She was old fashioned herself, that old soul, loving rustic, vintage things and the stories they had to tell. Audrey loved the character of old steamer trunks. She started collecting them, big and small, and filling almost every room, serving all kinds of purposes. Those old trunks held many things in their travels through life, but like us, we should only hold onto what's most important and unpack the rest.

In one of the listings, she found a few things she liked, all from one seller. She made a deal with him for two items, one was a stained-glass lamp that needed minor repair and another an Art Nouveau statue of a young lady holding a giant flower as a candle holder. A low price was agreed upon, and after work, Ethan planned to pick them up for her.

When Ethan got home, he was excited to show her that the lamp was in perfect condition, and he couldn't wait to turn it on. It filled the room with its warm light and glowing pink prairie roses. The statue was perfect to hold a small candle and found its home on Audrey's bookshelf. Ethan handed her another package and said the seller threw this in for free. It was a frame wrapped in old newspaper. When she finally saw what it was, she felt a warming of her heart, causing her shoulders to rise to her cheeks and her lips to curve into a broad smile. It was a very old and delicate poem that was from the 1920s, titled "Wonderful Pal of My Dreams":

Through the moments of gladness, or even of sadness,

Through all of life's varying themes,

You stand by me loyally, staunchly, and royally,

Wonderful Pal of My Dreams

Through problems that worry me, duties that hurry me,

Troubles that change all my schemes,

You're always a part of me, right in the heart of me,

Wonderful Pal of My Dreams

Something about this old piece resonated with her deeply. Almost as if she had seen it somewhere before. She wasn't one to collect many things other than feathers, but she began a collection of poems from that era. A piece of history. Perhaps her own.

She loved wingback chairs and found two in a dark tan, sandy color. Other than the color, they were quite different. One had just a plain tan velvet fabric that came with an ottoman. The other sat tall but reclined, having the most subtle flowers and poppies throughout the fabric.

Poppies always took her back to her grandparents' garden. Much like her mother's enchanted garden, her grandma had a special touch with plants as well. They lived in downtown Clovis near main street, on a very old lot that was much larger than usual. Back in the time when Audrey's grandparents were just married, they had the whole corner lot to raise animals and farm the land. It was home for poor folk from Oklahoma, but their bellies were full of good food, and their family was kept close. Their homes were small, built by their own hands, but brimming with love. Audrey's grandma's father was a butcher and fed the family well, but Wesley had his vices. Audrey remembered hearing stories of her great-grandfather going to the opium dens in downtown Fresno, Chinatown, California. He also struggled with alcoholism. His vices contributed to his cancer diagnosis and early passing. But he brought a memento home from his visits to Chinatown that bloomed every spring in grandma's garden, opium poppies.

Audrey eagerly anticipated every spring for these magnificent flowers to sprout from the earth, their pale green, tall, thin stalks and jagged leaves, and at the very top was a round bulb bursting with pink frills. It looked like layers upon layers of soft silk, finally unfolding under the sun. Audrey knew they held a poison in them that would make good men go mad. Her grandma showed her what the Chinese people would do to their poppies, slicing the orbs and waiting for the white liquid to seep out. Grandma knew Audrey would never join the opium trade, so there was no harm in demonstrating. Those poppies at first were specifically planted in areas away from the street view. Soon the poppies were popping up wherever they pleased, and that light pinkish orange hue could be seen throughout their property. Her grandma always wondered what the Clovis police would do if they knew a little old lady was growing an innocent opium poppy garden. They probably wouldn't do anything at all, but it was something that Audrey and her grandma laughed about and kept as their little secret. Sitting in her poppy-covered wingback chair always reminded her of some of the happiest times in her life, springtime in her grandma's garden.

There was a great room in Audrey's home that had a peaked ceiling and exposed beams. It was all covered in the same type of wood, a ceiling she had rarely been under, except for in a church or two. It had a warm sanctuary feel to it, with large, bright windows displaying the crepe myrtle trees that bloomed in bright pink in the backyard. At the entrance of the room, just below the peak where the beams met the beige colored walls, Ethan hung a large cross that Audrey had bought. It was made of iron in long lines and scrolls. It definitely felt like her sanctuary now.

Audrey's faith, though her foundation and saving grace, was usually kept private. There was so much she was still learning about, so she kept it tight to her vest and was open to the wisdom God gave so generously, which came from unpredictable directions. She wasn't the type to yell Hallelujah when great things happened, but echoing in her temple within was God is so good. Ethan was raised in a Christian home, but it wasn't a priority or practice, and over the years, he had become indifferent. Every now and then, when curiosity struck, he'd ask questions about the Bible and things of that nature. That's just how things go. As a Christian, you don't have all the answers, which is why they say we all walk by faith, though the more Word you read, the more questions you can answer.

Audrey's faith was a subtle side to her, a faint whisper that you'd have to lean in to hear. But that's how she felt about her relationship with her Creator, soft signs of His presence in her life, knowing what signs to look for, or they'd be missed altogether. There are ways God whispers He loves you. And it's not that we can hear the words, but it's more of a feeling we get when wonderful things happen. It's when no cell phone can capture it, no one to distract us from it, just a moment of beauty and timing and love all woven together. It's times of small miraculous occurrences, that if shared, might not be believed by others. But they happen right in front of you, to you, only for you. Those occurrences usually happen in the connection and solitude that nature can give us. So go outside without your phone, be still, and anticipate something wonderful.

When Ethan hung the cross in such a prominent spot, it was a comforting thought that the relationship he had with his Creator might be growing too and that she might get to see a hidden side to him begin to emerge.

The back door led directly to a cozy covered patio, just large enough for a table and chairs and a few flowerpots that only needed a dose of morning sun. In the corner of the backyard was a koi pond, the size of two Jacuzzis. It was trimmed in lava rock and happy plants, some whose roots dangled down into the water. The pond was loaded with slow-moving, happy, friendly fish. When you sat by this pond, you couldn't help but adopt its slow-moving flow. It had huge koi of all different colors, just seeming to be wise souls with their gentle glide and little moustaches. Surrounding them were their energetic and hungry little goldfish friends of all shapes and sizes. Audrey had never been around a koi pond before and found that even five minutes, sitting here, listening to the rushing water and watching their smooth swimming colors was captivating, cathartic. It was an escape. It was so much more.

The pond was surrounded by Japanese maple trees with smooth, shapely trunks and branches, adorned with tiny stems holding delicate, little, waving leaves. There was a queen palm tree that was about ten feet tall and greenery filled in all the spaces. The pond was its own little paradise. Next to the rocks of the pond was a green lawn, bordered by pink crepe myrtles along the fence line. When Audrey first moved in, she figured a simple watering routine would keep everything alive, but she wanted more than that. She wanted a garden of her very own. She finally had space for her own plants, and she considered setting up a herb garden, here and there in pretty pots, where maybe she could finally try to grow tomatoes. It was time to take that trip to the garden center she'd always been dreaming about.

There was one day when Audrey's mother decided to take a stroll through her local garden center. She had been on her own for a while now, divorced, children grown and flown. She was able to spend more time in her garden, returning it to its former glory. It had grown wild and unkempt in the years Adele spent working so hard to provide for the family, so she took her time, carefully and lovingly pruning back what was unnecessary, as in life, in order for the new growth to flourish. There were areas that needed new seeds planted and fresh flowers to take root, so she drove into town for just that. She parked her car on this bright, warm morning, sunny enough to expose a dime near the trunk of her car. She smiled, dropped it into her pocket, and looked up to the sky. All along the exterior of the garden center were pretty pots of happy flowers, all of which would love the chance to live their lives in her enchanted garden, but she kept making her way into the heart of it. Bees buzzed about, cheerful gardeners smiled at her as they passed by, and wide tables sprawled out in long straight lines, all covered in floral varieties. She stopped to look at the Gerbera daisies. They add such bright, cheerful life to any stretch of earth. As she returned the daisies to the table, a gleaming dime caught her eye. She had almost stepped on it, right by the toes of her left foot. She bent down to pick it up and quietly giggled. Now there were two dimes dropped into her pocket. She had wandered through the aisles slowly to really enjoy the calmness all this green flourishing life did to one's spirit, when she saw another dime, toward the back of the garden center now, near the tall fragrant vines. When she reached down to pick it up, she bumped into a man who was reaching for it too.

"You know these are signs from heaven," the man said, smiling, pinching the dime between his finger and thumb. He held it out toward her.

"I believe that too," Adele agreed with a wide smile, knowing exactly who was leaving dimes in her path. She opened her hand so he could drop the dime into it.

Funny how she thought she'd only find flowers that day. Adele and Ben, the man who gave her the third dime of the day, struck up a lovely conversation that flowed into lunch and into lengthy discussions on how they came to know dimes were signs from Heaven. They shared fun times together, personalities that complemented each other, and love was blooming. He was a tall, big guy with white hair and a white goatee. He was genuine, funny, handsome, and charming, hoping to find real love after all these years, just as Adele was. What Adele didn't know was that the smiling gardeners she passed in the aisles were her guardian angels, wearing t-shirts and jeans to blend in, one wearing a big sun-blocking straw hat. As Adele and Ben finally met over the dime that Diane, in a straw hat herself, had carefully placed in her path, Diane and the angels all stood together, watching their handiwork and celebrating the paths of two wonderful people finally crossing.

Audrey hadn't known much about gardening at first. Her grandma's yard was known as the garden ICU. Everyone could bring their sick and dying plants over, knowing she would somehow arrange their miraculous recovery. She had some secret to reviving plants and making them look better than they ever did before. Her grandma gave her some sage advice when she was a little girl about learning how to garden. Start out with a cactus and succulents. These plants just want to be left alone. They don't want a lot of water, so if you forget to water them, they'll forgive you most of the time. That's just what Audrey did. She had pots of all sizes of different "leave me alone" plants. Then she learned how to propagate the leaves, watching them sprout tiny pink roots and a whole new little plant from the main plant's cuttings. Her garden was expanding. She brought home a discounted agave that was pale green with yellow trim. He was having trouble and needed love, so she brought him home and named him Phillipe the agave. She became drawn to cacti and agave, more so than most people. After all, she had grown accustomed to companionship with things of prickly dispositions.

She had a Confederate jasmine that she named General Lee. She brought an aeonium, a purple rose succulent, back from a trip to Pismo Beach and, of course, called her Pismo.

All those years spent with her grandma in her garden greatly influenced Audrey. The cynefin, the querencia found there. She remembered the sage, the herb garden, and watching her grandma pick off stems of herbs for their dinner. She remembered her grandma picking up feathers from the ground and admiring them, big or small, and then sticking them up, next to a plant in a flowerpot. Throughout the garden, feathers were everywhere, causing curiosity. Her grandma told Audrey about their Lakota ancestry, and finally, all of the Indian décor in her grandma's house made sense. There were beautiful woven baskets, abalone shells with sage bundles, and hawk feathers in each room, large papooses hanging from the wall. One of them was what her grandma used to carry Audrey in as a baby. There were peace pipes, totems, little Indian dolls, bows and arrows, and other artifacts that her grandmother treasured. Her grandma was also fascinated by the ways of old Indian medicine, the use of herbs to heal and sage to cleanse. Audrey remembered being healed by those very herbs as a child, and it seemed a part of her deep down remembered the interests of a past life.

Audrey remembered going to a friend's house and sitting in the tiny patio of her apartment for some iced tea and catching up on lost time. Much of the conversation had been forgotten, but what she did remember was the tiny space, transformed by the presence of potted plants that grew long stems, which draped and swayed in the breeze. There were succulents and happy pathos plants in an array of pots that stole her attention away. It was a feeling of calmness, of the green living breathing life around her, refreshing her spirit. That was what Audrey wanted to recreate in her own garden, and she did just that.

Over time, her plants flourished and expanded, flowered and spawned. Life was happy in her own little space, whether scattered around in pots or rooted deep in the earth. Her garden had a charm and vibration all its own that would welcome and embrace any lost soul. There was a time when Audrey had wanted to travel the world, as most young people do. She wanted to see the Great Pyramids and the vast oceans and deep canyons. But things had changed once she created her little magical garden. It was her own paradise, and if the world needed her one day, the world would have to come find her.

Music was always playing around her. In the garden, the music was such that if you closed your eyes, you would think you were at a resort in the Mexican Riviera. Rich flamenco guitar trills and soft upbeat drums that made you want to break out into Latin dancing. On this quiet evening, the sun was setting into warm pinks and oranges, and she tuned the channel to play all her favorite songs. I had some ideas.

Audrey heard "The Promise" play first. Our song. She remembered the DJ's dedication as if it were yesterday, from Josh to his dream girl. She was on her knees in the garden, pulling weeds in an area where they had dug in deep. The garden had taught Audrey to slow down. Turn on the music, and do her work at a pace that wasn't daunting. Digging hands into the earth and walking barefoot in the grass was healing. Kindly rehoming earthworms and waving to scurrying lizards, enjoying ladybug landings and butterfly crossings. Next, I played "Someone to Watch Over Me" by Ella Fitzgerald. Audrey thought Ella's voice was as close to an angel singing as she'd ever heard on earth. Where is the shepherd for this lost lamb? If Audrey only knew. She heard this song and felt the significance of the two being played back-to-back. She paused the weeding and started to sing along, still feeling the cool soil break apart in her hands.

She was too busy pulling weeds to see the first stars appear and sparkle, so I gave her a reason to look up. "Shining Star" by The Manhattans caught her attention. She stopped weeding and got to her feet, dusting off her hands. She saw a dove feather in her path and gently tucked it into a flowerpot near her kitchen window. On a lounge chair that faced the pond, she listened to the words of that song and was starting to wonder if these songs all being played after "The Promise" could be…a message? Could it possibly be Josh saying hello from so far away?

The last song I played for her was "I'll Be Seeing You" by Billie Holiday. This was one of Audrey's favorites. It sang to her lonely soul like few songs do. It made her think of me, and tears escaped the side of her eyes as she gazed up at the moon. To my surprise, the progression of songs, her emotions and tears, the sight of the moon brought her to me again. She closed her eyes, calmed her mind as still water, and found me lying on the lounge facing her. A smile spread across my face.

"You're here," she whispered.

"Always."

Chapter Twelve

hat if you had the ability to create a set of unique beings and watch over them like you would a crate full of puppies? Wouldn't you want them to reach out to you when they feel hurt or alone or scared? Would it make you sad if they didn't? How quickly would you rush to fight their battles for them or fix their problems or clear obstacles in their path, if they would just ask?

We are not exactly puppies in a crate, but we do have a Creator who longs to hear from us. He knew us before we were formed in the womb; he knows our soul's name, the number of hairs on our head, and our needs before we ask for them. Audrey and I stood with our Creator, discussing the lessons we were to learn in this life. I remembered what Audrey wanted. She told Him that she wanted to learn to love like He does. I wanted to learn about promises and how to keep them like He does. We all spoke with our Creator this way, long ago. But in this world, it's easy to forget. So many of us feel disconnected from our Creator and rarely, if ever, reach out.

Prayer is a quiet and personal yet powerful force. People are blessed with grace whether they pray or not, but prayer, like the act of writing a thought down on paper, solidifies the intention. Prayer is a communication, a longing, a love letter to the Creator. It's a yin-yang balance to ask and to receive, so ask, and it will be given to you.

It does not need to be a formal, well-planned dialogue. Just as you would approach another living being, you spend time in their presence, getting to know them, getting used to their way of communicating. At first, my prayers were awkward and reserved, but I realized that we are made in His image, so why not just consider him a friend? A friend who wants to spend time with us, wants us to confide our troubles to Him, wants to earn our trust, and keeps His promises.

Most of us grow up thinking we have to do everything on our own, we have to make our own miracles, we have to be our own light and fight our own battles. That is a surefire way to burn out. We are not made to take on this world alone. That's too heavy a burden to put on yourself. The world is too dark. After some time, Audrey formed a deepening connection with her Creator. A work in progress, an open line, where she could ask questions, and in His own way, He would answer. Audrey believed that by asking, trusting, and waiting, doors would be opened for her, ways would be made, and barriers would be removed. She began to learn that the stronger her connection to the Creator, the bigger the doors were opened, and heavenly signs were far less subtle. A spiritual world was revealing itself to her, one that she always felt was there, like a concert being held behind high walls, and she was finally being awarded her pass of entry.

For some time, the garden had become the perfect dwelling. Four large wooden posts held up the roof of her patio, which sheltered a rustic wooden table and chairs and provided just enough cover for those delicate "morning sun only" plants. Each ivory-colored post was trimmed with twisting vines of jasmine. Between each post hanging high on the connecting beam was a hook that held a hummingbird feeder. With great pleasure each week, and daily in the peak of summer, Audrey would put her kettle on and mix four cups of hot water with one cup of sugar. This mixture kept her little swarm of hummingbird families happy all day. It made her laugh, the thought that she always wanted to own her own little bar, cantina, watering hole, but the one God gave her was a lot smaller than she expected. She could just sit back and watch those jet-set little birds drop into her humming cantina all day, admiring their colors and mannerisms, courting habits, and high-speed dog fights. It was the best show in the garden. The birds, bright sun, and music playing left little room for darkness, though the occasional dark clouds were welcome, only if rain came with them. Audrey would also pray for rain through the long, dry California summers. The only thing about the sky that Audrey loved more than new stars appearing in the deepening blue was dark, heavy rain clouds. Californians are rain-starved souls, and gardeners and farmers are even more so, tormented by the dry terrain. Any heavy rain cloud is just about enough to make them run out in the open and dance until drenched.

Audrey painted a large scene of a farmer's tilled land in rows that led to an orchard with soft, golden rolling hills in the background, dark rain clouds, and the occasional windswept palm tree along the horizon. It was that indigo that the clouds turn during a storm that looked so striking in contrast to the bright oranges of the sunlit earth. In all the rows were puddles of rain that had collected as one of the storm clouds passed by. She called it "Praying for Rain," and the puddles that had collected were clear signs of prayers answered. Audrey painted it, not only because it was a beautiful scene, but because it reminded her of the farmland that surrounded our homes. Audrey and her father would ride their horses through the soft tilled fields when he got off work some nights and on weekends. It was one of the only things that they did together. Her father wasn't a man of many words with her. He'd just saddle up and have the horses ready, then go inside the house to find her. She never turned down an opportunity to ride her horse. She would follow his lead out the double gates and down their long driveway, across the quiet country road, and into the fields. Sometimes they'd walk through the orchards of peach trees, but wherever they rode, their two dogs would always follow close behind. There's nothing like riding horses. They are big puppies, following the commands we give them. They are happy to go somewhere new, they are sad if they get left behind, and they are excellent judges of character. They are large and quiet animals for the most part, but never underestimate their ability to feel and sense, to challenge and play. Horses were sometimes the only beings on earth that ever reached the hidden heart of her father.

She painted "Praying For Rain" for her father's birthday that year, but before that date in July rolled around, she heard of an art group that met in her new town once a month. They also had an art show twice a year, in the spring and the fall. Their spring show was only a couple of weeks away, and being in a new town, Audrey thought this would be a fun way to meet new, like-minded people, so she entered a piece of artwork in almost every event in the competition. Most of them ribboned. "Praying For Rain" won first place in the oil paint category and went on to win the Best of Show. This was her first big art award. Now that the piece was an award winner, she was even more excited to give it to her father, but before she let him see it, she simply asked him if he would like to have the Best of Show winner she painted for him. He had always been a confusing man to her, but Audrey actually expected him to answer just the way he did. Sadly, he just didn't seem to have the room for it. So the painting remained on her wall, not as a rejected gift, but as a reminder of a simpler time in her life, her accomplishments, and inspiration to create more award winners. That's exactly what she did.

One afternoon, Audrey went to the local Michaels arts and crafts store. They had huge canvases there, and lucky for her, they were running a sale. She stocked up on all different sizes, but the giant canvases required a store associate to bring them down from the high wall. A woman with short gray hair in a red t-shirt approached her and started handling the canvases, leaning them against the wall. Audrey struck up a conversation with the woman, who was slightly older and shorter than Audrey was. Audrey asked if she liked working there to get a sense of their work environment. The woman asked her if she needed a job, and Audrey told her she was new in town and was looking for employment. Little did she know, she was talking with the store manager, who insisted she apply and would be perfect for an artistic position that had just opened up.

This was one of those moments that Audrey walked away from, knowing her angels had a hand in it. She felt guided right into Michaels and their sale that day. She felt urged to ask that woman the right questions, which eventually got her hired. She knew there couldn't be any other explanation when events went this smoothly, and she was right. When things fall into place, when it's easy and doesn't need to be forced or coerced, there are usually angel prints all over it.

She began her new job as the Floral Designer for her local Michaels store in September, as the air began to change, waving goodbye to summer and ushering in a new season. Her first shift began before dawn, with the truck team, a group of goofy characters most customers never got the chance to encounter. They were a rowdy and quirky, tight-knit group of singing and yelling, joke-telling and most often foul-mouthed, and possibly inebriated group of hard workers. They were the reasons the trucks got unloaded, and the shelves were so well stocked. They unloaded all the boxes from the trucks in the large square bins they called shark tanks. Once all the boxes were unloaded and sorted, each truck team member took their shark tank to their section, and in a cloud of bubble wrap, paper, and shreds, the merchandise was placed onto the shelves with care. All the debris disappeared before 9:00 a.m. in a giant trash compactor in the back storeroom, and as customers strolled in, the truck team was already done for the day and headed home. On this particular day, Audrey's shark tank was filled with fall silk flowers. She got to see how they arrived, zip-tied carefully inside their box, sometimes wrapped in plastic. Her job was removing them from their wrapping and bringing them to life, a bend here, a fluff there. With little attention, the silk flowers were ready to be dropped in their new homes, narrow galvanized tin buckets that held about twenty flowers of each variety in rows. When she was finished, it made an extraordinary display of every color under the sun, fall colors accentuated in wines, ambers, pale rose, and soft greens.

The real reason the store manager hired Audrey was that they needed an award-winning artist to make floral arrangements for their upcoming holiday season. It was a huge business. The store purchased premade floral arrangements from China, but they just couldn't compare to the artistic flair that Audrey added to each piece. Tucked away in the middle of the store, surrounded by thousands of stems of silk flowers, was her worktable. It was a tall stainless steel counter with drawers and storage spaces beneath. People could walk by her counter, typically covered in creative disarray, and watch a floral arrangement come together, stem by stem. Most of the time, people would stop and ask directions on where to find certain items in the store. Audrey memorized the aisles and contents to direct traffic more easily. Other people would stop and ask questions, wondering how to make arrangements themselves. Audrey was more than happy to show them. A container, dry floral foam, hot glue, silk flowers, and wire cutters were all that was really needed, but her creativity was why Audrey had the job of floral designer and others didn't.

Audrey loved her job. She could walk the entire store full of fun, artistic things and turn any number of them into a masterpiece. Fall was just beginning, and people wanted arrangements and wreaths with sunflowers and turning leaves, harvest, and pumpkins. There were splashes of fall throughout the store, and Audrey had more ideas than time. Her arrangements always seemed to have their own spirit about them. If you looked closely into her creations, you would see a bird's nest full of eggs artfully tucked away as a bird in the garden would do. Some arrangements would have butterflies looking like they had just fluttered through the store and lit upon those flowers. So much character and personality, telling a silk story.

She had creative talent, but paired with her instincts, or what I knew to be her angels whispering in her ear, it was pure magic. She couldn't finish a piece fast enough to meet the demand. Countless orders were being placed. People were excited to have her make their wedding arrangements. She made countless bouquets. I watched Audrey begin this job with so much anxiety. She wondered if she'd be good enough, if people would like her arrangements enough to buy them, if she would make the store any money, and so many other silly things. It wasn't just that she was good enough or made the store lots of money, but people loved her. They loved her work. It went far beyond her talent for flower arranging, but she poured from the soul. That's what made her work different than anything else.

Pouring from the soul. Most people aren't aware of this gift if they have it, and it is certainly not something everyone is capable of. Meraki. It means to create something and leave a part of yourself in it, injecting pure love and soul into your creations. It's an act of alchemy, taking the negativity, the pain one collects through life, internalizing it, allowing it to ferment, melting it down, purifying it by fire. The alchemist internally forges a new energy from it. A dull to a shimmer, a bad to good, a darkness to light. This was the work Audrey did with her hands and her heart. This was why people walked by her work sitting on a shelf and just felt that there was something very unique and special about it. Her work was only just beginning.

She also helped the new artists get set up with all the right materials. It's a scary thing to start something new. Walking down the paint aisle, wondering where to begin, would be overwhelming for anyone, but it was fun for Audrey to help them pick out what they needed. In just one visit with them in the aisle, she gave them tips to begin that made them want to paint as soon as they got their supplies home. It reminded her of her early days, each anxious time she had tried out a new medium. From drawing and studying grid lines, facial features, and hands, since those were the most difficult. She'd then studied photo realism, believing that to be s ome of the greatest training an artist can have, recreating a drawing that resembles a photo as closely and realistically as possible.

She'd gotten her hands dirty working with charcoal and playing with those gray, kneaded erasers. She tried chalk pastel and then oil pastel, very different but a huge leap into the world of color. She was intimidated by color at first. It's easy to create shading with gradients of black and white. Color was masterful magic she never thought she'd be able to learn. That's the best part of trying things that scare you, conquering the fear, silencing that voice in your mind that tells you that you can't do it, but realizing that you can do it and really quite well.

It was watercolor and oils that she felt the most comfortable with. Watercolors are delicate, and painting with them involves washes of transparent color using special techniques and doing your best to work light to dark. Oils are thick and heavy; they have a ghastly chemical smell that takes some getting used to but are relatively easy to work with, easy to fix mistakes, and if you don't like what you've done, you just paint over the whole thing.

As her skills in each medium kept improving over time, her style started emerging. One might call it a style, but it was just her comfortable way of doing things. The more comfortable she was with something, the easier it was to pour from the soul. And as she began to enter her work in competitions, it was a whole new education. To Audrey, it was not enough to copy a photo perfectly, because after all, it's just a reproduction in another medium. So you can copy a photo, what then? Does it have personality? She was drawn to work that may not have been just like a photo but depicted a scene through the lens, the eye, the experience, the pain, the wisdom, the love of an artist. Art is the unique view that you offer to people, which only you can show them.

There's so much nonsense in modern art. Some people call

themselves artists because they splatter paint on a canvas in a matter of moments, swirl the paint around in a weird way, and think that because it's abstract, some hipster will walk by it in a gallery and describe the piece in some obscure way, as if it means something far more than just thoughtless smears. When Audrey came across modern art of this sort, she wondered if she'd be more inclined to buy it if it were painted by a talented elephant, penguin, or monkey, or a gifted German Shepherd named Monkey. Years ago, she'd traveled to San Francisco to visit the Museum of Modern Art with her college art history class. One of the first pieces she saw was a white paper in a simple frame. On the paper was a rolled-up piece of scotch tape with a long hair stuck to it. She stared at that piece, wondering why on earth the museum would find this to be worthy of display. In her mind, she felt that it was just framed garbage. Something like that was easily found on the floor of her home every Christmas when she wrapped up all her presents. When they got back to their classroom and discussed what they saw, Audrey asked her teacher why a piece of rolled-up tape would be on display. Her teacher responded, "Because you didn't think of it."

Another painting that stood out from the rest was a giant piece from Africa. It had scenes of villages, people, elephants, and other wildlife, created using paint and mixed media. Some of the media used was elephant poop. There were giant piles that the artist used as rocks, and they gave depth to the piece. She had never seen a painting that used feces before and hoped that she never would again. However, those two pieces of art were the only two that stuck in her memory. Maybe that's why they were there, as works of art. They were memorable.

So, what makes a work of art win a competition? It needs dynamic lighting and subject matter, flawless and creative technique, and it has to stand out above the rest. What makes someone want to buy your work? Over time, Audrey learned how to please judges, but attracting a buyer was a little different. While it was still good to have all those things a judge looks for, the most important thing a painting needed to have was the artist's soul poured into it. Buyers and admirers had to see it, and it would have to speak to their own soul. This would make it remembered. Generally, people like scenes that catch their attention, something that makes them remember a time or feeling in their lives that they loved. The pieces that Audrey sold weren't painted to please judges or to be trendy or political. They were the simple scenes she painted for herself, the ones she wanted to hang in her bedroom, to be able to gaze into and get lost in. Those were the ones that buyers paid good money for.

Audrey's father inspired greatness in her, even if he wasn't the nurturing, supportive teacher she wanted. Those teachers are good, but they don't drive you to be your best. The kind that pushed you forward were the critics, the honest, harsh, insensitive ones, those who get under your skin, hurt your feelings, irritate and piss you off so much that you want to "show them." So, take that criticism, get pissed off good. Then go to work and level up. Her dad saw talent. He saw enough talent to be honest about where she needed improvement. We should be grateful to our critics, and the work we do for ourselves as a result of them.

There will always be critics. You cannot please everyone, no matter how good you are. So work until you are proud of it. Work until you meet the high standards you set for yourself. And ultimately, make art that pleases you, that you want to hang in your bedroom and gaze into every day, that has your soul mixed into the media, like the poop in that elephant painting. You cannot please everyone with your work, but they'll remember it.

Audrey's grandma gave her very special advice that stuck with her. She told Audrey to pray over her artwork. Her grandma wanted her to pray so that she would be able to accomplish what she set out to, that the ideas would flow and it would all go together smoothly. Audrey took her advice. In doing so, by the time Audrey was finished with a piece and all the prayers added up, the piece became a prayer itself. She prayed that her work would heal, and indeed, her work became beautiful, colorful catalysts for just that.

Unfortunately, there was a dark side to her job. People. No matter how fun her job description sounded, it still fell under the dreaded term…retail. Shoppers aren't kind to retail workers, no matter what the position. Usually, you only have a few minutes to spend with a person, help them find what they need, answer questions, offer a few tips, and you just hope that the whole exchange goes well. That's not always the case. More often than not, the shoppers were in a hurry, their patience worn thin, and their attitude off putting. The light that beamed from Audrey irritated dark people. She brought out the worst in people, and it wasn't anything she had any control over. It frustrated her. Drained her. She had to make peace with the fact that some people just want to be unhappy. In some cases, you can do everything you possibly can for a person, and if they are hell bent on being an ass, you just have to let them. Nothing to do with you.

This job taught Audrey how to protect her energy from people, the ones that siphon positive energy, called energy vampires. Since everything is energy, she read that a clever way to protect herself was to envision a protective bubble forming around your body. Then, when negative people interact with you, their negativity bounces off. She visualized the negative energy not only bouncing off of her bubble, but her bubble zapped that bad juju like a bug zapper. She could almost hear the cracking and sizzling of the zapped energy when she spoke to certain people. Often, she had to hide the inexplicable smile on her face. Anything to help her get through the day.

The demand for more and more arrangements was growing and so did the needs of fussy customers as the days grew shorter and cooler. Retail took its toll on her. The moment she could close her car door and sit in the silence of her car was the moment she longed for earlier and earlier each workday. By the end of her shift, she was covered in glitter and moss, her hands were singed from the tip of the hot glue gun, and her spirit frayed. With a few deep breaths, she'd start her engine and begin her drive home with the healing feeling of wind in her hair, a few good songs, and I, her DJ.

With the rigors of retail, meditation was a welcomed retreat, even if it began as the simple act of pouring a glass of wine, choosing the right music and sitting outside by the pond, and breathing deeply in the crisp fall air. Audrey sat on the edge of her lounge chair with her legs crossed, wrapped in her favorite green sweatshirt with the words Pismo Beach embroidered across the front. The lounge next to her seemed empty, but I was there with her. She still felt alone inside the house, inside her bedroom, inside her marriage, but out here in her garden, the spirit was different. While the only living human in her garden at that time, she was definitely not alone.

Over the summer, Audrey was drawn to a book about a woman who'd had a near-death experience. The author wrote about what she experienced on the other side and described it in great detail. The living rarely get a glimpse of what's beyond the veil, and the book captivated Audrey with every page. The author wrote about gardens, which particularly caught Audrey's attention. She wrote that gardens and the earth have spirits that keep watch over it, just the same as the living have guardian angels watching over them.

Every living thing has a guardian spirit watching over it. Animals do. Plants do. Forests are full of them. On this side of the veil, it's an astounding thing to witness. Just a stroll through the woods could lead to encountering hundreds of new friends. By reading about garden spirits, deep down Audrey prayed that the work she had been doing in the garden had pleased them all. I can attest to that; in fact, they were all so proud of her progress, and both plant and spirit were happy to be a part of her garden.

At dusk one evening, Audrey stepped out onto the patio and looked over all the plants, making sure they each had enough water and attention. The twinkle lights that lined the edge of the patio were glowing. The neighbors and traffic had quieted, and there was a calm to the evening. She just happened to pass by one of the large wooden beams that had spiraling jasmine vines up to the top of it. In the softening sunset light, on a branch slightly higher than her line of sight, she could see a sleeping hummingbird. This tiny sweet creature was in slumber, though never to wake again. Audrey gasped and covered her mouth in shock. At first, she wanted to cry at the heartbreaking scene, but then a feeling came over her. Audrey had been calmed with a peace she was becoming more familiar with. It was Em. Em whispered to her, "You have fed him, fed his children, and his children's children. Be glad knowing that your garden is where he has called home and chosen to be his final resting place."

With the sweetest of care, the little bird was returned to the earth with flowers, prayers, and Audrey's tears. It was from that day forward that whenever Audrey was in the garden, she noticed the hummingbirds flying closer to her. They would hover right by her face for a few moments, and the vibration and sounds of their wings, though startling sometimes, always made her smile. She treasured each of their visits and imagined that, maybe, they were thanking her for the kind burial of their patriarch. If only she knew that the hummingbirds see beyond the veil and are visiting with their patriarch, who had taken a liking to Audrey. If only she knew that the spirit of her hummingbird watched over her wherever she went, buzzing just over her shoulders, maybe she wouldn't feel so alone all the time. Oh, how different her walk through life would be, if she knew we all were with her.

Chapter Thirteen

Work, crowds, pressure, all grinding on a sensitive spirit. This time of year was too busy to sneak away to Pismo, where one long walk in the sand would have her right again. She would have to settle for small indulgences instead. One of them was exploring her favorite store after a long day's work. World Market had it all, interesting things from all over the world, but she always found herself drawn to the pieces from India. There were tapestries, pillows, and textiles in bright patterns, lanterns, clothing—all with beading and embroidery and an artistry unmatched. It was the bright colors that sang to her, particularly red. Could Audrey possibly remember a time when we were married in India, and the angel who helped it all happen?

It was the time of the British Raj. British military men and their families were stationed throughout my country, and a dark cloud had descended on my people. There were desperate pleas for sovereignty and dignity, but rays of light shine through even the darkest clouds.

Military men come and go, but on grand estates, it's the memsahibs, the fair-skinned military wives, who run the show. My father was the gardener for the Memsahib, and our home was located on the grounds of this wondrous place. Our family maintained the land, but it was Memsahib and my countrymen who maintained the house, the luncheons, dinners, parties, and guests. But Memsahib had very special help.

Memsahib was traveling to the estate for the first time, and what were normal, everyday scenes in my country could be a bit jarring, traumatic even for the fair ladies of England. Memsahib had to travel through many cities to finally arrive at the estate to meet her husband and see her new home, but it was a brief stop on the road, a chance encounter, that changed her life and the lives of many others, forever. She was overheated and exhausted while also suffering from a terrible condition that few knew about. Her condition was what made her so different from most of the fair ladies. Her vehicle stopped abruptly, a brief pause for livestock to cross the road, and while she waited, she peered out at what rested against a building. Many people walked past, never noticing what looked like a crumpled pile of rags. Her gaze lingered. The pile of rags moved. Her fingers gripped the top of the car window as she took a closer look. A very small and weary, dispirited child lay on the street. My country referred to them as the untouchables. Her car began to move, and a feeling of desperation overcame her. A maternal feeling, echoing what she'd always longed for but was physically denied.

She ordered her driver to stop the car and help her return to the child. The driver refused. She pleaded with him, and when that didn't work, she ordered him to leave her and all of her belongings there on the side of the road. The man knew what kind of trouble he'd be in if he abandoned Memsahib, so he reluctantly agreed. Her driver carried the young child to the back seat and placed her next to Memsahib. Eyes meeting. Misery meeting compassion.

The gates to the estate swung wide for their arrival, and besides the relief she felt in knowing her long journey was over, she was overcome by all of the flowers, colors, and scents. The gates closed behind them, and as she looked around at the grounds so lovingly kept, the rose garden, the jasmine vines, she felt an unfamiliar feeling stirring within. The garden was calling her.

The condition Memsahib suffered from was acute agoraphobia. As Memsahib decided to journey to her new home, a decision was made that her life would change dramatically. It was time to face her demons, with a vow that she was a prisoner of her own mind no longer. It was a bold act of taking control, believing in herself, knowing that she would rather step out bravely into the unknown than waste away in fear. It was that same boldness that ordered the driver to help that desperate child, boldness to order staff whom she'd never known to treat the child better than they were expected to treat her. She ordered the staff to make the appropriate accommodations for the child in her private quarters, a little girl who knew no name, no birthdate, no family, but only the brutality of her caste. Memsahib arranged for the finest medical care, nourishing food, and tailored clothes but still wondered what to call her.

Agoraphobia had seemed like a life sentence that only worsened when she learned she was unable to conceive a child. Her spirit retreated deeply within her. But as the doctors and nurses rushed around the child, she suddenly desired fresh air, for the first time in so long. She began to walk through the gardens, through the roses and vines, hoping to create a bouquet for the child, knowing how healing fresh-cut flowers could be. She stopped to admire the blooms when she saw my father working. It was out of character for a Memsahib to speak to a worker, a gardener, but she approached him and inquired about the grounds. It was a high honor for him to be her guide that day. She saw so much beauty that afternoon that her condition seemed like a passing storm cloud. Being a kind and gentle man who cherished working with the earth, flowers, and life there, it was no wonder that she felt safe and comforted in his presence. My father made her laugh and taught her the names of flowers she'd never seen before, told her of their many uses, and helped her create a most exquisite bouquet. Before she returned to the house, she asked for the name of his mother, my grandmother. He wasn't sure why she had asked such a question, but in the coming days, he would learn.

Memsahib returned to her room, placing the bouquet in a crystal vase on a table near the child. She sat on the child's bed, holding her frail little hand. A once filthy, discarded child, who had been washed clean, her skin treated with fragrant oils, her hair brushed, a broken spirit free to mend. Memsahib raised her free hand and held it to her chest, saying, "Clara." Then, with the same hand, she placed it upon the child's chest. "Veena." Clara repeated the gesture again. "It's wonderful to meet you."

In the next few years, Clara treated Veena not only as she would her own child, but more like a treasure. Veena grew into a polished, educated, and lovely young lady. The members of the estate began to appreciate certain unique qualities of Veena. She seemed to have empathic and psychic abilities. She had a way of just knowing things beforehand. The elders attributed her gifts to the traumas she'd experienced early in her life, perhaps giving her a glimpse through a thinned veil. The responsibilities of the estate were normally delegated to her. The staff of the house was treated far better than at any other estate. It was a working family. We were all very pleased and honored to work for Memsahib and Veena. A school for the children of the estate staff was created, which is where I was able to benefit. Veena treated me as if I were a little brother, watching over me, affording me tutors, an education, a broadening of the mind and talents I never knew I had. An opportunity that never would have been afforded to a working-class gardener's son otherwise.

It was lifetimes ago, but I remember it like it was yesterday. Audrey's parents were spending their summer in India, visiting their family friends who were diplomats in the region. Audrey's first visit to my country was when she was seven years old. She looked every bit as blond and beautiful as she did when I met her in this lifetime, though her accent was slightly different. Her family was one of the many guests at the sprawling estate. She had a room with her parents on the second floor, and her window was on the far-left corner, which seemed to anchor the sun as it rose above the rolling hills behind the house and set far deep into the horizon of the spectacular Indian countryside. I was just a little Indian boy running around the grounds, trying to stay out of trouble. My father, being the gardener of the estate, meant that I was usually put to work, helping him finish large jobs. India is a rich, fertile land, and the line between garden and jungle often blurs. My father was a proud man and loved his job, loved his family, and we all contributed to this place, growing within the vines of that garden.

There was a picnic in the main yard one day, and Audrey wandered away from the crowd. The inner grounds were known to be a safe haven, so parents allowed their children to roam just a little farther than they normally would. The parents were all drinking their wine and singing songs, laughing and enjoying their afternoon. The children also had games to play and dogs to chase, but Audrey just wanted to explore. There was a charm and mystery about every turn. It was part quaint English garden and part enchanting wild India. Audrey peered around tree trunks and ran her fingers along the twisting vines of jasmine that wrapped around the arbors the same way Indian women wear their silk sarees. This is when I met her. A cluster of white feathery jasmine blooms lay delicately in her little open hand, and she closely observed them.

"The Belle of India," I smiled. "You should smell it." Bringing a cluster of blooms to my nose, I introduced myself. Our names were different then, but names matter not when the soul remains unchanged. "My father is the gardener here. He has planted many kinds of jasmine, but this one is my favorite."

I was a lanky Indian boy, and she, a little shy British girl. It was funny how she looked similar to how she did back then, but I was so different. We spent the entire summer much like we did in this life, playing until the sun went down and wishing we had more hours in the day. We spent some days swimming in a small creek that ran through the corner of the estate. We seemed to have laughed more in those summers as children than many lifetimes put together. You just seem to know when you meet special souls, and she and I, deep down, always knew we were destined.

There were summers her family wasn't able to make the journey to India, and I was devastated. I had already known that the beautiful blond British girl had stolen my heart long ago, but now I knew I couldn't live without her. Those summers were not only blistering hot but grueling, and I counted the days till their end and a new season began. I distracted myself in any way I possibly could. Veena taught me proper etiquette and how to ballroom dance. I found I had a talent for writing. It's amazing what you can accomplish when you're determined to use it as an escape. I was slowly becoming an Indian gentleman and making my father and family very proud. Veena, especially. But I believe they all knew my intentions.

It was that time of year again when visitors arrived, and I was beginning to look for her in crowds. One day, Veena called me to the main house, maintaining a sober expression. I was unsure what I was about to walk into. She pointed to the ledger she was carrying in her arms. It was a small list of families that rooms were reserved for, and there was Audrey's name beside her usual room, the one that anchored the sun, the windowsill I'd watched her lean upon as thousands of colors of the Indian sunset illuminated her. We both shared eager smiles.

I had worked so hard and made sure to afford nice clothing

to impress her because we had become much older, and I knew that proper attire and manners were of the utmost importance. My father asked me one particular day to help him prepare the grounds for the guests, and I acquiesced. I feared being a dirty mess, that it would be her first impression of me after so long, but I hoped that maybe by the grace of the gods, her family would arrive late.

My father and I worked all morning and stopped to have lunch that my mother had prepared for us. The dinner table discussion was all about the guests arriving and if my old friend would be one of them. The anticipation was so much so that even my family could feel it. They were teasing that she might not recognize me. After lunch, we returned to our work, and the temperature only increased. It was sweltering. I unbuttoned my white shirt and draped it on the fence near me. I was doing heavy, demanding work. My body was covered in sweat, just streaming off of me. I stopped my work for a moment, resting my hand atop the handle of my rake, and used my other hand to wipe the sweat from my brow as a familiar voice greeted me from behind. It was her. I turned around in surprise, hoping the wide smile on my face was enough to distract her from the disgraceful rest of me. There she stood, this radiant young woman in a peach-colored dress, offering me a cool glass of water. When she had arrived, Veena had greeted her with a most cheerful embrace and warm words. They began chatting, and the conversation quickly shifted to me.

Veena watched her crane her neck, peering out windows to catch a glimpse of me. Veena knew right where to send her.

All the time I spent worrying about what clothing to wear when she first saw me again was all in vain. It turned out that she rather enjoyed seeing me working without a shirt. No longer the skinny boy, but rather a muscular Indian man. Years of jungle taming would do that to you. The ladies had become very fond of me. Mothers were trying to arrange marriages between their daughters and me, to no avail. I was in love with a blond angel in a peach-colored dress, holding a straw hat trimmed in a matching French ribbon and a cut crystal glass of cool water. I graciously accepted the drink. Isn't it strange how water can sometimes taste sweet?

"It's wonderful to see you. I'm so happy you're here," I started, nervous energy welling inside me.

"It's wonderful to be here. I'm happy to finally find you," she said, fidgeting with her hat.

"I had hoped you'd be seeing me fully dressed and less, well..." I trailed off, looking down at my state. "...But it seems your family arrived early." I stepped just a few feet away to a blooming pink rosebush and picked a perfect rose. I walked back, standing just in front of her, taking the hat from her hands. I placed the rose carefully into the bow on her hat. I held her hat in one hand and brought her delicate hand up to my lips with the other. She always had this little way about her; when something touched her heart, she would tilt her head, close her eyes, smile, and her shoulders would rise up to meet her cheek. I watched her do that very thing once again. And when she opened her eyes, she put her hat on with a slight curtsey. We spoke our own language growing up, and I could see that hadn't changed.

"Do you have plans this evening? I have something to show you," I asked expectantly. My father taught me that if you are pressuring someone to answer you, ask the question and then say nothing. Just look at them, don't even breathe. Wait for the answer like a tiger about to pounce.

She wasn't fazed by my tactics. "I'm having dinner with my family, and then I am free. What do you have in mind?" She was light as feathers. Her smile so serene, entire wars could end at the sight of it. I could've stood there gazing upon the sight of my angel for a millennium, but I had better plans.

"You will see!" I assured, buttoning my shirt. I gathered my tools and cleaned up for the day. My face hadn't stopped smiling since I saw her. I could feel the ache in my cheeks.

After a long day working on the grounds, I thought I'd be exhausted after I bathed, but I was a new man. The events of the day, meeting her again after so long, reeled in my mind. The girl of my dreams was here in my town, and somehow, I was going to parade her through it.

I was lucky to find work in journalism. I worked for the local newspaper. The paper had their favorite journalists, though I had aspirations of finding the perfect story someday that would land me on the front page. This job granted me many opportunities and opened doors that otherwise would have been closed to a young Indian man among British dignitaries. Dinner at the estate was one of those doors that opened—fine dining, proper formal dinner attire, etiquette, and British snobbery on holiday. Any regular Indian boy would be eaten alive in a room like that. How lucky I was to be educated not only on all the finery, but snobbery warfare as well. The British are hilarious with their brutal comments brilliantly disguised as flattery. If you're not paying attention, you'd hardly notice you've been sliced and diced and bleeding out, yet they say it all with the loveliest tone and smile. The goal is to always return fire and make people laugh at the same time. It's an art form.

None of those things mattered. I dressed with care, picked fresh flowers from my mother's garden, wildflowers, more roses like the one I tucked in the ribbon of her hat and, of course, the Belle of India. The walk to the estate house was sensual, the sun having just set, the sky alight with a masterful palette of colors. The sweet smell of jasmine and wildflowers from the gardens and spices drifting from the kitchen could be bottled up as intoxicating perfume.

Audrey was pleasantly surprised to see me at dinner. I could tell she was impressed with the transformation from disheveled gardener to besuited gentleman. Veena made arrangements with the staff to seat me directly opposite her on the long dining table. Veena also placed my bouquet of flowers in a vase on Audrey's nightstand. For my flowers, no note was needed. The jasmine said it all. The room was loud and lively, and the chatter, laughter, and sounds of clinking China, silver, and crystal limited conversation to only our dinner partners on our immediate left or right. While she and I were speaking to the people to our sides, we were looking across the table at each other. We raised our glasses to one another in a silent toast. Our gazes were long and deliberate, growing longer as the dinner progressed. There is an intimacy unmatched in eye contact; the eyes tell you everything. Her eyes were smiling as the evening began, but I knew that people drained her, and her journey had been long. I could see she needed rest just by the slow way she blinked, but you could never tell from her glow.

The wait staff buzzed around us, meeting our every need, filling our glasses, removing our plates, and all went as smoothly as expected. These wonderful people had trained for such a time as this. My Indian brethren were functioning as a symphony on this evening. And when the final course was served and the final dish removed from the table, the gentlemen adjourned to their study for cigars and coarse words of women and politics. The ladies tended to their children or grouped off into smaller gatherings for the latest gossip, sipping their port from tiny crystal glasses.

I had dazzling plans for the two of us. There was a street fair of art and food, music and colors in town, and I had planned on reacquainting my wonderful friend with the soul of my culture, but I could see in her eyes that tonight was not the night for that. Veena knew just what to do. My friends in the kitchen saved me a bottle of champagne and glasses, wrapped up in a shoulder bag, and stowed them away where only I could find.

While Audrey was finishing a conversation with another guest, I ducked out and found the bag that the staff had prepared for me. The vision that evening, the blooming rose, in a golden gown with accents of jade and violet, was the girl of my dreams, my jaan, and now that dinner had come to a close, she was finally mine.

We strolled down the steps of the estate and through the main yard, through the hedges and rose gardens, catching each other up on all the events we had missed in our lives. The conversation flowed as if we'd never lost touch, and she had been here with me the whole time. It was magical. The bright moon lit a path for us all the way to the gazebo I'd built years ago with my father. The vines had years to completely cover the entire structure. She gasped when she saw it, having the faintest glow of candlelight escaping through its entryways. Veena and the staff had arranged the whole scene, just for us.

Just as Audrey was in her current life, she was right at home in the garden. She felt closer to the spirit of the garden and nature than that of other people, and this night offered her reconnection on many levels. We drank the champagne, we told stories and laughed. We were silly and lighthearted as children and exchanged the heartbreaks and tears of time as well. She threw her arms around me several times in the night, and there was a time when we were talking that I sat on the settee, her head lay on my shoulder. Our lips begged to meet. We were about to burn this season down with the sparks surrounding us. I watched her gather up her dress as ladies do when they are about to scurry away, and the layers of her dress billowed in the breeze behind her until she disappeared into the field of roses and moonlight. My hand over my chest, my heart pained, as I missed her already.

It felt like my eyes had only closed for a moment on my pillow before I had to rush off to work in the morning, my mind careening from the exquisite evening I just shared with her. I couldn't focus on anything else but managed to get to my desk and appear as if I was busy working. The country was in an uproar. War and rumors of war, Indian people fighting for their independence and sovereignty from a far-overreaching and never-ending British occupation. The discourse was deafening, and it was my job to cover it all. Luckily, it was a quiet news day for me, and toward the end of the workday, most people left. The office was but a whisper. I rested my head in my arms upon my desk for what I thought would only be a minute.

I drifted off to dream of the evening in reverse. I saw her running toward the estate with the frills and sashes of her gown flowing behind her in soft motion. Then she was close to me with her head on my shoulder, my hand gently weaving her golden ringlets around my brown fingers. The range of emotions I watched her feel through the night as I felt them with her.

I was so deep in sleep that I didn't hear her enter my tiny office. She tiptoed through the room, looking at pictures on the walls. Small, colorful tapestries and Indian art to keep my spirits high and senses sharp were placed throughout the room. She stepped behind me near the window, first looking outside at the view of a busy street below and then turning her gaze to my desk. One thing caught her attention. A photograph sat on the left side of the desk, and she remembered when it had been taken. It was a sepia-toned photo of the two of us when we were younger, not even teenagers, and clearly one of the happiest times of my life. It was a moment captured in time when nothing was more wonderful than being in each other's company, when we knew everything about each other, what made us laugh and cry, our wildest dreams and aspirations. A time when I seemed to come to life by her visits into my world, and upon her leaving, I'd return to a solemn state of inanimation.

"I didn't know you wore glasses." She rubbed my shoulders lightly to wake me and walked toward the front of my desk.

"Oh, hello." Feeling the glasses on my face, I giggled. "They are only for reading and sleeping. They are the latest thing." I rubbed my eyes and tried my best to look presentable. "What brings you to town, jaan?"

"I like it when you call me that." Her shoulders raised toward her ears again. "I just needed some fresh air and a nice walk around town. Did you hear about the street fair?" she asked as she flipped through a stack of photographs on my desk. "We simply must go!"

I stood up and gathered my things to leave for the day. As we made our way back to the estate, we set a plan for the evening. I was to dine with my family and she with hers, and we would meet on the steps of the estate, just as we did the night before and spend the evening at the street fair.

We walked along the busy streets and through crowds of people, talking about news stories and the day's events, the growing turmoil and dangerous times my people found themselves in. A desperate fight for freedom, our sovereignty, our culture. But as soon as we were out of the chaos of town and closer to home, I grew quiet, and she followed my lead. I knew these paths. I took her hand and guided her through long hanging vines and leaves to a special place. I took her to see a tree I had been fascinated with my whole life. It was a grand Banyan tree standing tall enough to tickle the clouds, old and massive, with a sprawling canopy and innumerable roots that draped down from its branches like a thousand ribbons. I'd always felt a connection to this tree, in awe of its beauty and the stories it could tell from its long life. As a boy, I wanted to live in this tree as if I were a bird or monkey. I could close my eyes and feel its calming energy flowing. We stood under my old friend, the Banyan tree, enjoying the sound of the sudden wild winds sweeping through it. I watched as she placed her hand against the tree, as I had. She closed her eyes when the wind rushed and softly lifted her blond curls. I moved my hand closer to hers on the tree. I took her other hand up to my lips and kissed it. If the eyes could convey all the love we had amassed after all these years, we could see it all now. She took her hand from the tree and ran her fingers slowly through my black hair and then moved to hold the back of my neck. Time slowed, frame to frame. I watched a slight smile cross her lips before she kissed me. In that moment, fireworks blasted in my every artery. I had everything I had ever wanted, dreamed, and wished for. I was a king, I was a legend, I was in love, as was she. Is there anything more incredible in life than the feeling of being young and in love?

The sun was sinking into pools of colors and disappeared behind the Indian hills. I waited for her on our steps with a pink hibiscus flower in my hand. She smiled when she saw me holding it. She took the flower slowly from my hands and placed it behind her left ear. These gestures have meaning. A flower worn behind a woman's left ear reveals that she is spoken for. She wore my flower with intention. She held my hand from the last step to the edge of the estate and all the way to town. It's in the most dangerous times of war and conflict that the rarest love blooms. The love between an Indian man and a British woman would draw ire in my country, so in town, any closeness we shared was hidden, but for the grazing of my hand with her fingertips when she passed by. The air was filled with rich spices of curry, nutmeg, cardamom, clove, and cinnamon. Sheets of silk and batik fabric from a street vendor caught the breeze and flowed in an unimaginable, colorful scene, while the wild beats of the music played on, making all those who listened subconsciously move to it. Eventually we all ended up dancing that night at some point. We would throw our arms up in the air and clap to the beats, laughing all the while.

We passed by a man's table selling mirchi bajji, more than happy to serve his fiery Indian snack. It is a breaded and deep-fried hot pepper, stuffed with potato or cauliflower. You can dip it into a tomato sauce or chutney. The man saw the lovely blonde and knew that British ladies rarely could take the heat, so he waved his hand in front of his mouth to signal to her that it was way too hot. She nodded in agreement but then pointed to me, with a mischievous look. The man knew what she was up to. They both pressured me to eat this fried fireball. I laughed and declined, walking away hoping she would follow me, but she didn't. She made me eat the damn pepper. I love hot and spicy things, and I love this dish, but the man didn't give me chutney to dip it in. He drizzled a fiery curry called vindaloo over it all, with a chuckle. This was a sauce he reserved for certain special people he was displeased with or to tease others. The pepper was deceiving. At first, I thought I got away having little heat, but it snuck up on me. I started breathing heavier, sweat dripped from my brow, and my eyes watered. I was a burning mess, but seeing her laugh at me like that, I'd eat three more. The vendor's belly shook with his laughter.

We walked through tall structures with draped fabric and sarees that danced to and fro in the breeze. She held this deep green silk up to her eyes, covering her nose and mouth with it, eyes flirting. I was entranced by how the green complemented those eyes of hers. As she walked through the swathes of fabric, playfully running her hands across the fine silks, I purchased the green saree for her. I just simply had to. It belonged to her. But there was another saree that struck me. It was red, something you might see a bride wear at her wedding. They wrapped her green dress in tissue and tied it with a natural fiber. I continued to carry it under my arm. We got to the last piece of hanging fabric, and behind it was an empty spot, void of people, where she pulled me toward her and kissed me, most desirously. A secret kiss, forbidden, making each moment that it lasted, pure fire.

My blood raced through my body, still high from our first kiss that was just hours ago. There was a commotion of a thousand different things around us, and I could hear sounds of people in the distance laughing and dancing, but all my focus was on her. She smelled of jasmine and strawberries, and her lips were soft. I was in a daze as she drew away from me.

"My mouth is on fire!" She shouted, holding her hand over her mouth. Her eyes were big and starting to water.

I couldn't help but laugh. "This is all your fault, you know. You made me eat that pepper."

She was fanning her mouth now and breathing deeply.

"Are you enjoying your first mirchi bajji?" I bent over laughing, then ran a few steps down the corridor, finding her something to drink.

We grew tired of the festivities and returned to the estate where our little vine-covered oasis waited for us. It was once again candle lit, and the staff had left a bottle of wine with an opener and a vase full of jasmine blooms. The wine was smooth, the most delicious red, an Indian vintage from the south, which paired well with burning lips and sparking hearts. On this night, we told each other all the things we had held within our hearts, all these years. My people view intimacy differently from Westerners. We can reveal ourselves to the point of nakedness without disrobing. It can be captured in the eyes, with the hands, with words, with the soul. Raabta.

We spent the entire holiday together, inseparable and vowing to remain so. We swam in the deep pools of the creek just as we had when we were children. We had picnics in the garden under the canopy of rain trees, daydreaming of what our future might hold. I learned in that time that she saw God everywhere, in everything. She saw God even within me, and it was then that I came to know her God. I asked my questions, I cried out, I opened up, and never once had those gods and idols of our culture spoken to me, as her God had. Suddenly, all the gods, those little idols we keep everywhere, that I had grown up knowing, had lost their meaning to me and were forgone forever.

When she spoke of her God and her dreams of one day marrying me, she told me that her people view a marriage being a union of three. Some people believe that a braid is a union of mind, body, and spirit, but to her, it was the interlacing of man, wife, and Creator, forging an unbreakable bond. I shared my intention with Veena in a quiet conversation one afternoon, when my dream girl was spending time with her family. With Veena's heartfelt blessing, a plan was made. I was to buy a set of gold braided bands, and she was to buy a red beaded silk sari. I was surprised that she was so encouraging, feeling that our plans were hurried, and I asked her why it felt rushed. The smile on her face was replaced by a somber pause. She patted my hand and, with sympathy, said, "There is simply no time."

One night as the season drew to a close, a private bonfire was built for us. Emotions swelled in my chest as I watched my love, my jaan, descend the staircase of the estate in a jeweled red sari on this special night. I took her hand and led her to our steps where we always met, her topaz eyes glittering, her skin glistening with scented oils of jasmine and strawberries, her hands adorned with Veena's own henna designs. There she was, my bride. I asked my love to be my wife in this lifetime and eternity. She agreed, and I placed a braided gold band, exquisitely made for her, on her left ring finger. She placed the other band on my hand as well. Our ceremony began with a varmala.

For my people, we have many ancient rituals and ceremonies, especially surrounding weddings, but for this evening, with all things of war, timing, and cultures considered, I was only able to focus on the most important of them. Her father was happy to see his little girl making friends, even with natives, but when it came to marrying her, he would never allow it. We both were harrowed by the choices we were forced to make, but to us, in love, in a time of war and uncertainty, we held fast to our destiny and each other. It was a heavenly evening for a bonfire. Known as agni, bonfires are sacred and are believed in many cultures to consecrate, to purify and bless.

I took her hand and led her to a table draped in layers of silk. Lying on this table were two floral garlands, one for my bride and one for me. I took the first garland and gently laid the ring of fragrant wild Indian flowers around her neck, adjusting them to lie perfectly against that red silk sari. She took the other garland and held it up to me. Being much taller, I bowed for her, and she arranged the flowers just the same. The garlands of flowers represented our commitment to each other, a symbol of respect and love. The bonfire had its purpose. The Saptapadi, circling the fire together seven times, symbolizes the spiritual union of the bride and groom, with each turn focusing on a vow. So, we circled and we vowed before our Creator, we danced and kissed, and we were now two bodies, one soul, in a ceremony all our own.

Two weeks after our honeymoon, and the night before a special dinner was prepared at the estate, I heard the sound of a howling dog. It was a persistent, sad cry in distress, somewhere in the distance, an omen to my people, a troubling feeling I couldn't shake. The dinner was in celebration of the birth of the viceroy's son, even though he would not be in attendance. It was a formal affair, and I was able to attend. We collected in the great hall, me being so proud to dance with this exquisite woman before all of these most envious people. The string quartet was lovely, but as they rose for an interlude, I excused myself from my bride's company. I walked to the edge of the room and stepped behind groups of people to the grand piano situated to the left of the musician's chairs. I sat upon the piano's bench. I tightly clenched my fists and breathed ever so deeply before I began to play Debussy's first Arabesque. This was the song that played in my mind when I'd thought of her in those long, lonely intervals, in between her visits, or simply through the night. I began playing with my eyes on the keys, and by the time my nerves subsided and I could look up, the crowd parted, making way for my love to draw near to the piano. There were moments in the song when I could look up from the keys and our eyes could meet. She and others shared the look of astonishment. The proud Memsahib also watched, with tears filling her eyes as moments played in her mind like a film. Leaving the sadness behind her in dreary England, the pause in the road when she caught a glimpse of a lost soul, an angel in disguise. The moment Clara introduced herself to Veena for the first time.

And watching how Veena went on to bless others. Veena watched me perform with a quiet stream of tears, which she quickly brushed away, a knowing smile, with mixed emotions of elation, pride, and that Japanese word, yugen, describing the beauty of both happiness and pain, sweetness and bitterness, love and loss.

I chose this song because it sounded like what falling in love felt, even more beautiful when played for the only woman I had ever loved. I stood from the bench to roaring applause, the loudest coming from the house staff that all paused their duties to watch me perform the song I had learned in the estate. The proud moment Veena and the staff had all been waiting for, but I bowed only to my bride.

In this time, her visit to India marked so many perfect instances, the kiss under the banyan tree, the fiery embrace behind layers of flowing silks, our union of souls, but it was in this moment that her eyes glittered with emotions of surprise, pride, and love. The musicians returned to their seats and began to play a soft waltz, and our bodies swayed, our gaze held, her lips whispering, "I love you."

It was that romantic waltz we were dancing to when an explosion blasted through the walls. A massive bomb tore through the estate as if it were made of soft clay. In my mind, I could still hear Arabesque being played as the fragments of the blast seemed to fly through the air in slow motion. Smoke filled the rooms, and all I could hear were coughs and cries of fear and agony. I came to, in panic. I had to find her in all this madness. She was not far, but the room was nothing but rubble, smoke, and confusion, looking nothing like it once had. She was lying there peacefully, her eyes open, fixed on a moment in time when we were happy. There was a pool of blood silently spreading on the ground and soaking into her hair. She was already gone, her spirit waiting for mine. I held her and cried, tears rolling through the dust on my face.

It felt as if only breaths later, I found myself on the steps of the estate, dressed in white linens. I saw the damage done to the once towering stone building and the flowering vines that once covered it. I saw people running away from the estate, my own people who bombed this special place because of its British occupants. There was a jealousy of how workers of the estate were treated so well compared to elsewhere. My own people were trying to win their freedom, even if Indian blood was spilled to accomplish it. The culprits were never identified. Thirteen people lost their lives in the blast, and we were part of them, this being the reason I finally made the front page of the paper. I stood on those steps for the last time, my bride in a pure white dress, meeting me, looking beautiful as ever, restored and renewed. Belle of India worn behind her left ear. She took my hand and led me away from the rubble, through the main yard, past the hedges and rose garden to our vine-covered oasis where we spent the last few moments of our time on earth, in this lifetime together. Connecting with eyes, hands, words, and soul, forever.

Audrey bought a bottle of smooth red wine and a deep green shawl that brought out the color of her eyes that day from World Market. That weekend, she planted the newest addition to her garden, a new variety, the Belle of India, and something tells me, deep down, somehow, she remembers.

Chapter Fourteen

Though the world is cold and love is scarce, you are never truly alone. You have angels watching over you. They come in many forms. The stray on your doorstep, the kindness of a stranger, profound advice from a friend, and the wisdom of an elder. Chances are you've gone through your normal daily life and walked right past them. You might have talked to them, helped them get a can off a high shelf at the supermarket, or held the door open for them at the restaurant. They might be the pet sitting in your lap, led to you because you needed true companionship. Or they may have arranged a series of events to unfold in your favor. Angels go through life with us, but all we have to do is ask our angels each day for their help in our lives, a simple invitation. They revel in helping us, but most times, we forget to ask.

Summer never seems to fade away gracefully. It fights to the end in California and only seems to tire near the time people are celebrating Halloween. Halloween was fun as child, costumes and candy, but now that Audrey was older, the holiday seemed to become dark and disturbing. For someone who was so familiar with death and the nature of the spirit world, toy skulls and graveyards, mummies and goblins weren't so fun anymore. But there was one thing that she did like about the spooky season. Black cats everywhere. Audrey had a collection of black cat figurines and pictures that she displayed on a table in the foyer of her home. It was the Halloween display that wasn't. It was actually more of a black cat homage than anything, with a few apothecary bottles of potions. Black cat's hiss, Essence of Black Cat Whiskers, Love Potion #9, and Black Cat Label Poison. She loved the look of the bottles and little Romeos on the label. But the season was changing, and it was time for something new.

Above the table was a Renaissance-looking oil painting of her winged Romeo playing a lute. Across the hallway was another painting of both her cats as Raphael's cherubs, sitting at the table looking up. Wings were showing up in every room of her home without her consciously adding them.

The store had shifted gears from harvest and Halloween to all the Christmas trimmings. Everywhere you looked, it was Christmas. Stores like this had to usher holidays in early for all the crafters and creatives out there. There was an area of the store that had a dozen different twinkling Christmas trees, and one in particular kept calling her. After all her hard work over the last few months, Audrey bought a new tree and waited as time seemed to crawl, for the right time to put it up in the perfect spot and finally plug it in. Just a simple Christmas tree with white twinkling lights in darkness, so ethereal like a portal to the middle of the universe captured in her living room.

Audrey had such fun watching her cats create a playground out of the tree. They were fascinated with it. They both played beneath it, climbed up high, peaked their faces out of the branches, and just about knocked the whole thing over. She left the tree up without any trimmings for a couple of weeks until the cats lost interest, and it was during that time that she could really look around in the store and decide how to decorate this new tree for its first Christmas.

My mom decorated our tree very simply. It was a house full of men, and she knew she didn't have to do much to impress us. She had a collection of really nice wool blankets with Aztec patterns on them, all in bright colors that she wrapped around the base. She used horsehair hackamores as decoration, winding them around the tree. One year, we didn't have any balls to hang on the tree, so we used raffia to tie dog bones on the edges of branches. That year, the dogs learned how to strong-arm us all into giving them treats. All they had to do was walk over to the tree and sniff a bone. One of us would have to oblige him. One by one, when we weren't looking, our little decorations disappeared from the tree, but we all had fun with the idea.

I remember going to Audrey's house at Christmas time. Her mother had the whole house decorated magically, holly and ivy, garlands and bows everywhere you looked. Their Christmas tree was covered top to bottom in rocking horses. Every size, shape, and color, some were ceramic, some were leather, and all of them completely unique. It was a collection they began years ago, and it outgrew the tree. There were rocking horses everywhere you turned, each carefully crafted and collected from their travels. I could spend days here admiring each one, and it inspired me to want a holiday collection of my own someday. I wondered what Audrey and I would've collected together had we gotten the chance.

Christmas would always remind Audrey of the treasured memories she made on a holiday trip to New Orleans years ago with her mother. They both shared the same excitement for Christmas, and that allowed them to put aside their differences for a while. To them, it was never too early to put up the tree. They got more excited about buying presents for their loved ones than about what they might get in return. To them, the spirit of Christmas was intoxicating, the high of a collective cheer, and they just couldn't get enough. How fitting for the two of them to enjoy this enchanted city when draped in twinkle lights and bows, decorations lining the streets, and each storefront trying to out-Christmas the next. This was the time of the year that Audrey called the Season of Angels.

Their plane arrived just as the sun was setting. Once they took their bags to their rooms and ventured back out, the twinkling lights set the city aglow, offering the most bewitching of welcomes. Audrey and her mom, being empaths, felt the vibration of the city the second their feet hit the ground. It was a feeling unlike any other. The history here can be felt. The fire, the flood, the war, the mob, the voodoo, the danger, it's all here in a delicate balancing act. Then there is the charm, the art, the architecture, the French Quarter, and the spirit. Dare I say spirits? Audrey felt a supernatural presence here, a feeling of mystery. This trip had some surprises in store.

Audrey's mother thought they could use a couple of French Quarter favorites, the weary travelers they were, so they walked to the Quarter, where they found Pat O'Brien's sign that hung from a scrolling wrought iron rack, all lit up and seeming to wave them in. There was so much history in this place, and Audrey was curious about what kind of history her mother had there too. They made their way out to the courtyard where a rushing fountain was surrounded by very old and very charming brick buildings looking down on it. There at a table in that twinkling moonlit courtyard, they sat by the fountain and let the sound of the flowing water renew their spirits. Their server bought two tall, curvy glasses filled to the brim with a reddish-orange drink. Adele told Audrey all about the history of the famous Pat O'Brien Hurricanes. In World War II, whiskey was scarce, so the famous Pat O's created a drink with rum instead, and the drink got its name from the shape of the glass, looking like a hurricane lamp. The concoction starts out innocent enough with grapefruit and pineapple juice and a splash of grenadine, but then it takes a dangerous turn with its copious amounts of vodka, gin, rum, triple sec, amaretto, and more rum. It's as if you asked a drunk pirate to go behind the bar and make something light and refreshing. That might actually be where the drink came from; you just never know in this crazy city.

As they listened to the sounds of jazz music drifting through the courtyard, Adele leaned in and asked, "Did you know there was a serial killer here, named the Axeman?" Audrey shook her head as she sipped through her straw. "In 1918, a man was terrorizing the city, killing his victims with their own axes. After the Axeman had claimed many victims, the police believed they got a letter from the killer, saying that if he passed by a place that was playing jazz music, he promised he wouldn't attack them. The town flooded into the local bars and restaurants and remained there all night as they played jazz music to appease the madman."

"Did he keep his promise?" Audrey leaned in.

"Yep. There were no murders reported that night. Crazy, huh?"

They both sat quietly, feeling the jazz music and the city become a bit more haunting.

They took in every bit of the ambiance, the fire fountain, the breeze through the courtyard, the soft twinkling of lights, and the buzz from a strong drink on an empty stomach. They both sipped slowly until their fruity storm in a glass had passed them by. But now they both felt their little storm's aftermath. Perfect time for another French Quarter favorite, the Po Boy. They both got up from their table and walked out of Pat O'Brien's, their path a bit more crooked than before. Adele's memory of the French Quarter was good but had grown hazy with time. They weren't sure which street the restaurant was on, so they just walked in its general direction and left it to chance. Chance led them down a dark street. There were no twinkle lights; no, this was more like a dark alley, and some strange figure was walking toward them. He began to sway and dance. He twirled, putting on a show for them all while getting closer. Now he was right in front of Audrey. He was a short, heavy-set man dressed as a clown in full makeup, handing her a rose that he'd made from a palm leaf. Audrey was surprised by his actions. He waved the flower, encouraging, pressuring her to take it. Dark alley, strange man, eerie encounter, a general dislike of clowns. It was almost enough for Audrey to take off running and screaming, but she took the flower and thanked him. Immediately he stuck his palm in her face and, with a gravely deep voice, he croaked, "Five dollars."

Audrey was unsettled now, but she just wanted to be left alone. Stashed in the right pocket of her jeans was a folded five-dollar bill. She took it out of her pocket and smacked it into his hand, singeing him with her glare. He closed his hand with the bill in it, tipped his hat, and continued his bizarre clown dance down the street until he disappeared in the darkness. Adele and Audrey just stood there, almost in shock, until Adele began to laugh. They laughed and giggled about that weird grifter clown until they finally found the restaurant. It was packed, but they managed to be seated quickly. Adele delighted in telling Audrey the history of the loaded sandwich, famously known as the Po Boy. Bennie and Clovis Martin were streetcar conductors since 1910, but in the streetcar strike of 1929, they opened the Martin Brothers' Coffee Stand and Restaurant. Their sandwich, which was a classic French baguette loaded with either roast beef or seafood, smothered in a thick spicy sauce, became the talk of the town. Everyone had to have one. The Martin Brothers will always be remembered not only in New Orleans but the entire South, for their culinary genius, the Po Boy. It was just as delicious as Adele had described.

In the light of day, the city loses its arcane feel. One might almost forget that every now and then, after a massive flood, coffins of former French Quarter residents wash their way down the street. The city was buzzing with tourists and river boats, artisans and food vendors. After sleeping well and waking up hungry, Adele took Audrey out for the best breakfast in New Orleans. The Mississippi River, the second largest river in the United States, was to their right as they strolled into town. The architecture became more ornate and beautiful with each passing building as they drew closer to the French Quarter. The sun was bright, and the air was fresh off the water. Audrey wanted to bottle up the lively energy of the city and take it home with her.

They were walking down an open street, closed to through traffic, when Audrey saw a woman standing out from the crowd. She was a tall Native American woman in a suede-fringed jacket, with long, straight black hair. Her skin was a deep bronze, and she had light eyes with the slightest golden glow to them. This tall, beautiful Indian woman seemed to stare into Audrey's soul. Time slowed to a still, and it felt as though they were the only ones walking there for a moment. There was something surreal to the whole encounter. She asked, "Hey, did you see that Indian woman pass by us just now?"

Adele was too busy living in the moment, and when they both looked back to see her, the woman was gone. The encounter hovered in the back of Audrey's mind for the rest of the afternoon. It's not often you make eye contact with a person and you feel x-rayed.

Adele pointed to St. Louis Cathedral, a towering white church with turrets and three round black steeples. It's one of the most famous sites to see in the city, along with what is in front of it. It's a little fenced-in park, with a bronze statue and fountain in the middle of a courtyard. Talented artists set up booths all through Jackson Square, offering paintings to clothing and even fortune telling. They strolled through quickly on their way to breakfast, but Audrey knew this was a place she had to return to. This town was starting to feel like a home away from home. Art was in the lifeblood of this city, and it ran in every color, in all directions. There was no escaping it.   As they reached the end of the square, they came upon the place.

"This is Café Du Monde!" Adele presented. "We are about to have the best beignets you'll ever eat!" Her smile was the biggest smile of the whole trip so far. It made Audrey so happy to see her mother this way. This trip brought out fond memories she had filed away for far too long. The beignets were hot and fresh, delicate and sweet, melt in your mouth, straight from heaven, dusted in powdered sugar. Decadent, light and lovely, makes you glad to be alive, savoring every last bit, but where's the milk to wash this all down?

The sugar high launched the two shopping into the French Market, where everything could be found under the southern sun. There was a distinct smell of the fresh fish market, food vendors, and even alligator on a stick. It looked terribly greasy. Audrey declined that New Orleans delicacy and moved on to look at the jewelry and fun tourist trinkets and things. From the market, they moved on to the French Quarter and looked in every fun little shop they came across. Many of them had warning signs up by the door with a very voodoo vibe, reading, "Shoplifters will be Cursed!" Some even had chicken bones dangling from them. The voodoo and witchcraft items in the store gave a cold chill up Audrey's spine. She got a really bad feeling from all of it. Almost as if spirits were in the shop, watching her look at those things on the shelf. Malevolent spirits, which, if given enough time, would cause trouble. She was right about that. There were spirits there, but Em and Gavri were with her wherever she went. Spirits are no match for the power of angels. This is a battle being waged all our lives, all around us. It is being fought for our very soul, and we are usually blissfully unaware.

Witchcraft has been around forever. History is full of tales of evil witches or innocent women being mistaken for them, being burned at the stake. Witchcraft can be alluring, the idea that a simple mortal might be able to control powers as deities do. They believe their powers come from the earth and the universe, but it doesn't. Their spells do carry power, but that power is given to them, and payment, sacrifice, or blood is expected in return. You can tell that spellcasting comes with a high price when you see how unwell witches eventually look. Prayer is the opposite of spellcasting. It's powerful, it's intention and meditation, but it costs nothing. And often, it can be rejuvenating, healing, and promising. It just depends on where your heart is. I wanted to believe that spellcasters know this deep down and that the romanticism of the darkness eventually fades like a drunken night sours into a bad hangover by morning. I hoped they would find their way to the light.

Audrey and her mother dined on more street fare and wandered back to the hotel. While Adele needed rest, there was something still beckoning Audrey back to the French Quarter. She wrapped herself in a dark green shawl that brought out her eyes and headed straight for Jackson Square, admiring the changes the city took on as the sun moved across the sky, blooming in colors of a ripe peach. There was a shift in the city's energy. This was where she slowed down. She looked at every painting for sale. It was all so inspiring that she wanted to go buy paints that minute and set up her own little table right then and there. The artwork was beautiful, paintings, sketches of the city, sketches of you if you wanted. There was something for everyone.

Jackson Square is named after Andrew Jackson, the seventh president of the United States. Jackson was the first president to be a former prisoner of war, was nearly victim to the first presidential assassination attempt, and though he hated paper money, his face was featured on one of the most widely used bills, the twenty-dollar bill. Quite a unique man with a colorful life, and since he was a gambling man, I might wager that he'd be pleased that this wonderful place bears his name. The square is a nearly three-acre park in the heart of New Orleans in front of St. Louis Cathedral, with a paved perimeter where artisans gather to sell their work and perform a variety of talents.

When Audrey walked to the halfway mark around the square,

she found herself near the doors of the Cathedral. She took a moment to admire the architecture of the famous old church, stepping backward slowly while looking up. Windchimes in the twilight broke her concentration, and in that moment, she turned around and saw her. It was that Indian woman from earlier that morning. She was wearing the same suede brown beaded jacket. She had long, straight black hair and sharp features, with those unmistakable, glowing golden eyes. With an open hand motioning to the empty chair at her table, the woman warmly smiled, "Please, sit."

Audrey could clearly see that the Indian woman had a table set up to read palms and fortunes. She sat down and said hello. The woman placed her palms facing up on the table, an invitation for Audrey to present her hands to be read. Up until that point, Audrey could hear the merchants, artists, and tourists all around her. She could hear street musicians playing famous jazz tunes, wind chimes clinking in the fresh breeze, and distant riverboat horns honking. All that quieted when their hands met. The Indian woman who was giving Audrey the reading was actually Em. Audrey had seen Em walk past her earlier that morning. Em took her hands, quieted the world around them, closed her eyes, and breathed deeply. When her eyes opened, she had answers to give, which hadn't even been asked yet.

"You are a creative. A sensitive." Em's straight face turned to a slight smile, still in contemplation. "You're an empath. Have you ever heard that word before?"

"I don't think so." Audrey shook her head. She looked down at the table, tarot cards neatly stacked. Usually, her palm would be read or she'd be asked to cut the tarot deck while asking it questions she wanted answered, but there was no need for that.

This was a special reading. Most people with these gifts send their questions out into the universe, not knowing who their answers come from. We are warned not to seek the help of fortune tellers for two different reasons. The person charging you for their special insights might be a charlatan, brilliant at reading cues and manipulating people, or their answers could come from a dark source. Sometimes, negative energy is delivered to you, and you give it power over your future and allow it to make decisions. This is a recipe for disaster. In rare cases, the insights come from a good energy source, but how can anyone ever be sure?

"You have a light inside you, and you need to be careful who you share your energy with. Your energy is precious. There are people who will siphon it, deplete it." Em took one of Audrey's hands, pretending to read into it. "You have suffered great loss, but don't let that stop you. It is from the losses that you suffer that you will spin into your greatest strengths." Em took another deep breath. "You lost someone close to you, years ago."

Audrey nodded, knowing not to give psychics too much information.

"He's here with you. He watches over you with your angels." Em smiled in a familiar way.

Audrey drew a heavy breath.

I was standing by the table, listening to the whole thing. I was shouting things I wanted Em to tell her. I was screaming it at the top of my lungs. "Tell her I love her, Em!" The intensity of the moment was building, and we could all feel it. "Tell her I'm sorry. Tell her she's never alone." Pressure rising inside of me, I couldn't contain myself. This was my chance to tell her everything. We were so close. "Tell her about the music I send her. Tell her about the signs!" I paced, my hands running through my hair. "Tell her the dreams, our dreams are real, Em. Tell her!"

"Your angels are always with you too. We are—they're always happy to help you. All you have to do is ask." Em was trying to reassure an increasingly emotional Audrey.

Em was taking long, deep breaths, trying to listen to me and focus on what to say to Audrey without scaring the poor girl, but I was losing my patience. "He has some things to tell you. He wants to tell you that you feel alone, but you're not. He wants me to tell you that he's keeping his promise."

In that instant, Em and I watched as peach blossoms sparked and bloomed all around her, dazzling us. Our mouths dropped in spectacular surprise, but to Audrey, all it felt like was a dynamic chill up her spine.

Tears flooded Audrey's eyes. She wasn't expecting a message from me, Josh, the Wonderful Pal of Her Dreams. I was still shouting at Em. I had this moment to tell Audrey things that had been building up for years. "Em, please tell her I love her. Dammit, Em, if you don't tell her, I'm flipping the table! Tell her!"

I lost it. I flipped the table. I screamed and smashed anything and everything around me, but to the living, it was only a strong gust of wind from a strange direction. Their table didn't flip, but the wind blew their hair all around, and the stack of tarot cards caught the wind and went flying in all directions. The gust of wind seemed to only affect the two of them as they sat there holding hands.

"That was him," Em said with eyes wide, laughing. "He has so much to say to you."

"Really? Tell me. Please." Audrey laughed through her tears, mesmerized at the thought of me being so close to her. It was thrilling and wonderful. She took a moment to look around, as if to see me standing there. If only she could see me.

"Look for the signs. The songs, the lights. He visits you in your dreams. If you clear your mind, you can visit him too." Em tightened her grip on Audrey's hands. "He said that he's sorry for how things turned out. You two…are destined. But just remember he's watching over you. He loves you, Audrey. He always has and always will."

"Always." Audrey breathlessly whispered as the dam broke, and tears finally streamed down her cheeks.

Audrey sat quietly as her mind raced over all the things she'd dismissed as a silly coincidence, her wild imagination, peculiar events that could be explained away. Message received, finally. And I knelt beside her, watching her through tears of my own, smiling, as she searched the air around her for the slightest glimpse of me. I moved my fingers through her wind-blown hair and kissed her hand, Em watching us.

Em stood to her feet and hugged Audrey as tightly as she could. Em loves her too. She had been wanting to hug her every day, but today was the day Audrey would actually feel Em's arms around her. Audrey noticed how familiar the hug seemed to feel, as if hugging a dear friend for the umpteenth time. She tried to pay Em for the most unforgettable reading, a reading that would change her life forever, but Em refused to take her money. "You're surrounded by so much love. It's easy to feel alone in this world, but you have love all around you, and you have so much love within you. You are blessed beyond measure, young lady."

"Thank you for everything. This has been truly amazing," Audrey said, wiping the tears from her cheek, dimples as she smiled. Audrey put her hands on her cheeks, so moved by the magical day and all its revelations. She stood still, allowing the words to sink in while she watched Em wave goodbye and disappear into the crowd. She never saw that beautiful Indian woman again, but the memory of that evening has never left her.

Audrey rested her weary head on her pillow, her mind reexamining every word from her reading. She remembered the dedication on the radio that summer day, from Josh to his dream girl. With a smile and her hand on her heart, she finally accepted the truth, that it really was from me. Memories of when that song, "The Promise," would come on the radio at the perfect moment—she realized that those were my doing. And all those dreams, of my arms around her, were real. She closed her eyes and drifted into my arms again. I played her the perfect song for a mystical French Quarter evening with me, called "Haunt Me."

We met in a courtyard of our very own, lit by the radiant moon and soft twinkling lights, surrounded by bricks, wrought iron, and the sweet smell of climbing roses. As each step brought us closer, our gaze locked, and with it came an understanding. The expression on our faces matched, and our hearts were overwhelmed by the realization that this was it. The connection we both dreamed of. Our embrace, tighter. Sparks flew from the contact of our skin, our eyes telling the story of our deepest secrets and timeless love. It's all in the eyes, isn't it? Her eyes told me that she knew now. The longing, the devotion, and the flood of emotion captured in the moments of a kiss. Whether her waking self allowed her to believe it or not, deep down, she knew I'd been this close to her, all this time. My heart begged, "Please remember."

The next day, Adele and Audrey enjoyed more shopping in the

French Quarter and the French Market, working up an appetite for a big plate of creole seafood. The food was spicy and aromatic, but the waiter was terribly rude. He rushed them every chance he got, messed up their orders, and even smelled of alcohol. The tip Adele left the waiter reflected his poor performance. Moments later, down the street, they found a horse and buggy to take them around town in. As they were about to take off in the buggy, the waiter stopped them in the street and threw Adele's tip back at her. He croaked in his gravelly voice, "You obviously need this more than I do."

Adele was shocked at the nerve of this man, yelling, "You didn't deserve it!" The man acted like he didn't hear her, and he did a little dance as he scurried back to work.

"Mom, that's the weird clown grifter who took my money!" Audrey pointed. They erupted in laughter. They laughed at that clown all through the old streets. On their way through town, they pointed at the House of the Rising Sun and the other landmarks, always returning to laughter at their surreal, spooky, and fun time here in New Orleans. Audrey would never forget the supernatural encounters she'd felt while visiting the city, imagining this city's veil to the other side being a bit thinner than anywhere else. I happened to know that she was right. An old city so drenched in history has a veil worn thin. The rest of their trip took them into Mississippi to visit family, and a wonderful visit it was, but even on their flight home, they could still be heard laughing. Was it the charm of that old moonlit city that brought Adele and Audrey closer, even if it was only for a short time? Was it the thin veil that brought Audrey and me closer together than ever before, or was it this miraculous time of year that surrounds Audrey so lovingly, that she calls the Season of Angels? Whatever it was, Audrey wore a slight smile from that mystical evening in Jackson Square. The kind of smile one has when they carry a wonderful secret in their heart.

Audrey was placing her new arrangements on the display shelves at work when she saw a very old, little Asian lady needing help. She was having trouble getting around in her wheelchair, being cut off by holiday shoppers who just didn't see her there. Audrey asked the lady if she could help her find anything on her shopping list. The lady was relieved to have some help, so Audrey took her around the store and retrieved the items she needed, all the while talking to the little lady about her day and holiday plans. She was all alone and had a transit bus drop her off. She wanted to get some decorations for her room at the nursing home, where she lived alone. This sweet little old lady was all alone, and she had no one to take her shopping at the end of her days. As Audrey pushed her chair, she became heartsick for her. In the few moments that Audrey had control of her chair, she was going to help her anyway she could. Audrey pushed her chair swiftly and heard the little lady make a gleeful sound. This made them both laugh. She told the lady to make sure her feet were off the ground and to hang on, 'cause this ride was about to go faster. Audrey raced the little lady down the aisles, hearing her laugh probably louder than she had in years. They went down aisles, nearly smashing into people, slowed down around store managers, and then sped up again when the path was clear. It was nothing but big laughs from both of them. Then the time came when the little lady wanted to use the restroom before her ride back home, so in the meantime, Audrey called the transit to pick her back up. While she was waiting on the lady, Audrey put a twenty-five-dollar Michaels gift card in her shopping bags, with a card that thanked her for today, hoping to see her again and wishing her a very Merry Christmas.

Audrey was called away to do other things, still being on the clock and having to work, so she never got to say goodbye to the sweet little lady with whom she had such a fun time. She never saw her again after that day. Audrey hoped that she was able to spend her gift card on something special and that she had a wonderful Christmas. A verse came to mind: "Do not forget to show hospitality to strangers, for by so doing some people have shown hospitality to angels without knowing it" (Hebrews 13:2). She prayed for the little lady, that if she wasn't an angel, then she would have angels entertaining her, so she wouldn't be all alone at Christmas. This was, after all, the Season of Angels.

I got to see the little lady open her card. She was moved to tears, and her heart was touched by the generosity of a kind stranger. She never forgot Audrey and the fun they had. The little lady didn't come back into the store because she'd bought all that she needed. She gave the gift card to her friend in the nursing home who didn't have any money. Her friend took the same transit and was able to buy her granddaughter, the budding artist, a bunch of art supplies for Christmas.

Audrey felt closer to her angels than ever before, and one afternoon, she got the perfect idea what to decorate her tree with. It was so obvious. She bought all the angel wing ornaments in the store, and every year after that, her tree was so full of wings that it could take flight. We helped her decorate it every year. With all her favorite Christmas songs blaring, Audrey danced around, decking the halls with glittering angel wings, surrounded by cats climbing in the tree, most definitely entertaining her angels.

The best bridge between despair and hope is a good night's sleep.

—E. Joseph Cossman

Chapter Fifteen

So much happens to us when we are peacefully sleeping. You will learn that when you cross over. The living sink into a peaceful dream, and that is when angels, your subconscious, and even the Creator Himself speak to you. It is in dreams that you receive healing. In dreams, you can travel to far-off lands and explore other lives. You can contact the dead, or the dead can contact you.

It was in one of Audrey's dreams that I saw the Creator reveal something very special to her. We each have a home prepared for us beyond the veil. Audrey was shown her home, and I was honored to be her guide. On the other side, when she is called home, she has a cottage by the sea waiting for her. It is a cottage in every sense of the word, reminiscent of those dreamy homes that make Carmel-by-the-Sea so famous. It was cute and quaint, gardens and fountains, giant ripe tomatoes and thick winding jasmine vines, and, of course, peach trees blossoming. Rose bushes blooming in her presence, and the ocean roaring in the shimmering topaz blue down below. Horses appeared from behind the greenery to greet her in the courtyard. They were all her old friends. Mugs, the tall old quarter horse that was in many ways her babysitter; Pumpkin, the orange Appaloosa with so much love to give; and Rabbit's Dance, the lively little one that no one wanted because of its size. Audrey loved that little red mare, being the perfect size for a lonely little girl. It was a precious reunion. Then the dogs and cats ran out to greet her. Sam and the Rottweilers that loved and protected her all those years leaped into the air, yelping gleefully with kisses. There was Bednight, the fluffy black and white kitty whom I'd gotten to meet all those years ago. They all rushed to see Audrey, knowing that this visit was only for a moment. There was another black kitty that came to greet her. It ran up and weaved between her feet until she picked it up. I realized I'd seen this cat before.

Audrey woke from the dream with a rapping on her window. It was a tap tap tap that kept repeating every few seconds. She got out of bed and moved the white sheer curtain to see a mockingbird flee from the window. A mockingbird has distinct markings, a brown body with large white patches on the underside of its wings. It's a larger bird, so it made quite the racket.

Birds, like angels, are messengers. Birds have another reason for appearing on your windowsill, and it's not the sign you want to see. Birds can usher souls into the afterlife. I knew that this was the reason the mockingbird was knocking on Audrey's windows. He begins with a few taps, and by the time the end is near, the bird is practically breaking the glass to get in. It is best to leave the windows cracked, but it was the dead of winter, and Ethan and Audrey weren't ready for what was coming.

After a day trip into the mountains near Sonora, Columbia, and Jamestown, they returned to an extremely sick Romeo. He had had a grand mal seizure while they were away. He was still sleeping in the same spot they had left him, on her tan wingback chair with poppies on it, but he wasn't the same at all. When he woke, he roamed the house relentlessly searching for something, wandering aimlessly, never resting. He wouldn't eat or drink. The vet had grim news and told them they should think about putting Romeo down. They could never bring themselves to make that decision. He was still alive and possibly had a fighting chance. But time had passed, and his condition worsened. Ethan held him all through the night as he cried and squirmed to free himself until he tired and fell asleep. Ethan and Audrey were able to claim a few moments of rest here and there, but Romeo was an aimless vessel at this point. He was bumping into things and harming himself while trying to get past the barriers that they'd put up. His whole body was starting to shut down while Ethan got the news that he had to leave for a military obligation. Ethan left at 3:00 a.m., and Audrey found herself alone and helpless. All she could do was pray as hard as she could for her baby, though it seemed no amount of prayers could help him now.

All the memories of the helplessness she felt when she watched her grandpa pass away came rushing back, and it was too much to take. She lay by Romeo for hours, and by mid-morning, he was showing signs of succumbing to the seizure. "It's okay, baby. If it's your time to go, you can let go now. I love you. I love you, baby. I love you." Her face, neck, and clothes were soaked with tears. There under that big iron cross in their sanctuary, she lay on the floor with Romeo. The prayers she prayed could've raised the dead that day, but nothing changes the direction of those wild winds. She was there when he drew his last breath.

She sometimes wondered how she would feel at that moment, trying to prepare herself for that inevitable day somewhere in the future. She thought she'd be an inconsolable mess, but an intense and inexplicable feeling of gratitude overwhelmed her. She thanked God for the opportunity they both had, to love Romeo all the days of his life, since he was such a true blessing. I watched his spirit leave his body and join the mockingbird who was sent for him. The sight was truly beautiful, of light and music and freedom from the stronghold of illness that had silently plagued him for years, but for Audrey, she had just lost her baby, and the air was still, like a void of oxygen, and life, and hope. She'd lost a great love in her life, again. With her heart in pieces, she picked up her Romeo and placed him in his favorite bed, curled him up as he usually looked when sleeping, and then called Ethan to break the news.

Ethan was able to be excused for this tragic event, so he returned home on this intensely windy day. In his military uniform, he stoically carried his Romeo, the little kitten he'd found all those years ago, to the vet's office for cremation. Audrey had known Ethan for thirteen years and never seen him cry until that night. They poured shots of chilled tequila in his honor, remembering his little quirks and their favorite memories. They laughed through their tears and wounded hearts. There in the kitchen, they sank to the floor and lay on the big rug, sobbing together for hours, for as long as it took.

Romeo had been a ragdoll kitty. He was so trusting when Ethan and Audrey picked him up, he would completely relax and let them hold him however they wanted. Audrey and Romeo were often found dancing in the kitchen and snuggling in her wingback chair. He would dart under their feet when they were trying to eat something off the coffee table, seeming to use his tail as a food detector. He was a shoulder cat to Audrey. She always thought that if she were a pirate, he'd be her parrot. If she ever bent over to pick something off the ground, he would jump on her back, and that would always startle her into laughter. He'd loved fiercely and truly, living up to his namesake. Doing everything I asked of him. There were times she still felt him on her shoulders, caressing her face.

Her Romeo was still with her. He remained with her, slept on her pillow, and never left her side until it was his time to go to that home Audrey had waiting for her in the hereafter. There were times she'd be at work, making arrangements, when certain gifted individuals walked by. They could see the fluffy black cat balancing on her shoulders. Audrey wondered why these people gave her strange looks, but I knew why. I kept Romeo company during his wait. He had a reason to hang around, just as I did.

Audrey thought that she and Ethan had turned a corner in their relationship. She was desperate for signs of a deeper connection from him, and for a little while after Romeo's passing, they had it, but it was fleeting. People handle grief differently. They either feel everything all at once, or they put it away and feel nothing at all. Ethan chose to feel nothing and to go somewhere far away to ensure that. Without notice to Audrey, Ethan signed up for a year-long deployment in Iraq. The news came as a blow to her. She felt abandoned. Betrayed even, but there was nothing she could do but watch him pack his things and prepare to leave. They fought about his decision, which only pushed him further away from her. He left on uncertain, hopeless terms. All happening so fast, she dropped him off at his base, hugged him goodbye, and came home. She was facing her worst fears, being all alone.

She had a few friends in town, but none of them were close

enough to turn to. She was drowning in feelings of stress, grief, and fear. Emotions can act as a poison in the body. If they aren't released, they find a home in flesh, making it sick, and this was happening to Audrey. Her stomach was raw and ached anytime she ate or drank anything. Her back ached from the stress she carried from a precarious future. She had such awful headaches and dizziness that sometimes she had to pull off to the side of the road if she was driving. She felt at times she was about to pass out. Something had to be done about this, though none of her doctors had answers. She saw an antiquated doctor in her small town who tried to put every female patient of a certain age on antidepressants. Audrey refused. Sure, she was in a full-blown depression. But Audrey never looked at depression the same way as doctors did. Doctors seem to want to label a person with depression, as if it's a life sentence. Audrey watched doctors label her mother and sister with depression and give them pills and more pills, which only sedated them and curbed their zest for life. Depression isn't a lifelong affliction. It's like the tide. It comes and goes, but it will never leave a patient who is labeled and prescribed life-dulling, addictive medication.

Very late at night, when she couldn't sleep, Audrey sat up in her bed and started looking through her phone for a holistic doctor. She thought maybe they might have answers that these Big Pharma ones could not provide. That's when Em stepped in. Em whispered to her in her comforting way, "Why don't YOU learn holistic medicine and heal yourself?"

Audrey contemplated the idea for a moment. She'd always loved the old ways of healing her grandma had introduced her to. The herbs, the natural tonics, and salves instead of a foul-tasting pill. She remembered the map of the feet, the pressure points of reflexology, which her grandma had shown her when she was young. Old medicine, she'd called it. These old ways had a slow, comforting, natural way of healing, which slowed time and allowed the body and mind to rest while recovering. But there was that negative whisper again: You're not going to become a holistic doctor. Why do you think you need to learn all this at some school? This is a silly idea.

Still, she researched schools online and found one in the next town over. She kept the phone number in her pocket and heard Em's encouragement grow louder throughout the day, "You should call the school. Make an appointment." A battle of whispers raged in her mind all day at work, but by 3 P.M., Audrey finally gave in and made the call. She talked to the school director, June, a lovely woman who happily set a time for them to meet the next afternoon.

That evening, she sat in her poppy chair, with a glass of red wine and Roxy curled up in her lap. She tried to read the book about angels in her hand, but her mind was too busy with possibilities and the wild winds in crescendo.

A storm had blown in while she slept. She sipped warm chamomile lavender tea that morning, watching the downpour through the

French doors in her living room. The rain was battering her garden. Audrey was nervous about the meeting and the drive to get there, and there was that negative whisper: Guess you'll have to cancel your meeting then. You can't drive in this. With Em's reassurance, she drove into the small school's parking lot in Oakdale, California, admiring the peach-colored building and cream-colored trim. Tall and unique, the building had character for being in a cowboy town. It looked much more suited to be somewhere in Miami. Audrey pulled into the parking space closest to the door. It was pouring straight down. The lot was empty, as there was no school in session that day. She waited there for quite some time. A white SUV finally pulled in and parked a few stalls away from her. She was greeted by June, a tall red red-haired woman in her sixties, elegantly dressed in her own bohemian style. Her hubris was one that filled the whole building. This was probably something that rubbed unhealed people the wrong way, but Audrey felt drawn to her. She was a healer and teacher. She was most definitely a lightworker and empath, the same as Audrey was. June drove an hour through the torrential downpour to get to the meeting, then spent the entire afternoon with Audrey, sitting in her office, explaining the classes and talking about their gifts. Audrey drank in the information; she was learning from a kindred spirit, and she felt home. The things she was learning that day just seemed to resonate on a frequency of truth with her. She felt a familiarity with it all, in some strange way, so she signed up for the holistic medicine and massage courses. It was a big step to take when the path was still so uncertain.

June had been about to reschedule the meeting over the weather, but her angels had a clear message for her. "This girl needs to be in your class. Keep the appointment, however you can." June braved the elements and, in the meeting, realized why her angels were so adamant about her going that day. June saw far deeper than the nicely dressed and smiling exterior. She could see a very sick girl, a lost and lonely girl in desperate spiritual need. If there was ever a student to benefit from her school, it was Audrey. June could see the pain and loss, even the rejection that had settled in Audrey's body. She knew that when emotions did this, holistic medicine was the only way. No medical doctor treats the soul when it is wounded. You cannot print this in a textbook and test it. And you cannot make a pill that heals the soul, or the pharmaceutical companies would be trillions richer.

Healing the soul is old medicine. It's passed down through centuries by lightworkers, the awakened and intuitive beings. The only students who have a true calling to June's little school were lightworkers. Most of them didn't know it yet. That was the beauty of the school, putting a bunch of wounded empaths through a crash course of healing themselves and healing the world around them.

It was the first day of school, and nerves were high, making Audrey feel dizzy. She got to the classroom early and sat in the back row of tables set up in a large room. The lights were off, allowing natural sunlight to filter in through narrow windows that lined the east side of the building. One by one, students arrived and found their seats. It was about twenty women and one man who sat up at the front. June was late, giving the students time to get acquainted and settled.

Nerves were getting the best of all of them. Lightning flashed across the sky outside as the only lights that were on toward the farthest entryway flickered. That was what happened when you put a bunch of nervous empaths together. Electronics shorted out, weather shifted, electromagnetic fields clashed. Amid all the chaos beginning to happen, June walked into the classroom with her commanding and calming presence. It was her job that day to put everyone at ease. June, an old soul empath, absorbed the negative energy of the room within the hour, clearing it of chaos.

Her students were intrigued and laughing. Audrey felt the weight of her purpose being there. She heard a message from her angels saying, "No matter how sick you feel, just get to class and you will start healing." There were days when Audrey needed to stay in bed, her body was in pain, her head was spinning, but she made it to her seat in the center of the back row each day. One day, she wrote in her notebook, "I had to drag myself to school today. I was horribly sick, but I knew I needed to be attuned. That happened in the first half of class. I felt the vibration of June's hand. It made Reiki real for the first time. I felt so much better. Not right away, but in about ten minutes—no more dizziness. Not sick anymore."

June taught Reiki, the first phase of courses, all by design. There were six students who just couldn't understand energy work. It was of a deeply spiritual nature, and for those who hadn't decided to take the long journey inward, it could be too overwhelming. These students left them with a much smaller, close-knit class. June was a Reiki master teacher, having gone through all the levels of Reiki learning. When the class began, each student received an attunement in a prayer ceremony. They all sat around in a circle while June walked behind each of them. She placed her hands on their shoulders to connect, then a gentle hand was placed on the top of their head, and a series of Reiki prayers was offered over them. All heads were bowed, and eyes were closed. The class couldn't watch her perform the attunement, but I did.

As the students bowed their heads and closed their eyes, June was in the corner of the room, praying and engaging her hands. In Reiki, your hands are fine instruments, and during the course of a session, it would look as if your hand is grasping a large, clear, illuminated bubble. This is a form of healing of the hands. We had all heard of it but must have wondered if it really existed. It does. This particular way of healing that June taught had been passed down from a Japanese master, who had received not only tremendous healing from his own angel, but was given the knowledge of how to help heal others. Dr. Mikao Usui's angel helped him remember something we all know how to do, that our Creator instilled in us all, but have long forgotten.

Each student received three of these attunements. The attunement itself is a process of harnessing the flow of sacred energy, the chi. We were all born into this life with a silver cord that connects us to our Creator through the top of our heads. In a way, we are astronauts, out exploring a dangerous space, all the while tethered to the mothership. Within that silver cord is that flow of chi, the lifeforce, energy, communication from our Creator, wisdom, knowledge, enlightenment. Reiki masters are each attuned so that the silver cord is widened each time. By their final attunement, the flow of energy is a powerful force. Just by June's simple act of placing her activated hands on Audrey's shoulders in the quiet of that prayer, Audrey's sickness started healing that day. Audrey had felt so dizzy as it all began that she'd gripped the sides of her chair, feeling like she might fall onto the floor. The healing energy flowed from June's hands and concentrated in the areas Audrey needed it most. Her body drank the energy in.

Reiki is a flow of healing energy from one person to another. The healing energy flows from the Source, through the healer and into those needing healing. Can a person be healed through prayer alone? Sure. Sometimes our Creator sends healers out into the world to reach people who need more. The students were beginning their own Reiki treatments on one another. In their large classroom, they had several massage tables set up, draped in sheets, and soft meditation music playing. The room was dark, but I could see their hands activate, and lights, once dim, grew brighter. I stood in the lustrous light of their hands, experiencing one of life's miracles, wishing they could see it all as I did.

Before Reiki or any therapy begins, the Master must ground. That is a process of protecting your energy from transferring to another person or their energy transferring to you. Audrey's process of grounding was so visual, visceral. Grounding is imagining yourself growing deep roots that run down into the earth to keep your energy from drifting. Audrey always imagined that, wherever she sat, she still fell through the floorboards, all the way to the earth, and that's when she sat as if meditating and let the roots flow from her, deep into the ground. They grew until they came to a place in the earth that was an opening with giant geodes and amethyst crystals growing alongside massive tree roots, tethering herself to them. Audrey took the long journey inward and, ever since then, had been growing a garden inside. It's no wonder that she would have a magical place to ground such as this.

Audrey prayed over her hands that day, activating them in an ice blue glow, asking her Creator to guide her. That was all she needed to do. Reiki, or the healing of hands, is intuitive. As she connected with her fellow student lying supine on the table, she took a series of deep breaths while her hands lay gently on their shoulders. She slowly moved her hands, hovering slightly above their body, and even through their clothing, she could feel a strange sensation in her hands as they crossed over certain areas of the body. It felt like her hands were on the end of a vacuum cleaner hose, feeling a more subtle draw of energy. It was in those areas that the student later revealed they needed the most healing. Their body was siphoning the energy as fast as it could from Audrey's hands. That was the first moment she truly felt like a healer. At home, during meditation, she used her healing hands on her neck and back and stomach, where she felt most pain. Even her heart. She was noticing her pain subsiding.

The next course was reflexology. The entire body is mapped out on our ears, hands and feet. If you press on the map where you need healing, your body will benefit. Our feet need so much love and attention for all the work they do for us. When reflexology is performed, if it's done well, most recipients fall asleep, but the healing gained from this is similar to that of an entire night's rest. It's one of the most relaxing therapies and also one of the most ignored. Most people think they need to get a deep tissue massage to feel better. That's just not the case. Audrey came into this class feeling ill, a blank slate for this holistic medicine to work on. She got to experience each therapy and felt the healing effects of each one differently.

Her reflexology teacher was a short woman with big blond curls, maybe a bit older than June. She was a little Southern firecracker. This little lady reminded Audrey of Dolly Parton with her effervescent, positive attitude. Audrey thought of her as an Earth

Angel who cracked jokes and had little code words for anatomy. "When working on someone's foot, you'll come across those crunchies. They are little crystals that we develop in our feet, like stagnant energy or chi. So you just gotta get in there and work them crunchies out. And be careful to work on the colon clockwise, otherwise your client won't be able to poop for a week." She giggled. "Oh, and another thing, don't even go near the back of the ankle on pregnant women. Unless they are begging you to send them into labor. Just don't even go back there. You just gotta be real careful with them pregnant women."

Her teacher really liked Audrey as most of her teachers did. June and her instructor pointed to Audrey while she performed reflexology on another student. Audrey sat with her eyes closed, allowing her sense of touch to sharpen. On the last day of reflexology class, during the final exam, Audrey was not feeling well and got off on the wrong foot. She literally began the reflexology therapy on the wrong foot, starting with the person's left foot instead of their right. The teacher saw what she was doing and ever so quietly pointed to the correct foot. Audrey's eyes grew wide, her expression that of failure and embarrassment, but her teacher nonchalantly put her finger up to her lips and winked at her. No one knew what had happened, and it really didn't matter. Audrey completed the course and was sad to see her lovely teacher go.

The next teacher was a short, thin woman with a bob cut and

light brown hair. When she wasn't instructing the class on cranial sacral therapy, she was quiet and kept to herself. It was a far cry from the personality of her last teacher. But this was an important therapy, and the focus was on just that. It is a tension and pain-relieving therapy that boosts one's immune system. It is very gentle and relaxing and, if performed accurately, examines the flow of fluids in and around the central nervous system. It tends to the blockages in the body to restore the flow of fluid, chi, and restore balance.

Audrey paired up with a student who was having a tough time in class. In the first week of school, this student never spoke to anyone. She avoided conversation, kept her head down, and tuned out. The second week of school, there were no tables put up. The students could just grab a blanket and pillow from the closet and find a comfortable spot on the floor to learn from. Sitting in the back of the classroom put her near Sylvia, where she was able to start up a conversation with her. After a while, Audrey was able to learn that she had recently become a widow. Her husband had, nearly a year ago, had an asthma attack in their kitchen and passed away. She had returned from a trip out of town to find emergency vehicles and crew at her home, informing her of the terrible news. It wasn't only the fact that he died so suddenly that brought her so much pain; it was also the fact that they had a tremendous amount of unfinished business to take care of in their relationship. They'd left things in a fight. He'd been a conservative Christian while she a wild, tatted-up hippie who didn't believe in God or the afterlife. She was a cynic, but Audrey couldn't tell if she had always been a cynic or if losing her husband caused her to be. Her regret about their fights, constant arguing about how they should raise their children, their differences, how they'd left things—it was all crushing her. She, like Audrey, was learning to live on her own.

Audrey and Sylvia had a few things in common. The biggest things were that they were both in mourning for the loss of a loved one. Sylvia was mourning her husband, and Audrey was in mourning over someone still living. Ethan was alive, they were still married, but he was very much a ghost in her life, haunting her with memories of how things used to be but may never be again. He was a ghost who was living in her home with her, in the same room, but never close enough to touch. It was in that loneliness that Audrey could empathize with Sylvia. She was able to get Sylvia talking, voicing her frustrations to a friend, and it was helping.

Energy transfer is real. Audrey was performing cranial sacral therapy on Sylvia one day when she forgot to ground. She didn't protect her energy, so when the session was over, Sylvia went home in the best mood she'd felt in years. Audrey, on the other hand, went home screaming at the other drivers on the road, angry. She felt so miserable and sad. It was so unlike Audrey to be feeling that way, to that extent, and she was stunned to realize that those weren't her emotions. They were Sylvia's. In cases like that where energy transfers, June taught them to ask their angels to transmute the energy from bad to good. From negative to positive. If angels are helping in the healing process, they can heal the healer.

Knowing how important energy is and how easily it transfers, one must take that into consideration when choosing a massage therapist or any service that requires touch. Unless you always remember to ground before contact, consider the energy they give off and if you want that energy to blend with yours.

All the students were quirky and different, though all were there for a reason. There was Renee, who was a single mom, a recovering narcotics abuser, though eager to acquire tools to build a new life. This was her one chance to change her life for the better, and she made the most of it. There was Michelle, the tall Aussie. She was married, and her daughter was in high school. She'd worked for a chiropractic and physical therapy office for years, wanting to make a change and broaden her education. The class loved her accent, and whenever there was a time for something to be read out loud, Michelle's name was always volunteered. Audrey and Michelle became good friends. They were both tall, observing, genuine old souls who seemed to understand each other. Maybe that's what happened to people who had taken the long journey inward: they recognize each other from within. Namaste.

There was Ricki, a sweet girl trapped in a terribly overweight body. She refused to let anyone try any therapies on her, but she was an outstanding therapist. She had suffered a great deal of trauma in her life, which had caused her to retreat into her own body and build boundaries of flesh. She was confused about life, her sexual orientation, confused about her political and spiritual perspectives. She gravitated to Audrey and talked to her for hours. Audrey was a great listener and comic relief. To each one of the girls, they all got a side of Audrey and the friendship that they needed. It was amazing to see how each of the women transformed and healed in this class.

It was time for the class to learn deep tissue massage, which was taught by a tall, warm, lovely woman, about the same age as June, with short red hair and glasses that reminded Audrey of the 1950s. Audrey called her Miss Susan. A delight to learn from, funny, informative, and sweet. The class adored her. In the mornings, the class would study anatomy, sitting at the tables and coloring the nerves, ligaments, muscles, and bones with colored pencils. Everyone just filled theirs in with one blot of color, but Audrey, the artist, used several colors and values. It was just in her nature, finally, something right-brained where she could excel. All these girls were taking the massage courses to become massage therapists, but that wasn't Audrey's goal. Would she love to open a spa someday and paint the interior of it full of murals? Yes, but her focus was more on holistic medicine and healing herself first.

Deep tissue massage involves performing a therapy on another person's naked body while artfully maneuvering around the sheet that is covering them. Audrey was removed from this. She just didn't have her heart into it. All these students went home and practiced on their family and friends, husbands or boyfriends. Audrey didn't have anyone to practice on, so her technique stalled. Renee, the outspoken sober mom, was Audrey's partner one day. Audrey really was trying her best, but Renee yelled at her during the session in a silent classroom full of students. Audrey was humiliated. A week later, the same thing happened again. A rift had been growing between the two for quite some time, but this put it over the edge. It caused Audrey to want to quit the class. Miss Susan kept a close watch on the whole thing. She made it a habit to hug every student before they left class, at the end of the day. She knew they were all in a spiritual setting, doing spiritual work, and fighting spiritual battles. Behind Miss Susan's 50s-style glasses and warm smile, she carried the weight of loss and pain, hidden well from most, but Audrey could see it. Her pain aside, she knew which students needed her the most and cared for them, as angels do. Miss Susan's compelling hugs were the only thing that kept Audrey going. It was hugs from her teachers and friends in class that helped her get through Ethan's deployment and being so alone. God bless those teachers who inspire us, challenge us to reach new heights, and offer us kind words and understanding. I believe strength isn't measured by what we can bench press, but rather, it is measured by the amount of pain we can carry while lovingly lightening the load of others. That's what Miss Susan did. Miss Susan's hugs and encouraging words gave Audrey the strength to see it all through. It was amazing what one hug can do.

Shiatsu was different. Having had back pain all her life, Audrey was able to learn from each therapy. Most of them just seemed to offer a physical relief of the pain for a few hours. Shiatsu was an ancient Chinese practice; it wasn't as relaxing as deep tissue massage, and there was probably no way that a person could fall asleep during its application, but it worked for Audrey. Her back pain was relieved for days, maybe even weeks. The belief behind shiatsu is that a constant flow of energy, chi, sweeps through our bodies like a river, as long as we are living. Because we have stress, follow poor diets, or hold onto emotional baggage, sometimes our bodies develop blockages, and the flow of chi is disrupted. In this disruption, pain and physical issues begin to grow and worsen. Shiatsu, performed correctly, will restore the flow of chi, mentally and physically, while stretching the body, applying pressure to certain points, and moving it in ways that it hasn't been moved in a long time. These are all good things, and your body will thank you for it, but the next morning, your muscles might be sore, as if you worked out vigorously. When that fades, you're left with more flexibility and less pain. Sadly, most people just don't know enough about shiatsu and opt for the more popular therapies.

The class taught holistic medicine and massage therapy, and while that is what was on the curriculum, Audrey and the class learned so much more beyond what they paid for. Throughout the time in class, she was instructed by nothing short of Earth Angels. Healers awaken your own healing spirit that has been lulled asleep by the spells of the world. Her instructors were all so gifted and compassionate, assuming duties far beyond the call of an instructor. These women who taught at this little school, in the small town of Oakdale, California, were saving the world, one small class at a time. Audrey was healed by the time the class was over. She was healthier in mind, body, and spirit than she had been in years, possibly ever.

She had finally made connections with like-minded people. She was able to take baby steps, changing her diet slowly. Removing the unnecessary and unhealthy. Replacing the unnatural with the wholesome natural gifts of the earth. Holistic medicine is about what you absorb, from the food you eat to the deodorant you use, to even the television you watch. Some music is even set to a frequency to subconsciously upset you, though there are frequencies you can listen to that have healing effects for every aspect of your body and mind. Holistic medicine is about removing the bad and adding the good. Remove the toxins in your life, even if they are people. It's the steps we take to find and maintain a balance.

While attending the class, it was a learning experience on many levels. A crash course in healing methods of the world. She learned more about empaths. Unfortunately, empaths don't attract whole people. The people who are drawn to empaths are wounded and broken, finding themselves in a time trapped in darkness, searching for healing light. It's empowering knowing that. Being prepared for it. It caused her to view the people who came into and went out of her life with a new perspective. She used to think the people were in her life for a fleeting time, as they didn't care enough to stay. But perhaps there was a different reason altogether, a meaning to the temporary. To heal themselves, and once they were, they were free to continue on with their journey.

She learned how important her energy was and why she had to protect it. She was no longer just an empath. She was a healed and empowered empath. Even beyond that, I watched as Wohpe visited her in a dream, whispering the word "Heyoka." When Audrey woke, she researched this word she had never heard before. Heyoka, according to legend, is a lone wolf of a soul, never being the center of attention, though healing, playful, and humorous in ways that help people see life from a fresh perspective. They are different from most; they do strange things, and their ways are contrary to the ways of society because fitting in would not be honest to who they truly are. They are reclusive beings who feel tremendous sadness for the earth but are the most powerful of all empaths, and they only know they are heyoka when called upon. It is only when you truly know who you are, understand why you are the way you are, and accept these things that you can fulfill your purpose.

The word heyoka gave me perspective on Audrey, a broader understanding. She seemed to be suspended in a spiritual realm closer to the veil than most. This was evident only in conversations or workdays where she interacted as normal humans do, but mostly, the heyoka walks between worlds. Deep calls to the deep. She never shied away from tough conversations or topics that exposed deep wounds. It was just in her nature to feel things so deeply, but in doing so, the beauty and kindness and wonders of the world appeared far brighter and meant more. And when most people looked over those things as common, she saw them for what they really are, a windfall of blessings, a stream of favor and grace, everyday miracles. Yugen.

Acceptance. A powerful word if one can achieve it. Audrey's journey within demanded it. Most people make long lists of their New Year's resolutions, but Audrey only made one, and it didn't have to be the new year to do it. She resolved to look in the mirror without judgment. It seemed easy, but it wasn't. We don't realize how hard we are on ourselves. There's not a soul walking the planet today who is perfection. We all have flaws, but Audrey's resolution forced her to look in the mirror at herself with love. She no longer entertained those negative thoughts and whispers about her appearance. What purpose did they serve anyway? By accepting her reflection, by accepting herself, her whole thought process changed. It's not only when we stand in front of a mirror that we are hard on ourselves. Negative thoughts haunt us throughout the day. Gaining control over the negative thought process was a huge turning point for Audrey. She was never the same after that. How can we expect real healing unless we accept and love ourselves entirely?

I found this time in Audrey's life to be fascinating. I watched this transformation from "worldly beautiful" to "spiritually beautiful." The world holds ridiculous expectations for women to be considered beautiful, and the more I watched Audrey change, the less she fit into them. In fact, it was almost a rebellion. She loved not being part of the manufactured beauty fads, the hair extensions, the trendy clothes, the long nails, the fillers, and heavy makeup. Spiritual beauty isn't something that can be purchased and applied. It's the light that radiates from that battle-worn temple within you. I would argue that spiritual beauty far surpasses what the world offers. You can be born with natural beauty, you can buy things that enhance it, but spiritual beauty is an energy that emanates from within. It is found in the depths and wisdom of your eyes, the authenticity of your smile, the resonance of your words, and the nature of your energy. For a time, Audrey was worried that as she aged, Ethan wouldn't find her as beautiful as he once had. Women spend a lot of money trying to turn back the hands of time, but Audrey didn't want to do that. She just wanted to be healthy and real. The more time she spent in her own temple, the brighter the light shone from it. Her eyes weren't just a shade of green. They were somehow illuminated from the inside. She liked what she was seeing in the mirror, who she was becoming, and for once, it wasn't the world that was classifying her worth; it was her Creator.

Intention. Another powerful word, when you learn how to focus it. This was another game-changer. Instead of just drifting through life without purpose, Audrey learned to apply her intention to life, to the day, to the class or meeting. She lived with the intention to be a positive and supportive force for those in her life. She went to work with intention. She prayed with intention. She started playing a game she called "best case scenario." Her mother had a way of envisioning and obsessing over the worst way things could work out and then was unhappy when things turned out just that way. Audrey decided to believe differently. If something important was coming up, instead of envisioning the negative and letting it play out over and over in her mind, she thought of the best-case scenario. She focused on it. She took steps to ensure it. And to her surprise, what she envisioned was how things began to shift.

It was during her class that Audrey was able to be on her own and manage the house as she would see fit. It was a happy home. Ethan's deployment started off terribly for her. It seemed like everything that could go wrong did, and Audrey had to figure everything out on her own. But we never know how strong we truly are until we are forced to be. Audrey finally understood she could handle it all on her own, not that she wanted to, but she was certainly capable. There began a flow of happy energy through the house that wasn't there before. All her intention. This was her work in the house to usher in a new time, a new energy, a new era. Audrey and Roxy had gotten into a routine, and being just the two of them wasn't that bad after all.

Western medicine has always been a little cold and removed from real healing, if you ask me. Do you have an ailment? There's a pill for that. Boom, you're cured, and all it took was an uncomfortable office visit, a thirty-dollar copay, and waiting in line at your local pharmacy. But that's not really healing, is it? It's just a foul-tasting concoction of chemicals to make you forget that you ever had an ailment, until something else goes wrong. Having an illness is a sign to change something in your lifestyle. Holistic medicine isn't only about treating the physical body. The mind, body, and soul should be harmonious, but illness is a dissonance that affects all. Thinking, feeling, holding on, and letting go are all as important to the body as a good diet is. Sometimes it all comes down to that one thing we cannot get over. Hippocrates, the father of medicine, instructed, "Before you heal someone, ask him if he's willing to give up the things that make him sick."

The beauty of that little class taught by the eccentric, wonderful, wise women was that it was an introduction to how healing really works, all over the world. In India, Ayurveda is the belief that your diet and personality are closely related, and should you look into Ayurveda a little deeper, you might find that your personality craves certain foods, and you might already be drawn to them. Chinese medicine believes the body and its functions are connected to the elements, earth, water, fire, and air. But the most important part of healing in those cultures is the link between balance and spirit. Western medicine has no interest in your spirit. Maybe that's why Westerners are some of the most health-challenged in the world.

The little school opened Audrey's mind to healing practices. It helped the healer heal. Some cultures believe that medicine women are closer to the spirit world, and that is what sets them apart from others. Some believe they have magical powers to heal, or they have a direct connection to the Creator. But there's also a belief that healers hold a space for you while you heal yourself. I think that's my favorite. Holding a space. A healer is an Anam Cara, the friend you can tell anything to without judgment. It's those negative emotions, secrets, and pain that we bury deep that cause the most havoc within us. An Anam Cara is someone you can hand your emotional pain over to, in exchange for compassion. Clear a path and grow a garden inside, and then be an Anam Cara to those who need you.

Meditation, healing of the hands, yoga, and prayer. They are all powerful tools to communicate with a higher power. Christians are urged not to embrace new-age ways. There has been a big debate in the faith-based world about whether Christians should do yoga. They say it's not a Christian practice. The Christians who actually practice yoga don't agree and find no harm in it. But most of them aren't aware that each pose was formed to honor a deity. The sun salutation is really saluting the sun god. So if yoga is a tool to communicate with gods, make sure it's your intention to honor your own. Make sure that practicing new and exciting things of other cultures, which we might think are harmless, is not causing you to break the commandment of putting another god before your own.

Seasons were changing again, and the weather was getting cooler. It was time for a Halloween shopping event in one of the mountain towns, called Murphys. Audrey invited Michelle to go with her. It wasn't often that Audrey invited friends to go out, but this seemed to be a fun occasion with street vendors, musical performers, and good food. Audrey became more excited as the date approached, but the night before the event, Michelle cancelled. It seemed Michelle already had other plans with her husband. Audrey felt a little rejected and was disappointed. She broke down and asked God why it was so hard for her to find friends that she could let in. Every friendship she'd ever had ended in pain and disappointment, and even though this was just a small cancellation from a wonderful friend, it still made her sad. God didn't have an answer for her yet. After a few minutes, she was tired of crying, so she got up and showered her Roxy kitty with love and ear rubs. She opened a can of wet food for her, put it into a cute ceramic cat dish, and let Roxy eat it on the kitchen counter. That didn't always happen, but today was different, so why not?

When Audrey first moved into the neighborhood, she noticed that there were a number of stray cats that gravitated to her porch for shelter. One day, when the rain was pouring down, she peered out her window and saw several feral cats gathered there. They waited for the storm to pass and went on their way. Because of that, she decided to create the "Beastro," bowls full of dry food and clean water. She liked looking out the window throughout the day to see if she had any Beastro guests. Many strays were fed there, including an opossum, a raccoon, and a couple of bluejays. The morning she was supposed to go to Murphys, she noticed the bowls were empty, so she gathered a bag of food and a pitcher of water and opened the front door.

Sitting on the porch, just above the steps, was a little black kitten. Audrey and the kitten were equally shocked to see each other. They just stood there, frozen, wondering what to do next. After a few seconds had passed, Audrey slowly filled the food and water dishes. She didn't make any sudden movements or loud noises. She then brought a can of wet food back out for the little kitten, which was well received. The kitten ate as if it had been starved. Her coat was dull, and her belly was bloated. Those were sure signs of rough living. The kitten let Audrey pet her, beginning to purr while she was eating.

They met thirteen days before Halloween, serendipitously, because her plans had been changed at the last minute. That was God's answer. It wasn't a rejection at all. God had better plans, which is always the case.

She watched the kitten stay on the porch. She slept on the cushion of a wicker park bench outside the front window, where Audrey could keep an eye on her. It was a windy evening, and this little kitten, lying at the edge of the porch like a cold little loaf, made for a somber picture. That was when she decided she had to make a move. The next morning, she fed the kitten more wet food and was able to pet her a little more. When she was done eating, Audrey tried to pick her up. It was all going well, the kitten was fine with being picked up until she turned and made eye contact with Audrey. It made a loud squeal and squirmed, and Audrey did too, and down the kitty went. The kitten wasn't scared of her; it just didn't like too much pressure on her belly. Not even an hour later, Audrey had her front door open, and the kitten was walking right in. She spent the rest of the day and night getting acquainted with her new home and liking it. Roxy kitty didn't seem to mind the company either. Pretty soon, they were chasing each other back and forth down the hallway and napping on the same couch together.

Audrey wanted to give her kitten a spooky name since they'd met thirteen days before Halloween, so she named her Belladonna Deadly Nightshade, but we never call our cats by their real names, do we?

Audrey saw that her new little kitten was a runt or teacup panther, and Teacup was the name that felt right. By that same front window, Audrey and Teacup had morning tea and read the news together. It's an Irish blessing of good fortune to have a black cat appear on your doorstep. In most cultures, black cats are lucky. When God closes a door, he always opens a window, so it goes. It was Gavri who had placed Teacup on Audrey's doorstep, knowing she needed true companionship, and Roxy did too.

That wasn't the only kitty he left on the porch for Audrey. There was always a mama cat that came around to eat. She was too wild to get close to, so the best Audrey could do was offer her food, fresh water, and a prayer for her angels to watch out after her. She noticed that Mama Kitty started bringing her little boy with her. He was a big ginger tabby that looked like the end of his tail was missing. After a couple of weeks, the ginger kitty was living on the porch and sleeping on the same wicker bench. It was getting cold. One evening, Audrey put up the Christmas decorations outside. She did the same thing every year, hanging green garland and twinkle lights all along the railing and draping them between the posts. As the garland came up to each post, it was tied with a big red bow. The same red ribbon continued twirling up the post, looking like a candy cane. There were seven posts to decorate with ribbons, and the little ginger kitty was curious. It turned out he was a big fan of ribbons and bows.

She stayed outside, listening to Christmas carols and playing with the ginger tabby for hours. She noticed he meowed a lot, and when he did, he'd draw out his meow for a long time like a singer. She got a kick out of that and gave him a crooner's name, Frank. But he just wasn't a Frank. No, he was a Tony. And Tony was a ham. He peeked in the windows and begged for food and playtime. Audrey went out to the porch one evening and sat on the wicker bench. Tony was close by. He came closer. He leaned in against her affectionately, and she picked him up. She brought the big boy up to her lap and sat quietly, petting him. He turned toward her face and inched closer. This was still a wild cat that could claw her face or bite her in an instant. She was feeling a bit of panic until he leaned in and kissed her nose. That made Audrey laugh. She wrapped her arms around Tony, gave him a kiss on his head, and put him back down. If he was angling for a furever home, he'd just found one.

Ethan was finally on his way home. He knew all about the new kitten visitors and was excited to meet them. It took a good majority of their anxiety away from their reunion. Nothing breaks the ice like a couple of furry comic reliefs. She knew Tony and Ethan would get along tremendously. They were fast friends, buddies, amigos. And little Teacup slept on Audrey, where Romeo used to. Ethan had left his house in its darkest, saddest state and Audrey too. He was shocked at the transformation he found when he returned. They had a clean slate, a fresh start, a growing family, and good intentions.

Romeo had taken the place of a black kitty who was taken from Audrey long ago. The last one to greet her in the dream. I recognized that kitty because it was the one that had been staring at me from the side of the road the night I died.

Audrey's sister had a very pretty dress hanging outside her closet. The dress was of silk, long and flowing, but no match for the claws and playful nature of Audrey's Booboo kitty. Her sister found the cat standing on its hind legs, trying to reach the dress, snagging and tearing it terribly. Her sister was horrified. Her anger flamed as she grabbed the cat and took it on a drive in the country. That wasn't the first outfit the cat had destroyed, but it was to be the last. Her sister abandoned Booboo kitty on the side of the road and sped off. The cat wandered around for hours. It was lost and hungry. There had been a squirrel that met its demise in the middle of the road, and the cat had stopped for a moment to check it out. That was the fateful moment we met.

Life will take things from you unexpectedly, so love while you still can. I watched as Romeo finally crossed the rainbow bridge to Audrey's home on the other side. He waited for Gavri to deliver his replacements. He jumped on Audrey's shoulders once more, nuzzling her with all of his might. I watched as Audrey put her hand to her face. I knew she felt him. With a kiss, he leaped from her shoulders and ran across the bridge, being greeted by all the animals she had ever loved.

Sometimes we think that once we lose a pet, we will never be able to love again. The truth is, our hearts are crushed, but following our hearts' repair, they become bigger each time, able to hold even more love than before. So may you love grand while you still can. And may you have such good fortune that a black kitten waits for you on your doorstep.

Chapter Sixteen

I t was in another time and another place that I found her again. My uncle and I had been working very hard over the last few months, and it was just time to take a break and live a little, with the money we'd stashed away. We both had new suits tailored and bought sharp hats to match. That was the look then, of any gentleman, but we were just a couple of bootleggers from the California hills wanting to play the part. We didn't make the rotgut whiskey that any old rumrunner could make. Word got out that we made the best booze around, and we loved it. We loved the process, carefully tending to our batches and pouring love into what we did. You could taste the difference. We had to be smart, though. This was a dangerous business, and the feds were always out trying to ruin a good time. It got to a point where we were overworked, and the heat was a little too close, so we backed off from distribution for a bit and had some fun.

I put on my pale pink button-down shirt and my slate blue suit. I was drawn to darker-colored suits, but this one matched the color of my eyes, so I had to get it. In the tailor's shop, he had just bought bolts of silk brocade from the Orient. It was the most beautiful silk I had ever seen, intricately embroidered with silk threads in small blackberries and blossoms. He was happy to make me a vest, tie, and kerchief out of it. From the looks of me, you'd never guess I'd spent the last few years of my life evading the law, but things never are as they seem.

My uncle, John Joseph, dressed in his new tan suit and bone-colored vest, looked nothing like the contrabandist that he was, but he knew the passwords that unlocked the doors to the best speakeasies within a hundred miles. They rolled out the red carpet for us and gave us the best seats in the house wherever we went. It was the Canary Diamond Club and Casino we were off to that night. Just before I left my little house, I picked two roses to stick in the lapel of our jackets. It was often that men who were all dressed up had flowers on their lapel, so I picked two pink roses from the rose bushes that my mom, Joey's sister, had planted for me as a housewarming gift. It seemed like they bloomed with the beautiful spirit of her all year long, one on either side of the steps leading right to my door.

We got to the door of the establishment and knocked three

deliberate times. There was a much smaller door up at the top that opened, just large enough to show a sneering face peering out at us. He barked threats at us until my uncle quietly said the password. Domino. One little word, and the rattling of keys began to retract the bolts holding this massive door closed. It opened quickly, just enough for us to pass through, then closed and locked once again. A locked door behind me was unsettling. We had stepped into a different world now. It was a stunning, elegant place. The couches and chairs were a deep velvet. Chandeliers captured glints of light within their dangling crystals. The women's dresses looked like sparkling crystal chandeliers as well, and their gowns glistened with beads, feathers, and fringe. Everyone was happy and laughing, clinking their glasses and listening to the music.

Once we had gotten a drink at the bar and said a few hellos, we were led to a table down toward the front of the stage. We got settled and toasted to our health. I took a long sip of my drink and sat back in my chair, then I saw her. Standing before a five-piece band was the most exquisite, glittering, gleaming, singing songbird I'd ever seen. A spotlight illuminated the thousands of tiny diamond-like crystals on her champagne-colored gown. The gown was the same color as her skin and seemed to drape upon her figure like running water. It clung to her curves and spilled down around her feet. Her hair was the palest blond that seemed to absorb the light in her curls and glow. I knew that if angels did roam the earth,

I was encountering one at that moment. She sang to the depths of the room as I watched her every move. Her gaze drifted over the crowd until our eyes finally met. Adrenaline rushed through my body when this angelic creature looked at me. I had never found anything more intoxicating than the moments our eyes met, and it seemed she was singing to me. She performed three songs for the audience and then took a short break. Joey started talking about her and the songs while my eyes followed her off the stage and into the crowd. She had two men guarding her. They kept the drunkards at bay. Joey's glass was empty, and so was mine, so I volunteered to refresh our drinks at the bar. The bar was lively, but I saw a clearing and stood there, waiting for the bartender's attention. I was wondering where my songbird had flown off to, swirling the last sip in my glass when the smell of jasmine and strawberries romanced my senses. Just breathe. That's what I told myself when I looked up and saw her standing right beside me.

"Are you enjoying the show?" she asked while waving down the bartender with the slightest movement of her fingers. She wore gloves on her hands that matched her dress, with crystals trimming their edge.

"Very much so. It's my first time here." I could see that she was about to order a drink, and I was curious. "What is the lady drinking this evening?" I needed to know so that I could order for her.

"The lady is having champagne." She tilted her head, smiling.

"Always." I've never loved a word more than that word in that moment. I watched her red lips part as she said it, ending in a smirk. We exchanged our names, though names matter not when the soul remains unchanged. She was still my Audrey, with long blond curls and dimples in her cheeks. Her eyes were sparkling emeralds, bewitching me to the point I was breathless, but I only had a moment. I had to make an impression. It seems I already had, as she moved closer to me. I almost thought she was going to kiss me, but she leaned in and smelled the rose on my lapel. Her eyes closed as her lungs drew in the sweet smell of that special pink rose. "That's my favorite color of rose."

I pinched myself, having the feeling I'd dreamt this whole thing. The bartender finally approached us, handing the songbird a champagne coupe. "Thank you, Marty, and please, whatever the gentleman is having." She took a little sip, "It was a pleasure, Mr. Stroud. I hope we meet again soon."

She slipped away into the crowd and back toward the stage as Marty asked me what I wanted. Was the answer that obvious? Marty shook his head, "Sorry about your luck, buddy, but she's definitely taken. Spoken for. Capiche?"

"Oh, of course." I ordered our drinks, and while I was waiting, I asked, "So where is the lucky gentleman?"

Marty chuckled, "The owner." As he was drying a glass with a white cloth, I could see him look toward him, standing at the corner of the bar. He was of average height and broad shouldered. Surrounded by an entourage, I took one look at him and knew he was mafia. My uncle had done his best business with the mafia, but these are not the kind of people to cross. So, I thanked Marty and took our drinks back to the table and enjoyed the rest of the show. When she returned to sing, it was different this time. She performed for everyone in the room, but she definitely sang to me. Our eyes met and lingered. There were times she performed her songs and picked a random gentleman in the audience to sing to, I'm sure, but this time it wasn't random. She was mesmerizing. Even Joey was watching her sing to me with a puzzled look on his face. His eyes switched back and forth between the songbird and me.

The more precious a time is, the shorter it seems. The songbird took a graceful bow amid cheers from an inebriated room and made her exit. She gave me one last smile before disappearing.

"Joey, old chap…what a night! We must do this again soon." I said laughing.

Joey just side-eyed me, "Uh-huh." Nervous about what kind of trouble this evening might lead to.

We were talking in Joey's truck when we saw the songbird being escorted to a car. We both looked at each other with the same thoughts. It was part of our job to watch people, see where they went, and get to know who we were about to do business with. But this was different, a simple curiosity about what tree the songbird nested in.

Not far from the Canary Club was her tree, and it appeared to have a guard out front. The men parked their car, saw the songbird just inside her door, and then left. For such an eventful evening, it was a quiet drive home. Joey dropped me off in my driveway, just down the road from his own house. I lay in bed replaying the evening over in my mind. I had to see her again.

Joey and I went back to the club the next night. We were disappointed to find a different singer in her place. We were shown the same treatment and the same table. I was sitting close to the stage and looking everywhere else. I watched the bar for a stunning blonde, but she never showed. Joey and I still had a good time, but it just wasn't the same. We tried to get some details out of Marty, but he wasn't forthcoming. He just told us that she'd be back in a few days.

My Aunt Bee was a short, sharp-witted, lovely culinary genius. She was a little God-fearing spitfire, and it was a good thing. She kept my uncle in good health and spirits and provided a balance in his life. I was grateful to her for allowing us to blow off steam at the gin joints after all the hard work we'd been doing, but that all came with a price. She'd remind us with a hand on her hip, "You can go have your fun on Friday and Saturday nights, but you're all mine on Sunday."

The first order of business on Sunday was Auntie Bee's big breakfast: eggs, sausage, hot biscuits, and fresh-picked fruit from her garden. Next, we piled into my uncle's truck and drove down the road to a little chapel. My uncle and I were both good men, but even good men needed to hear a little Word now and then. Well-dressed people gathered by the church doorsteps, a very cheerful and welcoming bunch. Would they still be so welcoming of us if they knew what we did for a living? My Uncle Joey and I had been judged harshly by church folks before. He was uneasy stepping into a church ever since, struggling with the idea of his own forgiveness. He loved and provided for his family, and for him, for now, that had to be good enough.

We sat close to each other on little creaky wooden pews. We all had to squeeze in to make room for everyone, and I recalled never seeing a church this filled before. I looked around at all the smiling faces, the whispering couples, the stained-glass windows, and the high-peaked ceiling. I just let my eyes wander, taking in all the sights around me in the Lord's house until I felt Uncle Joey tap my leg. He pointed to the front of the church, "I didn't know songbirds sing in church too."

There in a pale blue dress, my songbird stood with three other ladies, leading the church in the singing of hymns. Her resounding, unmistakable voice within the walls of this little chapel demonstrated to me for the first time what worshiping should really feel like. I noticed Joey was whispering to Aunt Bee, pointing to the songbird and looking back at me. Aunt Bee's excited smile meant only one thing. For the last few years, she had taken a more personal interest in finding a nice young woman for her nephew to marry.

It hadn't gone well so far. Dastardly, in fact. Would Aunt Bee approve of this girl if her first impression was of her up on stage in that champagne gown?

I watched her sing, and when she looked out upon the crowded pews and saw me, a smile came over me like never before. It made her smile too. Uncle Joey's elbow hit me in the ribs when he saw her recognize me. The sermon was a good one. Strange how the message always seemed to apply to each and every one of us, though our lives were so different. The pews emptied, ladies visited, the men were shaking hands, and my eyes searched the crowd for the color of light blue and her blond curls.

The songbird stood in a group of people, but as they left for the door, and our eyes finally met, I approached her. With my hat in hand and shyness overcoming me, I cleared my throat and said, "Miss Day, it's very nice to see you again. Let me introduce my Aunt Bee and Uncle Joey." Aunt Bee shook her hand, praising her singing.

"Did you enjoy the service?" she asked me.

"I sure did. The singing, particularly."

The pastor caught the songbird's attention and wanted to introduce her to people, but before she left, she looked at Aunt Bee and Joey. "It was a pleasure meeting you." She looked at me and smiled, placing her hand lightly on my arm as she walked away.

Miss Day was the topic of the ride back home. I never thought I'd see the day that my little Aunt Bee would want to go to the

Canary Club, but now she was insisting.

I needed new furniture in my house. I was beginning to wonder what I needed in this old place, should I ever entertain people, or the songbird even. She deserved something better than a bootlegger's den, so off to town I went, but before I left, I cut a handful of pink roses, tying them up with ribbon we usually tied on bottles for our special customers. It was a wide, dark blue satin ribbon that tied up the flowers perfectly. As I walked up to the man at her door, he seemed as if he'd been expecting me. "Ah, yes, good day, sir. You must be here to see Miss Day."

Deep down, I was surprised, but I'd played my share of poker. He asked, "You're Miss Day's attorney, yes? She's been expecting you. I just saw the dark blue ribbon and flowers. It's really quite thoughtful, sir. Pink roses are her favorite. Pity the only roses she has delivered here are red."

"Thank you, sir." I tipped my hat to the most helpful gentleman. In a slight case of mistaken identity, I was about to walk into her home. A million thoughts raced through my mind. What was I doing? Was it terrible timing? I wondered what had happened.

I choked down all the anxiety that I had. I knew I just had to be myself, be kind, give her the flowers, tell her how magnificent she was, in so many words, and be on my way. I knocked a few times on the black lacquered door, taking deep breaths. The door was swung open by a short woman with a flapper cut. "Hello there, how can I help you?"

"Ma'am, I'm here to give these to Miss Day. May I see her?" I smiled while she judged my bouquet with squinted eyes.

"Please do come in. I'm Birdie, her assistant. Who may I say is calling?" she asked, walking toward the hallway. I recognized her from the church, singing with the songbird.

"Uh, you can tell her that Mr. Stroud was just dropping by to say hello."

She went into a back room, and while I waited, I noted how she'd decorated her home. It was much like the Canary, with velvet furniture. I could see colors of purple and chartreuse throughout. Flowers were everywhere, enormous bouquets, dozens of roses in bright reds, yellows, and white. It didn't seem like a cheerful group of bouquets. It was in sympathy. What had I just walked into?

Birdie returned and told me it would be just a few more minutes. She gathered her notebooks and papers to leave. "Nice meeting you, Birdie."

"Likewise, Mr. Stroud. Good day," she said quickly and closed the door behind her.

My songbird was a vision, gliding down the hallway in her long, dark blue silk dress and bare feet. Her eyes were sad, but she smiled when she saw me standing there.

"Well, this is quite the surprise, Mr. Stroud." She took the flowers from me and lifted them up to her nose. With a deep breath, her smile grew. "Thank you," she said quietly. Looking up at me was a very different woman than the performer I had first met nights ago. She moved to a cabinet where she pulled out a crystal vase, small enough to make my roses look like they had been arranged just for it. She went into the kitchen, filling the vase with water.

"I just wanted to say hello, and it seems I should offer my condolences. Your doorman offers the same. He was really quite helpful. I had just planned to leave these flowers with him, but he mistook me for someone else, I suppose," I said loud enough for her to hear in the next room.

"I just had my meeting rescheduled. It's just family business. I'm not in the mood to talk about all of that today." She shook her head. "But I'm happy to see you. Your timing couldn't be any better." She made her way gracefully to the velvet couch and tapped her hand on the cushion, inviting me to sit down with her. It was there on that couch and under that dark cloud of sadness that we talked like we were old friends. We laughed and told stories about our families and upbringing. It was all kept quite polite, and a gentleman knows not to overstay his welcome, so after some time passed, I stood up and thanked her for the lovely time. She could see all over my face that I was hopelessly falling in love with her. Seeing her so sad just made me even more so. I wished I could be the man in her life, making her happy every day. I would grow her an endless garden of pink roses. I would learn to make her the most exquisite champagne. She would never know a day without love. Yet, here I was, walking ever so slowly toward the black door.

"I had a wonderful time with you. Let's do this again soon, my songbird," I said as I brought her hand to my lips. She closed her eyes and tilted her head; her shoulders rose up to her cheeks. It was that thing she always did when something touched her heart. I called her my songbird, and I would from now on. I wrote down my address and phone number, telling her to contact me anytime. She read the paper and held it to her chest as if to protect it.

"Until we meet again, Miss Day," I murmured, tipping my hat.

In the time that had passed since the last day I saw her, I stayed busy. I found new furniture and bought a new record player. When I saw her last, I had schemed my way into her home and left her a way to contact me. With any luck, if she felt the way I felt about her, maybe she would find me this time. I would extend my hand and hope for a songbird to light upon it.

A tree had fallen down the slope of the back of my property. I hadn't even noticed until Joey, always keeping watch over me with his binoculars, saw it happen. It was a windy day, and I was tucked away inside in my old, comfortable reading chair, lost in the pages of a delightful book. I suppose the entire police force could come rolling up to my door, and I'd be entranced by the pages of a good story, but Joey would sure see it. He's given me a scare a few times. In minutes, he'd be roaring up through the driveway with a cigar in his mouth, cocking his shotgun. I wouldn't have had it any other way.

I took my axe down the slope but didn't feel like I was making any progress on that fallen tree. I was covered in sweat and chips of wood, looking up for a moment to see an angel watching me. Striking the tree kept me from hearing her car drive up. My songbird stood up the slope a bit, the breeze causing the frills in her peach-colored dress to dance. She was holding a picnic basket with her little white gloves. "Thirsty, Mr. Stroud?"

"Always!" Smiling that big church smile, I took a rag from my back pocket and dusted myself off the best I could. She looked more radiant than ever, standing in a clearing I was sure that Joey could see well.

"Lovely day for a picnic, wouldn't you say?" She smiled from under the brim of her hat.

"Yes, it is. Hey, do me a favor, would ya?" I pointed to the next hill, "My Uncle Joey is over there checking on me with his binoculars. Let's give him a little wave."

She set the basket on the grass and, with both hands, gave a big theatrical wave. Just for fun, since she knew we had an audience, she grabbed my dusty hands and began to dance with me. With twirls and a dip, I had us both laughing. We gave Joey a big bow to end the performance. It all made her laugh, and butterflies swirled inside of me. She had a way of turning the simplest things into pure magic. I was in awe, trying my best to hide it.

I excused myself while I cleaned up inside the house. When I returned, she had spread out a checkered blanket and emptied the contents of her wicker picnic basket. She'd brought breads and cheeses, fruits and jams, and even a bottle of wine. I sat down in front of her, admiring everything, her especially. She had removed her shoes and was leaning on one arm with her legs stretched out together, her toes just barely touching the blades of grass. It was the first time I had seen her wearing a hat. The weave of the hat filtered the sunlight onto her nose and cheeks in pretty little diamonds. This scene should have been a Renaissance painting; it was so perfect. We briefly spoke of the weather and other pleasantries. Then we dove a little deeper, talking about how I came to live here, my family, and a hint of what I did. I couldn't tell her everything; that's just not what bootleggers do, but Joey had a forge and did repairs for people with my help. That was usually just enough to quell suspicion.

"I saw your pink rose bushes when I first got here. They're beautiful," she told me, bringing her glass of red to her lips.

"My mom planted them for me a few years before we lost her." It was my turn to take a sip. "She was a free spirit, very lively and kindhearted. Very much like you are, from what I can see. One day, she was taking a walk in the hills, and as you know, these hills have been known to have rattlers. She got bit but was rushed to the hospital and treated. We thought she was going to be all right, but for some reason, she became extremely sick one night with a bad fever and never recovered." My hands fidgeted as I told the story, with my eyes turned down the whole time. After a deep breath, I said, "I feel her spirit all around us, watching over us all the time. Those roses are definitely connected to her."

"I was happy to see you at church, Mr. Stroud." She used my last name flirtatiously.

"I was happier, Miss Day. My Aunt Bee gave us no choice, but it wasn't as bad as I thought."

"Good. So we'll be seeing more of you on Sundays."

"I'll go anywhere to hear you sing."

"The rose you were wearing the night we met, that's why I saw you. It's so strange. In a very dark room, with lights shining in my eyes, it seemed like something was twinkling around the rose on your lapel. It caught my attention, so when I saw you at the bar, I wanted to get a closer look. Did you have some sort of contraption with a rose on it? Something to distract me with?"

"Well, I don't need a contraption. My dashing good looks are distracting enough," I was barely able to say with a straight face. Anything to make her laugh.

Our laughing continued, but then she grew serious again. "Do you ever find yourself wanting to run away?"

"Do you want to run away, Miss Day?" I took her hand and held it.

"Always," she said, looking down. She began to pack up the basket. We folded the blanket together, and I took her hand again as we walked back toward the house.

As we got to the pink rose bushes at the top of the steps, she paused and smelled them. "Please come in," I invited. I pulled her hand and tilted my head, breathlessly waiting for her answer.

She paused and, with a hesitant smile, answered, "Just for a moment."

She looked around my place. There were old photos of the family, candles here and there, books I had read and was planning on reading. She took her time sweeping through my living room as if it told the story of who I really was. Perhaps it did. When she made her way back to me again, I began to bare my soul to her. "I think I loved you from the moment we met. No, from the moment I saw you there, sparkling on stage. My songbird. You don't have to run away. Just be with me."

She smiled widely, and I thought she was happy until I saw a tear run down her cheek. What is love if it's not pure peace in chaos? She rushed toward me, arms around my neck, kissing me. It was a kiss that didn't end for the next forty-eight absolutely amazing hours. She stayed with me in my little house, which I had seemed to prepare just for her. For two days, we were close, playful, silly, vulnerable, one. But the more precious a time is, the shorter it seems.

"Must you leave me?" I asked sadly.

"I have a performance tomorrow night. I hope to see you there." She leaned in for another kiss.

"Oh, I'll be there, my songbird."

Missing her was an affliction my heart wasn't used to. It was even worse now, being so close, yet not quite close enough. I caught Joey up on how our picnic went. The rest of the details were secrets a gentleman kept. He warned me of the dangerous waters I was swimming in. More like up shit creek. We had a good laugh at my expense, and then I told him we were going back to the Canary Diamond Club tomorrow night, to hear my songbird sing again. He told me I was plum crazy.

I put on a dark suit for this night. It was special. I put on a blackberry vest and tie over a white button-down shirt and a special pink rose in my lapel. I picked one rose, saving it for later. Joey and Aunt Bee picked me up, and we headed into town. My Aunt Bee put on one of her finest, dazzling dresses, not looking remotely like the apron-wearing, weed-pulling auntie I had gotten used to. "Domino" opened the door, and Marty gave us our drinks. Our table was waiting. My songbird wore a deep emerald green dress that night, with peacock feathers and shimmering crystals. She looked more beautiful every time I laid eyes on her. She gave a vibrant performance; her voice was smooth and deep, romancing the room with every verse. When she looked at me, I could tell something wasn't right. Something was worrying her. As the final song of the set came to a close and she left the stage, I raced to the bar. I asked Marty to have two coupes of champagne ready. Marty was a good chap, and he did everything I asked. I watched him place the drinks on the bar just before I stepped up to it. Without anyone seeing, I reached into my breast pocket for the diamond ring I'd bought. As I motioned to pick up the glass, I dropped her ring inside it and watched it tumble down through the bubbles. With the coupe in one hand and the pink rose in the other, I saw her come closer. People were stopping her, praising her talent, but finally, for a moment, she was mine.

"Champagne for my songbird. I do hope you like it." My words were soaked with intention.

She nodded her head and smiled. "Always." She sipped from the glass, and while it was up close to her, she raised the glass as if to toast. Her eyes widened when she saw the ring. Her worrisome expression faded, and a calm came over her like I hadn't seen before.

Before she left for the stage with glass and her rose in hand, she asked, "Another picnic tomorrow?"

I agreed and watched her gown flow behind her as she navigated the crowd.

There in my seat, sipping my drink and watching my songbird sing, I was the happiest I've ever been. She placed her hand on the microphone, and the light illuminated the diamond ring on her finger. She was wearing my ring, singing to me. We were in love, and it felt like we were the only two people in the room, in the world. My soul sighed finally, because I'd found her, my destined one.

Joey and Aunt Bee dropped me off that evening with a hug and a

"We love ya, kid. See ya tamorra."

I walked into my dark house, emptying my pockets and loosening my tie. The room was eerily quiet, reminiscent of the woods, signaling a predator. Something was off. When I went to light a lamp, I was tackled and thrown to the floor. There were four men waiting for me. They tied me to a chair, taking turns beating the hell out of me. They cracked my ribs and spilled my blood. I just knew it was his mafia boys. I knew I'd crossed a line. I deserved it. And you know what, she was worth it all.

One of them finally lit the lamp and revealed who they really were. Things aren't always as they seem. These boys weren't mafia at all. I got the shit beat out of me by the feds. Turns out they had been investigating the Canary Diamond Club owner for some time and were using my Songbird to get close to him. I had become a problem. They couldn't have their informant running away with a bootlegger, could they?

The next morning, there was a knock at my door. I had passed out in the chair I was still tied to. The feds invited Miss Day inside. She screamed when she saw me. She rushed to my side, but they pulled her away and held her back. They told her that it was almost time, but there was still some work to be done. Murder, racketeering, a long list of offenses, but they needed her to commit to bringing down a powerful man. If she did not, they were going to kill me. She agreed to do whatever they wanted, so they let her go. She was crying, and my arms couldn't hold her. Out of all of this, that is what hurt me the most.

She got into her car and drove off but didn't go back to the Canary Club as they'd anticipated. She drove over to the next hill, looking for Joey. She saw Joey working outside on his old truck as she pulled into his driveway. She ran to him and told him everything. She told him about the four feds in my house with shotguns and bad tempers. Joey knew what to do. He asked Aunt Bee to look after Miss Day, as Joey rounded up the boys.

The boys were our men, four brothers, who had a general distaste for authority and an axe to grind. These boys had old Indian blood coursing through their veins. They all went by predatory bird names. The eldest brother was Eagle, then Owl, Falcon, and Hawk. They worked together seamlessly, knowing how to draw the enemy out. They were savage, but luckily, Joey and I were family. When you offer a good man a more than fair wage and all the alcohol he can drink, you're family, whether you like it or not. They were probably the reason we had been so successful in our illicit trade thus far. We already owed them our lives, and they were about to save my skin again.

The boys loaded for bear and climbed the mountain to my house from all directions. I knew they were outside when I heard their bird calls, signs to each other, an old Indian language all their own. I'd heard each of those calls while working with them, even in town or sitting by a fire.

The feds could hear their calls but disregarded them, though they were unable to shake a growing trepidation. The calls got louder and more deliberate until, one by one, the feds went out to investigate. The boys subdued each man with a blow to the head. With the men lying on the ground unconscious, the boys pulled their sharp blades from their scabbards and, in one swift motion, sliced their throats. The third man wouldn't come outside until he heard glass breaking. Eventually, he cautiously walked out until he found the broken glass and fellow feds, and his throat was cut too. One fed remained, and he stood over me. Eagle crawled through the window in my bedroom. He pushed a stack of books from the table onto the floor, making a racket, so the last fed cautiously walked to the hallway, cocking his pistol.

When more noise came from the bedroom and the fed finally walked down the hallway, Owl crept through the front door and untied me. The last fed returned to the room I was in, to see me being freed. He shouted, "Don't move!" Owl was behind me. Eagle was right behind the last standing fed, driving a long blade through the center of his body. Blood poured from him as he dropped to his knees and to the ground. They had a call that was for victory, and Falcon and Hawk came running at the sound of it. Joey did too and struggled not to break down into tears when he saw me. I was soaked in my own blood. He scooped me up and carried me to my truck and dropped me on the passenger seat. The boys knew what to do. They took their time cleaning up my house like nothing had ever happened. The bodies disappeared, and their murders went unsolved, though the department suspected the mafia boys, not mine.

Joey drove me over the hill to his place, where Auntie and my songbird cleaned me up and cared for me. I was in bad shape, but nothing time and a kiss or two couldn't cure. The Canary Diamond Club and Casino was shuttered for good soon after that.

I married my songbird later that year in that small chapel in the hills. She wore a flowing white dress and carried Mama's pink roses. Joey, Aunt Bee, and all the boys were there. It was the sweetest little ceremony anyone could ask for, and as the sun began to set, people from all around began to show up to celebrate with us. Both from the bar and from church. It was the party of the century with all of our best customers and all of her fans, our friends, and family. The band played, and my songbird sang. We danced the whole night through and welcomed the morning light as husband and wife. My songbird mentioned the work we did in our forge to the congregation, and it drew so much business from the church folks that Uncle Joey and I could step away from the bootlegging business for good. It was time, we'd had our fun and made plenty of money. We handed our business to the boys who, it turns out, were far better businessmen than we'd ever expected. It all happened in a matter of weeks, but it was the raabta. Our souls remained unchanged, and deep down, we remembered.

Chapter Seventeen

Season to season, stores have to make sacrifices to keep the doors open. Part of those sacrifices was Audrey's floral job. The store insisted on keeping her but not in a way she had hoped. She was to be the last smiling face that guests would see upon leaving.

This job wasn't ideal. People. People in a hurry and stressed out, with fussy kids and an appointment they're late for. It was more bad energy she had to protect herself from, but until she found another job, she made the most of it. She made people laugh, made friends, and memorized names. Some guests would be near tears, buying flowers for the grave of a loved one, or had just received a bad diagnosis. She never let those who needed a hug leave without one. She even held people as they cried, and as they realized that they were crying in a store and felt embarrassed by it, she'd say something funny, and laughter would replace the tears. I called it an alchemist's exchange. They would trade their pain for her bright energy, which flowed within her like those drinking fountains in Italy.

There were wonderful people who came through the line at the register, and then there were others. She was growled at, she had things thrown at her, men came through that said offensive things that no lady should have to hear, a man tried to lure her out to his van, and several times the metal detectors were set off by men with duffel bags. Audrey felt the peace of her angels' hands as a very agitated man came up to her with a strange bag, trying to provoke a fight. He was sweating, his breathing was stressed, and Audrey became alarmed. Em whispered instructions to Audrey, telling her to be as kind and polite, asking questions, distracting the man from his true intention, of suicide by a cop. He had decided to commit atrocities before that happened. Forty-eight hours later, he pulled a gun on a gas station owner who blasted a hole in the man, leaving him to bleed out in the potato chip aisle.

There were also the unsavory encounters with those snooty women. These women bought their things and looked down on the people working so hard, overstressed amid typical staff shortages. After several condescending comments, an older, very well-dressed woman asked Audrey, "Why do you even work here?"

Audrey had no answer for her. She went home that night, asking herself the same question, though. Why was she working in a position that took so much fire for such little compensation? She even asked God if He had a reason for her remaining there at that store. God answers those questions we have, but it's never in the way we'd expect.

There were people with strange energy that came through her line. There was the rude college-age guy in noticeably short shorts, a white purse and matching long white nails and heels, appearing to roll his eyes while judging her. He'd offer her a squint and a fake smile. She wondered what was going through his mind. There were the older ladies who were never happy; nothing could appease these bitter women, no matter what. Audrey could've easily been in her own mind, cursing at these ill-mannered people, wondering, what the hell is wrong with you? To be honest, she did at first, but at least she knew that accomplished nothing. With a helpful whisper from Em, she began to pray for these wayward souls, realizing that the more ill-mannered and off-putting a person was, the more help they were in need of. She prayed for the women to find happiness once again, so much so that they spread it wherever they went. Audrey wondered what was going through that man's mind when he stood there with his purse and long nails, seeming to judge her. I can tell you, he was judging her for a bracelet she wore, thinking, look at this Christian judging me. I bet she thinks I'm going straight to hell, while the real sin is that ugly floral blouse she's wearing. But that wasn't what she was thinking at all. She wondered if people had hurt him so much with their judgment for his lifestyle that he'd lost himself, the real soul somewhere, that he could not even offer a genuine smile back when it was offered. If he knew his Creator loved him, would it still matter what others thought of him? Would he be so concerned about one facet of his life, when there was so much more of himself to offer that he kept hidden behind high walls? All of those people just seemed to be missing joy, this certain type of joy that only came from the love of their Creator.

We all judge. And by that, I mean we assess each other, our clothes, our expressions, cars, homes, jewelry. It's as natural as dogs sniffing the ground. It's just because we are all so different. All the people that we are so quick to judge so harshly are in the most need of urgent prayer, and maybe it just takes one nonjudgmental person to pray for them and change someone's life.

Every day on her way to work, she started praying that her day would be blessed and she would be protected. She prayed that everyone who came through her line or came near her who needed a miracle, be it money, health, love, a job, or a car, would receive it. Whatever it was that they were worried about, praying for, or desperately needed, she prayed that God would supply that need and rain miracles.

She wore a thick leather band on her right wrist that had a copper-stamped fish symbol on it. It was the Ichthus, the Jesus fish.

She thought it was fitting to wear since wearing crosses and religious symbols in the workplace was frowned upon. The fish was a symbol that ancient Christians would draw in the sand to safely identify one another. One person would draw one side of the fish, and the other person would draw the rest. She loved it from the moment she first put it on. It was one of those spontaneous purchases from Etsy. When the package containing the bracelet had arrived, she'd been surprised to realize that the craftsman lived in Poland. The craftsman had been happy to receive Audrey's rave review. She wore this bracelet without fail, every day since she'd gotten it. It made her appreciate it even more, knowing it came from an artisan so far away, from such historically persecuted people. The true value she placed on it was the prayers she prayed over it. She prayed that everyone who saw that bracelet would walk away, curious, maybe even eager to open the door when the Savior came knocking. Audrey received compliments on the leather and copper Ichthus bracelet every single day she worked at that store.

It was in meditation that God answered her question. She was still working at that store...to pray over people. These were people who probably needed prayer most, and she was the only one who crossed their path who could offer it. The message was clear. So she continued.

She was becoming more adept at meditation. It wasn't some strange notion of sitting in a cross-legged position in a serene environment, hands contorted, and soft music playing. Sure, sometimes if the situation permits, that was all nice. A serene environment is lovely, but meditation is where you create the environment within, so meditation can happen anywhere. Meditation music enhances, as music does with any experience. "He who dwells in the shelter of the Most High will abide in the shadow of the Almighty" (Psalm 91:1), and "He will cover you with His feathers, and under His wings you may seek refuge" (Psalm 91:4). These verses helped Audrey meditate. That was where she usually went, under his wings, in the shelter of the Most High, closing her eyes, clearing her mind.

It was after a long day at work that Audrey came home to an overwhelmed Ethan. He had been drinking and was angry at the day's events at work, wanting to be left alone. After long days, she just wished she could come home to Ethan and make some sort of emotional connection, but that wasn't happening. She'd always hoped for a big hug after work, to make dinner together, and laugh off the day's mishaps. Instead, she poured herself a glass of her favorite blackberry wine and closed herself off in her art studio. She put soft soothing music on and sat on the floor, surrounded by all of her paintings, big and small, colorful and deep. She took sips, savoring the ever-so-slightly sweet wine and allowed the tense muscles in her body to begin to relax. She closed her eyes and breathed deeply, calming her mind like still waters.

In meditation, you can get lost. You can allow your mind to take you anywhere. After all, meditation is a tool to connect. Audrey closed her eyes and drifted off to Pismo. In a flowing white sundress, she walked the shoreline. She could feel the wet sand crush beneath her feet. She let the cool tide rush around her ankles to and fro and felt the rays of the sun warm her face. The air was salty and fresh, filled with the sounds of seagulls and happy beachcombers. They say that the person you think of when you watch a sunset is the person you truly love. Her mind wandered and settled on the veil and those she loved and missed every day just beyond it. And then something extraordinary happened. Her focus turned to me. She found me.

I found myself experiencing the tide and sun and the sand, all with this vision of her, and part of me wondered if what I was seeing was real, but there were all the telltale signs. The wild winds I had been feeling became suspended, my heartbeat calmed, my breath deepened, and there it was. The pull of the cord of the prairie rose that bound us, willing us closer, and into my arms again.

"Hi." She said quietly.

Her smile widened, and she began walking toward me, her eyes locking with mine. The soft wind-swept sundress, her arms curling around me, the smell of jasmine and strawberries. I held her as long as she needed me to, still surprised to see her. Without words, we just stood there together, with the motion of the wind and waves flowing around us. She buried her head in my chest, searching for escape, the safest place she could think of. I was her refuge. I had always been.

I squeezed her hand tightly and ran with her, feet in the shallow sweeping waters, fleeing from roaring waves, and laughing when the waves caught us. Out beyond the crashing and rolls of the current, there was a stiller water where we waded. We stilled ourselves and embraced. As the sun descended, when most people pause to witness the evolving colors of the fiery ether and reflecting waters, thinking of the person they hold dearest in their hearts, we held each other. This wasn't one of the dreams that I controlled, where I was forgotten at the sound of her alarm in the morning. She was here, and she was controlling this moment. She would remember this. But as I was about to speak, tell her I love her, and the countless other things I wish she knew, she was gone.

Audrey's cats were always attracted to her when she's meditating, and it was then that her little Teacup climbed into her lap and altered her focus. There is something about cats and your state of meditation. Being interdimensional beings, I think Teacup just wanted to go where her mom was going. In an instant, Audrey was gone from my arms, and my heart suffered from missing her. I should've said something. I should've kissed her. If only I had more time.

Things aren't always as they seem. To Audrey, our encounter was simply explained away as her active imagination, but I could assure you I felt the warmth of her holding me. I still remembered her smelling of jasmine and strawberries. If she only knew how powerful the mind was and where it could take you when you shut the world out. If she only knew how easy it was to find me, maybe she'd come right back. Maybe she'd stay longer.

Things aren't always as they seem, like the bad news about her floral job. She was in tears over losing it, but bad news is usually a cloaked opportunity. God put her where He needed her, where the people needed her. That city was a miserably dark place, and Audrey brought her light to it, as difficult as that was for her, every day. And so often we think our prayers go unheard and unnoticed. That's just not the case. I wish the living could see what different prayers look like. Some prayers are soft and simple, like a candle in a paper lantern rising in the sky, millions of them all rising up into the heavens out of the darkness. If you knew how beautiful prayer is, you would pray all the time. Then there are those powerful prayers one prays when a miracle is desperately needed. There is power in the Name, and those that know how to pray emit such a bright, commanding light that it looks like lightning bolts sent from earth to Heaven and to the feet of the Creator Himself. Prayers are so powerful, especially when one stranger prays for another, such as Audrey while working in the store. Prayers even change the chemistry of our food before we eat it. If simply speaking kind words changes the chemistry of water or helps your plants grow bigger and healthier, just imagine how a prayer can bless and change lives.

Things aren't always as they seem. Audrey suffered a heartbreaking loss when Romeo crossed the rainbow bridge, but Teacup and Tony came to fill the empty space in her life. Audrey lived out her life with the aching feeling of loneliness. She felt so alone without friends or Ethan really being there for her. If she only knew how I'd never left her side. If she only knew how it was actually the two of us watching the stars come out at night, sipping wine, and listening to the music I played for her. If she only knew that she has more angels than friends, she'd never feel alone again.

Even marriage. Things aren't always as they seem. Audrey believed she'd married a man who was in love with her and that kind of love would last. She thought that marrying a good man who loved her, and just having one, just one person in her corner, would allow her to accomplish great things. Ethan was a lost soul, though. He didn't know himself, he didn't really know her, and he certainly didn't know what would make him happy. It is only if we know and love ourselves well, with a certain level of self-awareness, that we are able to know and love other people. For Audrey, it was different. How long could you love a man who didn't return the sentiment? There were times I heard her heart cry out to him, "Love me, so I can love myself again." She stayed, hoping that a connection could be made again someday, that he would be happy again someday. But her marriage was an endless winter season, with unpredictable weather, spontaneous downpours, tornadoes without warning, while she longed for signs of spring.

Wild winds swept the hands of the clock faster and faster. Seasons came and went, and soon Audrey and Ethan found themselves in October, receiving notice from their landlord that the home they had loved for almost seven years was being sold out from under them. They had nowhere to go. Prices of apartments were outrageous. Other rental homes were even worse, if you could find them. They began to look into buying a home but far enough away to be affordable. Anything remotely close to the Bay Area had only grown in price. Half a million dollars for a tiny, run-down house was common. It was cheap, actually. But this was California, and everything comes at a high price.

They looked in Valley Springs, a small, dry town up in the foothills. It was miles and miles of oak trees and soft rolling golden land. After some consideration, they decided they just needed to look for more green grass and trees and signs of life. Audrey looked up the prices in those charming mining towns they loved to visit. She looked for homes in Jamestown, Sonora, Columbia, and even Twain Harte. Though the commute would be a long one for Ethan, the area grew on them. Pines and oaks, green grass, deer, and wild turkeys. The pace was a bit slower, and the people seemed friendlier and happier.

They were referred to a real estate agent named Ted, who must've shown them four or five houses every weekend. The closer they came to the holidays, the more hostile their landlord became. She was eager to move Audrey and Ethan out, but it wasn't to sell. She wanted to hike the rent up another couple of thousand dollars a month. She'd lied to them, already having new renters lined up. She became threatening and harassing to hasten their move.

In this chaotic time of house hunting, there were wonderful moments on certain weekends when Adele, Ben, Audrey, and Ethan went house hunting together and then went out to lunch after seeing the last house on the list. Audrey invited them on these lunch dates in hopes of changing Adele's mind about moving to Mississippi. California was home. She had hoped that in seeing how beautiful the rolling golden hills dotted with tall oaks, the towering pines and green glades, the deer grazing in warm meadows, and the simple alluring beauty of a woodland path, Adele would be reminded of why she chose to call California home, year after year. It was working. All four of them began to dream of the possibilities of living close by, helping each other, sharing Sunday dinners and morning tea. Audrey and Ethan planned to buy a large lot so that in time, Adele and Ben could build a little cottage nearby, close enough to ride golf carts from one door to another. Adele and Ben were getting older and needed looking after. Ethan made dinner each night, more than enough for the two of them. Audrey had hopes of sharing Ethan's home-cooked meals, delivering them to their doorstep on the nights her mother and Ben didn't feel like cooking.

Audrey helped Adele list her house, Audrey's childhood home, the enchanted garden, and the home so close to my own, and a flurry of offers was received within days. It seemed like all their stars were aligning, and the fresh start for Audrey and Adele was in full swing. They spoke almost every day, checking in on each other, laughing as if Aunt Diane was on the phone, having the mother-daughter friendship that Audrey had so longed for.

Audrey and Ethan made an offer on a place, but it seemed to be a strange bidding war with the owner. They gave her their best offer, but it just never felt right. Though the place was tucked deep in the woods and on a private driveway, it had an unusable and awkward backyard, the neighbors happened to be in a war with themselves, and red flags were waving. But Audrey and Ethan were more desperate with each passing day. They had no prospects. They were losing hope, and the pressure to move was crushing.

One early evening, Audrey sat outside by her pond with her guitar in hand. As she strummed the chords of a gentle melody, she looked around at the yard she had loved so much. She'd become a gardener here, learned to work with the land to grow food and flowers. She kept the company of koi and goldfish, birds and cats. She kept the company of so much more than she'd ever realize. The soft resonance of the melody she played swirled around her as if caught in the wind and rose to the sky. From high above her, orbs of garden spirits with the hearts that she had touched while tending this little garden drew near. Only I could see how she drew us all close to her with her song. I could see the glowing orbs, the specs of light, one by one, gather all around in the ether, until there must have been hundreds. I wish she could see this. She spent time that evening with gratitude for all her memories in this wonderful home. She thanked it for being her shelter through so many storms, her escape and oasis, the literal form of holding a space. With a heavy heart and tears in her eyes, she was saying goodbye.

She searched the real estate listings, even though they both felt like giving up. But it was in the early hours of the morning that Audrey saw a picture of a little house on seven acres, high atop a mountain, surprisingly in their price range. She sent the link to Ethan at work. He made the call to Ted, and by the grace of God, they were the first potential buyers to view it.

It was a warm, sunny fall day when Ted led Audrey and Ethan through the property. Ted mentioned that the owner was selling because his wife had passed away, and he was planning on moving to Virginia to be with family. Audrey could see signs of his wife at almost every turn. She had planted a rose garden showing off its final blooms of the season. A photo was left on a shelf in one of the rooms, and Audrey gazed at it for a moment. It was a photo of the owners, Tim and Deb. They were older, Tim with his wisdom and

Deb with her warm smile. Audrey felt a connection with them.

Audrey, Ethan, and Ted walked the sprawling acres. There was a road carved through the woodsy land's perimeter, a path weaving through the trees, inspiring long evening walks and morning adventures. At first, Ethan was nervous that it might be too much land, that they might be getting in over their heads. They walked out the back door and were greeted by a group of hungry little barn cats. Two were just kittens, looking a lot like Roxy and Romeo as little ones. The cats ranged from tabbies to black cats, long and short hair, some friendly and some feral. The kittens rushed to Ethan's shoes and looked up at him, hoping he had some food. Before they left that day, they arranged for their offer to be submitted.

The owner was happy to receive their offer but decided to wait through the week to see if more offers would come in. The place was being seen by many people. Panic and worry grew, so they prayed together. It wasn't only that Audrey prayed to God for the opportunity to love this place and call it home. Each day that passed, as Audrey packed up her belongings, she spoke to Deb, the rose gardener and previous owner. She told Deb her hopes and dreams of the place. She talked to her about her garden and how she'd love to be the one to care for it, for her.

The passing days were agony. Finally, that weekend, Audrey and Ethan got the good news that their offer had been accepted. There were many more hurdles to jump to make sure that they could move out of their old home and into their new one in a timely fashion. They prayed together for miracles, and miracles were granted. Everything worked out seamlessly. Angel prints all over it.

I can attest that Deb heard every word. Deb weighed heavily on Tim's heart, which prompted him to choose the offer from the kids. Deb was so happy to hear that her garden would live on and be l oved. Deb's spirit was very much alive in this garden and through the land, and she was honored to be seen by Audrey and not just as some woman who had lived there once upon a time. What Audrey and Ethan didn't know was that even though they had their hearts set on a couple of other places, made offers and said prayers, no other home would've been theirs. But things aren't always as they seem. This place was set aside for them. This place chose them. When they started giving up and losing hope, fearing they'd never find a place in time that would be what they wanted or could afford, it was God aligning the stars according to His plan. It was all a redirection. He led them on a path that brought them home, this home.

On Audrey's birthday, a chilly day in mid-December, she and Ethan spent the whole day moving, much like every day before and after that. They emptied the boxes from the moving truck, and as the sun went down, they drove a few miles into downtown Columbia for the best pizza around. The truck was so big that they had to find an empty parking lot at the edge of town to park it. They walked down Main Street of the very old goldmining town, dimly lit by flickering street lanterns. The stores were all closed, but in the not-too-far distance was the glowing St. Charles Saloon.

They rested their tired bones in the old saloon, waiting for their gourmet pizza, amid the lively regulars. They all knew each other and gave warm greetings each time the door opened. Audrey and Ethan sat at a table beside the bar, looking all around at the historical memorabilia, the antique upright piano, sepia-toned photos, and the waitstaff dressed for the late 1800s. There was a drunk old timer at the bar beside their table who swayed back and forth. At times, he looked like he was about to fall fast asleep, but he'd sway too far and wake himself up. Audrey protected her drink in her hand and alerted Ethan about him. They both watched him sway and giggled. They wondered if, at some point, the guy would lean too far from the bar and land in the middle of their table. Eventually his cab arrived, and the regulars made sure he got home all right by passing him down the bar like a Chinese fire drill and finally out the door. The birthday pizza was delicious and lived up to the reviews. They toasted to Audrey's birthday and how far they'd come. They toasted to their new home and to all that the future holds.

As they left the St. Charles Saloon, they walked hand in hand through the dark street. Pitch black, spooky alleyways to either side, but some were illuminated only by the lit ends of cigarettes and chatter. On the winding road that led back to the valley, Audrey was tired but thankful. There were a million times throughout this move where she and Ethan could've fought like the titans they once were. But she was grateful for how much they'd changed. They were too tired to fight, they were too scared of being thrown out on the street with nowhere to go, that it forced them to grow closer and work together. They were older and wiser; they had begun a new chapter, all just in time.

Adele and Ben drove up to visit, bringing housewarming gifts of tasty snacks and Audrey's favorite blackberry wine that Ben insisted on buying for her. Before they all set out into town to get some lunch, Ethan drove all of them down the perimeter path, pointing out potential places for their cottage to be built. Ethan's truck was a four-wheel-drive, so he drove them up hills, around sharp corners and down steep embankments all to hear their laughter. It was an adventure after all. They ate at their favorite Mexican food restaurant and spoke of their exciting plans for the future. Adele and Ben loved the place and were ready to get moving. Sadly, it would be the last visit Ben and Adele would make to their home.

Ben encouraged Adele to call Audrey to catch up most days, but when they were done talking, Ben would want to talk to Audrey as well. Over the years, they had become wonderful friends and could talk about almost anything. They both had a sense of humor, laughing the time away, but they were also able to talk about real topics, politics and faith, sadness, illness, all the things that can burden the soul. All throughout Ben's life, he'd avoided asking the big questions about the afterlife and God. He was a big, tough guy and usually felt immortal, but over the last few years, the sense of his mortality set in. He told Audrey about his fears, that because of his past, he may not get into heaven. Audrey spent hours talking with him, sharing with him the process she went through to become closer to her Creator. She told him how a counselor at her church had met with her, giving her spiritual guidance and helping her through the dark night of the soul. She mentioned that saying the sinner's prayer and being baptized might be something that would make him feel better about where his soul was headed. He asked Audrey how to say the prayer. There are many versions, but this is the prayer she shared with him that day.

Jesus, I know that I'm a sinner and I ask You for Your forgiveness.

I believe You died for my sins and rose from the dead.

I invite You to live in my heart, and I promise to commit

My life to You.

In saying this simple prayer and believing it, from that moment on, you are transformed into a new being. Your sins are forgiven, your past is forgotten. There are a lot of people who struggle with the idea that two thousand years ago, God took human form to make a new covenant with His people. That this man took on the sins of the world by taking the punishment and death of humanity, that you may have eternal life. He wasn't born to a king in a castle; he was born in a manger. He didn't arrive in Jerusalem on a white horse, but rather on the back of a humble donkey. Instead of using his powers to create riches for himself, he risked his life healing others. I find that to be so beautiful.

Saying this prayer doesn't mean that you have to have everything figured out. In fact, you might be confused now more than ever, but God wants you to be open to the wisdom He's about to give you. He just wants you to have the faith of a tiny mustard seed and believe. That's the beauty of this walk with Him. Amazing how scripture written thousands of years ago can impact one's life today. It gives you strength and renews your hope. It transforms you. In the darkest of Audrey's days, sometimes she felt like the only things she had left were His promises. But they are unfailing. They comforted her more than anything else could. Ben, after all these years, had just become a believer. When he said those words and opened his heart, a miraculous light began to flow from it.

Ben felt a real sense of urgency now, and their conversations grew in depth. In one phone call, he revealed to Audrey the things that tormented him from his past. In his younger days, he had been good looking, played sports, driven a hot rod, and lived a charmed California teenage life. After high school, he joined the army and was soon deployed. During one of his trips back home, he had a fun night out with friends and was intimate with a shy girl named Caroline who had secretly always loved him. He returned to his base and went on about his life, but a year later, when it was time to come back home, there on his mother's doorstep was Caroline, sitting with Ben's mother, who was holding her grandchild. Caroline had gotten pregnant from their one-night stand and had a child, though never telling him until that day. He did the honorable thing. He married Caroline. They raised two sons together. He was a good husband and father to his boys, but his heart remained with someone else. In his time away, he fell in love with a nurse named Betty. She was a firecracker. She was a stunning beauty with a dynamic personality, vastly different from the woman Ben was obligated to marry. Through the years, his marriage became troubled. It was failing, and Ben decided to leave Caroline, but tried with all of his heart to be there for his sons in any way they needed. The whole story was heartbreaking for Ben. He had a chance to finally revive his romance with nurse Betty, but time had changed them, and they couldn't get back what they once had. He begged her to stay, but Betty found a job in San Francisco and decided to move on.

Ben found himself alone. Nurse Betty was gone from his life. Caroline had always been in love with Ben, but he just never felt the same way for her. His sons were witnesses to all of this, and no matter how much time, money, and effort he devoted to his sons, they never forgave him for leaving their mother. He went through most of his life under the burden of crushing guilt. Alcohol, women, and other vices were never enough to ease the pain, so he focused all that he had left on his work until one day he was led on a stroll through the garden center to look at the flowers and found dimes instead.

Ben began meeting with a church counselor, Brother Rodriguez, and great progress was made. Ben bought his very first Bible and read a little each day. Audrey told him that sometimes one verse is enough to keep her going through the day, that there were blessings disguised as letters on a page in the book of good news, and she was right. God is within the words. When you hold close to the promises He made to us, life becomes a little easier to bear. Brother Rodriguez and Ben agreed it was time for him to be baptized, and as the day grew closer, Ben was more excited about it. There's a miracle that happens to all of us when we are baptized. We enter the water a mortal, and as the Holy Spirit shines upon us as we rise from the water, we are given the gift of eternal life.

Two days following his baptism, he developed a cough that escalated into double pneumonia. Two weeks later, he was rushed to the emergency room, having terrible difficulty breathing. When Audrey heard the news, she came to their aid the best way she knew how. She spoke with his medical team and became Ben's health advocate, while Adele was spiraling out of control. Adele was wrought with anxiety, wondering if that was the last time she'd see her "blue eyes" again. She was nearly inconsolable, but as soon as Audrey could, she drove down to offer support and stay with her mom in her childhood home. Audrey spoke to the doctors and nurses daily, but days turned into weeks, and his condition worsened. It was on Audrey's last phone call with Ben that she told him she loved him and that he needed to get better, that they had too many fun plans for the future, and she needed more time with him. She stood at the edge, a steady drop off as the glade in her yard began and heard his voice for the last time. She remembered how beautiful the stars looked that cold February evening, and that very spot would always remind her of the last connection she had with her very dear friend.

A deep divide between Adele and Audrey grew, as it became apparent that Adele needed to step up and answer the doctor's calls but failed to do so. She was his wife, and decisions had to be made by her in the end. Adele was falling apart and felt let down by Audrey, forgetting everything Audrey had done for her up to that point. Just as easily as it was in the past, Adele turned against Audrey. In vicious words, the way a wounded animal lashes out at people trying their best to help, she told Audrey she never wanted to see her again. All the ugliness of the past was dredged up, blame was cast, and Audrey was shunned once again by her mother. Somehow Audrey was to blame for her loss and for all of her pain. None of that was true, but feeling the rejection of her mother all over again, a very deep wound reopened, yet this time, the wound was beyond mending.

Audrey had lost touch with her mother and sister for many years after she moved out at eighteen. Lost though she was, it was still better than being in toxic family relationships. The whole reason for Audrey and her mother reconciling these last few years was because of Ben. He disliked Audrey's sister, for the same reasons I did, but she had long since moved away on yet another grand hunt for love, men, and money. Ben knew that this was the time for second chances, a time when Adele and Audrey could have time together without the poison of a jealous sister around. He was trying to give Adele and Audrey the chance at a relationship that he so desperately wanted with his own children. Audrey would always love him for that. In the end, her greatest regret was not spending more time with him. She can still hear his caring voice on the line and his words of encouragement.

It's hard to speak sensibly with irrational people. Her mother cut ties for the last time. Audrey erased her text messages and emails. She cried harder than ever before, her heart shattered, having lost both her mother and Ben at the same time. Things aren't always as they seem. I understood it now. The ewe that rejected the lamb. Audrey seemed like the rejected lamb, but it wasn't all about her mother's rejection. It was about the love of her shepherd. With a rejected lamb, the shepherd must care for the lamb, feed her, and tend to her needs for its survival. But this time it was Audrey's shepherd that wanted to be the one who cared for her, mending her broken heart, holding her close, surrounding her with love. So now, finally, she would truly be able to know the depths of His love for her.

Ethan was the most comforting he had ever been. Time had changed him in wonderful ways. Amazingly enough, the job he dreaded taking by joining the military once again had softened him. Sure, he was the tough soldier, but by being in charge of many other soldiers with real problems, it was an education in empathy and compassion. Counseling these men and women through their problems had helped him understand Audrey better. He had also felt loss many times in his own life and knew what kind of support Audrey needed. He offered words of his wisdom, knowing what it took to deal with the pain of losing a loved one. He held her close when she cried, he cooked for her and took care of her as well as he could, but Audrey's depression was setting in. She wasn't sleeping or eating, she was self-medicating with alcohol and regretting it each morning.

She often sat outside quietly contemplating life in its flowing hourglass. The stress of the move, the news of the world in growing turmoil, and the gravity of loss crushed her spirit. She wandered through the house with little energy and will to do anything. The cleaning piled up, the to-do list kept growing, and the pressures of life in general grew, making her ever so weary. She wondered where her peace and free spirit had flown off to. And wondered if it might ever return.

She fed the tribe of hungry little lions outside her door, and while outside, feeling the warm sunlight on her face, she wandered just beyond the front garden gate, where the old swing with new cushions invited her to rest. She sat quietly, absorbing the sounds of nature all around her. Songbirds flying in and out of her garden with full bellies, singing happy early spring songs. She watched a gray squirrel leap from tree to tree, eating food with its little hands and giggling as they do. She closed her eyes to the sound of the gentle wind combing the tallest branches, through the pine needles and oak leaves.

With eyes closed and heart open, she began to pray over her family, her husband, her babies, and herself. She thanked Him for all the gifts He had given her, and the blessings on their way. She lifted Ben up in prayer and placed him in God's healing hands. She accepted that the events had all gone according to His plan and perfect timing. As we mourn the dying, as they lie in a bed, a fraction of the being they once were, their spirit may have already been taken home. The body, the empty temple is what is left here on earth. It is still to be honored.

Life truly is a treasure. Soon she stood from that old swing and walked across the driveway and down into the glade. She wasn't sure where her boots were taking her, but just being out in the green grass and tall trees was healing. She decided to take this long walk through the property, and no matter how far she had to walk, how tired she might become, or how cold she might feel, she decided to keep walking through this healing land until she was herself again. And by the time she returned from this walk, she was determined to start living. Solvitur Ambulando is Latin. It means it is solved by walking.

When we lose a loved one, it may not be that we want to die, but we lose the will to go on living without them. A part of us is missing. There's no escaping that. But the loved ones we lost would never want us to live in sadness. We begin to feel through our loss that living joyfully, fully, boldly doesn't honor them. But that sadness is lying to you. Our loved ones don't want you to waste your breaths in sorrow, in their name. It is so much the contrary. We wanted you to savor your days and live and breathe and love because we no longer can but wish we could.

So honor your loved ones in this: go outside and listen to all of the life, God's creations all around you, fill your lungs with deep breaths of fresh air, go on long walks through nature and marvel at His work, allow yourself to feel small on a big planet spinning in the universe, knowing that God wanted you to be a part of it all, give freely, wrap your arms around your loved ones until they know how treasured they are to you, make peace and bury hatchets, feed the birds and plant a garden—watching life thrive because you had a hand in it all. Live so boldly in love and savor life that even the slightest encounters with strangers make an indelible mark on their lives, that whoever is lucky enough to know you aspires to live boldly too. That's how you honor your loved ones beyond the veil. We'll be watching. We'll be so proud and cheer for you and celebrate your victories and watch you grow. And we'll be waiting to greet you in paradise once your purpose in life has been fulfilled, and you are called home. But you must live in love boldly now, right now, for there will never be enough time.

Chapter Eighteen

S torms have many different spiritual meanings. Native Americans believe that there are two primal forces represented in a storm: destruction and creation. Lakota believed that perhaps some storms are the spiritual world's intention of connecting with the natural world, and in some way, the rumbles of thunder and the heartbeat of the earth are trying to attune with its people. Eastern philosophy teaches that storms come to remind us of the impermanence of things in our lives, to lighten our grip and let go if we must, and to embrace our ever-changing environment. Some storms destroy, some cleanse, some transform. But the wild winds were up to something, and Audrey could feel it.

She had an eye for noticing patterns. Some were subtle, but these two seemed more obvious than others. Whenever Ethan left for a military obligation, something strange inevitably happened. It was something so predictable that they just began to laugh at it but didn't dare speculate about, for fear of giving fate any ideas. The other pattern she realized was that in the middle of storms, births are far more likely.

A terrible storm was headed straight for their little town of Columbia. A small tornado had formed, the likes of winds Audrey had never seen before. Things that weren't tied down were caught by the wind and moved or disappeared entirely. Ethan and Audrey had put a portable carport together just before he left. Not having enough time to secure it into the ground, he tied it to railroad ties and an old engine stand, weighing hundreds of pounds. Through the night, Audrey peered out the windows, watching the wind ravage the trees and land outside and the carport fill with air as if it were about to lift off at any moment. Sure enough, later that night, it did. It just wasn't anchored enough, and the carport had blown and tumbled a hundred feet away.

Ethan arrived back home to see the storm's aftermath, and they worked to put everything back together. They laughed at the strange happenings always occurring in his absence. Once all the work was done, they ventured into the garden. Just by chance, Ethan happened to look down and see something dark and furry underneath the branches of a magenta potted rosebush. Upon closer inspection, he began to hear tiny squeaks from the little furballs, and his mouth gaped open in shock to see it was a new litter of kittens. The mother was a skittish barn cat that they had tried to befriend, but all their efforts failed, and she hid in the bushes with watchful eyes as Audrey came to see why Ethan waved her over. They both looked into the large pot in wonder, but they knew not to handle the kittens and quietly stepped away, letting the new mama have her space and time.

The next day, Audrey peered into the rose bush, but the kittens had been moved. The fearful mother had moved them somewhere still in the garden. Audrey could hear those tiny squeaks. There was a place that the mother perhaps prepared for them. They were found behind a line of large pots, deep within tall stalks of spring wildflowers. It was this perfect place where the stalks of flowers had been trampled just enough to fit the little family, this pile of tiny furry babies, all sleeping against one another, so soundly. They were all black, but Audrey had already fallen in love with the one and only smoky baby that looked an awful lot like Roxy.

The weather became much warmer, and the kitten family had been moved once again, but this time, the momma kitty found a cozy spot for them in the carport. Audrey had an idea that the cats would love to take shelter on the many piled boxes inside, so she placed towels and rugs in various places to keep her little outdoor friends comfortable. Though weeks went by, Ethan and Audrey were still curious about how the little crew was doing. One night, as they placed plates of wet food down for the outside cats, they saw a little shadow streak and scurry about. They wondered if it was a mouse. It moved too fast for them to get a good look. Some of the kittens had grown old enough to venture out and look for more solid food. But there was this tiny kitten, the runt of the litter, the smoky baby, which was starving for food but just too shy to step up to the plates. The plates would be licked clean by the time the tiny baby would work up the nerve.

The hungrier he became, the closer he would come to Audrey and Ethan. They noticed he was terribly skinny, a tiny body and giant ears. He became their obsession. Ethan was able to put plates out at night and come close enough to pick the little guy up. Ethan nicknamed him Munchkin and would hold his little body in his big hands for as long as Munchkin would allow. A little longer each time, though with strays, you're always taking a few steps forward and then several steps back. Ethan was determined to catch Munchkin and make him part of the family, one way or another.

One day, Munchkin wasn't moving as fast as he normally did. He was becoming sick. Animals have a funny way of being feral until they have no choice but to ask for help. Ethan held baby Munchkin in his arms as Audrey drove to the vet. He was fading fast. Audrey was so worried that she stayed in the car while Ethan carried him inside the vet's office. She prayed as tears rolled down her cheeks. After a while, he returned with Munchkin with a concerned look on his face. The vet had given Munchkin a 50/50 shot at survival. He had an upper respiratory infection, was severely malnourished, and had parasites.

The vet had offered to put him down, but Ethan had protested. Absolutely not, he told them. From then on, their mission was to save their little Munchkin.

He slept on Ethan's chest and kneaded through his t-shirt and into his skin, leaving lots of little red scratches. Ethan didn't care; he was a proud dad and held him every chance he got. Some nights, Audrey's back would hurt, and she would find the chairs in the living room more comfortable to sleep in. Munchie would find her there. He would struggle to climb up the blankets to get to her. She soon put a little set of steps to make it easy for him, and in those nights, he would crawl up onto her chest and back up as closely under her chin as he could. That's where he decided to sleep every night. It was hard for him to breathe, but after all of this, they knew he was a tough little dude.

The meds had worked. First, the worm medicine kicked in, causing a ten-inch white worm to work its way partially out of him. Ethan held Munchie as Audrey, with tissues in hand, pulled a giant, warm parasite from his back end. Once the worms were gone, Munchie began to grow. His cough disappeared, and his fur filled in. He became so fluffy and began to grow into those big ears of his, revealing a whole new side to his personality. He looked like their little wolf now. He had the bushiest tail that swayed and waved as his little body strutted around the house. Audrey decided he needed a new name to match the massive personality that filled their home.

She named him Wolfgang, Wolfie for short. He snuck up onto their laps while they watched the movie Amadeus, sleeping on dad's chest for a while and then finally snuggling up under mom's chin.

It was never a dull moment on Blessed Mountain for them. Often it felt like they were putting one fire out while another sparked. They had become tired and overwhelmed with life but still managed to go to work and cook dinner, but all they really wanted to do was hold Wolfie. He had a way of making everything okay. He walked into a room, and they would both call out his name and watch him strut around and climb the chairs up to the kitchen counter to beg for treats. He would sit with one front paw raised up. He knew exactly what he was doing, being irresistible. It worked every time. Ethan and Audrey still treasured all their cats, spoiled them, and showered them with love, but when it came to Wolfie, it was different. They'd saved him from the brink, and that set him apart.

Wolfie was fussy about being picked up. He didn't like too much pressure on his little round belly. He still scurried about and played with the other cats, but he was, by far, the most loving. As soon as either of them sat down, he would climb into their laps and sit there proudly, swishing his giant, fluffy tail about. They got through the frosty winter months together, sitting in those chairs in the evening, multiple cats piled on their blankets and Wolfie right in the middle.

Audrey looked back on her phone to that day when she took the video of the little sleeping family nestled down under the cover of wildflowers. It had already been a year, and they celebrated his birthday with special cat treats and wet food. Audrey shared the special occasion on social media as Wolfie had gained quite the following. A year with Wolfie, she titled the post, unaware of the storm that was coming.

Audrey began to notice Wolfie would sleep a lot. He stopped playing and running around the house. He just wanted to be held more. Audrey always knew when her kids were sick. They both took him to the vet and put him on antibiotics. Then another round, and another. Nothing worked. He had a terrible runny nose and soon couldn't breathe out of his nose at all. It kept him from sleeping. He was fading fast, but they couldn't bring themselves to believe it. They decided to take him to a different vet, and maybe a second opinion might save his life. They were desperate.

Audrey's prayers were endless. She prayed like she'd never prayed before. She lit the heavens with bolts of lightning, she pleaded, she bargained, she begged. Ethan did the same. But Audrey was wondering why her prayers were going unanswered. She prayed harder, louder, she made sure the heavens heard every word, though the heavens were silent. She was beginning to feel abandoned by God. Where was He when she needed Him most?

Audrey cried the whole way to the appointment, and while she cleaned her face up in the car, Ethan took Wolfie inside the vet's office. Once Audrey stepped outside their truck, she was greeted by an old cowboy walking to his truck door. He made a funny statement about his parking, and Audrey giggled, even though she didn't feel like it. She stopped and stared at the black lab that was standing in the bed of the old man's truck. The big black lab looked into Audrey's eyes with so much compassion. It looked at her with more empathy and sadness than she had ever encountered from a human before. The old man said that he hoped she had a wonderful day, trying to say something kind to the woman with a red face from crying. The lab bowed his head. Somehow, he just knew.

When Audrey entered the vet's exam room, she saw little Wolfie's eyes looked very strange. The color had turned a dark yellow ochre, and they weren't dilated the same. The infection had spread through his body, and his liver wasn't functioning. One look into his eyes and she knew.

Over the course of the next few days, little Wolfie was losing his battle. Their hearts were crushed. Ethan grieved differently from Audrey. While Audrey's tears were endless, Ethan still held onto hope that Wolfie would pull through, that a miracle would happen, just as it had the first time. The night they had been dreading had come, and as Wolfie was breathing his last breaths, he lay in the center of their big bed, surrounded by Audrey and Ethan, and all the other cats. They lay there in silence, in unspeakable pain, until the very end.

It was now Ethan's turn to break apart. All hope had been lost.

Prayers went unanswered. Confusion, anger, and a deep darkness, settling in for both of them. They both drowned their sorrows. Tears fell as they raised their glasses to toast little Wolfie.

I watched as Audrey felt more abandoned than ever. She still prayed to God, but she was full of questions. "Are you there? Are you even listening? Do you even care? Say something to me, dammit!" But God remained quiet. I had never seen her in more despair. It's one thing to lose a baby. Wolfie was her baby; he slept under her chin and loved her with all his heart, and losing him was pure devastation, but feeling that her God turned away from her was a whole new level of pain. I watched the light of her faith diminish almost entirely. She doubted her ability to pray. She wanted for so long to be a prayer warrior as generations past but felt as if she'd failed. She felt like she'd failed Wolfie. Failed Ethan too.

What do you do when you're faced with crippling pain and loss of the likes most will never know? She poured a round of the strongest alcohol she could stomach and then another and then another, until she was numb enough to somehow continue living. Wrapped up in Audrey's favorite scarf and placed gently into a bed, Ethan and Audrey drove Wolfie down to the vet's office for cremation. They were both quiet and just stared far into the distance. I wished they knew what I knew, though. I wished they saw what I saw. Wolfie was no longer in the box. His spirit was all around them. He climbed up on Ethan's chest and kneaded with enthusiasm and kissed his cheek. Then he climbed over to Audrey and snuggled up under her chin. He nuzzled her cheek, and as tears began to fall from her eyes, she tilted her head and leaned into him. She felt him there. She felt his love, but she just thought it was her imagination. Wolfie jumped back and forth between them as they went about their entire day.

Religions all over the world revere the grieving. Lakota considers the grieving to be holy, that in their time of mourning, their prayers are most powerful, their connection with the afterlife profound.

There is no elegant way to grieve. There are books and beliefs on how one should cope with loss, but grief is something that can't be structured. It feels as if those wild winds circle around you, envelop you, swallow you whole. In the chaos of flying memories and swirling senses, you cry and wail and hit things and curse and drink and bleed. You just have to. Lock the door behind you and get it all out. Cry all you need to, until your eyes are swollen and empty and your head aches. It's not pretty. It's not supposed to be. But as I sat beside those grieving me, I felt all their love, every bit of it, from beginning to end, and that was beautiful.

On this side of the veil, our hearts feel a tug when you think of us. We know. And if the living only knew how wonderful the afterlife is, it wouldn't be such a heartbreaking end, but merely a I'll see you soon. It would make letting go maybe a little easier. There is no elegant way to grieve, but there is grace in letting go.

Later in the day, Audrey stepped to the edge of the glade and looked out at the beautiful spring view and all the life that surrounded her. She spoke to her little man, saying, "Thank you for loving us. Thank you for being such a huge part of our lives. We will always always, always love you." It was after that moment that I watched Wolfie and his big, fluffy tail walk across the rainbow bridge halfway. He turned back, wanting to run back to her, but bowed his head and continued crossing over.

They went back to work. The distraction of people and their happier energy was a good thing. It helped a little. But all that pain Audrey was feeling, that didn't get drowned out, got buried deep within her and began a storm of its own.

Several days later, the vet called with the results of the tests taken on Wolfie's last visit. The vet told them that it just came down to bad genes. He was predisposed to a weak immune system, and it was nothing short of a miracle that he survived the first infection.

Miracle. Yes, it was. Instead of God taking him when he was that little Munchkin scurrying about in the carport, in what should've been no time at all, God gave them a year with him. And Wolfie knew it. Wolfie knew that he didn't have much time, so he loved them as much as he could, every single day. He gave them all of his attention and made them laugh and made the most of every minute, the best way he knew how. The time they had with him was a gift. The time we have with each other is a gift. We just never know for how long.

Audrey's prayers were heard and considered, and appreciated, but after a year, he was called back home. It was his condition; it was his sick little body that perished. Her prayers had nothing to do with it. God heard every word. He collected her every tear. He bandaged her heart. And slowly I watched as He reminded her of how much He loved her, no matter what happened. Despite her anger, despite her confusion and doubt, He was there with her all along.

Her angels tried to communicate to her that her prayers were still heard. They were still powerful. They were still worth praying for. Don't stop praying just because you didn't get the answer you wanted. Pray through it. Ask the questions. Seek the answers. Don't give up.

Ethan and Audrey had a couple of weeks to calm themselves and try to return to some sense of normalcy before Ethan had to leave for another month-long trip, an important class he needed for promotion. There was a sense of worry deep within Audrey. She wasn't strong enough to handle anything strange happening while Ethan was away, and there was no rescheduling this trip.

They worked hard for days, making sure most of the big tasks had been handled so Audrey wouldn't have too much around the house to worry about. The time came for him to pack up his things and leave home. His training and classes were planned so he would be closer to advancement. He wasn't excited about leaving home, but it would shift his focus, something he very much needed to be able to heal. And just like the deployment after they lost Romeo, a change of scenery, being around other like-minded people, would do him well. But just as Audrey had to stay at home alone during the deployment, seeing all the places where Romeo slept and played, she was surrounded by memories of little Wolfie, weighed down by a shattered heart instead of his weight under her chin. Oh, how she loved that feeling of him sleeping there on her chest. Most nights, she would fall asleep with her hand where he used to be. Her little Teacup began to sleep on her chest, to her surprise. Something she had never done in the past, but what a wonderful feeling it was, a love on her chest again.

Audrey valued the peace and quiet in the house. She played the meditation music and sat on the porch with the kitties, watching them chase each other in the grass and pounce from behind pots. The roses were in full bloom, the garden abuzz with bees and bumbles, butterflies and dragonflies. I sat with her there on the steps of the porch as her mind wandered to that heavenly home, waiting for her on this side of the veil. She imagined little Wolfie playing with Romeo, his tail high in the air, swishing about. She wished the rainbow bridge offered visiting hours. How fun that would be.

It was late at night when Audrey awoke from horrible pains. In the last few weeks, she would have had about an hour of excruciating pain that radiated from her back, in the area of her kidneys. She spoke with her doctor, and they decided it was most likely kidney stones that she was passing. But that late-night pain she experienced carried on into the morning, and by 11:00 a.m., she was driving to the emergency room, alone. She pulled into the parking lot and cursed the other drivers for how horribly they had all parked their cars. She had to circle about to find a space and slowly walked toward the entrance.

After checking in at the desk, she sat among the young and old, those in pain and suffering. There were a couple of little children who had broken bones. There was an older man dressed in motorcycle gear who had a terrible cough and trouble breathing. There was an older woman with shoulder-length gray hair who offered everyone a compassionate smile. Audrey kept to herself, her pain level rising, worried that this might be something serious, that she was having to handle it all on her own. She put one earphone in an ear and played music that calmed her. Gavri, Em, and I were right there beside her. All the patients in the waiting room were surrounded by their angels. Hospitals are crowded places, but spiritually speaking, they are overflowing.

Audrey watched the other patients being called before her according to the severity of their condition. As she waited, she prayed for each and every one of them. She blessed them all.

One of her prayers was interrupted when she looked out the front windows and saw a woman who looked like she had come straight from her garden. She was in jean shorts, a tank top, hiking boots, and garden gloves. She held her wrist close to her chest. When she entered the emergency room and checked in, she finally began to sob. Her sobbing made Audrey begin to cry. She wanted to console the woman but wasn't sure if it was her place to do so. Audrey's prayers centered on this woman now, to ease her suffering and calm her heart.

After a few moments, the old lady with the compassionate smile asked if she could change seats to elevate her foot. She wanted to move to a seat close to Audrey. As she got up to walk, Audrey saw that she was unstable and got up in an instant to steady her. Once seated, the lady became a chatterbox about, of all things, cats. Audrey assumed this woman was nervous, and talking was calming her nerves. It was a welcome distraction. The woman had a terribly swollen foot from a spider bite. She was older and had bruises or splotches all over her exposed skin. She clearly had problems with her health, but she sat there and told funny stories and laughed with Audrey until she was called away by the nurse.

The ER was quiet again. She had noticed that she was surrounded by women who had to drive themselves there. These women didn't have husbands who were alive to drive them. Anytime Ethan had an opportunity, he'd text or call Audrey for an update. He was worried but believed they would run some tests, give her some medicine, and she'd return home soon.

That wasn't exactly how things happened. The nurse finally called her name and led her to her own room. She finally could lie down and rest her back. She was in terrible pain but was now being examined, stuck with needles, and had her blood drawn. She was weak and tired, wearing a hospital gown with a light hospital blanket wrapped around her body. She kept wondering what the problem was, what they were going to do to her, and was this as serious as it felt? Different staff would lead her into exam rooms for a CT scan, then an ultrasound. The lady with the spider bite was lying on a gurney in the hallway, and as Audrey was being wheeled passed her, they would wave at each other and offer words of encouragement each time. It was a small comfort for them both. Doctors would enter the room and press deeply into her abdomen, ruling out appendicitis and pancreatitis. The CT scan showed no signs of kidney stones, but the ultrasound showed that she had gallstones. It also showed that the bile duct from her gallbladder was dilated more than it should be. Her blood test revealed that her liver enzymes were quite high and rising, and that made the doctors uneasy.

It was easy to yell at the doctors from where I was. I could see it all plain as day. I knew what she needed. I began to think that if I yelled loud enough, they'd hear me. They'd give her medicine for her pain and an IV for dehydration. That they would offer her an extra blanket since she looked so cold there on that bed. I sat beside her, rubbing her forehead lightly with the palm of my hand. I held her hand and hugged her. We never left her side.

It was getting dark, and the doctor returned with no answers to give her. He was stumped. But the pain she was feeling worried him. With a consultation from his supervisor, he returned with unpleasant news. The doctors believed that she had a stone lodged in her bile duct and that it would need to be removed by an endoscopic procedure. She would need to be sedated and wouldn't leave the hospital for days. She informed the doctor that there was no one to look after her animals; she was the only one. Her husband was out of town, and he wouldn't be here to take her home and take care of her.

They came up with a plan. She returned home and put bowls of water and food out for the cats, left the windows open for fresh air, and packed an overnight bag. She called her physician on the way home for a second opinion, but he wasn't available. She called Ethan and told him what the doctors wanted to do. Audrey believed that surely the class would allow him to visit his wife in the hospital, but they wouldn't. He had a choice to either stay and finish the course or drop out completely.

Audrey ate dinner after being so hungry all day at the hospital, but it only made her feel worse. She reluctantly left her home and babies to return to the ER, where by midnight, they would admit her into the actual hospital overnight for more tests and monitoring.

It was becoming clearer that the doctors intended to perform emergency surgery to remove her gallbladder altogether. Audrey was terrified. She didn't want to be put under. She didn't want to go through a surgery and be stuck at a hospital all alone. And most importantly, she didn't want her babies to go without food and water. The treatment she was about to receive hinged on two things, the enzyme levels of her liver and the results of one final test. Both would take place that next morning, but there was a lot of time for worry and panic to settle in until then.

The nurse who moved her from the ER was a funny girl who was terrible at navigating her gurney. She bumped into other patients' beds, knocked over equipment, and narrowly missed other patients' IV drips. Audrey's eyes were wide and anxious, white knuckling the handles all the way to Room 330. She was happy to finally walk the rest of the way to the other bed. The funny nurse made sure she was still hooked up to her IV and new machines, wished Audrey well, and rushed back to the ER.

Many nurses tended to Audrey in her stay at the hospital, but Moses was by far her favorite. Moses was a young man from Kenya. He lived in Sacramento but commuted to work in Sonora. He worked hard to be able to send money back to his family on the eastern edge, in his fishing village. Audrey has always loved the sound of African music, the choirs of voices and harmonies sound like angels singing in heaven. She would often paint to that music and loved the happy mood it put her in. Moses had that same vibe as the music did. He was very soft spoken but had much to say. He was happy to talk about his home, his upbringing, and his family, but he was a Christian man and saw a very scared girl lying in a hospital bed all alone. He spoke to her about God, prayer, faith, and his own testimony. He ministered to her and brought her more peace than a room full of her family and Ethan ever could. He checked in on her and made sure she had all the meds, water, and comforts she needed. Most importantly, she asked him to pray with her, and when he did, it was a glorious sight. Our Creator says that when two or more gather together in prayer, He is there with them, and I witnessed it. The once dimly lit hospital room glowed a magnificent heavenly light that enveloped them both. It was because of his care and prayers that she made it through the night without panicking and was finally able to rest.

Early morning brought a shift change, and the new nurses weren't as kind. Audrey felt a moment of weakness. She called Ethan and begged him to come home. She cried about being all by herself, going through this, and said she needed him by her side. She cried about her fears of the surgery, about the wellbeing of their kitties, and just about her exhausted soul.

Ethan pleaded with his instructors, but the military had strict rules. His only option was to drive home after class, check in on the cats and feed them, and then try to see Audrey before driving back to the base, an eight-hour round-trip, before his class began the next day. AWOL.

Her doctor was a young Indian man who was genuinely concerned about her condition. He told her that it was most likely that she'd have to have surgery. Her enzymes had only gotten worse, and if it was not a gallstone obstruction causing her liver to act up, the diagnosis might be far more grave than he wanted to admit.

In her waiting, Audrey was still praying for the patients of the entire hospital, their family, and their care. She made herself feel better by praying for others. With prayer and time, she was able to think logically. She told Ethan she had a weak moment, demanding that he be there. She didn't want him to abandon all that he'd accomplished up to that point. She told him the game plan. She still had tests to take; it wasn't over and decided yet. There was still time for both of them to pray for a miracle. That's what she needed. She needed the MRI to show no obstruction and for her enzymes to go down, and if that happened, the doctor, against his better judgment, agreed to write her discharge papers.

I could hear her prayers, you know, those powerful ones. She didn't usually feel comfortable about praying for herself. She used her most powerful prayers to heal others, but today, the heavens heard her. She did have an obstructed bile duct, but it had passed in the night after Moses prayed with her, but no one else knew it yet.

The MRI placed an already anxious Audrey into a very tight tube with loud noises. The test's success was contingent on her breathing pattern, which was shallow at best. The test took an agonizing twenty minutes, and the last five minutes felt as if they were an hour. Finally, the test was finished, and she was wheeled back to her room to wait for the results. She prayed more, she texted Ethan, she read scripture on her phone, and clung to the words, by your faith, you are healed.

The new nurse came in to check her vitals, and Audrey asked about the results of the MRI. The nurse was curious, so she signed into the computer in her room and started searching. In an apathetic manner, she told Audrey that there was no sign of obstruction. No sign of obstruction meant no surgery. The prayers were working. But the doctor wouldn't release her until her enzymes improved, and she wasn't scheduled to have another blood test until the morning. The stress Audrey had been suffering from had caused her enzymes to rise, but the news of the MRI and knowing she wouldn't have to have surgery allowed her whole body to relax. She was smiling again. She felt that her prayers were being heard and answered. She requested an earlier blood test. She asked if they could just give her a test around 7:00 p.m. The doctor knew she needed to return home, so he surprised her with a 4:00 p.m. blood test, and the results had wildly improved. The doctor wrote her discharge papers, and they had her wheeled out the door before sunset.

She had never been happier to walk through her door than that night. She fed her kitties, sat on the front porch, and expressed pure gratitude.

Gavri and Em still had to comfort me. They had to calm me. Because when she laughed, I laughed, but when she cried, I cried. And when she hurt, I hurt and I screamed out for help, for her. Though her angels stood by her side, always, stoically in their powerful peace, the human side of me wanted to fight for her. I was still that neighbor kid who was just having fun every day with my good friend, when I realized how alone this little girl felt and the weight I felt from that, being one of the only cheerful companions in her life. Back then, she told me that her worst fear was being all alone and needing help. In her little prayers before bed, she'd cry herself to sleep, alone in the dark.

As she got older, her prayers changed. She prayed over tests she had to take and piano recitals. She prayed over her home and wished that her family would be a family again. She prayed that her mother would love her, and her parents would work out their troubles. Then prayers shifted to her future, fears that all her friends were finding their way through life with big plans and college and changes, but she was that boat adrift in a raging sea, that leaf caught up in the wind. She prayed for love. She prayed for just that one person to love her enough that she felt grounded to the earth. She prayed for her grandpa, those lightning bolts crashing through heaven and shaking its foundation.

I watched as she prayed for her marriage. I'd never seen so

many lights, those paper lanterns prayers rising in the sky. I saw that the older she became, the more important prayer was to her. She had seen her share of miracles from those prayer warriors in her family before her. She prayed that her prayers might one day be that powerful. She still prayed for wisdom and guidance, forgiveness and love. She prayed paper lantern prayers over herself and asked God to give her success one day, and I heard God reply to her, saying, "I won't give you success. I will give you victory." I know she heard His words. I watched her write them down.

This marked the beginning of her awakening. It was from the moment He answered her that her mission began. Her angels held her hand, leading her like a toddler learning to walk. And finally, all those years as a curious youth, questioning God's timing, questioning God's reasoning, and His presence, all my questions were answered with four words. He keeps His promises.

When Audrey was that little girl praying for fear of being left all alone, He promised to always be with her. It was so much more than that. Your angels are always there as well, but He sends His helpers to comfort you along your way. The lady in the ER with the swollen foot, the one who distracted her from her fears, made her laugh, and waved to her in the hallway. Moses, the nurse who told her stories and spoke of his homeland, the one who held her hand and prayed with her. God's plans are orchestrated so perfectly, precisely, as if we are all at some point called to serve, and when we do, we are musicians playing our part in a magnificent symphony, which we all get to witness when our time comes.

When we were those little Lakota children playing in the fields of sweet grass, but our families were going hungry, and she prayed for provision, He promised to take care of all of our needs. And when she was living in that Mexican river town at her father's estate, while praying desperately for the safety of her family and herself, He promised to protect her. When Ethan and Audrey were forced to move out of their home, she prayed for a way, because it just looked as if they had run out of options. They would still be in that little sage green house with ivory trim had it not been for God's gentle nudge in the right direction. It only looked as if their world was crumbling, but He kept His promise to work everything out for good.

And as she lay in that hospital bed, her body in pain, her soul exhausted, her eyes empty of tears, feeling so alone, she prayed for an answer. He kept his promises, all of them. Her angels comforted me and calmed me by saying, "Be still." And with the faintest smile from his lips, Gavri said, "He is working."

All of the promises, to be with you, to protect you, to take care of all of your needs, to work everything out for your good, to strengthen you, to give you rest, and most importantly, to answer your prayers. I watched it all happen throughout the course of her life and, then, suddenly, all of them, all at once.

What I learned from storms is, big or small, be still. God is working.

Chapter Nineteen

How do you measure success at the end of one's life? We are led to believe that money and power make you successful. But to whom? When you are on the other side, will it matter how much money you made, what side of town you lived on, or what designer suit you were buried in?

On the other side of the veil, success is measured very differently. We are sent into this world for a purpose, and every strange power in the world will work against you trying to fulfill it. Many people fail. Many come remarkably close, but their time is cut too short. That's the enemy's job, to convince you that you have plenty of time, so you lose focus. He'll convince you that you are insignificant in the world. He'll convince you that you're powerless. Is he succeeding?

The Earth and its inhabitants are our Creator's masterpiece, and our existence and interconnectedness ring out as a symphony through the universe. Within each of us lies a purpose, and just by being our truest selves, that purpose can be reached, but the enemy tries to convince us otherwise. He'll tell you, "Don't be yourself, no one will like you that way," helping you build your façade. "Don't be yourself, you have to be this, or that." This world is filled with misguided souls longing for their genuine selves to be accepted. If only they knew that by being their own unique self, their true gifts rise to the surface, no matter what age, no matter who or where they are.

I could see glimmers of Audrey's former lives shine through into this one. Feathers in her path were treasures and still had meaning. She was still innately connected to the spiritual realm around her. Certain things called to her like the twinkling stars at night, healing, color, music, and blooms. She still searched for me, connecting with me on levels yet to be explained on her side of the veil. She continued through this life without me, and though it seemed that our red thread had been severed, she still found me at the end of it. Losing me had shattered her heart, but she continued on alone, knowing deep down, there was a purpose to be fulfilled, beyond all understanding. Even her own.

A cyclone had developed near Alaska and was battering the west coast with heavy rain. After weeks of blistering heat, 115 degrees at one point, their Blessed Mountain witnessed a shift in the weather as well. It began with wild winds making music as it swept through tall treetops. Dark clouds moved in, and drops of water fell on the dry clay land. It soaked the water right in. In her green coat with the hood over her head, Audrey hung the filled hummingbird feeders on their hooks and stepped over to the edge of the glade. Sometimes it was nice just to stand in the rain, breathe, and give thanks. But she couldn't help but wonder what those wild winds were up to.

Ethan and Audrey spent the afternoon fixing a shelter for their porch kitties. A sturdy structure, with a soft bed, warm blankets, and a tarp to keep it all dry. After a while, they walked out the back door and around to the front gate to get a sneak peek of all the kitties curled up in the bed they had just made for them. They wanted to know that their kitties were cozy. It's those little things that warm the heart, after all.

While Ethan was deployed years back, Audrey's father sold his house in Clovis and his mother's house too. It all happened so fast. The home that she grew up in, the home that her grandparents had built with their bare hands, with her grandma's garden and the playhouse they built for Audrey when she was so young—it was all gone before Audrey could say a proper goodbye. What broke Audrey's heart was that in the last years of her grandma's life, she was torn from the home she shared with her husband, which housed so much love and memories. It was the home she wanted to spend her last moments in, just as her husband did.

Her grandma's most precious things got lost in the shuffle of who gets what and what goes where. Her father and stepmother bought a house in Nevada and, in a big hurry, left Audrey's things in a storage facility and moved without leaving a forwarding address. Audrey always wondered if her father really loved her. I wish children never had to wonder about this. But that close connection she saw with her friends and their fathers was so different. Leaving without a forwarding address was probably a silly oversight, a ridiculous mistake, but these things do carry weight with them, unfortunately.

Weeks ago, Ethan drove Audrey to Nevada, to a hospital that her grandma wasn't expected to ever leave. Her father was surprised to see them but quickly left the hospital room, allowing Audrey and her grandma precious time. Audrey gently held her grandma's frail, bruised little hand, and with her free hand, she lightly ran her fingers over her grandma's forehead. Audrey always thought that was one of the most comforting gestures, especially when you don't feel good. Her grandma's eyes closed, and Audrey could feel her tense little muscles relax.

What do you say to someone in your last moments with them? As best as Audrey could, she told her grandma how much she loved her. That she had been the best mom and grandma a lost little girl could ask for. They talked about memories that made them both laugh. They tried to keep things light, holding hands and being close the entire time. She could tell that her grandma was growing very tired and needed to rest, so with hugs and kisses and I love yous, Audrey and Ethan left the hospital and drove back home.

Audrey kept an eye on her phone, expecting that dreaded call from her father. One night, I watched as Audrey's grandpa met her in a dream. He had his old Chevy truck, Bluebell, all packed up, and he was wearing his usual mountain gear, wranglers with a leather belt that his son, the leather crafter, had made for him, and his short-brimmed cowboy hat. Her grandpa was pacing back and forth. He told Audrey that he was waiting to pick her grandma up, but for some reason, there was a delay. "What's taking her so long?" he asked before walking back to his truck.

"Destined, aren't they?"

Audrey looked to her right, to find me. Perplexed by that word, as if she hadn't heard it in a lifetime, but oh, how it resonated.

Audrey was informed by her father that her grandma had been moved back home, where he could care for her. When Audrey visited her grandma, she told her that she didn't want to stay in the hospital. She wanted to go back home and be in her own bed. That's just what she did. Once she was taken back home and finally able to rest, she was surrounded by her angels. When she was ready, the angels helped her cross over, her husband picked her up in Bluebell, and they drove to the mountains, where he showed her the A-frame cabin he'd built for her and the prairie roses he'd planted. This was where he had been waiting for her, all this time.

Back on Blessed Mountain, after days of rain and wild winds, Audrey spotted a break in the clouds and a rainbow spreading across the sky. She and Ethan and the herd of little lions walked out to the edge of the glade. Audrey took pictures and videos of the rainbow, the playing cats, and of Ethan holding some of them in his arms. It was a moment Audrey knew was very special. They hadn't seen a rainbow up there at all since they moved in.

Once they returned inside, Audrey got a call from her rarely emotional father. He abruptly told her the news and couldn't get off the phone soon enough. A text message the following day informed her of the upcoming graveside service schedule.

Audrey cried for her grandma, but after the dream she had of her grandpa, she carried this bittersweetness, the yugen, in her broken heart. Saying goodbye would always be painful, but she kept seeing images flash in her mind of her grandparents laughing and catching up, honeymooning, and holding each other close after years of loneliness and longing. Those images were given to Audrey. They wanted her to know they were happy and finally together. And it didn't matter where her grandma had spent her final days. Grandpa still found her. They'd met and fallen in love while picking apples as teenagers, and here it was, apple-picking season, meeting again. I was able to see them drive to the A-frame cabin he built, just beyond the veil, on a green hillside, with a garden ready for her to get planting, and surrounded by all the pets they'd loved in their lifetime together.

A week after she got the call from her father, they held the graveside service at Academy Cemetery. It is a quiet little old cemetery in the middle of soft, golden rolling hills and tall oaks. As the pastor spoke of her grandma, she closed her eyes and could actually see what I saw. Audrey could see her grandma, beaming with pride and gratitude, standing next to every soul that came to her service. Though Audrey had tears flowing, and her heart was aching, there was a small measure of peace as she saw the images of her grandma, smiling and looking up at everyone.

I know this place well. While Audrey stood there at her grandma's service, she had no idea that my parents had laid me to rest here, just yards away. It was one of the most beautiful old country cemeteries her family could've chosen for her grandparents' final resting place, but Audrey knew that this was a place to hold their former temples. This place was to be honored, but their spirits were up in the mountains, riding horses to fishing holes, campfires by night, and their love emanating through the veil.

Her father was cold and broken hearted. Audrey just held his hand. There was so much she wanted to say to him, fearing this was the last time they'd see each other again. But she let it all go. There was a time in her life when she had been living in survival mode. She'd made a lot of bad decisions; she'd disappointed her family, and her father never forgave her for things she'd done in a very dark time in her life. Sadly, although she had worked through her childhood trauma, survived the dark night of the soul, and was a new person, her father would never know the new her. There was a brief time when she'd moved into her father's house when she was in her early twenties and going to junior college. She'd made him dinner most nights, and they became good friends, but all that was lost when a woman from his past entered his life again. She was a jealous woman, and the bitterness that was rooted in her heart caused her to have a sour expression. She'd had an opportunity to step into Audrey's life and be a close friend to her, but instead, she slowly poisoned Audrey's father against her.

Audrey could've fought to hang onto the connection she finally made with her father, but it would be a losing battle. She let him go. She let him be happy with this woman and wished them well.

The tears that Audrey was crying were because she realized the only two people who'd ever truly loved her unconditionally, as if Audrey were their own daughter, were gone. She felt like an orphan. Her parents wanted nothing to do with her. Painful memories, blame, and bitterness kept any connection from happening. Her parents were raw, unhealed, and weighed down by the drags of poison they carried for other people. It was in her own healing that she learned that people can only love others if they have the capacity to love themselves. She forgave them, though. Sometimes all you can do for people is pray for them, forgive them, and love them from afar.

That's why the Creator stresses the importance of forgiveness. Forgive those who have wronged you. Don't seek revenge and carry hate in your heart. He will deal with those people for you, and it's always better than anything you could do on your own. Forgive them and embrace the healing that follows. And if we can forgive our enemies, our Creator can forgive us for the hurtful things we do. Most importantly, life begins when we are able to forgive ourselves.

She wanted so desperately for her father to reach out to her, even if it took decades, and say certain things we all need from our parents. I'm so proud of you, or you do good work, or I love you, I miss you, praise of any kind, words of kindness—she would have treasured anything. It hurt Audrey so much that her father would never know the woman she'd worked so hard to become. But I knew that someday, when it was his time to cross over, he would see it all, and only until he was made whole again on this side of the veil, would he truly be able to love Audrey, to be proud of her, as I am. I just wish it could've happened sooner.

Her life was full of heartbreak. When I died, she lost her destined one, which was why almost every romantic love she ever knew was not quite right. In the longing for rare human connection, she connected with the earth, animals, art, music, and spirit. She confronted demons, made peace with her past, and embraced her angels. She shed the façade that her world expected and, instead, grew a garden inside. In a dark world that lusts for power and control, she surrendered. She let the light, the love, and the wisdom of her Creator lead her. And when her marriage was falling apart and her husband was a mere apparition, when the world encouraged divorce and giving up, and even I wanted her to break free, she held on. Knowing that nearly everything in her life was out of her control, she lifted her cares up to her Creator and placed them into His hands, trusting that whatever His will was for her life would always be better than anything she could imagine. And if it wasn't, then He wasn't finished yet. Maybe the goal in life isn't the success we strive for, but in how we served and who we loved, and by loving, success is found in who around us felt safe enough to heal.

Her life was rarely easy. It was filled with loss and loneliness and a longing for a home she'd never known. Her heart shattered more times than I could stand, but perhaps because of that, she got to encounter so much more of the spirit world, miracles, dreams, messages, and connections that most will never have the pleasure of knowing. Ernest Hemingway wrote that the world breaks everyone, but many are strong in the broken places. Kintsugi, also known as the golden repair, is a Japanese custom of repairing broken pottery, piecing it all back together with gold. Instead of hiding the flaws, the cracks are accentuated with the golden repair, making it even more beautiful having been broken. Such as in life—we begin as a mound of clay, formed into a vessel that the cruel world invariably breaks, but our Creator never leaves us broken and empty. We are carefully reconstructed with gold, being made stronger, our capacity to love expanding and becoming more precious each time.

Audrey had lost many pets, but losing little Wolfgang was a pain she might never heal from. The tiny scurrying creature with those giant ears. It was only until he was extremely sick that he was finally able to ask for help and trust and let Ethan and Audrey fight his battle for him. But once he did, his whole life changed. Our Creator is just waiting for us to draw near, speak to Him, trust Him, and let our battles be His now. Our Creator loves us more than we'll ever know, immeasurably so, but we're much like that little feral kitten, scared to reach out, but when we do, life really begins.

Before we chose this life together, our Creator asked Audrey and me what we wanted to learn this time. Always being curious and having questions, I wanted to learn about how He works in our lives; I wanted to learn about promises and how to keep them like He does. God granted me a time of observation, watching the beautiful ways He flowed through each day of Audrey's life. When Audrey was asked what she wanted to learn, she said, "Teach me how to love like You." Although, in this life, she doesn't remember asking for that, but I've watched her life and struggles and how she had transformed pain into wisdom. How does one learn how to cherish if not to suffer loss? How does one become a healer without suffering their own wounds? How is one to love others unless they first learn to love themselves? How does one become a prayer warrior without fighting many battles?

Not a closed fist but an open hand—that was the toughest lesson. It was the hardest to do. You find a rare treasure in this life, you want to tighten your grip, hold it as close to you as you can. They say love is not meant to last. In a way that's true, but it's more accurate to say it changes. So this precious love we feel for another never really disappears. It transforms and transforms you along with it. You're blessed with it, that love that warms you, blooms you, comforts you, however long in this form it's given.

Take it from me, no matter how much time you think you have—it will never be enough. Audrey was given time with people, and these little creatures in her life, and one by one, in their time, they were called back home. The lesson is in the release. There's grace in letting go, as we are told. She reluctantly opened her hand and released them to go home. That means to cry and feel the pain of your broken, empty heart, and knowing that it is okay. Open your hand and release their ashes, release their suffering and pain, knowing that once they took their last earthly breath, their spirit crossed over, their body renewed, and a new season begins.

Life involves keeping an open hand, where one blessing sweeps out and another is swept in. Letting go of the old to make room for the new. With that, you're suddenly aware of the flow of the universe, the blood, the energy, the chi, the wild winds all around you, through you, within you. She finally learned that is how God loves us, with an open hand, open arms, and open heart.

All Audrey's life, she knew she was an artist. Paints and brushes were somehow woven into her DNA strands, and she believed it was a blessing. Being an artist made her feel special, a kind of alchemist, spinning pain into works of art that people could heal from. But to the world, she lacked an education without finishing a degree and was a nobody because her art didn't sell for tens of thousands of dollars out of New York galleries. They'd tell her she needed to get a real job. Some looked down on her. Even some of her own family. The beautiful thing about artists is that they feed off of that negativity. Audrey would lock herself in her studio, only to create healing masterpiece after masterpiece. Pain was fuel. The painting she created for her father all those years ago represented a rejection for quite some time. One afternoon, it was revealed to her why God wanted her to keep this painting. Every evening, she gazed into the painting, the pools of rainwater, the answered prayers. She realized that what she was looking at was earth, water, sunlight, all gifts from God. The question was posed to her: With all these things I've given you, what are you going to grow?

Being in their new home, high on what Audrey named Blessed Mountain, beauty surrounded them. Inspiration grew wildly. They watched as the first spring revealed all of the flowers that Deb planted. Her rose bushes bloomed in every color, fruit trees flourished in the orchard, and daffodils dazzled in all directions. Blue bells, forget-me-nots, and grape hyacinth. Then the purple irises bloomed along with thousands of wildflowers in lavenders, violets, and aubergine. Little thorned vines grew from the clay soil in the most unexpected of places, her home grown over with wild pink prairie roses. Audrey's reading chair and her wing-backed recliner with poppies sat near a large sunny window. It was the perfect place for morning tea and bird-watching. Audrey placed a birdseed dish and a hummingbird feeder just outside the window, which were always kept full. The cats lounged in those chairs all day watching "bird vision." Just outside the big window was a tree that slowly grew green leaves and eventually little purple buds. Audrey had always wanted a lilac tree. That was one of the first things she intended to plant here, besides jasmine, and to her surprise, Deb had that same idea. And it wasn't just any garden. A healer planted this garden with edible and countless medicinal plants still yet to be discovered by Audrey, and a healer would continue the good work. Springtime on Blessed Mountain was a time of gifts at every turn unwrapping themselves. Instead of ribbons and bows, it was stems and petals.

Ethan's to-do list was long, but the first thing he wanted to build was an art studio for Audrey. They never had a ton of money, but just as Audrey's grandparents broke ground on their home with forty dollars, they didn't let finances get in the way. There's a saying that those who care to move mountains begin by moving small stones. Audrey's favorite is that God delights in small beginnings. Ethan made his artist an art studio cottage, library, and music room. He built it large enough so that her dream of having a baby grand piano could come true as well. Her art studio was built in the Tudor style, with Dutch doors, much like the playhouse her grandparents built for her, all those years ago.

Ethan's dream of having a big shop up on the hill also came true. He finally had a place to work on cars, make repairs, and forge iron into creative things. Tim and Deb moved to Blessed Mountain later in life and didn't have enough time to realize their dreams here, but thankfully, Audrey and Ethan would. They made things together just as her grandparents did. They planted lemon, plum, and more peach trees and roses. There in Deb's garden was a brown birdbath that looked like a tree stump with carved squirrels on it. They kept it full of birdseed, sunflower seeds, peanuts, and corn, and it became a most popular place for the strutting wild turkeys and groups of deer to visit. They loved looking out their windows, watching all of the wildlife around them. They even saw the less lovable bears and mountain lions, bobcats, skunks, raccoons, foxes, opossums, and the occasional garden snake. They often wondered what strange thing they'd be seeing next.

We are all difficult to love at times in our lives. She could have filed for divorce and left Ethan behind her, but she left it all up to her Creator. Believing that if He wanted her to move on, He'd offer her the opportunity. Until then, she held on and prayed, worked on herself, and painted every empty canvas she could find. That's just the little secret to making things work; you just hold on and keep busy. She was given the task to just love him, faults and all, and I finally learned why. Her loyalty was one of the most devastatingly beautiful things about her, and I watched as it all eventually was worth it.

Ethan held to his mask the longest. Any time that he felt his mask slipping, he'd become defensive, especially with the person who knew him best. Those who see past masks are a threat to our delicate reality. Few can be so brave as those who destroy the walls of the façade around them, to reveal the bare bones, the raw and bleeding, wounded truth of the genuine self. When Ethan finally did, his whole life changed. His marriage healed. His relationships with others improved. It's a scary thing, removing the mask, wondering if the same people will still love you, once you do. But real friendships are built on truth. Real friends love you for who you are, not for the mask you once wore.

The trials we face in life bring us closer to our purpose. Ethan was so hesitant to rejoin the military. He felt he had served long enough, but he wasn't being called by the Department of Defense;

he was being called to serve his Creator. During his deployment, he would wake in the night to gunfire. It wasn't enemy gunfire, but it was a soldier's own gun, turned on himself. Another soldier lost. After deployment, he would learn the news of his best friend losing his life in a similar way. But our trials have a way of revealing our purpose. Ethan used the lessons he had learned to become a counselor to struggling soldiers. He would never know how many he saved, but I do.

For so many years, Ethan compartmentalized his life and his feelings. He boxed up the unhealed parts of himself, instead of facing them head on as Audrey did. If there is distance created between us and ourselves, it makes intimacy virtually impossible with another person. All these years it caused so much trouble in his life and relationships. But he finally had a constant in his life, someone who loved him, supported him, and held on. That made all the difference. There was some meaning to the song he was playing when they first met, "Patience." The healing and happiness he needed in his life were finally happening.

The grizzly bear that was once Audrey's husband became the gentleman she always knew he truly was. In her marriage, she longed to be loved. I remember her heart crying out, "Love me, so I can love myself again." But one of her greatest lessons in life was not how to heal others, but learning to love herself, especially if she felt no one else did. She also learned that in times when you're waiting for things to get better in a relationship, God wants you to shift your focus and work on yourself. That's how I knew Ethan was the perfect man for her. Ethan was the only one who could've helped her learn this lesson. God knew I would've surrounded her with so much love that she never would've learned how to love herself the way that God intended. And with everything seeming to be stripped away from her life, she learned most importantly, how immeasurably much God truly loves her.

The unpacking of what we carry is a good thing. Decide what to hold on to and let go of the rest. Digging through old boxes can take you back in time. As Audrey was looking for something in her garage, she came across boxes of photos of old friends. She found a love letter from Jack. He was quite the romantic in his time. After Audrey and Jack split up, he married a girl with her same name, who shared the same religion as him, and they had two beautiful children together. He tried so hard to make Audrey fit into his life, and it was only until he stopped trying so hard that his true love found him.

Anthony found Audrey on social media, and Audrey was able to watch his daughter, the perfect likeness to her father, grow into a gorgeous, talented young lady. Anthony still wrote to Audrey every so often, baring his soul, still loving her after all these years. But because of Audrey, he learned that it was safe to drop the mask. Once he did, he wasn't in hot pursuit of money, power, and shiny things. He committed his life to being the best father and a loving companion to the woman who gave him his daughter, the best gift of his whole life. As a family, they raise fat cattle in South Carolina. Audrey loves to see posts of their green garden, and she laughs at the videos of Anthony driving his tractor in his California flip-flops.

Inside a very dusty box, forgotten in the corner, was a green-and-white pinstriped button-down with a name written on the collar, B. Rogers. Below the shirt was a small stack of photos of a long-forgotten era of Beau and Audrey, when they were both tan, young, and in love. Beau tracked her down on social media as well. They were able to catch up a bit. After they parted ways, he finished his degree and became a college professor and polo coach. He fell in love with a wonderful woman named Melanie, a forensic psychologist. Not long after they were married, she developed a persistent cough. Having never smoked a cigarette and being the picture of physical health, Melanie learned that her cough was lung cancer. She went through a battery of treatments. She lost her lovely light blond hair. After her treatments ended, they decided to take a long road trip through the country, to take their minds off the heaviness of life. They drove from state to state, stopping at vistas, landmarks, for shopping and good food. Melanie was brave and determined. She didn't wear a wig or a hat to conceal the story of her life as she was living it. She lived boldly, her little bald head exposed for all to see. As their road trip drew to a close, they stayed at Beau's Morro Beach house for a little rest and fresh air. Her cough returned, and the cancer had spread. In a matter of days after they returned home, she was seen by specialists, admitted into the hospital, and then gone from this earth, far too soon. It left Beau in pieces, and he is still recovering.

In the grand scheme of things, maybe that's why he had always been surrounded by his close friends. His life hadn't been easy, and he was blessed to have such support in his life. Several years had passed since Melanie's farewell. Beau has a new girlfriend now, a teacher at the same school, and they are raising a family of French Bulldogs. Beau went on to become a published author and started a charity in his late wife's honor. He swims from Alcatraz to the shore every year, braving the great whites of the Bay, to raise money for her scholarship fund. Audrey loves the posts he shares of young students, scholarship recipients that have poignant stories and bright futures.

While they were catching up, he shared with her a photo of a painting hanging in his home, in a special place. It was a watercolor Audrey had painted years ago for Beau. He had a close relationship with his dad, the fireman, the coach, and his best friend. She painted it from a photo that Beau treasured, showing Beau on the football field in full gear and his dad beside him, giving him sage advice. Beau had kept the painting all these years. He gazed upon it countless times, especially now that his father had passed on. If only Beau knew that his father still stands beside him, guiding him, supporting and loving him, just as the painting depicts. Melanie keeps a close watch over him too, leaving him love notes in the memories, the songs, and the occasional meeting in dreams.

Sometimes, small things still remind her of Beau. Like the time he asked her to run to the store and get a bundle of cilantro for dinner. She'd accidentally grabbed a bundle of parsley instead. He lost his temper and threw a little fit over her silly mistake. She probably made it worse by laughing. He was trying to impress her by attempting to cook dinner. Something he was just learning, back in the day, putting a lot of pressure on himself to make it perfect. She'd now formed a habit of smelling the cilantro before buying it, giggling to herself whenever that memory surfaced. He's had to endure so much pain in his life, that life he was destined for, without her. But he's a writer and a coach now. For those professions, one must draw from a deep well of experience, and great wisdom is needed. A road he needed to travel alone. She holds the memories of the past in a special place in her heart. And she'll always remember fondly those who loved her when she felt most unlovable.

She still struggled with friendships. After her dark night of the soul, having lost the façade she once carried, she became more of a mirror. Every single person she meets will eventually see their own reflection revealed by her. People living behind masks and façades never like actually seeing them. People came and went from her life, unable to form close relationships because if she had formed a close circle of friends around her, she wouldn't be the healer I know her to be today. In her solitude, she is able to speak to strangers, she has time to welcome the travelers, as I call them, the ones who need a space held for them, if only for the time it takes to confide in her the pain they're feeling, until they're whole again and can continue on their life paths.

She used to think that her isolation was punishment, but in time, she found it to be what it truly was, a form of protection. Hardships are not always God's judgment, but rather a dose of wisdom. He is growing you, expanding you for your big calling. Sometimes you must be buried deep to grow tall and fruitful. And if you are one of those souls who often feels alone and can't seem to sleep at night, the ones who feel things so deeply and care too much, you might be an alchemist too. Deep calls to the deep. Perhaps that's why you feel so lost. You're an alchemist who hasn't done the work. You've trapped the pain inside you for so long but haven't transmuted your energy into light, your gift, yet. Find your gift and develop it, and find ways to give it away. The whole process will heal you from within. I hope that in time you learn how special this gift is.

Audrey went grocery shopping one afternoon to get a few little things for a new recipe. She was making vodka pasta sauce from scratch to pour over plump tortellini. Ethan called her while she was down one of the aisles. She was listening to him talk about his day, as she tossed a few things into her cart, when she raised her head and saw a man who looked just like Ben. He was his height, he had Ben's white hair and goatee, the ballcap and the dark gray t-shirt. It was all there. It took her breath away. Ethan thought he'd lost her on the phone: "Hello, are you there?"

Audrey had a kind smile that she offered people in passing. It could turn anyone's day around. She smiled warmly at him, and he smiled back. She knew it wasn't Ben, but just the sight of the man made her heart skip a little. She was still talking to Ethan, telling him about the encounter with Ben's lookalike. She made a large loop around the store and realized she needed one last thing. She passed the aisle where the man was. She chose a clear aisle to the back, grabbed what she needed, and headed for the register. Strangely, the man passed Audrey once again with a smile. It wasn't your usual flirty grocery store smile from men. This was a different smile. It was a fatherly smile, as if it were from Ben himself.

Once she prepared all the vegetables and had everything simmering, she went online to kill some time before Ethan drove in the driveway. As she scrolled, a post appeared in the feed that listed all the signs that showed your loved one was trying to reach you from the beyond. Right in the middle of the page, one of the signs listed was lookalikes. Audrey rose up in the chair and gasped. She had become familiar with the signs, and by now she thought she knew all about them, but she had never heard about lookalikes until that moment. And there it was. How funny that just after Ben's lookalike appeared to her, she read about that sign, quite specifically. By now, Audrey rarely believed things were coincidences. She believed Ben was saying hello and had given her an encouraging smile when she really needed one. Message received.

And that's what we, on this side of the veil, truly want. We want you to hear that song that reminds you of us, and instead of feeling sad, we want you to listen to the words with a smile, knowing that it's a sign that we are close and thinking of you. The memories that flash in your mind out of nowhere aren't being played to bring you down. It's your loved ones reaching out beyond the veil, in the only ways they know how, to show you their love. So maybe now, you won't think of your loved ones as gone forever, but just beyond the veil, just out of sight, but not as far from you as once believed. Look for the dimes and the feathers, the signs that remind you of them, and when you find them, smile and tell them you love them too.

It wasn't long after that lookalike sighting that Audrey's mother reached out to her. The lines of communication were opened, and there was forgiveness, healing, and love. Ben had a hand in all of it, even from the beyond.

On most cool nights, Ethan and Audrey play their guitars by firelight, entertaining the spirits of Blessed Mountain, me being one of them. I never left her side in all these days of her life, being the perfect song on the radio, the butterfly nearby, the ladybug on her hand. But she is mine at eventide, in the twilight, as her eyes close and her spirit is free to wander.

I take her hand in dreams, and we travel the world. We've seen the Great Pyramids, the deep canyons, and the vast oceans. We traveled to every place she had ever dreamed of seeing, but we saw them together. We ran through the tall grass of the plains below the Black Hills, we swam in the river near our old Mexican estate, and we drank champagne in our vine-covered gazebo deep within the Indian countryside. We walked the shoreline of Pismo Beach, searching for sand dollars, and we slow danced in the headlights of my old truck. Most importantly, we remembered.

I could tell you about her final moments on earth and how her story on her side of the veil ends, because I can see it all now, though her story continues. Her last days haven't happened yet. She has no idea when her time will run out, but until then, she is still that woman who lives and loves boldly, in bright healing colors, planting lilac trees for lilac wine in the springtime, lining hillsides with lavender, feeding her birds, and sowing her garden. She rises each morning to feed her little tribe of lions, indoors and out, and then walks to the edge of the glade to talk to her Creator and soak in the views of His creation, feeling so blessed to be a part of it. Her spirit is still renewed by wild winds, bodies of water, good music, and the raabta, that ever so elusive connection.

She will forever be excited by the possibility a blank canvas holds, and treasures the sense of accomplishment each time she signs her name on a finished piece. And by the time her signature appears on the canvas, her prayers for healing have soaked and saturated it, the alchemy of her craft, and all the love she has poured from her soul. Her art studio is filled with bright sunlight by day and candlelight by night, always with the music I play for her. It is kept in that creative disarray that she learned from her grandpa. They both drop in from time to time to see her progress, leaving a feather on her doorstep before they go. Memories they shared come to mind when they're near, red wagons, picking wildflowers, mountain picnics, summer strawberries—she always says a few words to them. Somewhere over the rainbow, he plays music for her too. I think she's learning to sense when old friends drop by.

She helped heal many as they came through her line at the art store. Thousands saw that leather bracelet while she was working. She helped heal as heyoka. She helped mend the broken, as in kintsugi. Those so desperate for miracles were blessed with them. That is how success is measured on this side. She changed the lives of countless strangers with simple prayers and a kind heart. Sillage is a French word that describes the trace of one's scent, the trail in the water, or the impression one leaves behind them. What a lovely word. We never know the impact of what we leave behind us. If we knew, we'd be inspired to leave more, to leave better. If you are blessed with gifts, you should use them. It's not that you should create art or beauty just to create, but you should create beautiful things because the whole world is counting on you to do so.

Few things are more pleasing in life than being surrounded by her garden, grown over with love and roses. She plants things to mark special occasions. Isn't that a lovely way to live? Planting a garden of memories, so even long after we have gone, the space in one's heart where we used to live, is still blooming. For the rest of her days, she will savor the moments when she feels a connection from beyond the veil. She feels it in the beauty of the earth, sunrise, sunset, the butterfly crossings, the ladybug landings, the hummingbird visits, and in the wild winds. Her Season of Angels, over time, has become much more than just a holiday season but more about how she lives, how life blooms around her, and the messages received.

I had the greatest honor in a span of lifetimes of knowing Audrey, and though we were separated in death, I shadowed her life, watching over her with the most exquisite of beings. She was carefully guarded, not just by her angels and me, but her Savior walked with her too. Always reaching for her hand. Once a lost lamb, she had been found and favored. No matter how hard I screamed and yelled at the iniquities in her life, the course of those wild winds cannot be changed. I questioned God in the early days of my life, as we all do. My Season of Angels was God answering my questions. The storms that came to drown Audrey were divinely altered to water her roses. The time with her angels and watching the work they have done in her life, the things they taught me, the experiences we shared, and the relationships we built—this is my Season of Angels. Miracles and the mizpah. It's more than words can express. It will be sad to see our season come to an end, but then, a new one will begin.

When it is time for Audrey to cross over, her passing will be swift. Beyond the veil, she'll finally see the life around her as she always knew it to be, in her heart. She'll see the colorful auras around each living being. Life is a glistening, singing miracle. An artist of her caliber will be mesmerized by the colors that flood her senses. The scents from her garden will overwhelm her. The spirits of the garden will peek out from behind their hiding places to introduce themselves. All the wonders of the world that she always suspected were there, will finally be on full display. She will be air, she will be water, she will be fire, and she will be earth. The tide of the universe will sweep over her with its wisdom.

Gavri and Em will soon greet her. She'll know them already; these two have been by her side longer than I have. They have protected her and loved her every moment of her being. I really can't express what a momentous occasion it is when you finally meet your angels and realize how often you've seen them throughout your life. Over the years, in Audrey's research of angels, she had become familiar with their presence, their signs, their voices, and calming spirits. And they'll all be together, soon enough.

She will be met with family and friends she had long since forgotten. She'll be embraced and celebrated. There will be happy tears. She'll see her grandpa and grandma holding prairie roses. He'll hug her the same way he did in the dream, before he crossed the veil. Her Aunt Diane will be there to hug her too, smiling through happy tears, welcoming Audrey home with her southern accent. Audrey will meet Deb after all those years of tending to their healing garden, greeting Audrey with a handful of lilacs, colorful roses, daffodils and forget-me-nots. Ben will be there too, his blue eyes smiling.

She'll see me standing there, patiently waiting for my turn. The bittersweet moment. I had watched her create this wonderful life all on her own, without me, and I just know how wounded and darker the world will be without her in it. She'll walk up to me the same as she did when we were kids, then she'll run those last few steps until she's close enough for me to finally wrap my arms around her. The red thread, the Destined Ones, together again. But the heavens will fill with what sounds like thunder, but it's actually the footsteps of the crowd of animals rushing to greet her. Birds of the air, springing cats, leaping dogs, and even horses surrounding her with their excitement of being reunited again.

Audrey is still adding to the film of her life, as are you, and there's still just enough time to make it a really good one. There's still time to work on you; there's still time to forgive and mend old wounds. You still have time to defeat your demons, and take that long journey inward, and grow a garden inside. There's still time to get to know your Creator and angels; after all, that's the most important thing we can do in this life.

There's still time to pray. Prayer is so simple. It's just you asking questions, asking for what you need, communicating with your Creator, who so desperately wants to hear from you. I watched as Audrey's power in prayer grew. From the slowly rising paper lantern prayers to the crashing lightning bolts that illuminated the heavens, she became a prayer warrior from a long line of prayer warriors. And when she prays, mountains move, and miracles are delivered. Windfalls of blessings move in the ways she directs, all because she keeps the line of communication open with the being who loves her even more than I do, her Creator. So don't be intimidated by prayer. Be empowered by it.

Don't let the evils of this world dilute your memory that all living things have the breath of life in them, one breath away from your Creator. Honor yourself and your battle-worn temple and the long journey you've taken to find it. Grow a garden inside. Look back on your past with love, the good and bad, and all those who played a role in your film, knowing that it all had to happen the way it did to bring you to this extraordinary time in your life. Honor your days and your purpose and the time you have left to fulfill it.

This spinning rock with fire in its belly, this earth with eight billion people on it, a time such as this—there is a purpose for you. There's a reason God said that the world needs you and your calling. The enemy will try his damnedest to derail you from your destination. He'll tell you you're not good enough, smart enough, attractive enough, young enough, or rich enough. But the enemy speaks only in lies. If the enemy is telling you those things, it's because you ARE enough, more than enough. You are a threat to the darkness, and knowing that, shine brighter.

Bright lights scare people; you may lose friends and family, and that's okay. Shine brighter. You might irritate demons that people don't even know they have. Demons fear bright light. Shine brighter.

Some people are lost in the darkness and are looking for a way out, for a sign, for a miracle. You might be the only light they see. Shine brighter. The world is cold, and love is scarce, the reason for people like us to bring love back into it, to leave a spark of light before we go, even if in some lives, we are forced to go alone. Audrey had to go through life without me, but her light was never dimmed. She walks with angels and I around her, messages received, connections made, and promises kept.

I look forward to catching glimpses of her most evenings, after the sun sets, running with her wolves, dropping stars in the sky, and leaving her footprints in the deepening blue, just as those holy men described, lifetimes ago. Until then, we are still tethered, that red thread tied to our fingers, the Destined Ones, the golden cord of the prairie rose, bound tighter than ever before. Until then, I'll be longing for the day when I can finally hold her and never let go, never to be separated by this veil I've tried so hard to shred. Until then, I'll play her music and hold her hand, whispering, I love you, always. I'll be watching over her, as angels do, keeping my promise.

Check out the next book in
The Destined Ones Series!

The Gatekeeper

Follow authorjaimekimbler on
instagram to keep up with new releases!

About The Author

Jaime Kimbler is an author, award-winning artist, and founder of Destined Press—a creative imprint devoted to mythic storytelling, divine calling, and eternal love. Drawing from a rich artistic heritage, Jaime's work is both personal and transcendent: a healing journey expressed through lyrical prose, symbolic imagery, and emotionally charged narratives.

A rescue mom, military wife, and lifelong creator, Jaime weaves beauty and meaning into every detail. Her debut novel, Season of Angels, launches The Destined Ones series—a poetic exploration of soul-bound connection, spiritual awakening, and love that defies fate.

Through Destined Press, Jaime champions creative autonomy and artistic legacy, offering stories that inspire, uplift, and reconnect readers to the divine. Whether watching the stars, playing guitars, or crafting timeless worlds, Jaime lives to make beautiful things—and hopes each creation helps others heal.

Jaime and Teacup

www.ingramcontent.com/pod-product-compliance
Lightning Source LLC
Chambersburg PA
CBHW020009120726
47903CB00004B/1209